A Celestial Omnibus

A Celestial Omnibus

SHORT FICTION ON FAITH

Edited by
J. P. Maney and Tom Hazuka

Beacon Press
Boston

We are indebted to our associate, Jill Maney,
for her help in shaping this book.

Beacon Press
25 Beacon Street
Boston, Massachusetts 02108-2892
http://www.beacon.org

Beacon Press books
are published under the auspices of
the Unitarian Universalist Association of Congregations.

Printed in the United States of America

02 01 00 8 7 6 5 4 3

Text design by John Kane
Composition in Monotype Dante by Wilsted & Taylor Publishing Services

Library of Congress Cataloging-in-Publication Data
A celestial omnibus : short fiction on faith / edited by J. P. Maney and Tom Hazuka.
p. cm.
Includes index.
ISBN 0-8070-8334-8 (cloth)
ISBN 0-8070-8335-6 (paper)
1. American fiction—20th century. 2. Faith—Fiction. 3. Short stories, American. I. Maney, J. P. (Jonathan Paul), 1956– . II. Hazuka, Tom.
PS648.F24C45 1997
813′.0108382—dc21 97-11824

For Ruth T. Maney,
John and Jean Hazuka,
and Christine Perkins

Dedicated to
the memory of
Maren Partenheimer

Contents

Introduction

> I think of what it is to write stories. It is a completion. It is discovering something you didn't know you'd lost. It is finding an answer to a question you never asked.

In these words, American writer Harriet Doerr describes how a story creates a bridge between the known and the unknown, the familiar and the strange. Writers imagine themselves into situations with roots in the familiar, where completion requires the creative acts of exploring and searching the unknown. Through these acts, writers—and their readers—make a double discovery. Finding, they know what they have lost; locating answers, they know the questions they should ask.

This spirit of discovery is what we believe distinguishes the fiction represented here; it is what guided us as we read hundreds of stories from the beginning of the twentieth century to the present. This book is designed for those who want to explore the mystery and value of life, to consider complex moral issues, to find meaning in their experience. The reader should be warned, however, that the stories in this collection are not easy or simple. They are frequently hard and unsentimental; they challenge assumptions, force us to cross unlikely bridges, take us to new country, and sometimes leave us wondering what to do with the answers and questions we have found.

As editors, our own process of discovery began when we looked for writers who do not hold that good and evil are merely subjective, that actions are morally indeterminate, or that the powers of soul are irrelevant to contemporary life. We chose stories from a variety of faith traditions. We looked for authors whose characters move toward moral or ethical crises which pressure them into making difficult and revealing decisions. We hoped to find a small but robust group of these stories, stalwarts against the modern tide of cleverness, nihilism, and meaninglessness. Instead, we discovered hundreds of them. These were stories with substance, some of the most powerful stories of our time.

A few years ago at Hobart and William Smith Colleges I had the opportunity to teach a course about the relationship between the Bible and contemporary literature. I selected stories by Flannery O'Connor, Bernard Malamud, John Updike, and many others. I noted with some surprise that students responded differently to this material than they had to the readings in my other English classes. Their course journals revealed a genuine contact between student and story—by this I mean jolts and shocks from encounters that could not simply be digested, paraphrased, and discarded. Believing that learning often proceeds by such shocks, I encouraged students to write papers about what bothered them in what we read, and, little by little, they began to shed the false sophistication that is often their armor, dodge, and refuge.

One book can only suggest the scope of religious experience in fiction, not fully represent it. The stories we have selected here testify to the survival of both faith and art, and the connection between them. Both art and religion examine the mystery of human experience, discover meaning, and reveal value. Religion and art reflect our aspirations and terrors, as well as our experiences of transcendence. This collection of fiction invites readers to explore the vital connection between art and religion.

Flannery O'Connor, no stranger to this vital connection, wrote that "Fiction is the concrete expression of mystery—mystery that is lived." *Mystery* is therefore the first of the five themes in this book. *Doubt* is the second, because without it there can be little of the creative exploration that deepens or develops belief. *Evil* is the third theme, because its existence is a major problem in the life of the world and is, for many, the main obstacle to faith. Fourth is *The Supernatural*, the source of wonder, of all that exceeds human understanding. The last theme, *Reconciliation*, encompasses the qualities of mercy and holiness, and brings the reader to the crossing between extinction and eternal being. We invite you to use these themes, not as definitive labels, but as starting places for considering each story's many facets and sometimes contradictory meanings.

Recently, Pulitzer Prize-winning novelist N. Scott Momaday told an audience in northern New Mexico that reinventing the sacred in our increasingly fragmented technological society is the central issue facing us today. This is what the writers featured in this anthology set out to do. Each of their stories reveals fundamental truths about human experience. All point toward the importance of making meaning. In its way, each story is a hallowed place, a church, mosque, synagogue, or sacred mountain, where the mystery and meaning of our humanity is explored, deepened, and above all, valued.

J. P. Maney
1997, Geneva, New York

MYSTERY

The unknown is the largest need of the intellect.

Emily Dickinson,
in Mabel Loomis Todd, ed.,
Letters of Emily Dickinson

What if the universe
is not about
us? Then what?
What
is it about
and what
about
us?

May Swenson, "The Universe,"
To Mix With Time

The veil between us and the divine is more permeable than we imagine.

Sue Patton Theole,
The Woman's Book of Courage

Now comes the mystery.

Henry Ward Beecher, last words

Little Miracles, Kept Promises

SANDRA CISNEROS

Exvoto Donated as Promised

On the 20th of December of 1988 we suffered a terrible disaster on the road to Corpus Christi. The bus we were riding skidded and overturned near Robstown and a lady and her little girl were killed. Thanks to La Virgen de Guadalupe we are alive, all of us miraculously unharmed, and with no visible scars, except we are afraid to ride buses. We dedicate this retablo to La Virgencita with our affection and gratitude and our everlasting faith.

Familia Arteaga
Alice, Texas
G. R. (Gracias Recibido / Thanks Given)

Blessed Santo Niño de Atocha,

Thank you for helping us when Chapa's truck got stolen. We didn't know how we was going to make it. He needs it to get to work, and this job, well, he's been on probation since we got him to quit drinking. Raquel and the kids are hardly ever afraid of him anymore, and we are proud parents. We don't know how we can repay you for everything you have done for our family. We will light a candle to you every Sunday and never forget you.

Sidronio Tijerina
Brenda A. Camacho de Tijerina
San Angelo, Texas

Dear San Martín de Porres,

Please send us clothes, furniture, shoes, dishes. We need anything that don't eat. Since the fire we have to start all over again and Lalo's disability check ain't much and don't go far. Zulema would like to finish school but I says she can just forget about it now. She's our oldest and her place is at home helping us out I told her. Please make her see some sense. She's all we got.

Thanking you,
Adelfa Vásquez
Escobas, Texas

Dear San Antonio de Padua,

Can you please help me find a man who isn't a pain in the nalgas. There aren't any in Texas, I swear. Especially not in San Antonio.

Can you do something about all the educated Chicanos who have to go to California to find a job. I guess what my sister Irma says is true: "If you didn't get a husband when you were in college, you don't get one."

I would appreciate it very much if you sent me a man who speaks Spanish, who at least can pronounce his name the way it's supposed to be pronounced. Someone please who never calls himself "Hispanic" unless he's applying for a grant from Washington, D.C.

Can you send me a man man. I mean someone who's not ashamed to be seen cooking or cleaning or looking after himself. In other words, a man who acts like an adult. Not one who's never lived alone, never bought his own underwear, never ironed his own shirts, never even heated his own tortillas. In other words, don't send me someone like my brothers who my mother ruined with too much chichi, or I'll throw him back.

I'll turn your statue upside down until you send him to me. I've put up with too much too long, and now I'm just too intelligent, too powerful, too beautiful, too sure of who I am finally to deserve anything less.

Ms. Barbara Ybañez
San Antonio, TX

Dear Niño Fidencio,

I would like for you to help me get a job with good pay, benefits, and retirement plan. I promise you if you help me I will make a pilgrimage to your tomb in Espinazo and bring you flowers. Many thanks.

César Escandón
Pharr, Tejas

DEAR DON PEDRITO JARAMILLO HEALER OF LOS OLMOS

MY NAME IS ENRIQUETA ANTONIA SANDOVAL I LIVE IN SAN MARCOS TX I AM SICK THEY OPERATED ME FROM A KIDNEY AND A TUMOR OF CANCER BUT THANKS TO GOD I AM ALIVE BUT I HAVE TO GET TREATMENTS FOR A YEAR THE KIMO I AM 2½ YEARS OLD BUT MY GRANDMA BROUGHT ME THAT YOU AND OUR LORD WHO IS IN THE HEAVENS WILL CURE ME WITH THIS LETTER THAT I AM DEPOSITING HERE ITS MY GRANDMA WHO IS WRITING THIS I HOPE EVERYBODY WHO SEES THIS LETTER WILL TAKE A MINUTE TO ASK FOR MY HEALTH

ENRIQUETA ANTONIA
SANDOVAL
2 AND A HALF YEARS OLD

I LEOCADIA DIMAS VDA. DE CORDERO OF SAN MARCOS TX HAVE COME TO PAY THIS REQUEST TO DON PEDRITO THAT MY GRANDDAUGHTER WILL COME OUT FINE FROM HER OPERATION THANKS TO GOD AND THOSE

WHO HELPED SUCH GOOD DOCTORS THAT DID THEIR JOB WELL THE REST IS IN GODS HANDS THAT HE DO HIS WILL MANY THANKS WITH ALL MY HEART.

YOUR VERY RESPECTFUL
SERVANT
LEOCADIA

Oh Mighty Poderosos, Blessed Powerful Ones,

You who are crowned in heaven and who are so close to our Divine Savior, I implore your intercession before the Almighty on my behalf. I ask for peace of spirit and prosperity, and that the demons in my path that are the cause of all my woes be removed so that they no longer torment me. Look favorably on this petition and bless me, that I may continue to glorify your deeds with all my heart—santísimo Niño Fidencio, gran General Pancho Villa, bendito Don Pedrito Jaramillo, virtuoso John F. Kennedy, and blessed Pope John Paul. Amen.

Gertrudis Parra
Uvalde, Tejas

Father Almighty,

Teach me to love my husband again. Forgive me.

s.
Corpus Christi

Seven African Powers that surround our Savior—Obatala, Yemaya, Ochún, Orunla, Ogun, Elegua, and Shango—why don't you behave and be good to me? Oh Seven African Powers, come on, don't be bad. Let my Illinois lottery ticket win, and if it does, don't let my cousin Cirilo in Chicago cheat me out of my winnings, since I'm the one who pays for the ticket and all he does is buy it for me each week—if he does even that. He's my cousin, but like the Bible says, better to say nothing than to say nothing nice.

Protect me from the evil eye of the envious and don't let my enemies do me harm, because I've never done a thing wrong to anyone first. Save this good Christian who the wicked have taken advantage of.

Seven Powers, reward my devotion with good luck. Look after me, why don't you? And don't forget me because I never forget you.

Moises Ildefonso Mata
San Antonio, Texas

Virgencita de Guadalupe,

I promise to walk to your shrine on my knees the very first day I get back, I swear, if you will only get the Tortillería la Casa de la Masa to pay me the $253.72 they owe me for two weeks' work. I put in 67½ hours that first week and 79 hours the second, and I don't have anything to show for it yet. I calculated with the taxes deducted, I have $253.72 coming to me. That's all I'm asking for. The $253.72 I have coming to me.

I have asked the proprietors Blanquita and Rudy Mondragón, and they keep telling me next week, next week, next week. And it's almost the middle of the third week already and I don't know how I'm going to do it to pay this week's rent, since I'm already behind, and the other guys have loaned me as much as they're able, and I don't know what I'm going to do, I don't know what I'm going to do.

My wife and the kids and my in-laws all depend on what I send home. We are humble people, Virgencita. You know I'm not full of vices. That's how I am. It's been hard for me to live here so far away without seeing my wife, you know. And sometimes one gets tempted, but no, and no, and no. I'm not like that. Please, Virgencita, all I'm asking for is my $253.72. There is no one else I can turn to here in this country, and well, if you can't help me, well, I just don't know.

Arnulfo Contreras
San Antonio, Tejas

Saint Sebastian who was persecuted with arrows and then survived, thank you for answering my prayers! All them arrows that had persecuted me—my brother-in-law Ernie and my sister Alba and their kids—el Junior, la Gloria, and el Skyler—all gone. And now my home sweet home is mine again, and my Dianita bien lovey-dovey, and my kids got something to say to me besides who hit who.

Here is the little gold milagrito I promised you, a little house, see? And it ain't that cheap gold-plate shit either. So now that I paid you back, we're even, right? Cause I don't like for no one to say Victor Lozano don't pay his debts. I pays cash on the line, bro. And Victor Lozano's word like his deeds is solid gold.

Victor A. Lozano
Houston, TX

Dear San Lázaro,

My mother's comadre Demetria said if I prayed to you that like maybe you could help me because you were raised from the dead and did a lot of miracles and maybe if I lit a candle every night for seven days and prayed, you might maybe could help me with my face breaking out with so many pimples. Thank you.

Rubén Ledesma
Hebbronville, Texas

Santísima Señora de San Juan de los Lagos,

We came to see you twice when they brought you to San Antonio, my mother and my sister Yolanda and two of my aunts, Tía Enedina and my Tía Perla, and we drove all the way from Beeville just to visit you and make our requests.

I don't know what my Tía Enedina asked for, she's always so secretive, but probably it had to do with her son Beto who doesn't do anything but hang around the house and get into trouble. And my Tía Perla no doubt complained about her ladies' problems—her ovaries that itch, her tangled fallopians, her uterus that makes her seasick with all its flipping and flopping. And Mami who said she only came along for the ride, lit three candles so you would bless us all and sweep jealousy and bitterness from our hearts because that's what she says every day and every night. And my sister Yoli asked that you help her lose weight because I don't want to wind up like Tía Perla, embroidering altar cloths and dressing saints.

But that was a year ago, Virgencita, and since then my cousin Beto was fined for killing the neighbor's rooster with a flying Big Red bottle, and my Tía Perla is convinced her uterus has fallen because when she walks something inside her rattles like a maraca, and my mother and my aunts are arguing and yelling at each other same as always. And my stupid sister Yoli is still sending away for even stupider products like the Grasa Fantástica, guaranteed to burn away fat—It really works, Tere, just rub some on while you're watching TV—only she's fatter than ever and just as sad.

What I realize is that we all made the trip to San Antonio to ask something of you, Virgencita, we all needed you to listen to us. And of all of us, my mama and sister Yoli, and my aunts Enedina and Perla, of all of us, you granted me my petition and sent, just like I asked, a guy who would love only me because I was tired of looking at girls younger than me walking along the street or riding in cars or standing in front of the school with a guy's arm hooked around their neck.

So what is it I'm asking for? Please, Virgencita. Lift this heavy cross from my shoulders and leave me like I was before, wind on my neck, my arms swinging free, and no one telling me how I ought to be.

Teresa Galindo
Beeville, Texas

Miraculous Black Christ of Esquipulas,

Please make our grandson to be nice to us and stay away from drugs. Save him to find a job and move away from us. Thank you.

Grandma y Grandfather
Harlingen

M3rlc5l45s Bl1ck Chr3st 4f 2sq53p5l1s,

3 lsk y45, L4rd, w3th 1ll my h2lrt pl2ls2 wltch 4v2r Mlnny B2nlv3d2s wh4 3s 4v2rs21s. 3 l4v2 h3m 1nd 3 d4n't kn4w whlt t4 d4 lb45t 1ll th3s l4v2 sldn2ss lnd sh1m2 th1t f3lls m2.

B2nj1m3n T.
D2l R34 TX

Milagroso Cristo Negro de Esquipulas,

Te ofrezco este retrato de mis niños. Wáchelos, Dios Santo, y si le quitas el trago a mi hijo te prometo prender velitas. Ayúdanos con nuestras cuentas, Señor, y que el cheque del income tax nos llegue pronto para pagar los biles. Danos una buena vida y que les ayudes a mis hijos a cambiar sus modos. Tú que eres tan bondadoso escucha estas peticiones que te pido con todo mi corazón y con toda la fe de mi alma. Ten piedad, Padre mio. Mi nombre es Adela O.

Elizondo,
Cotulla TX

Milagroso Cristo Negro,

Thank you por el milagro de haber graduado de high school. Aquí le regalo mi retrato de graduation.

Fito Moroles
Rockport, Texas

Cristo Negro,

Venimos desde muy lejos. Infinitas gracias, Señor. Gracias por habernos escuchado.

Familia Armendáriz G.
Matamoros, Tamps. México

Jesus Christ,

Please keep Deborah Abrego and Ralph S. Urrea together forever.

Love,
Deborah Abrego
Sabinal, Texas

Blessed Virgen de los Remedios,

Señora Dolores Alcalá de Corchado finds herself gravely ill from a complication that resulted after a delicate operation she underwent Thursday last, and from which she was recovering satisfactorily until suffering a hemorrhage Tuesday morning. Please intercede on her behalf. We leave her in the hands of God, that His will be done, now that we have witnessed her suffering and don't know whether she should die or continue this life. Her husband of forty-eight years offers this request with all his heart.

Señor Gustavo Corchado B.
Laredo, Tejas

Madrecita de Dios,

Thank you. Our child is born healthy!

Rene y Janie Garza
Hondo, TX

Saint Jude, patron saint of lost causes,

Help me pass my English 320, British Restoration Literature class and everything to turn out ok.

Eliberto González
Dallas

❖

Virgencita . . .

I've cut off my hair just like I promised I would and pinned my braid here by your statue. Above a Toys "Я" Us name tag that says IZAURA. Along several hospital bracelets. Next to a business card for Sergio's Casa de la Belleza Beauty College. Domingo Reyna's driver's license. Notes printed on the flaps of envelopes. Silk roses, plastic roses, paper roses, roses crocheted out of fluorescent orange yarn. Photo button of a baby in a *charro* hat. Caramel-skinned woman in a white graduation cap and gown. Mean dude in bandanna and tattoos. Oval black-and-white passport portrait of the sad uncle who never married. A mama in a sleeveless dress watering the porch plants. Sweet boy with new mustache and new soldier uniform. Teenager with a little bit of herself sitting on her lap. Blurred husband and wife leaning one into the other as if joined at the hip. Black-and-white photo of the cousins *la* Josie *y la* Mary Helen, circa 1942. Polaroid of Sylvia Rios, First Holy Communion, age nine years.

So many *milagritos* safety-pinned here, so many little miracles dangling from red thread—a gold Sacred Heart, a tiny copper arm, a kneeling man in silver, a bottle, a brass truck, a foot, a house, a hand, a baby, a cat, a breast, a tooth, a belly button, an evil eye. So many petitions, so many promises made and kept. And there is nothing I can give you except this braid of hair the color of coffee in a glass.

Chayo, what have you done! All that beautiful hair.
Chayito, how could you ruin in one second what your mother took years to create?
You might as well've plucked out your eyes like Saint Lucy. All that hair!

My mother cried, did I tell you? All that beautiful hair . . .

I've cut off my hair. Which I've never cut since the day I was born. The donkey tail in a birthday game. Something shed like a snakeskin.

My head as light as if I'd raised it from water. My heart buoyant again, as if before I'd worn *el* Sagrado Corazón in my open chest. I could've lit this entire church with my grief.

I'm a bell without a clapper. A woman with one foot in this world and one foot in that. A woman straddling both. This thing between my legs, this unmentionable.

I'm a snake swallowing its tail. I'm my history and my future. All my ancestors' ancestors inside my own belly. All my futures and all my pasts.

I've had to steel and hoard and hone myself. I've had to push the furniture against the door and not let you in.

What you doing sitting in there in the dark?

I'm thinking.

Thinking of what?

Just . . . thinking.

You're nuts. Chayo, ven a saludar. *All the relatives are here. You come out of there and be sociable.*

Do boys think, and girls daydream? Do only girls have to come out and greet the relatives and smile and be nice and *quedar bien*?

It's not good to spend so much time alone.

What she do in there all by herself? It don't look right.

Chayito, when you getting married? Look at your cousin Leticia. She's younger than you.

How many kids you want when you grow up?

When I become a mommy . . .

You'll change. You'll see. Wait till you meet Mr. Right.

Chayo, tell everybody what it is you're studying again.

Look at our Chayito. She likes making her little pictures. She's gonna be a painter.

A painter! Tell her I got five rooms that need painting.

When you become a mother . . .

Thank you for making all those months I held my breath not a child in my belly, but a thyroid problem in my throat.

I can't be a mother. Not now. Maybe never. Not for me to choose, like I didn't choose being female. Like I didn't choose being artist—it isn't something you choose. It's something you are, only I can't explain it.

I don't want to be a mother.

I wouldn't mind being a father. At least a father could still be artist, could love some*thing* instead of some*one*, and no one would call that selfish.

I leave my braid here and thank you for believing what I do is important. Though no one else in my family, no other woman, neither friend nor relative, no one I know, not even the heroine in the *telenovelas,* no woman wants to live alone.

I do.

Virgencita de Guadalupe. For a long time I wouldn't let you in my house. I couldn't see you without seeing my ma each time my father came home drunk and yelling, blaming everything that ever went wrong in his life on her.

I couldn't look at your folded hands without seeing my *abuela* mumbling, "My son, my son, my son . . ." Couldn't look at you without blaming you for all the pain my mother and her mother and all our mothers' mothers have put up with in the name of God. Couldn't let you in my house.

I wanted you bare-breasted, snakes in your hands. I wanted you leaping and somersaulting the backs of bulls. I wanted you swallowing raw hearts and rattling volcanic ash. I wasn't going to be my mother or my grandma. All that self-sacrifice, all that silent suffering. Hell no. Not here. Not me.

Don't think it was easy going without you. Don't think I didn't get my share of it from everyone. Heretic. Atheist. *Malinchista. Hocicona.* But I wouldn't shut my yap. My mouth always getting me in trouble. *Is that what they teach you at the university? Miss High-and-Mighty. Miss Thinks-She's-Too-Good-for-Us.* Acting like a *bolilla,* a white girl. *Malinche.* Don't think it didn't hurt being called a traitor. Trying to explain to my ma, to my *abuela,* why I didn't want to be like them.

I don't know how it all fell in place. How I finally understood who you are. No longer Mary the mild, but our mother Tonantzín. Your church at Tepeyac built on the site of her temple. Sacred ground no matter whose goddess claims it.

That you could have the power to rally a people when a country was born, and again during civil war, and during a farmworkers' strike in California made me think maybe there is power in my mother's patience, strength in my grandmother's endurance. Because those who suffer have a special power, don't they? The power of understanding someone else's pain. And understanding is the beginning of healing.

When I learned your real name is Coatlaxopeuh, She Who Has Dominion over Serpents, when I recognized you as Tonantzín, and learned your names are Teteoinnan, Toci, Xochiquetzal, Tlazolteotl, Coatlicue, Chalchiuhtlicue, Coyolxauhqui, Huixtocihuatl, Chicomecoatl, Cihuacoatl, when I could see you as Nuestra Señora de la Soledad, Nuestra Señora de los Remedios, Nuestra Señora del Perpetuo Socorro, Nuestra Señora de San Juan de los Lagos, Our Lady of Lourdes, Our Lady of Mount Carmel, Our Lady of the Rosary, Our Lady of Sorrows, I wasn't ashamed, then, to be my mother's daughter, my grandmother's granddaughter, my ancestors' child.

When I could see you in all your facets, all at once the Buddha, the Tao, the true Messiah, Yahweh, Allah, the Heart of the Sky, the Heart of the Earth, the Lord of the Near and Far, the Spirit, the Light, the Universe, I could love you, and, finally, learn to love me.

❖

Mighty Guadalupana Coatlaxopeuh Tonantzín,

What "little miracle" could I pin here? Braid of hair in its place and know that I thank you.

Rosario (Chayo) De Leon
Austin, Tejas

A Father's Story

ANDRE DUBUS

My name is Luke Ripley, and here is what I call my life: I own a stable of thirty horses, and I have young people who teach riding, and we board some horses, too. This is in northeastern Massachusetts. I have a barn with an indoor ring, and outside I've got two fenced-in rings and a pasture that ends at a woods with trails. I call it my life because it looks like it is, and people I know call it that, but it's a life I can get away from when I hunt and fish, and some nights after dinner when I sit in the dark in the front room and listen to opera. The room faces the lawn and the road, a two-lane country road. When cars come around the curve northwest of the house, they light up the lawn for an instant, the leaves of the maple out by the road and the hemlock closer to the window. Then I'm alone again, or I'd appear to be if someone crept up to the house and looked through a window: a big-gutted gray-haired guy, drinking tea and smoking cigarettes, staring out at the dark woods across the road, listening to a grieving soprano.

My real life is the one nobody talks about anymore, except Father Paul LeBoeuf, another old buck. He has a decade on me: he's sixty-four, a big man, bald on top with gray at the sides; when he had hair, it was black. His face is ruddy, and he jokes about being a whiskey priest, though he's not. He gets outdoors as much as he can, goes for a long walk every morning, and hunts and fishes with me. But I can't get him on a horse anymore. Ten years ago I could badger him into a trail ride; I had to give him a western saddle, and he'd hold the pommel and bounce through the woods with me, and be sore for days. He's looking at seventy with eyes that are younger than many I've seen in people in their twenties. I do not remember ever feeling the way they seem to; but I was lucky, because even as a child I knew that life would try me, and I must be strong to endure, though in those early days I expected to be tortured and killed for my faith, like the saints I learned about in school.

Father Paul's family came down from Canada, and he grew up speaking more French than English, so he is different from the Irish priests who abound up here. I do not like to make general statements, or even to hold general beliefs, about people's blood, but the Irish do seem happiest when they're dealing with misfortune or guilt, either their own or somebody else's, and if you think you're not a victim of either one, you can count on certain Irish priests to try to change your mind. On Wednesday nights Father Paul comes to dinner. Often he comes on other nights too, and once, in the old days when we couldn't eat meat on Fridays, we bagged our first ducks of the season on a Friday, and as we drove home from the marsh, he said: For the purposes of Holy Mother Church, I believe a duck is more a creature of water than land, and is not rightly meat. Sometimes he teases me about never putting anything in his Sunday collection, which he would not know about if I hadn't told him years ago. I would like to believe I told him so we could have philosophical talk at dinner, but probably the truth is I suspected he knew, and I did not want him to think I so loved money that I would not even give his church a coin on Sunday. Certainly the ushers who pass the baskets know me as a miser.

I don't feel right about giving money for buildings, places. This starts with the Pope, and I cannot respect one of them till he sells his house and everything in it, and that church too, and uses the money to feed the poor. I have rarely, and maybe never, come across saintliness, but I feel certain it cannot exist in such a place. But I admit, also, that I know very little, and maybe the popes live on a different plane and are tried in ways I don't know about. Father Paul says his own church, St. John's, is hardly the Vatican. I like his church: it is made of wood, and has a simple altar and crucifix, and no padding on the kneelers. He does not have to lock its doors at night. Still it is a place. He could say Mass in my barn. I know this is stubborn, but I can find no mention by Christ of maintaining buildings, much less erecting them of stone or brick, and decorating them with pieces of metal and mineral and elements that people still fight over like barbarians. We had a Maltese woman taking riding lessons, she came over on the boat when she was ten, and once she told me how the nuns in Malta used to tell the little girls that if they wore jewelry, rings and bracelets and necklaces, in purgatory snakes would coil around their fingers and wrists and throats. I do not believe in frightening children or telling them lies, but if those nuns saved a few girls from devotion to things, maybe they were right. That Maltese woman laughed about it, but I noticed she wore only a watch, and that with a leather strap.

The money I give to the church goes in people's stomachs, and on their backs, down in New York City. I have no delusions about the worth of what I do, but I feel it's better to feed somebody than not. There's a priest in Times Square giving shelter to runaway kids, and some Franciscans who run a bread line; actually it's a morning line for coffee and a roll, and Father Paul calls it the continental breakfast for winos and bag ladies. He is curious about how much I am sending, and I know why: he guesses I send a lot, he has said probably more than tithing, and he is right; he wants to know how much because he believes I'm generous and good, and he is wrong about that; he has never had much money and does not know how easy it is to write a check when you have every thing you will ever need, and the figures are mere numbers, and represent no sacrifice at all. Being a real Catholic is too hard; if I were one, I would do with my house and barn what I want the Pope to do with his. So I do not want to impress Father Paul, and when he asks me how much, I say I can't let my left hand know what my right is doing.

He came on Wednesday nights when Gloria and I were married, and the kids were young; Gloria was a very good cook (I assume she still is, but it is difficult to think of her in the present), and I liked sitting at the table with a friend who was also a priest. I was proud of my handsome and healthy children. This was long ago, and they were all very young and cheerful and often funny, and the three boys took care of their baby sister, and did not bully or tease her. Of course they did sometimes, with that excited cruelty children are prone to, but not enough so that it was part of her days. On the Wednesday after Gloria left with the kids and a U-Haul trailer, I was sitting on the front steps, it was summer, and I was watching cars go by on the road, when Father Paul drove around the curve and into the driveway. I was ashamed to see him because he is a priest and my family was gone, but I was relieved, too. I went to the car to greet him. He got out smiling, with a bottle of wine, and shook my hand, then pulled me to him, gave me a quick hug, and said: "It's Wednesday, isn't it? Let's open some cans."

With arms about each other we walked to the house, and it was good to know he was doing his work but coming as a friend, too, and I thought what good work he had. I have no calling. It is for me to keep horses.

In that other life, anyway. In my real one I go to bed early and sleep well and wake at four forty-five, for an hour of silence. I never want to get out of bed then, and every morning I know I can sleep for another four hours and still not fail at any of my duties. But I get up, so have come to believe my life can be seen in miniature in that struggle in the dark of morning. While making the bed and boiling water for coffee, I talk to God: I offer Him my day, every act of my body and spirit, my thoughts and moods, as a prayer of thanksgiving, and for Gloria and my children and my friends and two women I made love with after Gloria left. This morning offertory is a habit from my boyhood in a Catholic school; or then it was a habit, but as I kept it and grew older it became a ritual. Then I say the Lord's Prayer, trying not to recite it, and one morning it occurred to me that a prayer, whether recited or said with concentration, is always an act of faith.

I sit in the kitchen at the rear of the house and drink coffee and smoke and watch the sky growing light before sunrise, the trees of the woods near the barn taking shape, becoming single pines and elms and oaks and maples. Sometimes a rabbit comes out of the treeline, or is already sitting there, invisible till the light finds him. The birds are awake in the trees and feeding on the ground, and the little ones, the purple finches and titmice and chickadees, are at the feeder I rigged outside the kitchen window; it is too small for pigeons to get a purchase. I sit and give myself to coffee and tobacco, that get me brisk again, and I watch and listen. In the first year or so after I lost my family, I played the radio in the mornings. But I overcame that, and now I rarely play it at all. Once in the mail I received a questionnaire asking me to write down everything I watched on television during the week they had chosen. At the end of those seven days I wrote in *The Wizard of Oz* and returned it. That was in winter and was actually a busy week for my television, which normally sits out the cold months without once warming up. Had they sent the questionnaire during baseball season, they would have found me at my set. People at the stables talk about shows and performers I have never heard of, but I cannot get interested; when I am in the mood to watch television, I go to a movie or read a detective novel. There are always good detective novels to be found, and I like remembering them next morning with my coffee.

I also think of baseball and hunting and fishing, and of my children. It is not painful to think about them anymore, because even if we had lived together, they would be gone now, grown into their own lives, except Jennifer. I think of death, too, not sadly, or with fear, though something like excitement does run through me, something more quickening than the coffee and tobacco. I suppose it is an intense interest, and an outright distrust: I never feel certain that I'll be here watching birds eating at tomorrow's daylight. Sometimes I try to think of other things, like the rabbit that is warm and breathing but not there till twilight. I feel on the brink of something about the life of the senses, but either am not equipped to go further or am not interested enough to concentrate. I have called all of this thinking, but it is not, because it is unintentional; what I'm really doing is feeling the day, in silence, and that is what Father Paul is doing too on his five-to-ten-mile walks.

When the hour ends I take an apple or carrot and I go to the stable and tack up a horse. We take good care of these horses, and no one rides them but students, instructors, and me, and nobody rides the horses we board unless an owner asks me to. The barn is dark and I turn on lights and take some deep breaths, smelling the hay and horses and their manure, both fresh and dried, a combined odor that you either like or you don't. I walk down the wide space of dirt between stalls, greeting the horses, joking with them about their quirks, and choose one for no reason at all other than the way it looks at me that morning. I get my old English saddle that has smoothed and darkened through the years, and go into the stall, talking to this beautiful creature who'll swerve out of a canter if a piece of paper blows in front of him, and if the barn catches fire and you manage to get him out he will, if he can get away from you, run back into the fire, to his stall. Like the smells that surround them, you either like them or you don't. I love them, so am spared having to try to explain why. I feed one the carrot or apple and tack up and lead him outside, where I mount, and we go down the driveway to the road and cross it and turn northwest and walk then trot then canter to St. John's.

A few cars are on the road, their drivers looking serious about going to work. It is always strange for me to see a woman dressed for work so early in the morning. You know how long it takes them, with the makeup and hair and clothes, and I think of them waking in the dark of winter or early light of other seasons, and dressing as they might for an evening's entertainment. Probably this strikes me because I grew up seeing my father put on those suits he never wore on weekends or his two weeks off, and so am accustomed to the men, but when I see these women I think something went wrong, to send all those dressed-up people out on the road when the dew hasn't dried yet. Maybe it's because I so dislike getting up early, but am also doing what I choose to do, while they have no choice. At heart I am lazy, yet I find such peace and delight in it that I believe it is a natural state, and in what looks like my laziest periods I am closest to my center. The ride to St. John's is fifteen minutes. The horses and I do it in all weather; the road is well plowed in winter, and there are only a few days a year when ice makes me drive the pickup.

People always look at someone on horseback, and for a moment their faces change and many drivers and I wave to each other. Then at St. John's, Father Paul and five or six regulars and I celebrate the Mass.

Do not think of me as a spiritual man whose every thought during those twenty-five minutes is at one with the words of the Mass. Each morning I try, each morning I fail, and know that always I will be a creature who, looking at Father Paul and the altar, and uttering prayers, will be distracted by scrambled eggs, horses, the weather, and memories and daydreams that have nothing to do with the sacrament I am about to receive. I can receive, though: the Eucharist, and also, at Mass and at other times, moments and even minutes of contemplation. But I cannot achieve contemplation, as some can; and so, having to face and forgive my own failures, I have learned from them both the necessity and wonder of ritual. For ritual allows those who cannot will themselves out of the secular to perform the spiritual, as dancing allows the tongue-tied man a ceremony of love. And, while my mind dwells on breakfast, or Major or Duchess tethered under the church eave, there is, as I take the Host from Father Paul and place it on my tongue and return to the pew, a feeling that I am thankful I have not lost in the forty-eight years since my first Communion. At its center is excitement; spreading out from it is the peace of certainty. Or the certainty of peace. One night Father Paul and I talked about faith. It was long ago, and all I remember is him saying: Belief is believing in God; faith is believing that God believes in you. That is the excitement, and the peace; then the Mass is over, and I go into the sacristy and we have a cigarette and chat, the mystery ends, we are two men talking like any two men on a morning in America, about baseball, plane crashes, presidents, governors, murders, the sun, the clouds. Then I go to the horse and ride back to the life people see, the one in which I move and talk, and most days I enjoy it.

It is late summer now, the time between fishing and hunting, but a good time for baseball. It has been two weeks since Jennifer left, to drive home to Gloria's after her summer visit. She is the only one who still visits; the boys are married and have children, and sometimes fly up for a holiday, or I fly down or west to visit one of them. Jennifer is twenty, and I worry about her the way fathers worry about daughters but not sons. I want to know what she's up to, and at the same time I don't. She looks athletic, and she is: she swims and runs and of course rides. All my children do. When she comes for six weeks in summer, the house is loud with girls, friends of hers since childhood, and new ones. I am glad she kept the girl friends. They have been young company for me and, being with them, I have been able to gauge her growth between summers. On their riding days, I'd take them back to the house when their lessons were over and they had walked the horses and put them back in the stalls, and we'd have lemonade or Coke, and cookies if I had some, and talk until their parents came to drive them home. One year their breasts grew, so I wasn't startled when I saw Jennifer in July. Then they were driving cars to the stable, and beginning to look like young women, and I was passing out beer and ashtrays and they were talking about college.

When Jennifer was here in summer, they were at the house most days. I would say generally that as they got older they became quieter, and though I enjoyed both, I sometimes missed the giggles and shouts. The quiet voices, just low enough for me not to hear from wherever I was, rising and falling in proportion to my distance from them, frightened me. Not that I believed they were planning or recounting anything really wicked, but there was a female seriousness about them, and it was secretive, and of course I thought: love, sex. But it was more than that: it was womanhood they were entering, the deep forest of it, and no matter how many women and men too are saying these days that there is little difference between us, the truth is that men find their way into that forest only on clearly marked trails, while women move about it in like birds. So hearing Jennifer and her friends talking so quietly, yet intensely, I wanted very much to have a wife.

But not as much as in the old days, when Gloria had left but her presence was still in the house as strongly as if she had only gone to visit her folks for a week. There were no clothes or cosmetics, but potted plants endured my neglectful care as long as they could, and slowly died; I did not kill them on purpose, to exorcise the house of her, but I could not remember to water them. For weeks, because I did not use it much, the house was as neat as she had kept it, though dust layered the order she had made. The kitchen went first: I got the dishes in and out of the dishwasher and wiped the top of the stove, but did not return cooking spoons and pot holders to their hooks on the wall, and soon the burners and oven were caked with spillings, the refrigerator had more space and was spotted with juices. The living room and my bedroom went next; I did not go into the children's rooms except on bad nights when I went from room to room and looked and touched and smelled, so they did not lose their order until a year later when the kids came for six weeks. It was three months before I ate the last of the food Gloria had cooked and frozen: I remember it was a beef stew, and very good. By then I had four cookbooks, and was boasting a bit, and talking about recipes with the women at the stables, and looking forward to cooking for Father Paul. But I never looked forward to cooking at night only for myself, though I made myself do it; on some nights I gave in to my daily temptation, and took a newspaper or detective novel to a restaurant. By the end of the second year, though, I had stopped turning on the radio as soon as I woke in the morning, and was able to be silent and alone in the evening too, and then I enjoyed my dinners.

It is not hard to live through a day, if you can live through a moment. What creates despair is the imagination, which pretends there is a future, and insists on predicting millions of moments, thousands of days, and so drains you that you cannot live the moment at hand. That is what Father Paul told me in those first two years, on some of the bad nights when I believed I could not bear what I had to: the most painful loss was my children, then the loss of Gloria, whom I still loved despite or maybe because of our long periods of sadness that rendered us helpless, so neither of us could break out of it to give a hand to the other. Twelve years later I believe ritual would have healed us more quickly than the repetitious talks we had, perhaps even kept us healed. Marriages have lost that, and I wish I had known then what I know now, and we had performed certain acts together every day, no matter how we felt, and perhaps then we could have subordinated feeling to action, for surely that is the essence of love. I know this from my distractions during Mass, and during everything else I do, so that my actions and feelings are seldom one. It does happen every day, but in proportion to everything else in a day, it is rare, like joy. The third most painful loss, which became second and sometimes first as months passed, was the knowledge that I could never marry again, and so dared not even keep company with a woman.

On some of the bad nights I was bitter about this with Father Paul, and I so pitied myself that I cried, or nearly did, speaking with damp eyes and breaking voice. I believe that celibacy is for him the same trial it is for me, not of the flesh, but the spirit: the heart longing to love. But the difference is he chose it, and did not wake one day to a life with thirty horses. In my anger I said I had done my service to love and chastity, and I told him of the actual physical and spiritual pain of practicing rhythm: nights of striking the mattress with a fist, two young animals lying side by side in heat, leaving the bed to pace, to smoke, to curse, and too passionate to question, for we were so angered and oppressed by our passion that we could see no further than our loins. So now I understand how people can be enslaved for generations before they throw down their tools or use them as weapons, the form of their slavery—the cotton fields, the shacks and puny cupboards and untended illnesses—absorbing their emotions and thoughts until finally they have little or none at all to direct with clarity and energy at the owners and legislators. And I told him of the trick of passion and its slaking: how during what we had to believe were safe periods, though all four children were conceived at those times, we were able with some coherence to question the tradition and reason and justice of the law against birth control, but not with enough conviction to soberly act against it, as though regular satisfaction in bed tempered our revolutionary as well as our erotic desires. Only when abstinence drove us hotly away from each other did we receive an urge so strong it lasted all the way to the drugstore and back; but always, after release, we threw away the remaining condoms; and after going through this a few times, we knew what would happen, and from then on we submitted to the calendar she so precisely marked on the bedroom wall. I told him that living two lives each month, one as celibates, one as lovers, made us tense and short-tempered, so we snapped at each other like dogs.

To have endured that, to have reached a time when we burned slowly and could gain from bed the comfort of lying down at night with one who loves you and whom you love, could for weeks on end go to bed tired and peacefully sleep after a kiss, a touch of the hands, and then to be thrown out of the marriage like a bundle from a moving freight car, was unjust, was intolerable, and I could not or would not muster the strength to endure it. But I did, a moment at a time, a day, a night, except twice, each time with a different woman and more than a year apart, and this was so long ago that I clearly see their faces in my memory, can hear the pitch of their voices, and the way they pronounced words, one with a Massachusetts accent, one midwestern, but I feel as though I only heard about them from someone else. Each rode at the stables and was with me for part of an evening; one was badly married, one divorced, so none of us was free. They did not understand this Catholic view, but they were understanding about my having it, and I remained friends with both of them until the married one left her husband and went to Boston, and the divorced one moved to Maine. After both those evenings, those good women, I went to Mass early while Father Paul was still in the confessional, and received his absolution. I did not tell him who I was, but of course he knew, though I never saw it in his eyes. Now my longing for a wife comes only once in a while, like a cold: on some late afternoons when I am alone in the barn, then I lock up and walk to the house, daydreaming, then suddenly look at it and see it empty, as though for the first time, and all at once I'm weary and feel I do not have the energy to broil meat, and I think of driving to a restaurant, then shake my head and go on to the house, the refrigerator, the oven; and some mornings when I wake in the dark and listen to the silence and run my hand over the cold sheet beside me; and some days in summer when Jennifer is here.

Gloria left first me, then the Church, and that was the end of religion for the children though on visits they went to Sunday Mass with me, and still do, out of a respect for my life that they manage to keep free of patronage. Jennifer is an agnostic, though I doubt she would call herself that, any more than she would call herself any other name that implied she had made a decision, a choice, about existence, death, and God. In truth she tends to pantheism, a good sign, I think; but not wanting to be a father who tells his children what they ought to believe, I do not say to her that Catholicism includes pantheism, like onions in a stew. Besides, I have no missionary instinct and do not believe everyone should or even could live with the Catholic faith. It is Jennifer's womanhood that renders me awkward. And womanhood now is frank, not like when Gloria was twenty and there were symbols: high heels and cosmetics and dresses, a cigarette, a cocktail. I am glad that women are free now of false modesty and all its attention paid the flesh; but, still, it is difficult to see so much of your daughter, to hear her talk as only men and bawdy women used to, and most of all to see in her face the deep and unabashed sensuality of women, with no tricks of the eyes and mouth to hide the pleasure she feels at having a strong young body. I am certain, with the way things are now, that she has very happily not been a virgin for years. That does not bother me. What bothers me is my certainty about it, just from watching her walk across a room or light a cigarette or pour milk on cereal.

She told me all of it, waking me that night when I had gone to sleep listening to the wind in the trees and against the house, a wind so strong that I had to shut all but the lee windows, and still the house cooled; told it to me in such detail and so clearly that now, when she has driven the car to Florida, I remember it all as though I had been a passenger in the front seat, or even at the wheel. It started with a movie, then beer and driving to the sea to look at the waves in the night and the wind, Jennifer and Betsy and Liz. They drank a beer on the beach and wanted to go in naked but were afraid they would drown in the high surf. They bought another six-pack at a grocery store in New Hampshire, and drove home. I can see it now, feel it: the three girls and the beer and the ride on country roads where pines curved in the wind and the big deciduous trees swayed and shook as if they might leap from the earth. They would have some windows partly open so they could feel the wind; Jennifer would be playing a cassette, the music stirring them, as it does the young, to memories of another time, other people and places in what is for them the past.

She took Betsy home, then Liz, and sang with her cassette as she left the town west of us and started home, a twenty-minute drive on the road that passes my house. They had each had four beers, but now there were twelve empty bottles in the bag on the floor at the passenger seat, and I kept focusing on their sound against each other when the car shifted speeds or changed directions. For I want to understand that one moment out of all her heart's time on earth, and whether her history had any bearing on it, or whether her heart was then isolated from all it had known, and the sound of those bottles urged it. She was just leaving the town, accelerating past a night club on the right, gaining speed to climb a long, gradual hill, then she went up it, singing, patting the beat on the steering wheel, the wind loud through her few inches of open window, blowing her hair as it did the high branches alongside the road, and she looked up at them and watched the top of the hill for someone drunk or heedless coming over it in part of her lane. She crested to an open black road, and there he was: a bulk, a blur, a thing running across her headlights, and she swerved left and her foot went for the brake and was stomping air above its pedal when she hit him, saw his legs and body in the air, flying out of her light, into the dark. Her brakes were screaming into the wind, bottles clinking in the fallen bag, and with the music and wind inside the car was his sound, already a memory but as real as an echo, that car-shuddering thump as though she had struck a tree. Her foot was back on the accelerator. Then she shifted gears and pushed it. She ejected the cassette and closed the window. She did not start to cry until she knocked on my bedroom door, then called: "Dad?"

Her voice, her tears, broke through my dream and the wind I heard in my sleep, and I stepped into jeans and hurried to the door, thinking harm, rape, death. All were in her face, and I hugged her and pressed her cheek to my chest and smoothed her blown hair, then led her, weeping, to the kitchen and sat her at the table where still she could not speak, nor look at me; when she raised her face it fell forward again, as of its own weight, into her palms. I offered tea and she shook her head, so I offered beer twice, then she shook her head, so I offered whiskey and she nodded. I had some rye that Father Paul and I had not finished last hunting season, and I poured some over ice and set it in front of her and was putting away the ice but stopped and got another glass and poured one for myself too, and brought the ice and bottle to the table where she was trying to get one of her long menthols out of the pack, but her fingers jerked like severed snakes, and I took the pack and lit one for her and took one for myself. I watched her shudder with her first swallow of rye, and push hair back from her face, it is auburn and gleamed in the overhead light, and I remembered how beautiful she looked riding a sorrel; she was smoking fast, then the sobs in her throat stopped, and she looked at me and said it, the words coming out with smoke: "I hit somebody. With the *car.*"

Then she was crying and I was on my feet, moving back and forth, looking down at her, asking *Who? Where? Where?* She was pointing at the wall over the stove, jabbing her fingers and cigarette at it, her other hand at her eyes, and twice in horror I actually looked at the wall. She finished the whiskey in a swallow and I stopped pacing and asking and poured another, and either the drink or the exhaustion of tears quieted her, even the dry sobs, and she told me; not as I tell it now, for that was later as again and again we relived it in the kitchen or living room, and, if in daylight, fled it on horseback out on the trails through the woods and, if at night, walked quietly around in the moonlit pasture, walked around and around it, sweating through our clothes. She told it in bursts, like she was a child again, running to me, injured from play. I put on boots and a shirt and left her with the bottle and her streaked face and a cigarette twitching between her fingers, pushed the door open against the wind, and eased it shut. The wind squinted and watered my eyes as I leaned into it and went to the pickup.

When I passed St. John's I looked at it, and Father Paul's little white rectory in the rear, and wanted to stop, wished I could as I could if he were simply a friend who sold hardware or something. I had forgotten my watch but I always know the time within minutes, even when a sound or dream or my bladder wakes me in the night. It was nearly two; we had been in the kitchen about twenty minutes; she had hit him around one-fifteen. Or her. The road was empty and I drove between blowing trees; caught for an instant in my lights, they seemed to be in panic. I smoked and let hope play its tricks on me: it was neither man nor woman but an animal, a goat or calf or deer on the road; it was a man who had jumped away in time, the collision of metal and body glancing not direct, and he had limped home to nurse bruises and cuts. Then I threw the cigarette and hope both out the window and prayed that he was alive, while beneath that prayer, a reserve deeper in my heart, another one stirred: that if he were dead, they would not get Jennifer.

From our direction, east and a bit south, the road to that hill and the night club beyond it and finally the town is, for its last four or five miles, straight through farming country. When I reached that stretch I slowed the truck and opened my window for the fierce air; on both sides were scattered farmhouses and barns and sometimes a silo, looking not like shelters but like unsheltered things the wind would flatten. Corn bent toward the road from a field on my right, and always something blew in front of me: paper, leaves, dried weeds, branches. I slowed approaching the hill, and went up it in second, staring through my open window at the ditch on the left side of the road, its weeds alive, whipping, a mad dance with the trees above them. I went over the hill and down and, opposite the club, turned right onto a side street of houses, and parked there, in the leaping shadows of trees. I walked back across the road to the club's parking lot, the wind behind me, lifting me as I strode, and I could not hear my boots on pavement. I walked up the hill, on the shoulder, watching the branches above me, hearing their leaves and the creaking trunks and the wind. Then I was at the top, looking down the road and at the farms and fields; the night was clear, and I could see a long way; clouds scudded past the half-moon and stars, blown out to sea.

I started down, watching the tall grass under the trees to my right, glancing into the dark of the ditch, listening for cars behind me; but as soon as I cleared one tree, its sound was gone, its flapping leaves and rattling branches far behind me, as though the greatest distance I had at my back was a matter of feet, while ahead of me I could see a barn two miles off. Then I saw her skid marks: short, and going left and downhill, into the other lane. I stood at the ditch, its weeds blowing; across it were trees and their moving shadows, like the clouds. I stepped onto its slope, and it took me sliding on my feet, then rump, to the bottom, where I sat still, my body gathered to itself, lest a part of me should touch him. But there was only tall grass, and I stood, my shoulders reaching the sides of the ditch, and I walked uphill, wishing for the flashlight in the pickup, walking slowly, and down in the ditch I could hear my feet in the grass and on the earth, and kicking cans and bottles. At the top of the hill I turned and went down, watching the ground above the ditch on my right, praying my prayer from the truck again, the first one, the one I would admit, that he was not dead, was in fact home, and began to hope again, memory telling me of lost pheasants and grouse I had shot, but they were small and the colors of their home, while a man was either there or not; and from that memory I left where I was and while walking in the ditch under the wind was in the deceit of imagination with Jennifer in the kitchen, telling her she had hit no one, or at least had not badly hurt anyone, when I realized he could be in the hospital now and I would have to think of a way to check there, something to say on the phone. I see now that, once hope returned, I should have been certain what it prepared me for: ahead of me, in high grass and the shadows of trees, I saw his shirt. Or that is all my mind would allow itself: a shirt, and I stood looking at it for the moments it took my mind to admit the arm and head and the dark length covered by pants. He lay face down, the arm I could see near his side, his head turned from me, on its cheek.

"Fella?" I said. I had meant to call, but it came out quiet and high, lost inches from my face in the wind. Then I said, "Oh God," and felt Him in the wind and the sky moving past the stars and moon and the fields around me, but only watching me as He might have watched Cain or Job, I did not know which, and I said it again, and wanted to sink to the earth and weep till I slept there in the weeds. I climbed, scrambling up the side of the ditch, pulling at clutched grass, gained the top on hands and knees, and went to him like that, panting, moving through the grass as high and higher than my face, crawling under that sky, making sounds, too, like some animal, there being no words to let him know I was here with him now. He was long; that is the word that came to me, not tall. I kneeled beside him, my hands on my legs. His right arm was by his side, his left arm straight out from the shoulder, but turned, so his palm was open to the tree above us. His left cheek was clean-shaven, his eye closed, and there was no blood. I leaned forward to look at his open mouth and saw the blood on it, going down into the grass. I straightened and looked ahead at the wind blowing past me through grass and trees to a distant light, and I stared at the light, imagining someone awake out there, wanting someone to be, a gathering of old friends, or someone alone listening to music or painting a picture, then I figured it was a night light at a farmyard whose house I couldn't see. *Going,* I thought. *Still going.* I leaned over again and looked at dripping blood.

So I had to touch his wrist, a thick one with a watch and expansion band that I pushed up his arm, thinking *he's left-handed,* my three fingers pressing his wrist, and all I felt was my tough fingertips on that smooth underside flesh and small bones, then relief, then certainty. But against my will, or only because of it, I still don't know, I touched his neck, ran my fingers down it as if petting, then pressed, and my hand sprang back as from fire. I lowered it again, held it there until it felt that faint beating that I could not believe. There was too much wind. Nothing could make a sound in it. A pulse could not be felt in it, nor could mere fingers in that wind feel the absolute silence of a dead man's artery. I was making sounds again; I grabbed his left arm and his waist, and pulled him toward me, and that side of him rose, turned, and I lowered him to his back, his face tilted up toward the tree that was groaning, the tree and I the only sounds in the wind. Turning my face from his, looking down the length of him at his sneakers, I placed my ear on his heart, and heard not that but something else, and I clamped a hand over my exposed ear, heard something liquid and alive, like when you pump a well and after a few strokes you hear air and water moving in the pipe, and I knew I must raise his legs and cover him and run to a phone, while still I listened to his chest, thinking *raise with what? cover with what?* and amid the liquid sound I heard the heart, then lost it, and pressed my ear against bone, but his chest was quiet, and I did not know when the liquid had stopped, and do not know now when I heard air, a faint rush of it, and whether under my ear or at his mouth or whether I heard it at all. I straightened and looked at the light, dim and yellow. Then I touched his throat, looking him full in the face. He was blond and young. He could have been sleeping in the shade of a tree, but for the smear of blood from his mouth to his hair, and the night sky, and the weeds blowing against his head, and the leaves shaking in the dark above us.

I stood. Then I kneeled again and prayed for his soul to join in peace and joy all the dead and living; and, doing so, confronted my first sin against him, not stopping for Father Paul, who could have given him the last rites, and immediately then my second one, or, I saw then, my first, not calling an ambulance to meet me there, and I stood and turned into the wind, slid down the ditch and crawled out of it, and went up the hill and down it, across the road to the street of houses whose people I had left behind forever, so that I moved with stealth in the shadows to my truck.

When I came around the bend near my house, I saw the kitchen light at the rear. She sat as I had left her, the ashtray filled, and I looked at the bottle, felt her eyes on me, felt what she was seeing too: the dirt from my crawling. She had not drunk much of the rye. I poured some in my glass, with the water from melted ice, and sat down and swallowed some and looked at her and swallowed some more, and said: "He's dead."

She rubbed her eyes with the heels of her hands, rubbed the cheeks under them, but she was dry now.

"He was probably dead when he hit the ground. I mean, that's probably what killed—"

"Where was he?"

"Across the ditch, under a tree."

"Was he—did you see his face?"

"No. Not really. I just felt. For life, pulse. I'm going out to the car."

"What for? Oh."

I finished the rye, and pushed back the chair, then she was standing too.

"I'll go with you."

"There's no need."

"I'll go."

I took a flashlight from a drawer and pushed open the door and held it while she went out. We turned our faces from the wind. It was like on the hill, when I was walking, and the wind closed the distance behind me: after three or four steps I felt there was no house back there. She took my hand, as I was reaching for hers. In the garage we let go, and squeezed between the pickup and her little car, to the front of it, where we had more room, and we stepped back from the grill and I shone the light on the fender, the smashed headlight turned into it, the concave chrome staring to the right, at the garage wall.

"We ought to get the bottles," I said.

She moved between the garage and the car, on the passenger side, and had room to open the door and lift the bag. I reached out, and she gave me the bag and backed up and shut the door and came around the car. We sidled to the doorway, and she put her arm around my waist and I hugged her shoulders.

"I thought you'd call the police," she said.

We crossed the yard, faces bowed from the wind, her hair blowing away from her neck, and in the kitchen I put the bag of bottles in the garbage basket. She was working at the table: capping the rye and putting it away, filling the ice tray, washing the glasses, emptying the ashtray, sponging the table.

"Try to sleep now," I said.

She nodded at the sponge circling under her hand, gathering ashes. Then she dropped it in the sink and, looking me full in the face, as I had never seen her look, as perhaps she never had, being for so long a daughter on visits (or so it seemed to me and still does: that until then our eyes had never seriously met), she crossed to me from the sink and kissed my lips, then held me so tightly I lost balance, and would have stumbled forward had she not held me so hard.

I sat in the living room, the house darkened, and watched the maple and the hemlock. When I believed she was asleep I put on *La Bohème,* and kept it at the same volume as the wind so it would not wake her. Then I listened to *Madama Butterfly,* and in the third act had to rise quickly to lower the sound: the wind was gone. I looked at the still maple near the window, and thought of the wind leaving farms and towns and the coast, going out over the sea to die on the waves. I smoked and gazed out the window. The sky was darker, and at daybreak the rain came. I listened to *Tosca,* and at six-fifteen went to the kitchen where Jennifer's purse lay on the table, a leather shoulder purse crammed with the things of an adult woman, things she had begun accumulating only a few years back, and I nearly wept, thinking of what sandy foundations they were: driver's license, credit card, disposable lighter, cigarettes, checkbook, ballpoint pen, cash, cosmetics, comb, brush, Kleenex, these the rite of passage from childhood, and I took one of them—her keys—and went out, remembering a jacket and hat when the rain struck me, but I kept going to the car, and squeezed and lowered myself into it, pulled the seat belt over my shoulder and fastened it and backed out, turning in the drive, going forward into the road, toward St. John's and Father Paul.

Cars were on the road, the workers, and I did not worry about any of them noticing the fender and light. Only a horse distracted them from what they drove to. In front of St. John's is a parking lot; at its far side, past the church and at the edge of the lawn, is an old pine, taller than the steeple now. I shifted to third, left the road, and, aiming the right headlight at the tree, accelerated past the white blur of church, into the black trunk growing bigger till it was all I could see, then I rocked in that resonant thump she had heard, had felt, and when I turned off the ignition it was still in my ears, my blood, and I saw the boy flying in the wind. I lowered my forehead to the wheel. Father Paul opened the door, his face white in the rain.

"I'm all right."

"What happened?"

"I don't know. I fainted."

I got out and went around to the front of the car, looked at the smashed light, the crumpled and torn fender.

"Come to the house and lie down."

"I'm all right."

"When was your last physical?"

"I'm due for one. Let's get out of this rain."

"You'd better lie down."

"No. I want to receive."

That was the time to say I want to confess, but I have not and will not. Though I could now, for Jennifer is in Florida, and weeks have passed, and perhaps now Father Paul would not feel that he must tell me to go to the police. And, for that very reason, to confess now would be unfair. It is a world of secrets, and now I have one from my best, in truth my only, friend. I have one from Jennifer too, but that is the nature of fatherhood.

Most of that day it rained, so it was only in early evening, when the sky cleared, with a setting sun, that two little boys, leaving their confinement for some play before dinner, found him. Jennifer and I got that on the local news, which we listened to every hour, meeting at the radio, standing with cigarettes, until the one at eight o'clock; when she stopped crying, we went out and walked on the wet grass, around the pasture, the last of sunlight still in the air and trees. His name was Patrick Mitchell, he was nineteen years old, was employed by CETA, lived at home with his parents and brother and sister. The paper next day said he had been at a friend's house and was walking home, and I thought of that light I had seen, then knew it was not for him; he lived on one of the streets behind the club. The paper did not say then, or in the next few days, anything to make Jennifer think he was alive while she was with me in the kitchen. Nor do I know if we—I—could have saved him.

In keeping her secret from her friends, Jennifer had to perform so often, as I did with Father Paul and at the stables, that I believe the acting, which took more of her than our daylight trail rides and our night walks in the pasture, was her healing. Her friends teased me about wrecking her car. When I carried her luggage out to the car on that last morning, we spoke only of the weather for her trip—the day was clear, with a dry cool breeze—and hugged and kissed, and I stood watching as she started the car and turned it around. But then she shifted to neutral and put on the parking brake and unclasped the belt, looking at me all the while, then she was coming to me, as she had that night in the kitchen, and I opened my arms.

I have said I talk with God in the mornings, as I start my day, and sometimes as I sit with coffee, looking at the birds, and the woods. Of course He has never spoken to me, but that is not something I require. Nor does He need to. I know Him, as I know the part of myself that knows Him, that felt Him watching from the wind and the night as I kneeled over the dying boy. Lately I have taken to arguing with Him, as I can't with Father Paul, who, when he hears my monthly confession, has not heard and will not hear anything of failure to do all that one can to save an anonymous life, of injustice to a family in their grief, of deepening their pain at the chance and mystery of death by giving them nothing—no one—to hate. With Father Paul I feel lonely about this, but not with God. When I received the Eucharist while Jennifer's car sat twice-damaged, so redeemed, in the rain, I felt neither loneliness nor shame, but as though He were watching me, even from my tongue, intestines, blood, as I have watched my sons at times in their young lives when I was able to judge but without anger, and so keep silent while they, in the agony of their youth, decided how they must act; or found reasons, after their actions, for what they had done. Their reasons were never as good or as bad as their actions, but they needed to find them, to believe they were living by them, instead of the awful solitude of the heart.

I do not feel the peace I once did: not with God, nor the earth, or anyone on it. I have begun to prefer this state, to remember with fondness the other one as a period of peace I neither earned nor deserved. Now in the mornings while I watch purple finches driving larger titmice from the feeder, I say to

Him: I would do it again. For when she knocked on my door, then called me, she woke what had flowed dormant in my blood since her birth, so that what rose from the bed was not a stable owner or a Catholic or any other Luke Ripley I had lived with for a long time, but the father of a girl.

And He says: I am a Father too.

Yes, I say, as You are a Son Whom this morning I will receive; unless You kill me on the way to church, then I trust You will receive me. And as a Son You made Your plea.

Yes, He says, but I would not lift the cup.

True, and I don't want You to lift it from me either. And if one of my sons had come to me that night, I would have phoned the police and told them to meet us with an ambulance at the top of the hill.

Why? Do you love them less?

I tell Him no, it is not that I love them less, but that I could bear the pain of watching and knowing my sons' pain, could bear it with pride as they took the whip and nails. But You never had a daughter and, if You had, You could not have borne her passion.

So, He says, you love her more than you love Me.

I love her more than I love truth.

Then you love in weakness, He says.

As You love me, I say, and I go with an apple or carrot out to the barn.

Christmas

VLADIMIR NABOKOV

I

After walking back from the village to his manor across the dimming snows, Sleptsov sat down in a corner, on a plush-covered chair which he never remembered using before. It was the kind of thing that happens after some great calamity. Not your brother but a chance acquaintance, a vague country neighbor to whom you never paid much attention, with whom in normal times you exchange scarcely a word, is the one who comforts you wisely and gently, and hands you your dropped hat after the funeral service is over, and you are reeling from grief, your teeth chattering, your eyes blinded by tears. The same can be said of inanimate objects. Any room, even the coziest and the most absurdly small, in the little used wing of a great country house has an unlived-in corner. And it was such a corner in which Sleptsov sat.

The wing was connected by a wooden gallery, now encumbered with our huge north Russian snowdrifts, to the master house, used only in summer. There was no need to awaken it, to heat it: the master had come from Petersburg for only a couple of days and had settled in the annex, where it was a simple matter to get the stoves of white Dutch tile going.

The master sat in his corner, on that plush chair, as in a doctor's waiting room. The room floated in darkness; the dense blue of early evening filtered through the crystal feathers of frost on the windowpane. Ivan, the quiet, portly valet, who had recently shaved off his mustache and now looked like his late father, the family butler, brought in a kerosene lamp, all trimmed and brimming with light. He set it on a small table, and noiselessly caged it within its pink silk shade. For an instant a tilted mirror reflected his lit ear and cropped gray hair. Then he withdrew and the door gave a subdued creak.

Sleptsov raised his hand from his knee and slowly examined it. A drop of candle wax had stuck and hardened in the thin fold of skin between two fingers. He spread his fingers and the little white scale cracked.

2

The following morning, after a night spent in nonsensical, fragmentary dreams totally unrelated to his grief, as Sleptsov stepped out into the cold veranda, a floorboard emitted a merry pistol crack underfoot, and the reflections of the many-colored panes formed paradisal lozenges on the white-washed cushionless window seats. The outer door resisted at first, then opened with a luscious crunch, and the dazzling frost hit his face. The reddish sand providently sprinkled on the ice coating the porch steps resembled cinnamon, and thick icicles shot with greenish blue hung from the eaves. The snowdrifts reached all the way to the windows of the annex, tightly gripping the snug little wooden structure in their frosty clutches. The creamy white mounds of what were flower beds in summer swelled slightly above the level snow in front of the porch, and further off loomed the radiance of the park, where every black branchlet was rimmed with silver, and the firs seemed to draw in their green paws under their bright plump load.

Wearing high felt boots and a short fur-lined coat with a karakul collar, Sleptsov strode off slowly along a straight path, the only one cleared of snow, into that blinding distant landscape. He was amazed to be still alive, and able to perceive the brilliance of the snow and feel his front teeth ache from the cold. He even noticed that a snow-covered bush resembled a fountain and that a dog had left a series of saffron marks on the slope of a snowdrift, which had burned through its crust. A little further, the supports of a foot bridge stuck out of the snow, and there Sleptsov stopped. Bitterly, angrily, he pushed the thick, fluffy covering off the parapet. He vividly recalled how this bridge looked in summer. There was his son walking along the slippery planks, flecked with aments, and deftly plucking off with his net a butterfly that had settled on the railing. Now the boy sees his father. Forever lost laughter plays on his face, under the turned-down brim of a straw hat burned dark by the sun; his hand toys with the chainlet of the leather purse attached to his belt, his dear, smooth, suntanned legs in their serge shorts and soaked sandals assume their usual cheerful wide-spread stance. Just recently, in Petersburg, after having babbled in his delirium about school, about his bicycle, about some great Oriental moth, he died, and yesterday Sleptsov had taken the coffin—weighed down, it seemed, with an entire lifetime—to the country, into the family vault near the village church.

It was quiet as it can only be on a bright, frosty day. Sleptsov raised his leg high, stepped off the path, and, leaving blue pits behind him in the snow, made his way among the trunks of amazingly white trees to the spot where the park dropped off toward the river. Far below, ice blocks sparkled near a hole cut in the smooth expanse of white and, on the opposite bank, very straight columns of pink smoke stood above the snowy roofs of log cabins. Sleptsov took off his karakul cap and leaned against a tree trunk. Somewhere far away peasants were chopping wood—every blow bounced resonantly skyward—and beyond the light silver mist of trees, high above the squat izbas, the sun caught the equanimous radiance of the cross on the church.

3

That was where he headed after lunch, in an old sleigh with a high straight back. The cod of the black stallion clacked strongly in the frosty air, the white plumes of low branches glided overhead, and the ruts in front gave off a silvery blue sheen. When he arrived he sat for an hour or so by the grave, resting a heavy, woolen-gloved hand on the iron of the railing that burned his hand through the wool. He came home with a slight sense of disappointment, as if there, in the burial vault, he had been even further removed from his son than here, where the countless summer tracks of his rapid sandals were preserved beneath the snow.

In the evening, overcome by a fit of intense sadness, he had the main house unlocked. When the door swung open with a weighty wail, and a whiff of special, unwintery coolness came from the sonorous iron-barred vestibule, Sleptsov took the lamp with its tin reflector from the watchman's hand and entered the house alone. The parquet floors crackled eerily under his step. Room after room filled with yellow light, and the shrouded furniture seemed unfamiliar; instead of a tinkling chandelier, a soundless bag hung from the ceiling; and Sleptsov's enormous shadow, slowly extending one arm, floated across the wall and over the gray squares of curtained paintings.

He went into the room which had been his son's study in summer, set the lamp on the window ledge and, breaking his fingernails as he did so, opened the folding shutters, even though all was darkness outside. In the blue glass the yellow flame of the slightly smoky lamp appeared, and his large, bearded face showed momentarily.

He sat down at the bare desk and sternly, from under bent brows, examined the pale wallpaper with its garlands of bluish roses; a narrow office-like cabinet, with sliding drawers from top to bottom; the couch and armchairs under slipcovers; and suddenly, dropping his head onto the desk, he started to shake, passionately, noisily, pressing first his lips, then his wet cheek, to the cold, dusty wood and clutching at its far corners.

In the desk he found a notebook, spreading boards, supplies of black pins and an English biscuit tin that contained a large exotic cocoon which had cost three rubles. It was papery to the touch and seemed made of a brown folded leaf. His son had remembered it during his sickness, regretting that he had left it behind, but consoling himself with the thought that the chrysalid inside was probably dead. He also found a torn net : a tarlatan bag on a collapsible hoop (and the mus!in still smelled of summer and sun-hot grass).

Then, bending lower and lower and sobbing with his whole body, he began pulling out one by one the glasstopped drawers of the cabinet. In the dim lamplight the even files of specimens shone silklike under the glass. Here, in this room, on that very desk, his son had spread the wings of his captures. He would first pin the carefully killed insect in the cork-bottomed groove of the setting board, between the adjustable strips of wood, and fasten down flat with pinned strips of paper the still fresh, soft wings. They had now dried long ago and been transferred to the cabinet—those spectacular Swallowtails, those dazzling Coppers and Blues, and the various Fritillaries, some mounted in a supine position to display the mother-of-pearl undersides. His son used to pronounce their Latin names with a moan of triumph or in an arch aside of disdain. And the moths, the moths, the first Aspen Hawk of five summers ago!

4

The night was smoke-blue and moonlit; thin clouds were scattered about the sky but did not touch the delicate, icy moon. The trees, masses of gray frost, cast dark shadows on the drifts, which scintillated here and there with metallic sparks. In the plush-upholstered, well-heated room of the annex Ivan had placed a two-foot fir tree in a clay pot on the table, and was just attaching a candle to its cruciform tip when Sleptsov returned from the main house, chilled, red-eyed, with gray dust smears on his cheek, carrying a wooden case under his arm. Seeing the Christmas tree on the table, he asked absently:

"What's that?"

Relieving him of the case, Ivan answered in a low, mellow voice:

"There's a holiday coming up tomorrow."

"No, take it away," said Sleptsov with a frown, while thinking, "Can this be Christmas Eve? How could I have forgotten?"

Ivan gently insisted:

"It's nice and green. Let it stand for a while."

"Please take it away," repeated Sleptsov, and bent over the case he had brought. In it he had gathered his son's belongings—the folding butterfly net, the biscuit tin with the pear-shaped cocoon, the spreading board, the pins in their lacquered box, the blue notebook. Half of the first page had been torn out, and its remaining fragment contained part of a French dictation. There followed daily entries, names of captured butterflies, and other notes:

"Walked across the bog as far as Borovichi, . . ."

"Raining today. Played checkers with Father, then read Goncharov's *Frigate,* a deadly bore."

"Marvelous hot day. Rode my bike in the evening. A midge got in my eye. Deliberately rode by her dacha twice, but didn't see her. . . ."

Sleptsov raised his head, swallowed something hot and huge. Of whom was his son writing?

"Rode my bike as usual," he read on, "Our eyes nearly met. My darling, my love. . . ."

"This is unthinkable," whispered Sleptsov. "I'll never know. . . ."

He bent over again, avidly deciphering the childish handwriting that slanted up then curved down in the margin.

"Saw a fresh specimen of the Camberwell Beauty today. That means autumn is here. Rain in the evening. She has probably left, and we didn't even get acquainted. Farewell, my darling. I feel terribly sad. . . ."

"He never said anything to me. . . ." Sleptsov tried to remember, rubbing his forehead with his palm.

On the last page there was an ink drawing: the hind view of an elephant—two thick pillars, the corners of two ears, and a tiny tail.

Sleptsov got up. He shook his head, restraining yet another onrush of hideous sobs.

"I—can't—bear—it—any—longer," he drawled between groans, repeating even more slowly, "I—can't—bear—it—any—longer. . . ."

"It's Christmas tomorrow," came the abrupt reminder, "and I'm going to die. Of course. It's so simple. This very night. . . ."

He pulled out a handkerchief and dried his eyes, his beard, his cheeks. Dark streaks remained on the handkerchief.

". . . death," Sleptsov said softly, as if concluding a long sentence.

The clock ticked. Frost patterns overlapped on the blue glass of the window. The open notebook shone radiantly on the table; next to it the light went through the muslin of the butterfly net, and glistened on a corner of the open tin. Sleptsov pressed his eyes shut, and had a fleeting sensation that earthly life lay before him, totally bared and comprehensible—and ghastly in its sadness, humiliatingly pointless, sterile, devoid of miracles. . . .

At that instant there was a sudden snap—a thin sound like that of an overstretched rubber band breaking. Sleptsov opened his eyes. The cocoon in the biscuit tin had burst at its tip, and a black, wrinkled creature the size of a mouse was crawling up the wall above the table. It stopped, holding on to the surface with six black furry feet, and started palpitating strangely. It had emerged from the chrysalid because a man overcome with grief had transferred a tin box to his warm room, and the warmth had penetrated its taut leaf-and-silk envelope; it had awaited this moment so long, had collected its strength so tensely, and now, having broken out, it was slowly and miraculously expanding. Gradually the wrinkled tissues, the velvety fringes, unfurled; the fan-pleated veins grew firmer as they filled with air. It became a winged thing imperceptibly, as a maturing face imperceptibly becomes beautiful. And its wings—still feeble, still moist—kept growing and unfolding, and now they were developed to the limit set for them by God, and there, on the wall, instead of a little lump of life, instead of a dark mouse, was a great *Attacus* moth like those that fly, birdlike, around lamps in the Indian dusk.

And then those thick black wings, with a glazy eyespot on each and a purplish bloom dusting their hooked foretips, took a full breath under the impulse of tender, ravishing, almost human happiness.

Mr. Green

ROBERT OLEN BUTLER

I am a Catholic, the daughter of a Catholic mother and father, and I do not believe in the worship of my ancestors, especially in the form of a parrot. My father's parents died when he was very young and he became a Catholic in an orphanage run by nuns in Hanoi. My mother's mother was a Catholic but her father was not and, like many Vietnamese, he was a believer in what Confucius taught about ancestors. I remember him taking me by the hand while my parents and my grandmother were sitting under a banana tree in the yard and he said, "Let's go talk with Mr. Green." He led me into the house and he touched his lips with his forefinger to tell me that this was a secret. Mr. Green was my grandfather's parrot and I loved talking to him, but we passed Mr. Green's roost in the front room. Mr. Green said, "Hello, kind sir," but we didn't even answer him.

My grandfather took me to the back of his house, to a room that my mother had said was private, that she had yanked me away from when I once had tried to look. It had a bead curtain at the door and we passed through it and the beads rustled like tall grass. The room was dim, lit by candles, and it smelled of incense, and my grandfather stood me before a little shrine with flowers and a smoking incense bowl and two brass candlesticks and between them a photo of a man in a Chinese mandarin hat. "That's my father," he said, nodding toward the photo. "He lives here." Then he let go of my hand and touched my shoulder. "Say a prayer for my father." The face in the photo was tilted a little to the side and was smiling faintly, like he'd asked me a question and he was waiting for an answer that he expected to like. I knelt before the shrine as I did at Mass and I said the only prayer I knew by heart, The Lord's Prayer.

But as I prayed, I was conscious of my grandfather. I even peeked at him as he stepped to the door and parted the beads and looked toward the front of the house. Then he returned and stood beside me and I finished my prayer as I listened to the beads rustling into silence behind us. When I said "Amen" aloud, my grandfather knelt beside me and leaned near and whispered, "Your father is doing a terrible thing. If he must be a Catholic, that's one thing. But he has left the spirits of his ancestors to wander for eternity in loneliness." It was hard for me to believe that my father was doing something as terrible as this, but it was harder for me to believe that my grandfather, who was even older than my father, could be wrong.

My grandfather explained about the spirit world, how the souls of our ancestors continue to need love and attention and devotion. Given these things, they will share in our lives and they will bless us and even warn us about disasters in our dreams. But if we neglect the souls of our ancestors, they will become lost and lonely and will wander around in the kingdom of the dead no better off than a warrior killed by his enemy and left unburied in a rice paddy to be eaten by black birds of prey.

When my grandfather told me about the birds plucking out the eyes of the dead and about the possibility of our own ancestors, our own family, suffering just like that if we ignore them, I said, "Don't worry, Grandfather, I will always say prayers for you and make offerings for you, even if I'm a Catholic."

I thought this would please my grandfather, but he just shook his head sharply, like he was mad at me, and he said, "Not possible."

"I can," I said.

Then he looked at me and I guess he realized that he'd spoken harshly. He tilted his head slightly and smiled a little smile—just like his father in the picture—but what he said wasn't something to smile about. "You are a girl," he said. "So it's not possible for you to do it alone. Only a son can oversee the worship of his ancestors."

I felt a strange thing inside me, a recoiling, like I'd stepped barefoot on a slug, but how can you recoil from your own body? And so I began to cry. My grandfather patted me and kissed me and said it was all right, but it wasn't all right for me. I wanted to protect my grandfather's soul, but it wasn't in my power. I was a girl. We waited together before the shrine and when I'd stopped crying, we went back to the front room and my grandfather bowed to his parrot and said, "Hello, kind sir," and Mr. Green said, "Hello, kind sir," and even though I loved the parrot, I would not speak to him that day because he was a boy and I wasn't.

This was in our town, which was on the bank of the Red River just south of Hanoi. We left that town not long after. I was seven years old and I remember hearing my grandfather arguing with my parents. I was sleeping on a mat at the back of our house and I woke up and I heard voices and my grandfather said, "Not possible." The words chilled me, but then I listened more closely and I knew they were discussing the trip we were about to go on. Everyone was very frightened and excited. There were many families in our little town who were planning to leave. They had even taken the bell out of the church tower to carry with them. We were all Catholics. But Grandfather did not have the concerns of the Catholics. He was concerned about the spirits of his ancestors. This was the place where they were born and died and were buried. He was afraid that they would not make the trip. "What then?" he cried. And later he spoke of the people of the South and how they would hate us, being from the North. "What then?" he said.

Mr. Green says that, too. "What then?" he has cried to me a thousand times, ten thousand times, in the past sixteen years. Parrots can live for a hundred years. And though I could not protect my dead grandfather's soul, I could take care of his parrot. When my grandfather died in Saigon in 1972, he made sure that Mr. Green came to me. I was twenty-four then and newly married and I still loved Mr. Green. He would sit on my shoulder and take the top of my ear in his beak, a beak that could crush the hardest shell, and he would hold my ear with the greatest gentleness and touch me with his tongue.

I have brought Mr. Green with me to the United States of America, and in the long summers here in New Orleans and in the warm springs and falls and even in many days of our mild winters, he sits on my screened-in back porch, near the door, and he speaks in the voice of my grandfather. When he wants to get onto my shoulder and go with me into the community garden, he says, "What then?" And when I first come to him in the morning, he says, "Hello, kind sir."

He loves me. That is, I am the only person who can go near him without his attempting to draw blood. But he loved my grandfather before me, and there are times when he seems to hold the spirit of my grandfather and all his knowledge. Mr. Green sits on my shoulder and presses close to my head and he repeats the words that he has heard from my husband and my children.

My children even teach him English words. He says all these things, but without any feeling. The Vietnamese words of my grandfather, however, come out powerfully, like someone very strong is inside him. And whenever he speaks with my grandfather's voice, Mr. Green's eyes dilate and contract over and over, which is a parrot's display of happiness. Yesterday I tried to give him some drops that the veterinarian prescribed for him and Mr. Green said, "Not possible," and even though he is sick, his eyes showed how pleased he was to defy me.

When we all lived in Saigon at last, my grandfather discovered the bird market on Hàm Nghi Street and he would take me there. Actually, in the street market of Hàm Nghi there were animals of all kinds—dogs and monkeys and rabbits and turtles and even wildcats. But when my grandfather took my hand and said to me, "Come, little one," and we walked down Trân Hu'ng Đạo, where our house was, and we came to Hàm Nghi, he always took me to the place with the birds.

The canaries were the most loved by everyone who came to the market, and my grandfather sang with them. They all hopped to the side of their cages that was closest to my grandfather and he whistled and hummed and even sang words, songs from the North that he sang quite low, so that only the birds could hear. He did not want the people of Saigon to realize he was from the North. And the canaries all opened their mouths and the air filled with their sounds, their throats ruffling and puffing, and I looked at my grandfather's throat to see if it moved the way the throats of these birds moved. It did not move at all. His skin was slack there, and in all the times I saw him charm the birds, I never saw his throat move, like he didn't really mean the sounds he made. The people all laughed when they saw what he could do and they said that my grandfather was a wizard, but he would just ignore them.

The canaries seemed to be his favorite birds on Hàm Nghi, though he spent time with them all. The dark-plumed ones—the magpies and the blackbirds—were always singing on their own, especially the blackbirds with their orange beaks. My grandfather came near the blackbirds and they were gabbling among themselves and he frowned at them, like they were fools to be content only with their own company. They did not need him to prompt their songs. He growled at them, "You're just a bunch of old women," and we moved on to the doves that were big-eyed and quiet and he cooed at them and he told them how pretty they were and we looked at the moorhens, pecking at the bottoms of their cages like chickens, and the cranes with their wonderful necks curling and stretching.

We visited all the birds and my grandfather loved them, and the first time we went to Hàm Nghi, we ended up at the cages crowded with sparrows. He bent near their chattering and I liked these birds very much. They were small and their eyes were bright, and even though the birds were crowded, they were always in motion, hopping and fluffing up and shaking themselves like my vain friends. I was a quiet little girl, but I, too, would sometimes look at myself in a mirror and primp and puff myself up, even as in public I tried to hold myself apart a little bit from the other girls.

I was surprised and delighted that first day when my grandfather motioned to the birdseller and began to point at sparrows and the merchant reached into the cage and caught one bird after another and he put them all into a cardboard box. My grandfather bought twelve birds and they did not fly as they sat in the box. "Why aren't they flying?" I asked.

"Their wings are clipped," my grandfather said.

This was all right with me. They clearly weren't in any pain and they could still hop and they would never fly away from me. I wouldn't even need a cage for my vain little friends.

I'm sure that my grandfather knew what I was thinking. But he said nothing. When we got home, he gave me the box and told me to take the birds to show my mother. I found her on the back stoop slicing vegetables. I showed her the box and she said that Grandfather was wonderful. She set the box down and told me to stay with her, I could help her. I crouched beside her and waited and I could hear the chattering of the sparrows from the box.

We had always kept chickens and ducks and geese. Some of them were pecking around near us even as I crouched there with my mother. I knew that we ate those animals, but for some reason Hàm Nghi seemed like a different place altogether and the sparrows could only be for song and friendship. But finally my mother finished cutting the vegetables and she reached into the box and drew out a sparrow, its feet dangling from the bottom of her fist and its head poking out of the top. I looked at its face and I knew it was a girl and my mother said, "This is the way it's done," and she fisted her other hand around the sparrow's head and she twisted.

I don't remember how long it took me to get used to this. But I would always drift away when my grandfather went to the sparrow cages on Hàm Nghi. I did not like his face when he bought them. It seemed the same as when he cooed at the doves or sang with the canaries. But I must have decided that it was all part of growing up, of becoming a woman like my mother, for it was she who killed them, after all. And she taught me to do this thing and I wanted to be just like her and I twisted the necks of the sparrows and I plucked their feathers and we roasted them and ate them and my grandfather would take a deep breath after the meal and his eyes would close in pleasure.

There were parrots, too, on Hàm Nghi. They all looked very much like Mr. Green. They were the color of breadfruit leaves with a little yellow on the throat. My grandfather chose one bird each time and cocked his head at it, copying the angle of the bird's head, and my grandfather said, "Hello," or "What's your name?"—things he never said to Mr. Green. The parrots on Hàm Nghi did not talk to my grandfather, though once one of them made a sound like the horns of the little cream and blue taxis that rushed past in the streets. But they never spoke any words, and my grandfather took care to explain to me that these parrots were too recently captured to have learned anything. He said that they were probably not as smart as Mr. Green either, but one day they would speak. Once after explaining this, he leaned near me and motioned to a parrot that was digging for mites under his wing and said, "That bird will still be alive and speaking to someone when you have grown to be an old woman and have died and are buried in the ground."

I am forty-one years old now. I go each day to the garden on the bank of the bayou that runs through this place they call Versailles. It is part of New Orleans, but it is far from the center of the town and it is full of Vietnamese who once came from the North. My grandfather never saw the United States. I don't know what he would think. But I come to this garden each day and I crouch in the rich earth and I wear my straw hat and my black pantaloons and I grow lettuce and collards and turnip greens and mint, and my feet, which were once quite beautiful, grow coarse. My family likes the things I bring to the table.

Sometimes Mr. Green comes with me to this garden. He rides on my shoulder and he stays there for a long time, often imitating the cardinals, the sharp ricochet sound they make. Then finally Mr. Green climbs down my arm and drops to the ground and he waddles about in the garden, and when he starts to bite off the stalk of a plant, I cry, "Not possible" to him and he looks at me like he is angry, like I've dared to use his own words, his and his first master's, against him. I always bring twigs with me and I throw him one to chew on so that neither of us has to back down. I have always tried to preserve his dignity. He is at least fifty years older than me. My grandfather was eighteen when he himself caught Mr. Green on a trip to the highlands with his father.

So Mr. Green is quite old and old people sometimes lose their understanding of the things around them. It is not strange, then, that a few weeks ago Mr. Green began to pluck his feathers out. I went to the veterinarian when it became clear what was happening. A great bare spot had appeared on Mr. Green's chest and I had been finding his feathers at the foot of his perch, so I watched him one afternoon through the kitchen window. He sat there on his perch beside the door of the back porch and he pulled twelve feathers from his chest, one at a time, and felt each with his tongue and then dropped it to the floor. I came out onto the porch and he squawked at me, as if he was doing something private and I should have known better than to intrude. I sat down on the porch and he stopped.

I took Mr. Green to the veterinarian and he said that when parrots do this, it may be because they lack a certain vitamin or mineral. But more often the reason is that the bird is bored. I tried to convince myself that this is what it meant when Mr. Green stopped plucking his feathers as soon as I appeared on the porch. Keep him busy, the doctor said. So I got Mr. Green a new climbing tree with lots of fresh bark to peel and I spent more time with him. I took him to the garden even when he didn't ask to go and I brought my sewing and even some of my cooking—the preparation of the foods—out onto the porch, and while I did these household things, I talked to him. It was just idle chatter but there were plenty of words, and often Mr. Green looked at me sharply as I spoke and I could hear how I sounded, chattering away like a blackbird.

But I felt driven to do something for him. He was old and he was sick and I felt I had to do something. My grandfather took six months to die and he lay in a bed on the top floor of our house and Mr. Green was always on a perch beside him. I remember a wind chime at the window. It was made of brass and I've never had a wind chime in my home because when I hear one, another sound always comes with it, the deep rattling cough of my grandfather. I would visit him in his room with my mother and once he called me back as we were about to leave. I came to him and my mother had gone on out the door and I could hear her talking rapidly with my grandmother. My grandfather motioned me to come very near and he twisted his body in the bed. His face crumpled in pain as he did it, but he forced himself because he wanted to tell me a secret. I leaned close to him. "Do you hear them talking?" he said. He nodded toward the door and he obviously meant my mother and grandmother.

"Yes," I said.

He frowned. "How foolish they sound. Chattering and yammering. All the women sound like that. You don't want to grow up sounding like all these foolish women, do you?"

I did not know how to answer his question. I wanted very much to be like my mother, and when my grandfather said this, I felt the recoiling begin inside me and the tears begin to rise. But my mother called my name at that moment and I did not have to find an answer to my grandfather's question. I turned my back on him and ran across the room without saying a word. As I got to the door, however, Mr. Green cried, "What then?" and it sounded as if he had actually finished my grandfather's thought. You will grow up to be a woman—what then?

And maybe he did finish the thought. Parrots are very smart. Mr. Green in particular. And he knows more than just my grandfather's words. The Buddhists believe in the transmigration of souls, though I suppose it's impossible to transmigrate into some creature that's already alive. But after a few days of angry looks from Mr. Green when I filled the porch with talk that was intended to save his life, he began to cry, "Not possible" over and over until I stopped speaking. Perhaps a male voice would have been acceptable to him, but mine was not, and then Mr. Green began to pluck himself once more, even with me sitting there in the room. I went to him when he began to do this and I said, "Not possible," but he ignored me. He did not even raise his head to look at me but tore away at his feathers, each one making a faint popping sound as it came out. Then the next day he began to cough.

I knew the cough well. But I took Mr. Green to the veterinarian and he told me what I expected, that the cough was not the bird's. This was a sound he was imitating. "Did someone in your household recently have a cold or the flu?" the doctor said.

"It is my grandfather," I said.

On the last visit to my grandfather's room he began to cough. My mother went to him and he waved her away. She backed off and I came forward, wanting to help him. He was sitting up now and hunched over and the cough rattled deep inside his chest and then there was a sudden silence and I drew nearer, thinking that my step forward had actually helped, but my grandfather lifted his face and his eyes were very sad, and I knew he was disappointed. My brothers were not yet born and I held my breath so that this silence would go on, but the sound raked up from his chest and filled the room again.

This morning I went to the back porch and Mr. Green was pulling out a feather and he did not acknowledge me, even to taunt me by calling me "sir." He dropped the feather and began to pluck another from beneath his left wing. His chest was naked now and the skin looked as slack as my grandfather's throat. I stood before him and I offered my arm for him to come and sit on my shoulder. Yesterday he had said, "Not possible," but today he said nothing. He dropped a feather and leaned over and bit me hard on my arm. I bled. But I did not move my arm and he looked at me. His eyes were steady in their sadness, fully dilated, as if he was considering all of this. I pushed my arm to him again and he knew that he had no choice, so he climbed on, but he did not go to my shoulder.

I held my arm aloft and carried Mr. Green outside. The sun had still not burned the fog off the bayou and I went straight into the garden. My feet were bare, like a child's, and the earth was soft and wet and I crouched there and I quickly reached to Mr. Green and grasped him at his chest, lifted him and caught him with my other hand before he could struggle. His wings were pinned and he was bigger in my hands than I had ever imagined. But a Vietnamese woman is experienced in these things and Mr. Green did not have a chance even to make a sound as I laid him on his side, pinned him with my knee, slid my hands up and wrung his neck.

I pray for the soul of my grandfather. I do not bear him any anger. Sometimes I go to Mass during the week. Versailles has a Catholic church just for the Vietnamese and the Mass is celebrated in our language. I sit near the back and I look at the section where all the old women go. They take the Eucharist every day of their lives and they sit together wearing their traditional dresses and with their hair in scarves rolled up on their heads and I wonder if that is where I will finally end up, in the old women's section at Mass each day. No one in my church will likely live as long as a parrot. But our savior lived only thirty-three years, so maybe it's not important. There were women around Jesus when He died, the two Marys. They couldn't do anything for Him. But neither could the men, who had all run away.

The Man to Send Rain Clouds

LESLIE MARMON SILKO

They found him under a big cottonwood tree. His levi jacket and pants were faded light blue so that he had been easy to find. The big cottonwood tree stood apart from a small grove of winterbare cottonwoods which grew in the wide, sandy arroyo. He had been dead for a day or more, and the sheep had wandered and scattered up and down the arroyo. Leon and his brother-in-law, Ken, gathered the sheep and left them in the pen at the sheep camp before they returned to the cottonwood tree. Leon waited under the tree while Ken drove the truck through the deep sand to the edge of the arroyo. He squinted up at the sun and unzipped his jacket—it sure was hot for this time of year. But high and northwest the blue mountains were still in snow. Ken came sliding down the low, crumbling bank about fifty yards down, and he was bringing the red blanket.

Before they wrapped the old man, Leon took a piece of string out of his pocket and tied a small gray feather in the old man's long white hair. Ken gave him the paint. Across the brown wrinkled forehead he drew a streak of white and along the high cheekbones he drew a strip of blue paint. He paused and watched Ken throw pinches of corn meal and pollen into the wind that fluttered the small gray feather. Then Leon painted with yellow under the old man's broad nose, and finally, when he had painted green across the chin, he smiled.

"Send us rain clouds, Grandfather." They laid the bundle in the back of the pickup and covered it with a heavy tarp before they started back to the pueblo.

They turned off the highway onto the sandy pueblo road. Not long after they passed the store and post office they saw Father Paul's car coming toward them. When he recognized their faces he slowed his car and waved for them to stop. The young priest rolled down the car window.

"Did you find old Teofilo?" he asked loudly.

Leon stopped the truck. "Good morning, Father. We were just out to the sheep camp. Everything is OK now."

"Thank God for that. Teofilo is a very old man. You really shouldn't allow him to stay at the sheep camp alone."

"No, he won't do that anymore now."

"Well, I'm glad you understand. I hope I'll be seeing you at Mass this week—we missed you last Sunday. See if you can get old Teofilo to come with you." The priest smiled and waved at them as they drove away.

Louise and Teresa were waiting. The table was set for lunch, and the coffee was boiling on the black iron stove. Leon looked at Louise and then at Teresa.

"We found him under a cottonwood tree in the big arroyo near sheep camp. I guess he sat down to rest in the shade and never got up again." Leon walked toward the old man's bed. The red plaid shawl had been shaken and spread carefully over the bed, and a new brown flannel shirt and pair of stiff new Levis were arranged neatly beside the pillow. Louise held the screen door open while Leon and Ken carried in the red blanket. He looked small and shriveled, and after they dressed him in the new shirt and pants he seemed more shrunken.

It was noontime now because the church bells rang the Angelus. They ate the beans with hot bread, and nobody said anything until after Teresa poured the coffee.

Ken stood up and put on his jacket. "I'll see about the gravediggers. Only the top layer of soil is frozen. I think it can be ready before dark."

Leon nodded his head and finished his coffee. After Ken had been gone for a while, the neighbors and clanspeople came quietly to embrace Teofilo's family and to leave food on the table because the gravediggers would come to eat when they were finished. The sky in the west was full of pale yellow light. Louise stood outside with her hands in the pockets of Leon's green Army jacket that was too big for her. The funeral was over, and the old men had taken their candles and medicine bags and were gone. She waited until the body was laid into the pickup before she said anything to Leon. She touched his arm, and he noticed that her hands were still dusty from the corn meal that she had sprinkled around the old man. When she spoke, Leon could not hear her.

"What did you say? I didn't hear you."

"I said that I had been thinking about something."

"About what?"

"About the priest sprinkling holy water for Grandpa. So he won't be thirsty."

Leon stared at the new moccasins that Teofilo had made for the ceremonial dances in the summer. They were nearly hidden by the red blanket. It was getting colder, and the wind pushed gray dust down the narrow pueblo road. The sun was approaching the long mesa where it disappeared during the winter. Louise stood there shivering and watching his face. Then he zipped up his jacket and opened the truck door. "I'll see if he's there."

Ken stopped the pickup at the church, and Leon got out; and then Ken drove down the hill to the graveyard where people were waiting. Leon knocked at the old carved door with its symbols of the Lamb. While he waited he looked up at the twin bells from the king of Spain with the last sunlight pouring around them in their tower.

The priest opened the door and smiled when he saw who it was. "Come in! What brings you here this evening?"

The priest walked toward the kitchen, and Leon stood with his cap in his hand, playing with the earflaps and examining the living room—the brown sofa, the green armchair, and the brass lamp that hung down from the ceiling by links of chain. The priest dragged a chair out of the kitchen and offered it to Leon.

"No thank you, Father. I only came to ask you if you would bring your holy water to the graveyard."

The priest turned away from Leon and looked out the window at the patio full of shadows and the dining-room windows of the nuns' cloister across the patio. The curtains were heavy, and the light from within faintly penetrated; it was impossible to see the nuns inside eating supper. "Why didn't you tell me he was dead? I could have brought the Last Rites anyway."

Leon smiled. "It wasn't necessary, Father."

The priest stared down at his scuffed brown loafers and the worn hem of his cassock. "For a Christian burial it was necessary."

His voice was distant, and Leon thought that his blue eyes looked tired.

"It's OK, Father, we just want him to have plenty of water."

The priest sank down into the green chair and picked up a glossy missionary magazine. He turned the colored pages full of lepers and pagans without looking at them.

"You know I can't do that, Leon. There should have been the Last Rites and a funeral Mass at the very least."

Leon put on his green cap and pulled the flaps down over his ears. "It's getting late, Father. I've got to go."

When Leon opened the door Father Paul stood up and said, "Wait." He left the room and came back wearing a long brown overcoat. He followed Leon out the door and across the dim churchyard to the adobe steps in front of the church. They both stooped to fit through the low adobe entrance. And when they started down the hill to the graveyard only half of the sun was visible above the mesa.

The priest approached the grave slowly, wondering how they had managed to dig into the frozen ground; and then he remembered that this was New Mexico, and saw the pile of cold loose sand beside the hole. The people stood close to each other with little clouds of steam puffing from their faces. The priest looked at them and saw a pile of jackets, gloves, and scarves in the yellow, dry tumbleweeds that grew in the graveyard. He looked at the red blanket, not sure that Teofilo was so small, wondering if it wasn't some perverse Indian trick—something they did in March to ensure a good harvest—wondering if maybe old Teofilo was actually at sheep camp corraling the sheep for the night. But there he was, facing into a cold dry wind and squinting at the last sunlight, ready to bury a red wool blanket while the faces of his parishioners were in shadow with the last warmth of the sun on their backs.

His fingers were stiff, and it took him a long time to twist the lid off the holy water. Drops of water fell on the red blanket and soaked into dark icy spots. He sprinkled the grave and the water disappeared almost before it touched the dim, cold sand; it reminded him of something—he tried to remember what it was, because he thought if he could remember he might understand this. He sprinkled more water; he shook the container until it was empty, and the water fell through the light from sundown like August rain that fell while the sun was still shining, almost evaporating before it touched the wilted squash flowers.

The wind pulled at the priest's brown Franciscan robe and swirled away the corn meal and pollen that had been sprinkled on the blanket. They lowered the bundle into the ground, and they didn't bother to untie the stiff pieces of new rope that were tied around the ends of the blanket. The sun was gone, and over on the highway the eastbound lane was full of headlights. The priest walked away slowly. Leon watched him climb the hill, and when he had disappeared within the tall, thick walls, Leon turned to look up at the high blue mountains in the deep snow that reflected a faint red light from the west. He felt good because it was finished, and he was happy about the sprinkling of the holy water; now the old man could send them big thunderclouds for sure.

DOUBT

Faith and doubt both are needed—not as antagonists but working side by side—to take us around the unknown curve.

Lillian Smith, *The Journey*

There lives more faith in honest doubt,
Believe me, than in half the creeds.

Alfred, Lord Tennyson,
"In Memoriam"

Doubt is a necessity of the mind, faith of the heart.

Comtesse Diane, *Les Glanes de la Vie*

Doubts, like facts, are stubborn things.

L. E. Landon, *Romance and Reality*

The Expert on God

JOHN L'HEUREUX

From the start faith had been a problem for him, and his recent ordination had changed almost nothing. His doubts were simply more appropriate to the priesthood now. That was the only difference.

As a child of ten he was saying his evening prayers when it suddenly struck him that Catholics believed in three gods, God the Father, God the Son, and God the Holy Ghost. He blushed and covered his face. What if the kids at school found out? They were Protestants, and therefore wrong, but at least they had only one God. Instantly it came to him that there were three *Persons* in one God. It was a mystery. He was very embarrassed but very relieved, and he actually looked around to see if anyone had heard his thoughts, and for the rest of his life it remained for him a moment of great shame. At eighteen, when he entered the Jesuits, he got up his courage and told this story to his confessor, who laughed. Matters of faith, he decided then, were better kept secret.

There were other doubts. He doubted Christ's presence in the Eucharist. He prayed for faith, and some kind of faith came to him, because he left off doubting about the Eucharist and moved on to doubt other matters: the virginity of Mary, the divinity of Christ, and then later the humanity of Christ. At one time or another, he doubted every article of belief, but only for a while, and only one at a time. Faith demanded a different response to each mystery, he discovered, but doubt was always the same. The initial onslaught of doubt lasted for only a moment, a quick and breathtaking conviction that none of it was true, and then that conviction itself surrendered to doubt, leaving an awful lingering unspeakable ache.

In the end he doubted the love of God, and that doubt did not pass.

He was a popular priest but he had no friends. He kept other Jesuits at a distance, he forced them away. He had no time for the intimacies of his own kind, caught up as he was in his assault on God. He prayed for faith. And when that did not come, he prayed for hope. And when that did not come, he went on anyway, teaching, preaching, saying Mass at the odd parish whenever he was asked. That is how things stood with him on the day of the accident.

It was Christmas Day, not because Christmas is symbolic, but because that is when it happened. Snow had fallen for nearly a week, and then on Christmas Eve there had been hail and then rain and then a sudden freeze. The streets were ready.

He had said Mass at Our Lady of Victories and was driving back to the Jesuit house. It was almost noon and the sun was high. "It doesn't matter," he said. The air was clear and the day was bright after all that snow, and as he drove through the vast open countryside, he marveled again at the absence of God. "It doesn't matter anymore."

He had very nearly achieved a kind of trance, staring at the sun on the ice, trying to obliterate all thought. Suddenly, off to the side of the road, he saw a dark blue car turned half on its side and three boys huddled near it, looking at him as if he might be bringing help. He braked quickly, skidded in a half turn, and came to a stop. It was then that he noticed the tiny red sports car in the field on the opposite side of the road. It was crumpled nearly in two. The priest looked at the boys, but they only looked back, stunned. Finally one of them pointed to the red sports car.

He scrabbled through the glove compartment until he found the little vial of holy oils. He sprinted toward the car, following the wild track it had made as it spun through the snow, and when he got to it, he was not surprised to see the front end was completely demolished. He stooped and looked through the shattered window. The driver had been thrown to the side; the dashboard, crumpled back into the car, had pinned him, head down, in the passenger seat. The door hung on a single hinge, open a few inches but not wide enough for the priest to get in. The door would not give and he could not force it to open wider. He looked around a moment for help and saw that of course there was none; the boys huddling together across the street were too stupefied to help—or maybe they were injured, for all he knew.

He put the vial of oils in his pocket and jogged rapidly around the car. There was no way in. Somebody was inside, dying perhaps, and though he was only a few inches away, he could not reach him. It was maddening. He struck the car with his fist and sobbed suddenly in anger and frustration. Desperate then, he braced his back against the side of the car, pushing outward on the broken door and twisting, half crazy, until the hinge gave way. He squeezed himself into the car behind the driver's seat. He could hear a kind of gurgling sound from the man trapped beneath the dashboard. He edged across until he was behind the passenger seat and, with what strength he could muster, he pulled back on it until it snapped and broke loose. He climbed onto it so that he was behind the body. He squatted, doubled up, hunched over, scarcely able to breathe, but at last he got his arms around the body and eased it free of the dashboard.

It was a boy, in his new car, and he was still alive, or nearly. He made a sound that might have been a sigh or a groan. Blood trickled from his mouth. Still he did not die.

The priest held him in his arms. Crushed himself, he nonetheless managed to get the oils from his pocket and to wet his thumb with them and to place his thumb on the boy's bloody forehead, saying "I absolve you from all your sins. In the name of the Father and of the Son and of the Holy Ghost. Amen." Then he was silent.

There was no sound from outside the car, no ambulance wail, no curious viewers. They were in the middle of nowhere, he and this dying boy he held in his arms. He had touched the boy with the holy oils and he had offered him absolution for his sins, and something should have happened by now. Someone should have come to help. The boy should have died. Something. But there was silence only, and the boy's harsh, half-choked breathing.

He began to pray, aloud, which struck him as foolish: to be holding a dying boy in his arms and reciting rote prayers about our father in heaven, about holy Mary, mother of God. What could he do? What could he say at such a moment? What would God do at such a moment, if there were a God? "Well, do it," he said aloud, and heard the fury in his voice. "Say something." But there was silence from heaven.

His doubts became certainty and he said, "It doesn't matter," but it did matter and he knew it. What could anyone say to this crushed, dying thing, he wondered. What would God say if he cared as much as I?

He shook with an involuntary sob then, and as he did, the boy shuddered in agony and choked on the blood that had begun to pour from his mouth. The priest could see death beginning to ease across the boy's face. And still he could say nothing.

The boy turned—some dying reflex—and his head tilted in the priest's arms, trusting, like a lover. And at once the priest, faithless, unrepentant, gave up his prayers and bent to him and whispered, fierce and burning, "I love you," and continued till there was no breath, "I love you, I love you, I love you."

The Conversion of the Jews

PHILIP ROTH

"You're a real one for opening your mouth in the first place," Itzie said. "What do you open your mouth all the time for?"

"I didn't bring it up, Itz, I didn't," Ozzie said.

"What do you care about Jesus Christ for anyway?"

"I didn't bring up Jesus Christ. He did. I didn't even know what he was talking about. Jesus is historical, he kept saying. Jesus is historical." Ozzie mimicked the monumental voice of Rabbi Binder.

"Jesus was a person that lived like you and me," Ozzie continued. "That's what Binder said—"

"Yeah? . . . So what! What do I give two cents whether he lived or not. And what do you gotta open your mouth!" Itzie Lieberman favored closed-mouthedness, especially when it came to Ozzie Freedman's questions. Mrs. Freedman had to see Rabbi Binder twice before about Ozzie's questions and this Wednesday at four-thirty would be the third time. Itzie preferred to keep *his* mother in the kitchen; he settled for behind-the-back subtleties such as gestures, faces, snarls and other less delicate barnyard noises.

"He was a real person, Jesus, but he wasn't like God, and we don't believe he is God." Slowly, Ozzie was explaining Rabbi Binder's position to Itzie, who had been absent from Hebrew School the previous afternoon.

"The Catholics," Itzie said helpfully, "they believe in Jesus Christ, that he's God." Itzie Lieberman used "the Catholics" in its broadest sense—to include the Protestants.

Ozzie received Itzie's remark with a tiny head bob, as though it were a footnote, and went on. "His mother was Mary, and his father probably was Joseph," Ozzie said. "But the New Testament says his real father was God."

"His *real* father?"

"Yeah," Ozzie said, "that's the big thing, his father's supposed to be God."

"Bull."

"That's what Rabbi Binder says, that it's impossible—"

"Sure it's impossible. That stuff's all bull. To have a baby you gotta get laid," Itzie theologized. "Mary hadda get laid."

"That's what Binder says: 'The only way a woman can have a baby is to have intercourse with a man.' "

"He said *that,* Ozz?" For a moment it appeared that Itzie had put the theological question aside. "He said that, intercourse?" A little curled smile shaped itself in the lower half of Itzie's face like a pink mustache. "What you guys do, Ozz, you laugh or something?"

"I raised my hand."

"Yeah? Whatja say?"

"That's when I asked the question."

Itzie's face lit up. "Whatja ask about—intercourse?"

"No, I asked the question about God, how if He could create the heaven and earth in six days, and make all the animals and the fish and the light in six days—the light especially, that's what always gets me, that He could make the light. Making fish and animals, that's pretty good—"

"That's damn good." Itzie's appreciation was honest but unimaginative: it was as though God had just pitched a one-hitter.

"But making light . . . I mean when you think about it, it's really something," Ozzie said. "Anyway, I asked Binder if He could make all that in six days, and He could *pick* the six days he wanted right out of nowhere, why couldn't He let a woman have a baby without having intercourse."

"You said intercourse, Ozz, to Binder?"

"Yeah."

"Right in class?"

"Yeah."

Itzie smacked the side of his head.

"I mean, no kidding around," Ozzie said, "that'd really be nothing. After all that other stuff, that'd practically be nothing."

Itzie considered a moment. "What'd Binder say?"

"He started all over again explaining how Jesus was historical and how he lived like you and me but he wasn't God. So I said I under*stood* that. What I wanted to know was different."

What Ozzie wanted to know was always different. The first time he had wanted to know how Rabbi Binder could call the Jews "The Chosen People" if the Declaration of Independence claimed all men to be created equal. Rabbi Binder tried to distinguish for him between political equality and spiritual legitimacy, but what Ozzie wanted to know, he insisted vehemently, was different. That was the first time his mother had to come.

Then there was the plane crash. Fifty-eight people had been killed in a plane crash at La Guardia. In studying a casualty list in the newspaper his mother had discovered among the list of those dead eight Jewish names (his grandmother had nine but she counted Miller as a Jewish name); because of the eight she said the plane crash was "a tragedy." During free-discussion time on Wednesday Ozzie had brought to Rabbi Binder's attention this matter of "some of his relations" always picking out the Jewish names. Rabbi Binder had begun to explain cultural unity and some other things when Ozzie stood up at his seat and said that what he wanted to know was different. Rabbi Binder insisted that he sit down and it was then that Ozzie shouted that he wished all fifty-eight were Jews. That was the second time his mother came.

"And he kept explaining about Jesus being historical, and so I kept asking him. No kidding, Itz, he was trying to make me look stupid."

"So what he finally do?"

"Finally he starts screaming that I was deliberately simpleminded and a wise guy, and that my mother had to come, and this was the last time. And that I'd never get bar-mitzvahed if he could help it. Then, Itz, then he starts talking in that voice like a statue, real slow and deep, and he says that I better think over what I said about the Lord. He told me to go to his office and think it over." Ozzie leaned his body towards Itzie. "Itz, I thought it over for a solid hour, and now I'm convinced God could do it."

Ozzie had planned to confess his latest transgression to his mother as soon as she came home from work. But it was a Friday night in November and already dark, and when Mrs. Freedman came through the door she tossed off her coat, kissed Ozzie quickly on the face, and went to the kitchen table to light the three yellow candles, two for the Sabbath and one for Ozzie's father.

When his mother lit the candles she would move her two arms slowly towards her, dragging them through the air, as though persuading people whose minds were half made up. And her eyes would get glassy with tears.

Even when his father was alive Ozzie remembered that her eyes had gotten glassy, so it didn't have anything to do with his dying. It had something to do with lighting the candles.

As she touched the flaming match to the unlit wick of a Sabbath candle, the phone rang, and Ozzie, standing only a foot from it, plucked it off the receiver and held it muffled to his chest. When his mother lit candles Ozzie felt there should be no noise; even breathing, if you could manage it, should be softened. Ozzie pressed the phone to his breast and watched his mother dragging whatever she was dragging, and he felt his own eyes get glassy. His mother was a round, tired, gray-haired penguin of a woman whose gray skin had begun to feel the tug of gravity and the weight of her own history. Even when she was dressed up she didn't look like a chosen person. But when she lit candles she looked like something better; like a woman who knew momentarily that God could do anything.

After a few mysterious minutes she was finished. Ozzie hung up the phone and walked to the kitchen table where she was beginning to lay the two places for the four-course Sabbath meal. He told her that she would have to see Rabbi Binder next Wednesday at four-thirty, and then he told her why. For the first time in their life together she hit Ozzie across the face with her hand.

All through the chopped liver and chicken soup part of the dinner Ozzie cried; he didn't have any appetite for the rest.

On Wednesday, in the largest of the three basement classrooms of the synagogue, Rabbi Marvin Binder, a tall, handsome, broad-shouldered man of thirty with thick strong-fibered black hair, removed his watch from his pocket and saw that it was four o'clock. At the rear of the room Yakov Blotnik, the seventy-one-year-old custodian, slowly polished the large window, mumbling to himself, unaware that it was four o'clock or six o'clock, Monday or Wednesday. To most of the students Yakov Blotnik's mumbling, along with his brown curly beard, scythe nose, and two heel-trailing black cats, made of him an object of wonder, a foreigner, a relic, towards whom they were alternately fearful and disrespectful. To Ozzie the mumbling had always seemed a monotonous, curious prayer; what made it curious was that old Blotnik had been mumbling so steadily for so many years, Ozzie suspected he had memorized the prayers and forgotten all about God.

"It is now free-discussion time," Rabbi Binder said. "Feel free to talk about any Jewish matter at all—religion, family, politics, sports—"

There was silence. It was a gusty, clouded November afternoon and it did not seem as though there ever was or could be a thing called baseball. So nobody this week said a word about that hero from the past, Hank Greenberg—which limited free discussion considerably.

And the soul-battering Ozzie Freedman had just received from Rabbi Binder had imposed its limitation. When it was Ozzie's turn to read aloud from the Hebrew book the rabbi had asked him petulantly why he didn't read more rapidly. He was showing no progress. Ozzie said he could read faster but that if he did he was sure not to understand what he was reading. Nevertheless, at the rabbi's repeated suggestion Ozzie tried, and showed a great talent, but in the midst of a long passage he stopped short and said he didn't understand a word he was reading, and started in again at a drag-footed pace. Then came the soul-battering.

Consequently when free-discussion time rolled around none of the students felt too free. The rabbi's invitation was answered only by the mumbling of feeble old Blotnik.

"Isn't there anything at all you would like to discuss?" Rabbi Binder asked again, looking at his watch. "No questions or comments?"

There was a small grumble from the third row. The rabbi requested that Ozzie rise and give the rest of the class the advantage of his thought.

Ozzie rose. "I forget it now," he said, and sat down in his place.

Rabbi Binder advanced a seat towards Ozzie and poised himself on the edge of the desk. It was Itzie's desk and the rabbi's frame only a dagger's-length away from his face snapped him to sitting attention.

"Stand up again, Oscar," Rabbi Binder said calmly, "and try to assemble your thoughts."

Ozzie stood up. All his classmates turned in their seats and watched as he gave an unconvincing scratch to his forehead.

"I can't assemble any," he announced, and plunked himself down.

"Stand up!" Rabbi Binder advanced from Itzie's desk to the one directly in front of Ozzie; when the rabbinical back was turned Itzie gave it five-fingers off the tip of his nose, causing a small titter in the room. Rabbi Binder was too absorbed in squelching Ozzie's nonsense once and for all to bother with titters. "Stand up, Oscar. What's your question about?"

Ozzie pulled a word out of the air. It was the handiest word. "Religion."

"Oh, now you remember?"

"Yes."

"What is it?"

Trapped, Ozzie blurted the first thing that came to him. "Why can't He make anything He wants to make!"

As Rabbi Binder prepared an answer, a final answer, Itzie, ten feet behind him, raised one finger on his left hand, gestured it meaningfully towards the rabbi's back, and brought the house down.

Binder twisted quickly to see what had happened and in the midst of the commotion Ozzie shouted into the rabbi's back what he couldn't have shouted to his face. It was a loud, toneless sound that had the timbre of something stored inside for about six days.

"You don't know! You don't know anything about God!"

The rabbi spun back towards Ozzie. "What?"

"You don't know—you don't—"

"Apologize, Oscar, apologize!" It was a threat.

"You don't—"

Rabbi Binder's hand flicked out at Ozzie's cheek. Perhaps it had only been meant to clamp the boy's mouth shut, but Ozzie ducked and the palm caught him squarely on the nose.

The blood came in a short, red spurt on to Ozzie's shirt front.

The next moment was all confusion. Ozzie screamed, "You bastard, you bastard!" and broke for the classroom door. Rabbi Binder lurched a step backwards, as though his own blood had started flowing violently in the opposite direction, then gave a clumsy lurch forward and bolted out the door after Ozzie. The class followed after the rabbi's huge blue-suited back, and before old Blotnik could turn from his window, the room was empty and everyone was headed full speed up the three flights leading to the roof.

If one should compare the light of day to the life of man: sunrise to birth; sunset—the dropping down over the edge—to death; then as Ozzie Freedman wiggled through the trapdoor of the synagogue roof, his feet kicking backwards bronco-style at Rabbi Binder's outstretched arms—at that moment the day was fifty years old. As a rule, fifty or fifty-five reflects accurately the age of late afternoons in November, for it is in that month, during those hours, that one's awareness of light seems no longer a matter of seeing, but of hearing: light begins clicking away. In fact, as Ozzie locked shut the trapdoor in the rabbi's face, the sharp click of the bolt into the lock might momentarily have been mistaken for the sound of the heavier gray that had just throbbed through the sky.

With all his weight Ozzie kneeled on the locked door; any instant he was certain that Rabbi Binder's shoulder would fling it open, splintering the wood into shrapnel and catapulting his body into the sky. But the door did not move and below him he heard only the rumble of feet, first loud then dim, like thunder rolling away.

A question shot through his brain. "Can this be *me?*" For a thirteen-year-old who had just labeled his religious leader a bastard, twice, it was not an improper question. Louder and louder the question came to him—"Is it me? Is it me?"—until he discovered himself no longer kneeling, but racing crazily towards the edge of the roof, his eyes crying, his throat screaming, and his arms flying everywhichway as though not his own.

"Is it me? Is it me Me Me Me Me! It has to be me—but is it!"

It is the question a thief must ask himself the night he jimmies open his first window, and it is said to be the question with which bridegrooms quiz themselves before the altar.

In the few wild seconds it took Ozzie's body to propel him to the edge of the roof, his self-examination began to grow fuzzy. Gazing down at the street, he became confused as to the problem beneath the question: was it, is-it-me-who-called-Binder-a-bastard? or, is-it-me-prancing-around-on-the-roof? However, the scene below settled all, for there is an instant in any action when whether it is you or somebody else is academic. The thief crams the money in his pockets and scoots out the window. The bridegroom signs the hotel register for two. And the boy on the roof finds a streetful of people gaping at him, necks stretched backwards, faces up, as though he were the ceiling of the Hayden Planetarium. Suddenly you know it's you.

"Oscar! Oscar Freedman!" A voice rose from the center of the crowd, a voice that, could it have been seen, would have looked like the writing on a scroll. "Oscar Freedman, get down from there. Immediately!" Rabbi Binder was pointing one arm stiffly up at him; and at the end of that arm, one finger aimed menacingly. It was the attitude of a dictator, but one—the eyes confessed all—whose personal valet had spit neatly in his face.

Ozzie didn't answer. Only for a blink's length did he look towards Rabbi Binder. Instead his eyes began to fit together the world beneath him, to sort out people from places, friends from enemies, participants from spectators. In little jagged starlike clusters his friends stood around Rabbi Binder, who was still pointing. The topmost point on a star compounded not of angels but of five adolescent boys was Itzie. What a world it was, with those stars below, Rabbi Binder below . . . Ozzie, who a moment earlier hadn't been able to control his own body, started to feel the meaning of the word control: he felt Peace and he felt Power.

"Oscar Freedman, I'll give you three to come down."

Few dictators give their subjects three to do anything; but, as always, Rabbi Binder only looked dictatorial.

"Are you ready, Oscar?"

Ozzie nodded his head yes, although he had no intention in the world—the lower one or the celestial one he'd just entered—of coming down even if Rabbi Binder should give him a million.

"All right then," said Rabbi Binder. He ran a hand through his black Samson hair as though it were the gesture prescribed for uttering the first digit. Then, with his other hand cutting a circle out of the small piece of sky around him, he spoke. "One!"

There was no thunder. On the contrary, at that moment, as though "one" was the cue for which he had been waiting, the world's least thunderous person appeared on the synagogue steps. He did not so much come out the synagogue door as lean out, onto the darkening air. He clutched at the doorknob with one hand and looked up at the roof.

"Oy!"

Yakov Blotnik's old mind hobbled slowly, as if on crutches, and though he couldn't decide precisely what the boy was doing on the roof, he knew it wasn't good—that is, it wasn't-good-for-the-Jews. For Yakov Blotnik life had fractionated itself simply: things were either good-for-the-Jews or no-good-for-the-Jews.

He smacked his free hand to his in-sucked cheek, gently. "Oy, Gut!" And then quickly as he was able, he jacked down his head and surveyed the street. There was Rabbi Binder (like a man at an auction with only three dollars in his pocket, he had just delivered a shaky "Two!"); there were the students, and that was all. So far it-wasn't-so-bad-for-the-Jews. But the boy had to come down immediately, before anybody saw. The problem: how to get the boy off the roof?

Anybody who has ever had a cat on the roof knows how to get him down. You call the fire department. Or first you call the operator and you ask her for the fire department. And the next thing there is great jamming of brakes and clanging of bells and shouting of instructions. And then the cat is off the roof. You do the same thing to get a boy off the roof.

That is, you do the same thing if you are Yakov Blotnik and you once had a cat on the roof.

When the engines, all four of them, arrived, Rabbi Binder had four times given Ozzie the count of three. The big hook-and-ladder swung around the corner and one of the firemen leaped from it, plunging headlong towards the yellow fire hydrant in front of the synagogue. With a huge wrench he began to unscrew the top nozzle. Rabbi Binder raced over to him and pulled at his shoulder.

"There's no fire . . ."

The fireman mumbled back over his shoulder and, heatedly, continued working at the nozzle.

"But there's no fire, there's no fire . . ." Binder shouted. When the fireman mumbled again, the rabbi grasped his face with both his hands and pointed it up at the roof.

To Ozzie it looked as though Rabbi Binder was trying to tug the fireman's head out of his body, like a cork from a bottle. He had to giggle at the picture they made: it was a family portrait—rabbi in black skullcap, fireman in red fire hat, and the little yellow hydrant squatting beside like a kid brother, bareheaded. From the edge of the roof Ozzie waved at the portrait, a one-handed, flapping, mocking wave; in doing it his right foot slipped from under him. Rabbi Binder covered his eyes with his hands.

Firemen work fast. Before Ozzie had even regained his balance, a big, round, yellowed net was being held on the synagogue lawn. The firemen who held it looked up at Ozzie with stern, feelingless faces.

One of the firemen turned his head towards Rabbi Binder. "What, is the kid nuts or something?"

Rabbi Binder unpeeled his hands from his eyes, slowly, painfully, as if they were tape. Then he checked: nothing on the sidewalk, no dents in the net.

"Is he gonna jump, or what?" the fireman shouted.

In a voice not at all like a statue, Rabbi Binder finally answered. "Yes, Yes, I think so . . . He's been threatening to . . ."

Threatening to? Why, the reason he was on the roof, Ozzie remembered, was to get away; he hadn't even thought about jumping. He had just run to get away, and the truth was that he hadn't really headed for the roof as much as he'd been chased there.

"What's his name, the kid?"

"Freedman," Rabbi Binder answered. "Oscar Freedman."

The fireman looked up at Ozzie. "What is it with you, Oscar? You gonna jump, or what?"

Ozzie did not answer. Frankly, the question had just arisen.

"Look, Oscar, if you're gonna jump, jump—and if you're not gonna jump, don't jump. But don't waste our time, willya?"

Ozzie looked at the fireman and then at Rabbi Binder. He wanted to see Rabbi Binder cover his eyes one more time.

"I'm going to jump."

And then he scampered around the edge of the roof to the corner, where there was no net below, and he flapped his arms at his sides, swishing the air and smacking his palms to his trousers on the downbeat. He began screaming like some kind of engine, "Wheeeee . . . wheeeeee," and leaning way out over the edge with the upper half of his body. The fireman whipped around to cover the ground with the net. Rabbi Binder mumbled a few words to Somebody and covered his eyes. Everything happened quickly, jerkily, as in a silent movie. The crowd, which had arrived with the fire engines, gave out a long, Fourth-of-July fireworks oooh-aahhh. In the excitement no one had paid the crowd much heed, except, of course, Yakov Blotnik, who swung from the doorknob counting heads. "Fier und tsvansik . . . finf und tsvantsik . . . Oy, Gut!" It wasn't like this with the cat.

Rabbi Binder peeked through his fingers, checked the sidewalk and net. Empty. But there was Ozzie racing to the other corner. The firemen raced with him but were unable to keep up. Whenever Ozzie wanted to he might jump and splatter himself upon the sidewalk, and by the time the firemen scooted to the spot all they could do with their net would be to cover the mess.

"Wheeeee . . . wheeeee . . ."

"Hey, Oscar," the winded fireman yelled, "What the hell is this, a game or something?"

"Wheeeee . . . wheeeee . . ."

"Hey, Oscar—"

But he was off now to the other corner, flapping his wings fiercely. Rabbi Binder couldn't take it any longer—the fire engines from nowhere, the screaming suicidal boy, the net. He fell to his knees, exhausted, and with his hands curled together in front of his chest like a little dome, he pleaded, "Oscar, stop it, Oscar. Don't jump, Oscar. Please come down . . . Please don't jump."

And further back in the crowd a single voice, a single young voice, shouted a lone word to the boy on the roof.

"Jump!"

It was Itzie. Ozzie momentarily stopped flapping.

"Go ahead, Ozz—jump!" Itzie broke off his point of the star and courageously, with the inspiration not of a wise-guy but of a disciple, stood alone. "Jump, Ozz, jump!"

Still on his knees, his hands still curled, Rabbi Binder twisted his body back. He looked at Itzie, then, agonizingly, back to Ozzie.

"OSCAR, DON'T JUMP! PLEASE, DON'T JUMP . . . please please . . ."

"Jump!" This time it wasn't Itzie but another point of the star. By the time Mrs. Freedman arrived to keep her four-thirty appointment with Rabbi Binder, the whole little upside down heaven was shouting and pleading for Ozzie to jump, and Rabbi Binder no longer was pleading with him not to jump, but was crying into the dome of his hands.

Understandably Mrs. Freedman couldn't figure out what her son was doing on the roof. So she asked.

"Ozzie, my Ozzie, what are you doing? My Ozzie, what is it?"

Ozzie stopped wheeeeeing and slowed his arm down to a cruising flap, the kind birds use in soft winds, but he did not answer. He stood against the low, clouded, darkening sky—light clicked down swiftly now, as on a small gear—flapping softly and gazing down at the small bundle of a woman who was his mother.

"What are you doing, Ozzie?" She turned towards the kneeling Rabbi Binder and rushed so close that only a paper-thickness of dusk lay between her stomach and his shoulders.

"What is my baby doing?"

Rabbi Binder gaped up at her but he too was mute. All that moved was the dome of his hands; it shook back and forth like a weak pulse.

"Rabbi, get him down! He'll kill himself. Get him down, my only baby . . ."

"I can't," Rabbi Binder said, "I can't . . ." and he turned his handsome head towards the crowd of boys behind him. "It's them. Listen to them."

And for the first time Mrs. Freedman saw the crowd of boys, and she heard what they were yelling.

"He's doing it for them. He won't listen to me. It's them." Rabbi Binder spoke like one in a trance.

"For them?"

"Yes."

"Why for them?"

"They want him to . . ."

Mrs. Freedman raised her two arms upward as though she were conducting the sky. "For them he's doing it!" And then in a gesture older than pyramids, older than prophets and floods, her arms came slapping down to her sides. "A martyr I have. Look!" She tilted her head to the roof. Ozzie was still flapping softly. "My martyr."

"Oscar, come down, *please,*" Rabbi Binder groaned.

In a startlingly even voice Mrs. Freedman called to the boy on the roof. "Ozzie, come down, Ozzie. Don't be a martyr, my baby."

As though it were a litany, Rabbi Binder repeated her words. Don't be a martyr, my baby. Don't be a martyr."

"Gawhead, Ozz—*be* a Martin!" It was Itzie. "Be a Martin, be a Martin," and all the voices joined in singing for Martindom, whatever *it* was. "Be a Martin, be a Martin . . ."

Somehow when you're on a roof the darker it gets the less you can hear. All Ozzie knew was that two groups wanted two new things: his friends were spirited and musical about what they wanted; his mother and the rabbi were even-toned, chanting, about what they didn't want. The rabbi's voice was without tears now and so was his mother's.

The big net stared up at Ozzie like a sightless eye. The big, clouded sky pushed down. From beneath it looked like a gray corrugated board. Suddenly, looking up into that unsympathetic sky, Ozzie realized all the strangeness of what these people, his friends, were asking: they wanted him to jump, to kill himself; they were singing about it now—it made them that happy. And there was an even greater strangeness: Rabbi Binder was on his knees, trembling. If there was a question to be asked now it was not "Is it me?" but rather "Is it us? . . . Is it us?"

Being on the roof, it turned out, was a serious thing. If he jumped would the singing become dancing? Would it? What would jumping stop? Yearningly, Ozzie wished he could rip open the sky, plunge his hands through, and pull out the sun; and on the sun, like a coin, would be stamped JUMP or DON'T JUMP.

Ozzie's knees rocked and sagged a little under him as though they were setting him for a dive. His arms tightened, stiffened, froze, from shoulders to fingernails. He felt as if each part of his body were going to vote as to whether he should kill himself or not—and each part as though it were independent of *him.*

The light took an unexpected click down and the new darkness, like a gag, hushed the friends singing for this and the mother and rabbi chanting for that.

Ozzie stopped counting votes, and in a curiously high voice, like one who wasn't prepared for speech, he spoke.

"Mamma?"

"Yes, Oscar."

"Mamma, get down on your knees, like Rabbi Binder."

"Oscar—"

"Get down on your knees," he said, "or I'll jump."

Ozzie heard a whimper, then a quick rustling, and when he looked down where his mother had stood he saw the top of a head and beneath that a circle of dress. She was kneeling beside Rabbi Binder.

He spoke again. "Everybody kneel." There was the sound of everybody kneeling.

Ozzie looked around. With one hand he pointed towards the synagogue entrance. "Make *him* kneel."

There was a noise, not of kneeling, but of body-and-cloth stretching. Ozzie could hear Rabbi Binder saying in a gruff whisper, ". . . or he'll *kill* himself," and when next he looked there was Yakov Blotnik off the doorknob and for the first time in his life upon his knees in the Gentile posture of prayer.

As for the firemen—it is not as difficult as one might imagine to hold a net taut while you are kneeling.

Ozzie looked around again; and then he called to Rabbi Binder.

"Rabbi?"

"Yes, Oscar."

"Rabbi Binder, do you believe in God."

"Yes."

"Do you believe God can do Anything?" Ozzie leaned his head out into the darkness. "Anything?"

"Oscar, I think—"

"Tell me you believe God can do Anything."

There was a second's hesitation. Then: "God can do Anything."

"Tell me you believe God can make a child without intercourse."

"He can."

"Tell me!"

"God," Rabbi Binder admitted, "can make a child without intercourse."

"Mamma, you tell me."

"God can make a child without intercourse," his mother said.

"Make *him* tell me." There was no doubt who *him* was.

In a few moments Ozzie heard an old comical voice say something to the increasing darkness about God.

Next, Ozzie made everybody say it. And then he made them all say they believed in Jesus Christ—first one at a time, then all together.

When the catechizing was through it was the beginning of evening. From the street it sounded as if the boy on the roof might have sighed.

"Ozzie?" A woman's voice dared to speak. "You'll come down now?"

There was no answer, but the woman waited, and when a voice finally did speak it was thin and crying, and exhausted as that of an old man who has just finished pulling the bells.

"Mamma, don't you see—you shouldn't hit me. He shouldn't hit me. You shouldn't hit me about God, Mamma. You should never hit anybody about God—"

"Ozzie, please come down now."

"Promise me, promise me you'll never hit anybody about God."

He had asked only his mother, but for some reason everyone kneeling in the street promised he would never hit anybody about God.

Once again there was silence.

"I can come down now, Mamma," the boy on the roof finally said. He turned his head both ways as though checking the traffic lights. "Now I can come down . . ."

And he did, right into the center of the yellow net that glowed in the evening's edge like an overgrown halo.

Pigeon Feathers

JOHN UPDIKE

When they moved to Firetown, things were upset, displaced, rearranged. A red cane-back sofa that had been the chief piece in the living room at Olinger was here banished, too big for the narrow country parlor, to the barn, and shrouded under a tarpaulin. Never again would David lie on its length all afternoon eating raisins and reading mystery novels and science fiction and P. G. Wodehouse. The blue wing chair that had stood for years in the ghostly, immaculate guest bedroom, gazing through the windows curtained with dotted swiss toward the telephone wires and horse-chestnut trees and opposite houses, was here established importantly in front of the smutty little fireplace that supplied, in those first cold April days, their only heat. As a child, David had been afraid of the guest bedroom—it was there that he, lying sick with the measles, had seen a black rod the size of a yardstick jog along at a slight slant beside the edge of the bed and vanish when he screamed—and it was disquieting to have one of the elements of its haunted atmosphere basking by the fire, in the center of the family, growing sooty with use. The books that at home had gathered dust in the case beside the piano were here hastily stacked, all out of order, in the shelves that the carpenters had built along one wall below the deep-silled windows. David, at fourteen, had been more moved than a mover; like the furniture, he had to find a new place, and on the Saturday of the second week he tried to work off some of his disorientation by arranging the books.

It was a collection obscurely depressing to him, mostly books his mother had acquired when she was young: college anthologies of Greek plays and

Romantic poetry, Will Durant's *Story of Philosophy*, a soft-leather set of Shakespeare with string bookmarks sewed to the bindings, *Green Mansions* boxed and illustrated with woodcuts, *I, the Tiger*, by Manuel Komroff, novels by names like Galsworthy and Ellen Glasgow and Irvin S. Cobb and Sinclair Lewis and "Elizabeth." The odor of faded taste made him feel the ominous gap between himself and his parents, the insulting gulf of time that existed before he was born. Suddenly he was tempted to dip into this time. From the heaps of books piled around him on the worn old floorboards, he picked up Volume II of a four-volume set of *The Outline of History*, by H. G. Wells. Once David had read *The Time Machine* in an anthology; this gave him a small grip on the author. The book's red binding had faded to orange-pink on the spine. When he lifted the cover, there was a sweetish, attic-like smell, and his mother's maiden name written in unfamiliar handwriting on the flyleaf—an upright, bold, yet careful signature, bearing a faint relation to the quick scrunched blackslant that flowed with marvellous consistency across her shopping lists and budget accounts and Christmas cards to college friends from this same, vaguely menacing long ago.

He leafed through, pausing at drawings, done in an old-fashioned stippled style, of bas-reliefs, masks, Romans without pupils in their eyes, articles of ancient costume, fragments of pottery found in unearthed homes. He knew it would be interesting in a magazine, sandwiched between ads and jokes, but in this undiluted form history was somehow sour. The print was determinedly legible, and smug, like a lesson book. As he bent over the pages, yellow at the edges, they seemed rectangles of dusty glass through which he looked down into unreal and irrelevant worlds. He could see things sluggishly move, and an unpleasant fullness came into his throat. His mother and grandmother fussed in the kitchen; the puppy, which they had just acquired, for "protection in the country," was cowering, with a sporadic panicked scrabble of claws, under the dining table that in their old home had been reserved for special days but that here was used for every meal.

Then, before he could halt his eyes, David slipped into Wells's account of Jesus. He had been an obscure political agitator, a kind of hobo, in a minor colony of the Roman Empire. By an accident impossible to reconstruct, he (the small *h* horrified David) survived his own crucifixion and presumably died a few weeks later. A religion was founded on the freakish incident. The credulous imagination of the times retrospectively assigned miracles and supernatural pretensions to Jesus; a myth grew, and then a church, whose theology at most points was in direct contradiction of the simple, rather communistic teachings of the Galilean.

It was as if a stone that for weeks and even years had been gathering weight in the web of David's nerves snapped them and plunged through the page and a hundred layers of paper underneath. These fantastic falsehoods—plainly untrue; churches stood everywhere, the entire nation was founded "under God"—did not at first frighten him; it was the fact that they had been permitted to exist in an actual human brain. This was the initial impact—that at a definite spot in time and space a brain black with the denial of Christ's divinity had been suffered to exist; that the universe had not spit out this ball of tar but allowed it to continue in its blasphemy, to grow old, win honors, wear a hat, write books that, if true, collapsed everything into a jumble of horror. The world outside the deep-silled windows—a rutted lawn, a whitewashed barn, a walnut tree frothy with fresh green—seemed a haven from which he was forever sealed off. Hot washrags seemed pressed against his cheeks.

He read the account again. He tried to supply out of his ignorance objections that would defeat the complacent march of these black words, and found none. Survivals and misunderstandings more farfetched were reported daily in the papers. But none of them caused churches to be built in every town. He tried to work backwards through the churches, from their brave high fronts through their shabby, ill-attended interiors back into the events at Jerusalem, and felt himself surrounded by shifting gray shadows, centuries of history, where he knew nothing. The thread dissolved in his hands. Had Christ ever come to him, David Kern, and said, "Here. Feel the wound in My side"? No; but prayers had been answered. What prayers? He had prayed that Rudy Mohn, whom he had purposely tripped so he cracked his head on their radiator, not die, and he had not died. But for all the blood, it was just a cut; Rudy came back the same day, wearing a bandage and repeating the same teasing words. He could never have died. Again, David had prayed for two separate war-effort posters he had sent away for to arrive tomorrow, and though they did not, they did arrive, some days later, together, popping through the clacking letter slot like a rebuke from God's mouth: *I answer your prayers in My way, in My time.* After that, he had made his prayers less definite, less susceptible of being twisted into a scolding. But what a tiny, ridiculous coincidence this was, after all, to throw into battle against H. G. Wells's engines of knowledge! Indeed, it proved the enemy's point: Hope bases vast premises on foolish accidents, and reads a word where in fact only a scribble exists.

❖

His father came home. Though Saturday was a free day for him, he had been working. He taught school in Olinger and spent all his days performing, with a curious air of panic, needless errands. Also, a city boy by birth, he was frightened of the farm and seized any excuse to get away. The farm had been David's mother's birthplace; it had been her idea to buy it back. With an ingenuity and persistence unparalleled in her life, she had gained that end, and moved them all here—her son, her husband, her mother. Granmom, in her prime, had worked these fields alongside her husband, but now she dabbled around the kitchen futilely, her hands waggling with Parkinson's disease. She was always in the way. Strange, out in the country, amid eighty acres, they were crowded together. His father expressed his feelings of discomfort by conducting with Mother an endless argument about organic farming. All through dusk, all through supper, it rattled on.

"Elsie, I *know,* I know from my education, the earth is nothing but chemicals. It's the only damn thing I got out of four years of college, so don't tell me it's not true."

"George, if you'd just walk out on the farm you'd know it's not true. The land has a *soul.*"

"Soil, has, no, soul," he said, enunciating stiffly, as if to a very stupid class. To David he said, "You can't argue with a femme. Your mother's a real femme. That's why I married her, and now I'm suffering for it."

"*This* soil has no soul," she said, "because it's been killed with superphosphate. It's been burned bare by Boyer's tenant farmers." Boyer was the rich man they had bought the farm from. "It used to have a soul, didn't it, Mother? When you and Pop farmed it?"

"Ach, yes; I guess." Granmom was trying to bring a forkful of food to her mouth with her less severely afflicted hand. In her anxiety she brought the other hand up from her lap. The crippled fingers, dull red in the orange light of the kerosene lamp in the center of the table, were welded by paralysis into one knobbed hook.

"Only human indi-vidu-als have souls," his father went on, in the same mincing, lifeless voice. "Because the Bible tells us so." Done eating, he crossed his legs and dug into his ear with a match miserably; to get at the thing inside his head he tucked in his chin, and his voice came out low-pitched at David. "When God made your mother, He made a real femme."

"George, don't you read the papers? Don't you know that between the chemical fertilizers and the bug sprays we'll all be dead in ten years? Heart attacks are killing every man in the country over forty-five."

He sighed wearily; the yellow skin of his eyelids wrinkled as he hurt himself with the match. "There's no connection," he stated, spacing his words with pained patience, "between the heart—and chemical fertilizers. It's alcohol that's doing it. Alcohol and milk. There is too much—cholesterol—in the tissues of the American heart. Don't tell me about chemistry, Elsie; I majored in the damn stuff for four years."

"Yes and I majored in Greek and I'm not a penny wiser. Mother, put your waggler *away*!" The old woman started, and the food dropped from her fork. For some reason, the sight of her bad hand at the table cruelly irritated her daughter. Granmom's eyes, worn bits of crazed crystal embedded in watery milk, widened behind her cockeyed spectacles. Circles of silver as fine as thread, they clung to the red notches they had carved over the years into her little white beak. In the orange flicker of the kerosene lamp her dazed misery seemed infernal. David's mother began, without noise, to cry. His father did not seem to have eyes at all; just jaundiced sockets of wrinkled skin. The steam of food clouded the scene. It was horrible but the horror was particular and familiar, and distracted David from the formless dread that worked, sticky and sore, within him, like a too large wound trying to heal.

He had to go to the bathroom, and took a flashlight down through the wet grass to the outhouse. For once, his fear of spiders there felt trivial. He set the flashlight, burning, beside him, and an insect alighted on its lens, a tiny insect, a mosquito or flea, made so fine that the weak light projected its X-ray onto the wall boards; the faint rim of its wings, the blurred strokes, magnified, of its long hinged legs, the dark cone at the heart of its anatomy. The tremor must be its heart beating. Without warning, David was visited by an exact vision of death: a long hole in the ground, no wider than your body, down which you are drawn while the white faces above recede. You try to reach them but your arms are pinned. Shovels pour dirt into your face. There you will be forever, in an upright position, blind and silent, and in time no one will remember you, and you will never be called. As strata of rock shift, your fingers elongate, and your teeth are distended sideways in a great underground grimace indistinguishable from a strip of chalk. And the earth tumbles on, and the sun expires, and unaltering darkness reigns where once there were stars.

Sweat broke out on his back. His mind seemed to rebound off a solidness. Such extinction was not another threat, a graver sort of danger, a kind of pain; it was qualitatively different. It was not even a conception that could be voluntarily pictured; it entered him from outside. His protesting nerves swarmed on its surface like lichen on a meteor. The skin of his chest was soaked with the effort of rejection. At the same time that the fear was dense and internal, it was dense and all around him; a tide of clay had swept up to the stars; space was crushed into a mass. When he stood up, automatically hunching his shoulders to keep his head away from the spider webs, it was with a numb sense of being cramped between two huge volumes of rigidity. That he had even this small freedom to move surprised him. In the narrow shelter of that rank shack, adjusting his pants, he felt—his first spark of comfort—too small to be crushed.

But in the open, as the beam of the flashlight skidded with frightened quickness across the remote surfaces of the barn and the grape arbor and the giant pine that stood by the path to the woods, the terror descended. He raced up through the clinging grass pursued, not by one of the wild animals the woods might hold, or one of the goblins his superstitious grandmother had communicated to his childhood, but by spectres out of science fiction, where gigantic cinder moons fill half the turquoise sky. As David ran, a gray planet rolled inches behind his neck. If he looked back, he would be buried. And in the momentum of his terror, hideous possibilities—the dilation of the sun, the triumph of the insects, the crabs on the shore in *The Time Machine*—wheeled out of the vacuum of make-believe and added their weight to his impending oblivion.

He wrenched the door open; the lamps within the house flared. The wicks burning here and there seemed to mirror one another. His mother was washing the dishes in a little pan of heated pump-water; Granmom fluttered near her elbow apprehensive. In the living room—the downstairs of the little square house was two long rooms—his father sat in front of the black fireplace restlessly folding and unfolding a newspaper as he sustained his half of the argument. "Nitrogen, phosphorus, potash: these are the three replaceable constituents of the soil. One crop of corn carries away hundreds of pounds of"—he dropped the paper into his lap and ticked them off on three fingers—"nitrogen, phosphorus, potash."

"Boyer didn't grow corn."

"*Any* crop, Elsie. The human animal—"

"You're killing the *earth*worms, George!"

"The human animal, after thousands and *thou*sands of years, learned methods whereby the chemical balance of the soil may be maintained. Don't carry me back to the Dark Ages."

"When we moved to Olinger the ground in the garden was like slate. Just one summer of my cousin's chicken dung and the earthworms came back."

"I'm sure the Dark Ages were a fine place to the poor devils born in them, but I don't want to go there. They give me the creeps." Daddy stared into the cold pit of the fireplace and clung to the rolled newspaper in his lap as if it alone were keeping him from slipping backwards and down, down.

Mother came into the doorway brandishing a fistful of wet forks. "And thanks to your DDT there soon won't be a bee left in the country. When I was a girl here you could eat a peach without washing it."

"It's primitive, Elsie. It's Dark Age stuff."

"Oh what do *you* know about the Dark Ages?"

"I know I don't want to go back to them."

David took from the shelf, where he had placed it this afternoon, the great unabridged Webster's Dictionary that his grandfather had owned. He turned the big thin pages, floppy as cloth, to the entry he wanted, and read

> soul . . . 1. An entity conceived as the essence, substance, animating principle, or actuating cause of life, or of the individual life, esp. of life manifested in psychical activities; the vehicle of individual existence, separate in nature from the body and usually held to be separable in existence.

The definition went on, into Greek and Egyptian conceptions, but David stopped short on the treacherous edge of antiquity. He needed to read no further. The careful overlapping words shingled a temporary shelter for him. "Usually held to be separable in existence"—what could be fairer, more judicious, surer?

His father was saying, "The modern farmer can't go around sweeping up after his cows. The poor devil has thousands and *thou*sands of acres on his hands. Your modern farmer uses a scientifically-arrived-at mixture, like five-ten-five, or six-twelve-six, or *three*-twelve-six, and spreads it on with this wonderful modern machinery which of course we can't afford. Your modern farmer can't *afford* medieval methods."

Mother was quiet in the kitchen; her silence radiated waves of anger.

"Now now Elsie; don't play the femme with me. Let's discuss this calmly like two rational twentieth-century people. Your organic farming nuts aren't attacking five-ten-five; they're attacking the chemical fertilizer crooks. The monster firms."

A cup clinked in the kitchen. Mother's anger touched David's face; his cheeks burned guiltily. Just by being in the living room he was associated with his father. She appeared in the doorway with red hands and tears in her eyes, and said to the two of them, "I knew you didn't want to come here but I didn't know you'd torment me like this. You talked Pop into his grave and now you'll kill me. Go ahead, George, more power to you; at least I'll be buried in good ground." She tried to turn and met an obstacle and screamed, "Mother, stop hanging on my *back*! Why don't you go to *bed*?"

"Let's all go to bed," David's father said, rising from the blue wing chair and slapping his thigh with a newspaper. "This reminds me of death." It was a phrase of his that David had heard so often he never considered its sense.

Upstairs, he seemed to be lifted above his fears. The sheets on his bed were clean. Granmom had ironed them with a pair of flatirons saved from the Olinger attic; she plucked them hot off the stove alternately, with a wooden handle called a goose. It was a wonder, to see how she managed. In the next room, his parents grunted peaceably; they seemed to take their quarrels less seriously than he did. They made comfortable scratching noises as they carried a little lamp back and forth. Their door was open a crack, so he saw the light shift and swing. Surely there would be, in the last five minutes, in the last second, a crack of light, showing the door from the dark room to another, full of light. Thinking of it this vividly frightened him. His own dying, in a specific bed in a specific room, specific walls mottled with wallpaper, the dry whistle of his breathing, the murmuring doctors, the nervous relatives going in and out, but for him no way out but down into the funnel. *Never touch a doorknob again.* A whisper, and his parents' light was blown out. David prayed to be reassured. Though the experiment frightened him, he lifted his hands high into the darkness above his face and begged Christ to touch them. Not hard or long: the faintest, quickest grip would be final for a lifetime. His hands waited in the air, itself a substance, which seemed to move through his fingers; or was it the pressure of his pulse? He returned his hands to beneath the covers uncertain if they had been touched or not. For would not Christ's touch *be* infinitely gentle?

Through all the eddies of its aftermath, David clung to this thought about his revelation of extinction: that there, in the outhouse, he had struck a solidness qualitatively different, a rock of horror firm enough to support any height of construction. All he needed was a little help; a word, a gesture, a nod of certainty, and he would be sealed in, safe. The assurance from the dictionary had melted in the night. Today was Sunday, a hot fair day. Across a mile of clear air the church bells called, *Celebrate, celebrate*. Only Daddy went. He put on a coat over his rolled-up shirtsleeves and got into the little old black Plymouth parked by the barn and went off, with the same pained hurried grimness of all his actions. His churning wheels, as he shifted too hastily into second, raised plumes of red dust on the dirt road. Mother walked to the far field, to see what bushes needed cutting. David, though he usually preferred to stay in the house, went with her. The puppy followed at a distance, whining as it picked its way through the stubble but floundering off timidly if one of them went back to pick it up and carry it. When they reached the crest of the far field, his mother asked, "David, what's troubling you?"

"Nothing. Why?"

She looked at him sharply. The greening woods cross-hatched the space beyond her half-gray hair. Then she showed him her profile, and gestured toward the house, which they had left a half-mile behind them. "See how it sits in the land? They don't know how to build with the land any more. Pop always said the foundations were set with the compass. We must try to get a compass and see. It's supposed to face due south; but south feels a little more *that* way to me." From the side, as she said these things, she seemed handsome and young. The smooth sweep of her hair over her ear seemed white with a purity and calm that made her feel foreign to him. He had never regarded his parents as consolers of his troubles; from the beginning they had seemed to have more troubles than he. Their confusion had flattered him into an illusion of strength; so now on this high clear ridge he jealously guarded the menace all around them, blowing like a breeze on his fingertips, the possibility of all this wide scenery sinking into darkness. The strange fact that though she came to look at the brush she carried no clippers, for she had a fixed prejudice against working on Sundays, was the only consolation he allowed her to offer.

As they walked back, the puppy whimpering after them, the rising dust behind a distant line of trees announced that Daddy was speeding home from church. When they reached the house he was there. He had brought back the Sunday paper and the vehement remark, "Dobson's too intelligent for these farmers. They just sit there with their mouths open and don't hear a thing the poor devil's saying."

"What makes you think farmers are unintelligent? This country was made by farmers. George Washington was a farmer."

"They are, Elsie. They are unintelligent. George Washington's dead. In this day and age only the misfits stay on the farm. The lame, the halt, the blind. The morons with one arm. Human garbage. They remind me of death, sitting there with their mouths open."

"My *father* was a farmer."

"He was a frustrated man, Elsie. He never knew what hit him. The poor devil meant so well, and he never knew which end was up. Your mother'll bear me out. Isn't that right, Mom? Pop never knew what hit him?"

"Ach, I guess not," the old woman quavered, and the ambiguity for the moment silenced both sides.

David hid in the funny papers and sports section until one-thirty. At two, the catechetical class met at the Firetown church. He had transferred from the catechetical class of the Lutheran church in Olinger, a humiliating comedown. In Olinger they met on Wednesday nights, spiffy and spruce, in the atmosphere of a dance. Afterwards, blessed by the brick-faced minister from whose lips the word "Christ" fell like a burning stone, the more daring of them went with their Bibles to a luncheonette and smoked. Here in Firetown, the girls were dull white cows and the boys narrow-faced brown goats in old men's suits, herded on Sunday afternoons into a threadbare church basement that smelled of stale hay. Because his father had taken the car on one of his endless errands to Olinger, David walked, grateful for the open air and the silence. The catechetical class embarrassed him, but today he placed hope in it, as the source of the nod, the gesture, that was all he needed.

Reverend Dobson was a delicate young man with great dark eyes and small white shapely hands that flickered like protesting doves when he preached; he seemed a bit misplaced in the Lutheran ministry. This was his first call. It was a split parish; he served another rural church twelve miles away. His iridescent green Ford, new six months ago, was spattered to the windows with red mud and rattled from bouncing on the rude back roads, where he frequently got lost, to the malicious satisfaction of many. But David's mother liked him, and, more pertinent to his success, the Haiers, the sleek family of feed merchants and innkeepers and tractor salesmen who dominated the Firetown church, liked him. David liked him, and felt liked in turn; sometimes in class, after some special stupidity, Dobson directed toward him out of those wide black eyes a mild look of disbelief, a look that, though flattering, was also delicately disquieting.

Catechetical instruction consisted of reading aloud from a work booklet answers to problems prepared during the week, problems like, "I am the———, the ———, and the ———, saith the Lord." Then there was a question period in which no one ever asked any questions. Today's theme was the last third of the Apostles' Creed. When the time came for questions,

David blushed and asked, "About the Resurrection of the Body—are we conscious between the time when we die and the Day of Judgment?"

Dobson blinked, and his fine little mouth pursed, suggesting that David was making difficult things more difficult. The faces of the other students went blank, as if an indiscretion had been committed.

"No, I suppose not," Reverend Dobson said.

"Well, where is our soul, then, in this gap?"

The sense grew, in the class, of a naughtiness occurring. Dobson's shy eyes watered, as if he were straining to keep up the formality of attention, and one of the girls, the fattest, simpered toward her twin, who was a little less fat. Their chairs were arranged in a rough circle. The current running around the circle panicked David. Did everybody know something he didn't know?

"I suppose you could say our souls are asleep," Dobson said.

"And then they wake up, and there is the earth like it always is, and all the people who have ever lived? Where will Heaven be?"

Anita Haier giggled. Dobson gazed at David intently, but with an awkward, puzzled flicker of forgiveness, as if there existed a secret between them that David was violating. But David knew of no secret. All he wanted was to hear Dobson repeat the words he said every Sunday morning. This he would not do. As if these words were unworthy of the conversational voice.

"David, you might think of Heaven this way: as the way the goodness Abraham Lincoln did lives after him."

"But is Lincoln conscious of it living on?" He blushed no longer with embarrassment but in anger; he had walked here in good faith and was being made a fool.

"Is he conscious now? I would have to say no; but I don't think it matters." His voice had a coward's firmness; he was hostile now.

"You don't."

"Not in the eyes of God, no." The unction, the stunning impudence, of this reply sprang tears of outrage in David's eyes. He bowed them to his book, where short words like Duty, Love, Obey, Honor, were stacked in the form of a cross.

"Were there any other questions, David?" Dobson asked with renewed gentleness. The others were rustling, collecting their books.

"No.' He made his voice firm, though he could not bring up his eyes.

"Did I answer your question fully enough?"

"Yes."

In the minister's silence the shame that should have been his crept over David: the burden and fever of being a fraud were placed upon *him*, who was innocent, and it seemed, he knew, a confession of this guilt that on the way out he was unable to face Dobson's stirred gaze, though he felt it probing the side of his head.

Anita Haier's father gave him a ride down the highway as far as the dirt road. David said he wanted to walk the rest, and figured that his offer was accepted because Mr. Haier did not want to dirty his bright blue Buick with dust. This was all right; everything was all right, as long as it was clear. His indignation at being betrayed, at seeing Christianity betrayed, had hardened him. The straight dirt road reflected his hardness. Pink stones thrust up through its packed surface. The April sun beat down from the center of the afternoon half of the sky; already it had some of summer's heat. Already the fringes of weeds at the edges of the road were bedraggled with dust. From the reviving grass and scuff of the fields he walked between, insects were sending up a monotonous automatic chant. In the distance a tiny figure in his father's coat was walking along the edge of the woods. His mother. He wondered what joy she found in such walks; to him the brown stretches of slowly rising and falling land expressed only a huge exhaustion.

Flushed with fresh air and happiness, she returned from her walk earlier than he had expected, and surprised him at his grandfather's Bible. It was a stumpy black book, the boards worn thin where the old man's fingers had held them; the spine hung by one weak hinge of fabric. David had been looking for the passage where Jesus says to the one thief on the cross, "Today shalt thou be with me in paradise." He had never tried reading the Bible for himself before. What was so embarrassing about being caught at it, was that he detested the apparatus of piety. Fusty churches, creaking hymns, ugly Sunday-school teachers and their stupid leaflets—he hated everything about them but the promise they held out, a promise that in the most perverse way, as if the homeliest crone in the kingdom were given the Prince's hand, made every good and real thing, ball games and jokes and pert-breasted girls, possible. He couldn't explain this to his mother. There was no time. Her solicitude was upon him.

"David, what are you doing?"

"Nothing."

"What are you doing at Grandpop's Bible?"

"Trying to read it. This is supposed to be a Christian country, isn't it?"

She sat down on the green sofa, which used to be in the sun parlor at Olinger, under the fancy mirror. A little smile still lingered on her face from the walk. "David, I wish you'd talk to me."

"What about?"

"About whatever it is that's troubling you. Your father and I have both noticed it."

"I asked Reverend Dobson about Heaven and he said it was like Abraham Lincoln's goodness living after him."

He waited for the shock to strike her. "Yes?" she said, expecting more.

"That's all."

"And why didn't you like it?"

"Well; don't you see? It amounts to saying there isn't any Heaven at all."

"I don't see that it amounts to that. What do you want Heaven to be?"

"Well, I don't know. I want it to be *some*thing. I thought he'd tell me what it was. I thought that was his job." He was becoming angry, sensing her surprise at him. She had assumed that Heaven had faded from his head years ago. She had imagined that he had already entered, in the secrecy of silence, the conspiracy that he now knew to be all around him.

"David," she asked gently, "don't you ever want to rest?"

"No. Not forever."

"David, you're so young. When you get older, you'll feel differently."

"Grandpa didn't. Look how tattered this book is."

"I never understood your grandfather."

"Well I don't understand ministers who say it's like Lincoln's goodness going on and on. Suppose you're not Lincoln?"

"I think Reverend Dobson made a mistake. You must try to forgive him."

"It's not a *question* of his making a mistake! It's a question of dying and never moving or seeing or hearing anything ever again."

"But"—in exasperation—"darling, it's so *greedy* of you to want more. When God has given us this wonderful April day, and given us this farm, and you have your whole life ahead of you—"

"You think, then, that there is God?"

"Of course I do"—with deep relief, that smoothed her features into a reposeful oval. He had risen and was standing too near her for his comfort. He was afraid she would reach out and touch him.

"He made everything? You feel that?"

"Yes."

"Then who made Him?"

"Why, Man. Man." The happiness of this answer lit up her face radiantly, until she saw his gesture of disgust. She was so simple, so illogical; such a femme.

"Well that amounts to saying there is none."

Her hand reached for his wrist but he backed away. "David, it's a mystery. A miracle. It's a miracle more beautiful than any Reverend Dobson could have told you about. You don't say houses don't exist because Man made them."

"No. God has to be different."

"But, David, you have the *evidence*. Look out the window at the sun; at the fields."

"Mother, good grief. Don't you see"—he rasped away the roughness in his throat—"if when we die there's nothing, all your sun and fields and what not are all, ah, *horror*? It's just an ocean of horror."

"But David, it's not. It's so clearly not that." And she made an urgent opening gesture with her hands that expressed, with its suggestion of a willingness to receive his helplessness, all her grace, her gentleness, her love of beauty, gathered into a passive intensity that made him intensely hate her. He would not be wooed away from the truth. *I am the Way, the Truth . . .*

"No," he told her. "Just let me alone."

He found his tennis ball behind the piano and went outside to throw it against the side of the house. There was a patch high up where the brown stucco that had been laid over the sandstone masonry was crumbling away; he kept trying with the tennis ball to chip more pieces off. Superimposed upon his deep ache was a smaller but more immediate worry; that he had hurt his mother. He heard his father's car rattling on the straightaway, and went into the house, to make peace before he arrived. To his relief, she was not giving off the stifling damp heat of her anger, but instead was cool, decisive, maternal. She handed him an old green book, her college text of Plato.

"I want you to read the Parable of the Cave," she said.

"All right," he said, though he knew it would do no good. Some story by a dead Greek just vague enough to please her. "Don't worry about it, Mother."

"I *am* worried. Honestly, David, I'm sure there will be something for us. As you get older, these things seem to matter a great deal less."

"That may be. It's a dismal thought, though."

His father bumped at the door. The locks and jambs stuck here. But before Granmom could totter to the latch and let him in, he had knocked it open. He had been in Olinger dithering with track meet tickets. Although Mother usually kept her talks with David a confidence, a treasure between them, she called instantly, "George, David is worried about death!"

He came to the doorway of the living room, his shirt pocket bristling with pencils, holding in one hand a pint box of melting ice cream and in the other the knife with which he was about to divide it into four sections, their Sunday treat. "Is the kid worried about death? Don't give it a thought, David. I'll be lucky if I live till tomorrow, and I'm not worried. If they'd taken a buckshot gun and shot me in the cradle I'd be better off. The *world*'d be better off. Hell, I think death is a wonderful thing. I look forward to it. Get the garbage out of the way. If I had the man here who invented death, I'd pin a medal on him."

"Hush, George. You'll frighten the child worse than he is."

This was not true; he never frightened David. There was no harm in his father, no harm at all. Indeed, in the man's steep self-disgust the boy felt a kind of ally. A distant ally. He saw his position with a certain strategic coldness. Nowhere in the world of other people would he find the hint, the nod, he needed to begin to build his fortress against death. They none of them believed. He was alone. In that deep hole.

In the months that followed, his position changed little. School was some comfort. All those sexy, perfumed people, wisecracking, chewing gum, all of them doomed to die, and none of them noticing. In their company David felt that they would carry him along into the bright, cheap paradise reserved for them. In any crowd, the fear ebbed a little; he had reasoned that somewhere in the world there must exist a few people who believed what was necessary, and the larger the crowd, the greater the chance that he was near such a soul, within calling distance, if only he was not too ignorant, too ill-equipped, to spot him. The sight of clergymen cheered him; whatever they themselves thought, their collars were still a sign that somewhere, at some time, someone had recognized that we cannot, *cannot*, submit to death. The sermon topics posted outside churches, the flip, hurried pieties of disc jockeys, the cartoons in magazines showing angels or devils—on such scraps he kept alive the possibility of hope.

For the rest, he tried to drown his hopelessness in clatter and jostle. The pinball machine at the luncheonette was a merciful distraction; as he bent over its buzzing, flashing board of flippers and cushions, the weight and constriction in his chest lightened and loosened. He was grateful for all the time his father wasted in Olinger. Every delay postponed the moment when they must ride together down the dirt road into the heart of the dark farmland, where the only light was the kerosene lamp waiting on the dining-room table, a light that drowned their food in shadow and made it sinister.

He lost his appetite for reading. He was afraid of being ambushed again. In mystery novels people died like dolls being discarded; in science fiction enormities of space and time conspired to crush the humans; and even in P. G. Wodehouse he felt a hollowness, a turning away from reality that was implicitly bitter, and became explicit in the comic figures of futile clergymen. All gaiety seemed minced out on the skin of a void. All quiet hours seemed invitations to dread.

Even on weekends, he and his father contrived to escape the farm; and when, some Saturdays, they did stay home, it was to do something destructive—tear down an old henhouse or set huge brush fires that threatened, while Mother shouted and flapped her arms, to spread to the woods. Whenever his father worked, it was with rapt violence; when he chopped kindling, fragments of the old henhouse boards flew like shrapnel and the ax-head was always within a quarter of an inch of flying off the handle. He was exhilarating to watch, sweating and swearing and sucking bits of saliva back into his lips.

School stopped. His father took the car in the opposite direction, to a highway construction job where he had been hired for the summer as a timekeeper, and David was stranded in the middle of acres of heat and greenery and blowing pollen and the strange, mechanical humming that lay invisibly in the weeds and alfalfa and dry orchard grass.

For his fifteenth birthday his parents gave him, with jokes about him being a hillbilly now, a Remington .22. It was somewhat like a pinball machine to take it out to the old kiln in the woods where they dumped their trash, and set up tin cans on the kiln's sandstone shoulder and shoot them off one by one. He'd take the puppy, who had grown long legs and a rich coat of reddish fur—he was part chow. Copper hated the gun but loved the boy enough to accompany him. When the flat acrid crack rang out, he would race in terrified circles that would tighten and tighten until they brought him, shivering, against David's legs. Depending upon his mood, David would shoot again or drop to his knees and comfort the dog. Giving this comfort to a degree returned comfort to him. The dog's ears, laid flat against his skull in fear, were folded so intricately, so—he groped for the concept—*surely.* Where the dull-studded collar made the fur stand up, each hair showed a root of soft white under the length, black-tipped, of the metal-color that had lent the dog its name. In his agitation Copper panted through nostrils that were elegant slits, like two headed cuts, or like the keyholes of a dainty lock of black, grained wood. His whole whorling, knotted, jointed body was a wealth of such embellishments. And in the smell of the dog's hair David seemed to descend through many finely differentiated layers of earth: mulch, soil, sand, clay, and the glittering mineral base.

But when he returned to the house, and saw the books arranged on the low shelves, fear returned. The four adamant volumes of Wells like four thin bricks, the green Plato that had puzzled him with its queer softness and tangled purity, the dead Galsworthy and "Elizabeth," Grandpa's mammoth dictionary, Grandpa's Bible, the Bible that he himself had received on becoming a member of the Firetown Lutheran Church—at the sight of these, the memory of his fear reawakened and came around him. He had grown stiff and stupid in its embrace. His parents tried to think of ways to entertain him.

"David, I have a job for you to do," his mother said one evening at the table.

"What?"

"If you're going to take that tone perhaps we'd better not talk."

"What tone? I didn't take any tone."

"Your grandmother thinks there are too many pigeons in the barn."

"Why?" David turned to look at his grandmother, but she sat there staring at the burning lamp with her usual expression of bewilderment.

Mother shouted, "Mom, he wants to know why!"

Granmom made a jerky, irritable motion with her bad hand, as if generating the force for utterance, and said, "They foul the furniture."

"That's right," Mother said. "She's afraid for that old Olinger furniture that we'll never use. David, she's been after me for a month about those poor pigeons. She wants you to shoot them."

"I don't want to kill anything especially," David said.

Daddy said, "The kid's like you are, Elsie. He's too good for this world. Kill or be killed, that's my motto."

His mother said loudly, "Mother, he doesn't want to do it."

"Not?" The old lady's eyes distended as if in horror, and her claw descended slowly to her lap.

"Oh, I'll do it, I'll do it tomorrow," David snapped, and a pleasant crisp taste entered his mouth with the decision.

"And I had thought, when Boyer's men made the hay, it would be better if the barn doesn't look like a rookery," his mother added needlessly.

A barn, in day, is a small night. The splinters of light between the dry shingles pierce the high roof like stars, and the rafters and crossbeams and built-in ladders seem, until your eyes adjust, as mysterious as the branches of a haunted forest. David entered silently, the gun in one hand. Copper whined desperately at the door, too frightened to come in with the gun yet unwilling to leave the boy. David stealthily turned, said "Go away," shut the door on the dog, and slipped the bolt across. It was a door within a door; the double door for wagons and tractors was as high and wide as the face of a house.

The smell of old straw scratched his sinuses. The red sofa, half-hidden under its white-splotched tarpaulin, seemed assimilated into this smell, sunk in it, buried. The mouths of empty bins gaped like caves. Rusty oddments of farming—coils of baling wire, some spare tines for a harrow, a handleless shovel—hung on nails driven here and there in the thick wood. He stood stock-still a minute; it took a while to separate the cooing of the pigeons from the rustling in his ears. When he had focused on the cooing, it flooded the vast interior with its throaty, bubbling outpour: there seemed no other sound. They were up behind the beams. What light there was leaked through the shingles and the dirty glass windows at the far end and the small round holes, about as big as basketballs, high on the opposite stone side walls, under the ridge of the roof.

A pigeon appeared in one of these holes, on the side toward the house. It flew in, with a battering of wings, from the outside, and waited there, silhouetted against its pinched bit of sky, preening and cooing in a throbbing, thrilled, tentative way. David tiptoed four steps to the side, rested his gun against the lowest rung of a ladder pegged between two upright beams, and lowered the gunsight into the bird's tiny, jauntily cocked head. The slap of the report seemed to come off the stone wall behind him, and the pigeon did not fall. Neither did it fly. Instead it stuck in the round hole, pirouetting rapidly and nodding its head as if in frantic agreement. David shot the bolt back and forth and had aimed again before the spent cartridge had stopped jingling on the boards by his feet. He eased the tip of the sight a little lower, into the bird's breast, and took care to squeeze the trigger with perfect evenness. The slow contraction of his hand abruptly sprang the bullet; for a half-second there was doubt, and then the pigeon fell like a handful of rags, skimming down the barn wall into the layer of straw that coated the floor of the mow on this side.

Now others shook loose from the rafters, and whirled in the dim air with a great blurred hurtle of feathers and noise. They would go for the hole; he fixed his sight on the little moon of blue, and when a pigeon came to it, shot him as he was walking the ten inches of stone that would have carried him into the open air. This pigeon lay down in that tunnel of stone, unable to fall either one way or the other, although he was alive enough to lift one wing and cloud the light. It would sink back, and he would suddenly lift it again, the feathers flaring. His body blocked that exit. David raced to the other side of the barn's main aisle, where a similar ladder was symmetrically placed, and rested his gun on the same rung. Three birds came together to this hole; he got one, and two got through. The rest resettled in the rafters.

There was a shallow triangular space behind the cross beams supporting the roof. It was here they roosted and hid. But either the space was too small, or they were curious, for now that his eyes were at home in the dusty gloom David could see little dabs of gray popping in and out. The cooing was shriller now; its apprehensive tremolo made the whole volume of air seem liquid. He noticed one little smudge of a head that was especially persistent in peeking out; he marked the place, and fixed his gun on it, and when the head appeared again, had his finger tightened in advance on the trigger. A parcel of fluff slipped off the beam and fell the barn's height onto a canvas covering some Olinger furniture, and where its head had peeked out there was a fresh prick of light in the shingles.

Standing in the center of the floor, fully master now, disdaining to steady the barrel with anything but his arm, he killed two more that way. He felt like a beautiful avenger. Out of the shadowy ragged infinity of the vast barn roof these impudent things dared to thrust their heads, presumed to dirty its starred silence with their filthy timorous life, and he cut them off, tucked them back neatly into the silence. He had the sensation of a creator; these little smudges and flickers that he was clever to see and even cleverer to hit in the dim recesses of the rafters—out of each of them he was making a full bird. A tiny peek, probe, dab of life, when he hit it, blossomed into a dead enemy, falling with good, final weight.

The imperfection of the second pigeon he had shot, who was still lifting his wing now and then up in the round hole, nagged him. He put a new clip into the stock. Hugging the gun against his body, he climbed the ladder. The barrel sight scratched his ear; he had a sharp, garish vision, like a color slide, of shooting himself and being found tumbled on the barn floor among his prey. He locked his arm around the top rung—a fragile, gnawed rod braced between uprights—and shot into the bird's body from a flat angle. The wing folded but the impact did not, as he had hoped, push the bird out of the hole. He fired again, and again, and still the little body, lighter than air when alive, was too heavy to budge from its high grave. From up here he could see green trees and a brown corner of the house through the hole. Clammy with the cobwebs that gathered between the rungs, he pumped a full clip of eight bullets into the stubborn shadow, with no success. He climbed down, and was struck by the silence in the barn. The remaining pigeons must have escaped out the other hole. That was all right; he was tired of it.

He stepped with his rifle into the light. His mother was coming to meet him, and it tickled him to see her shy away from the carelessly held gun. "You took a chip out of the house," she said. "What were those last shots about?"

"One of them died up in that little round hole and I was trying to shoot it down."

"Copper's hiding behind the piano and won't come out. I had to leave him."

"Well don't blame me. *I* didn't want to shoot the poor devils."

"Don't smirk. You look like your father. How many did you get?"

"Six."

She went into the barn, and he followed. She listened to the silence. Her hair was scraggly, perhaps from tussling with the dog. "I don't suppose the others will be back," she said wearily. "Indeed, I don't know why I let Mother talk me into it. Their cooing was such a comforting noise." She began to gather up the dead pigeons. Though he didn't want to touch them, David went into the mow and picked up by its tepid, horny, coral-colored feet the first bird he had killed. Its wings unfolded disconcertingly, as if the creature had been held together by threads that now were slit. It did not weigh much. He retrieved the one on the other side of the barn; his mother got the three in the middle and led the way across the road to the little southern slope of land that went down toward the foundations of the vanished tobacco shed. The ground was too steep to plant and mow; wild strawberries grew in the tangled grass. She put her burden down and said, "We'll have to bury them. The dog will go wild."

He put his two down on her three; the slick feathers let the bodies slide liquidly on one another. He asked, "Shall I get you the shovel?"

"Get it for yourself; *you* bury them. They're your kill. And be sure to make the hole deep enough so he won't dig them up." While he went to the tool shed for the shovel, she went into the house. Unlike her, she did not look up, either at the orchard to the right of her or at the meadow on her left, but instead held her head rigidly, tilted a little, as if listening to the ground.

He dug the hole, in a spot where there were no strawberry plants, before he studied the pigeons. He had never seen a bird this close before. The feathers were more wonderful than dog's hair, for each filament was shaped within the shape of the feather, and the feathers in turn were trimmed to fit a pattern that flowed without error across the bird's body. He lost himself in the geometrical tides as the feathers now broadened and stiffened to make an edge for flight, now softened and constricted to cup warmth around the mute flesh. And across the surface of the infinitely adjusted yet somehow effortless mechanics of the feathers played idle designs of color, no two alike, designs executed, it seemed, in a controlled rapture, with a joy that hung level in the air above and behind him. Yet these birds bred in the millions and were exterminated as pests. Into the fragrant open earth he dropped one broadly banded in slate shades of blue, and on top of it another, mottled all over in rhythms of lilac and gray. The next was almost wholly white, but for a salmon glaze at its throat. As he fitted the last two, still pliant, on the top, and stood up, crusty coverings were lifted from him, and with a feminine, slipping sensation along his nerves that seemed to give the air hands, he was robed in this certainty: that the God who had lavished such craft upon these worthless birds would not destroy His whole Creation by refusing to let David live forever.

Watching Her Die

REYNOLDS PRICE

My father's last aunt moved in with us when I was ten and she was a thousand. Eighty-three, to be truthful, and virgin pure but sadly broke down. She'd lived near us, in her family home, all her life and mine. Only when she tried to rise one morning, stepped through a wormy board by her bed and stayed there trapped till my father found her just before supper, did she even consider giving up the old house.

Pure as she was, she'd raised my father when his own mother died; but once he got her foot unstuck, even he had to put the truth to her plain. "Dear Lock, time's up. You've outlived your house. We offer you ours."

Aunt Lock knew *we* did no such thing. Not if *we* included my mother, which it had to. Mother had dreaded Lock's arrival from the moment my father proposed. She always said "He popped the question, then showed me the fly in his ointment—he was duty-bound to see Miss Lockie to the grave in kindness, assuming he or anybody outlived her." To explain that my mother was known, statewide, as loving to a fault and a martyr to kindness is a quick way to say what Lock was like by then anyhow, that far gone in time.

Her short legs were bowed as any hoop. She stammered every word; and she understood less than any two geese, though she didn't know it. She thought she specialized in God and healing. You'd run in the house with a bleeding hand; she'd seize your wrist and say "Lick it, son!" When your mother protested that spit might infect it, Lock would tell her "Child, watch the animal kingdom. They lick everything that hurts and it *heals*." She'd of course known several people who cured the last stage of cancer with timely licks from a warm wet tongue, preferably their own.

With all the facts Lock knew about God, she was oddly silent in public with adults. It was mainly with me that she let them slip, when my parents were absent. I had the standard childhood way of avoiding my parents when I felt unhappy. Like other children I'd walk off alone or seek out somebody neutral but kind—like a maiden aunt in the dim back-room of the busy house. I'd lie on the hooked rug Lock set by her bed and let her pour what dammed up in her when my parents wouldn't listen. It was frequently memories of my father's boyhood. I asked for them often, not understanding I was near the age when I'd start being a man myself and would need to know how another boy managed to grow and make his own son.

I doubt Lock comprehended that, having changed so little through the length of her span. But something would make her tell a brief story about Dad's mischief and then let a quick strange moral appear in the empty air like a quirky motto stitched on a sampler. She'd tell about the time he stripped the setting from the supper table, plates and all, hid them in the sideboard and ran for the woods while the family were coming from the porch to eat. Once she described the empty table and the ten baffled faces, she might draw a feeble breath and say "God showed him tricks like that every day."

She'd never explain but move back to telling how warts were cured by words alone, in new-moon light. I doubt she expected me to think for an instant about God's purpose in teaching Dad tricks, but of course I'd think of little else for the rest of that day. And the several times she let me know how "God has promised I will not die"—no explanation—I turned the promise over all ways from there on out, for her life and mine. I'd seen a child die on the street beside school, and I felt no need to share the fate.

Those words about death were almost the strangest, except for the time I confessed to torturing a boy with a withered arm at school—I twisted it hard and watched his face. Lock heard me tell the whole miserable act; and when I expected at least a scolding, she almost smiled, looked far out the window and said "Keep it up if you need to—worse, if you must. You're making him better than you by far." So altogether from the day she joined us, Lock became even more a part of my mind than the rest of my family (I've acknowledged my parents, plus I had two sisters older than me).

In addition, more than anyone else I knew, I could always find her. Her room was behind a dark brown door right off the kitchen; she was generally there in a green rocker or—on a dry day when her asthma let up—she'd be on a walk through the deep back yard that passed through carefully tended grass into thick ranks of scarlet sage and then into pines, far as any strong boy could hope to walk, much less an old woman on miserable legs.

It was such a day, I'm recalling now. Mid-October, a spotless sky and air as dry as a bona-fide desert, though pleasantly cool. Despite all that, I'd had a miserable day at school. Because of the strange way Lock responded to my old confession of cruelty, I'd left the crippled boy alone. He'd even started bringing me gifts of dried fruit from his father's store on the edge of town where white-trash houses shaded into black with no firm line except in blood when a trespass occurred. Peaches, apricots, pears and figs. I didn't care for them; but I didn't say so, just gnawed them at recess along with the boy and watched him grin.

Yet on that grand October day for no discernible human reason—a day for brave deeds—I suddenly saw my hand reach out, take that boy's arm and wrench it behind him till I heard a serious crack on the air. The boy said not a word of complaint, though silent tears rolled down his face; and his eyes never blinked. Then I watched him walk to the edge of the playground by himself and slowly test if his arm was broke. His back was turned but, just by the slowness of how he moved I could guess the pain and the tears still rolling. His arm moved finally, straight out beside him like the school patrol; and then he just walked down the sideline and turned at the street and headed home, a quarter-past noon. As it turned out he stayed gone four more days.

By three forty-five on the guilty day, as I walked home, I knew I should climb to my white room, fall down on my back and beg the Lord, who'd memorized my meanness, to pardon me someway without demanding I find the boy and beg him first. His name was Zollicoffer Phipps, called Zollie. But since my path led through the back woods, I was deep in the cool shade, stroking through twigs and abusing my soul, when—Lord!—I heard my name out loud.

"Dalton Burke" in a high soft voice but keen as a sunbeam.

I stopped cold and tried to guess was it human. I'd had more than one communication from the unseen world, years before I was ten; so I had some grounds for judging the matter. But in five more seconds, I couldn't decide.

"Dal? Answer me." I'd also been asked to answer before by unseen voices that never spoke the question. But something made me guess it was a woman, even a girl—where the hell was she? (I'd started to cuss.) I turned every way. Just thicker leaves and deeper shade on every side. All my life, what I can't see, I seldom address; so I held my tongue.

"D-*Dal*."

Aunt Lockie out this far alone?

Exactly that, though it took awhile to find her. Ten yards away in a neat clearing I'd never noticed, Lock sat on a huge uprooted oak. It looked freshly killed. The roots were still damp, but we'd had no wind or lightning for a month. Anyhow it had landed at the right height for Lock. She was firmly seated, holding a limb; and for once her small feet touched the ground—in chairs they tended to dangle useless. She was cool as the day and not even panting, so I figured she'd been back here a good while. That, and the distance she'd covered, made me think she'd wrangled with Mother, badly this time. So I moved on closer. "You waiting it out?"

Lock even smiled and refused the question. "I'm 'fust-rate,'" she said, one of her numerous old-time replies that gave me a fit when school friends were near, though many of them had similar antiques in their own back rooms. In general back then children knew many more old people than now. Living near them, having to kiss and greet them, we learned far more about the speed and goal of life than children today. But I honestly doubt it made us gladder to know them or kinder. Anyhow there was nothing Aunt Lock had done that was really first-rate—or so I thought then—except raising Dad, and that was behind her.

That opened a path for me to say "I'm worse off than I've been in living memory."

Mother would have laughed at the solemn phrase; but Lock took me as she'd taken my father, dead-earnest at all times, even when we teased her. So now she pointed to the dry ground below, and when I sat she said "What's your plight?"

I told the whole story in her own way. Lock couldn't just say "It happened one afternoon last week." She had to back and haul a good deal to establish the day, the hour and weather. Then she'd dress whatever rooms were involved and give you descriptions of everybody with such precision that years ahead you could pick them out from an angry mob. I told her every fact she didn't know since I left her at breakfast—the disappointment I'd had in reading class and all the other extenuators. Then I painted my crime in grim detail and said "I've mentioned excuses, Lock. They don't count, do they?" I hadn't looked straight at her eyes for a while; and even when she started, I couldn't look.

She said "Very much to the contrary, Dal, th-they all count against you."

From then on she barely stammered again. She'd given me lengthy thumbnail sermons before on a lot more subjects than the powers of spit, but nothing had prepared me for what came next. She said two or three more sentences on the no-count nature of childhood meanness. Then she took a brief silent pause.

I risked a glance at her, but she was faced straight out beyond me at nothing but leaves, far as I could see.

Then still looking off she seemed to take a wide left-turn in her mind. She said "Now I'm asked to die for you, son."

She'd long since learned not to call me *son*; it riled my mother. So trying to grin, I said "I'm Dalton, your favorite great-nephew. And Dalton's asking for no such thing." Jokes from Lock were scarce as snow, but I thought somehow she was teasing me. Young as I was, I knew about Jesus dying for the entire human race; but I couldn't think Lock was meant to follow him. Bad as I felt about Zollie's arm, I didn't quite see myself in Hell. So I said "Lock, I've been died for, remember?"

At first she nodded. Then she thought awhile longer. By now she'd all but proved she was listening, so I watched her closely. She was not watching me; she still faced the woods. And with every second her face got paler and her skin got thinner. Soon a thousand hairline veins stood out in her spotty brow and down her throat. They turned dark purple as if her blood was desperate for oxygen, dying fast. In the space of two minutes, that seemed like a month, I had to believe my great-aunt was dying because she was asked.

She was somehow dying because of me and the cruel acts I couldn't stop doing, young as I was. Strangest of all, the change didn't scare me, though I finally said "Aunt Lock, hold back. You said God promised you'd never have to die." If she heard, it made no difference at all. So I finally made the painful offer I'd tried to shun. I said "I'm to blame." Still no good; she was past my reach.

By then her eyes had drifted shut, and soon they also started to die. The lids, that were always paper-thin, went nearly transparent till I could see the ghost of her pupils gazing through—thank God, not at me. And her lips, that had also thinned, drew up in a thorough smile of a sort I seldom saw on Lock unless my father bent to kiss her on Christmas morning or at the supper he always cooked for her birthday. More than once Mother said "Miss Lock's never known a whole happy day; and she means us to share her discontent." So while I estimated that her death was less than a minute ahead of us now, I asked "Are you happy?"

Any other time she'd have stammered badly at that big a question. And she did wait so long I thought she was gone. Then a voice, from farther out than she'd gone before, said plainly "Happy? No. But I'm honored, yes, and glad to serve." Another long wait while every cell of her skin went still as the dead oak she sat on.

I thought "Any second, she'll pitch over on me." And I braced to catch her.

But one more time that far voice spoke. "Shut your eyes now, son, and count to a hundred."

I not only shut my eyes; I bent way down and hid my face in my folded legs. I figured when she fell, I could roll her aside. Then I counted slowly. As always I got confused in the 60s and backtracked some; but from 95 on I spoke the last numbers. I thought if Lock was hearing me still, she'd say what next when I got to 100. But no word came, no sigh, no breath. Even the leaves all sounded dead. I shouldn't have been the least surprised since I almost never prayed anymore. I kept the decision a private fact; but at nine, I decided God had more work on his hands than my slim business. Still that October afternoon again I spoke out loud once more, "Sir, help me please." Then I looked.

I've said Lock never played tricks on us, but even the greatest actor on Earth couldn't have imitated death this well. I'd seen two old great-uncles dead and a friend of mine in the wreck of his bicycle near our school. Lock was dead all right; and I still wasn't scared or thinking ahead to what I'd tell my mother now, not to mention Dad when he got home. I put one finger out toward her, waited in midair to see if she'd flinch, then went the whole way and touched her wrist where it still gripped the limb.

Up till today she'd kept a steady heat, lukewarm and weird, like standing oatmeal; so I'd always shied off feeling her skin except when she absolutely required it. Now though she was cool and not weird at all, peaceful really. My finger stayed on her flesh so long, I felt her go maybe five degrees cooler with not a trace of pulse or twitch.

I stood up finally and stepped well back. No way on Earth I could get her home now with my schoolbooks and lunchbox. But I should stretch her out or she might fall—any breeze would tip her down in a heap. That's when I suddenly thought I should listen, listen at least as hard as Lock. Whatever voice had spoken to her might have some useful advice for me. Children this side of the early teens are still smart enough to know such things. I put both hands down calm at my sides, shut my own eyes and tried to slow my heart. It obeyed so soon that, for one cold instant I thought it was stopping too. But I stayed in place; and next I heard it thudding onward, slow but trusty.

Then a voice, the same old voice I'd heard in early years, said "Leave her here, boy. She's where I want her." I held on a good while, hoping it would offer some word on where I should go next, who I should hunt down and what I should say.

And eventually, once a crow had called, the voice said "Now you are free again; she saved your skin."

My mind was suddenly clean as a washed slate. I tried to think of my name but couldn't. I knew just one thing, *Haul your rusty ass* out *of here*. So young as I was, I hauled it home.

Mother was out, my sisters were on a field trip to Raleigh, the cook wouldn't be back till five o'clock. Dad, being a doctor, might come in early or not till past bedtime. For once I hated the house being empty, but I still wasn't what you could truly call scared. I believed the voice. I knew not to worry now about Zollie. He'd been repaid already by whoever ran the show, this peculiar day. Someway tomorrow or by Thanksgiving I'd make my amends. He and I would be friends for life; I'd be his protector.

In my own room though, my private belongings began to wake me. Familiar objects, like a Barlow knife and a silver dollar from the year I was born, stared back at me and saw my shame and my wild rescue. An actual human being just now had volunteered to be my scapegoat and pay some debt I owed to justice. I had felt bad enough just on my own; but nothing had made me understand how hard the sky or the voice behind it viewed my cruelty and all such acts here and elsewhere always. Being not just young but normally human, I hoped the voice would let me lead my parents to Lock and say no more than that I'd discovered her, coming from school, dead there in the woods. And since the last place I'd said a prayer was in my bed, I lay down there, got still again and asked if I could take my father to the woods and not explain why Lock died on me.

I thought the voice was ready to speak, but no word came that I could hear.

I told myself the answer was *Yes*. I still think it was.

The cook came in a while later and worked on, singing so high she woke the local bats before sundown. Soon after five Mother was suddenly downstairs with her, laughing and saying "No, no, *no*." I stayed in my room and finished my homework, praying that Dad would turn up shortly, then would climb up to take his evening leak and check on me. I honestly think, till the day he died, he thought I'd evaporate some unannounced morning between the time he left me at breakfast and touched me upstairs again at six. I 'd known forever he prized me more than both my sisters, I understood my disappearance would ruin his life, I mattered that much in all his plans. But I wouldn't know why till I had one satisfactory child of my own, the green-eyed daughter who rewards me still.

When I heard Dad finish washing his hands, I was still on the bed. I rolled to the wall and balled myself up to look like sleep.

He came in anyhow, sat on the edge and tapped my hip. "Sarge, you sick?"

Just before I had to respond, I suddenly wondered if that was it. Was this whole afternoon some kind of sick dream? Was I laid up now in a hospital bed with a record fever, a puzzle to science? Was I the dead person and this was eternity? Had Zollie gone home and prayed for justice and all I was going through now was just my strange but fair deserts? I'd been saved though; I still trusted that. So I turned to face Dad and said "No, tired."

Dad studied me to test my honesty. Then he nodded. "*School*-tired." He had disliked school as much as me, and he always said how amazed he was that he spent thirty years on something that bitter. Whatever, it had made him a first-rate surgeon, widely sought. Next he sat on quietly, watching his hands. He had told me more than once lately how much he was hoping they'd last him out till he had to retire. He thought sometimes they'd begun to quiver.

So I whispered clearly "Stop looking; they're *still*." It made me think of Lock dead of course, but I kept my secret.

He searched my face again and then laughed. "You know too much."

I said to myself *He's righter than ever* but I laughed too.

"How's Lockie feeling?" That was nothing strange. He knew how Lock and I most afternoons listened to the radio from four to five—*The Lone Ranger, Terry and the Pirates*. Lock's favorite was *The Phantom*, who knew "what evil lurks in the hearts of men." Every day without fail, Dad would see me first and ask about Lock—had we liked our programs? If I said yes and that Lock was normal, he could put off paying a before-supper visit to her back room and risking Mother's temper.

With him I always knew I could reach for the truth at once, no fooling around. I told him "You need to see something right now; but don't ask questions, not yet at least. Let's get downstairs, quiet as we can, and out to the woods."

The way he replied was the reason I'd loved him all my life and honor him still, long past his presence. He said "Then lead me."

Silent as braves we got outdoors, on through the yard and into the trees without so much as a yell from Mother, though she had to be watching at the kitchen window.

When we were a good ten yards into thicket, and our backs were hid, I stopped and faced Dad. I even asked him to step back a little. "I need to tell you something hard."

He'd after all had people die in his hands, his literal hands; so his face didn't frown, and he stepped well back.

When he pulled a red dogwood leaf to chew, I suddenly thought I'd spare him the mystery, Lock's awful merciful words before leaving. I said "Aunt Lockie has passed away. I found her body back deep in here when I came home from school. Her heart just stopped, no sign of blood. I couldn't lift her. She was peaceful and safe, so I didn't tell Mother but waited for you."

My father was strong on the order of iron, strong but ready to love what he loved. I'd seen him cry only once till then when a girl child died as he touched her heart to repair a valve. He climbed to my room that terrible evening, not stopping for Mother, and sat on my bed and said "This one finger *touched* her heart—for the first time, son, to give her the life she ought to have—and it stopped, stock-still." Here in the woods though, dusk coming down, he let my news pass into his eyes. Then he looked back awhile.

I thought he was hiding his grief this time—Lock was his mother to all intents—and I said "Don't mind. I won't tell a soul."

But he faced around and was smiling a little. He said "Have you told me the real truth, Sarge?"

I must have looked troubled.

"She's not been killed? You said no blood—"

I raised my hand in the standard boy's oath. "Sir, she's peaceful." That much was true.

Dad was no sunny-sider; he tended to frown. Till now I'd never heard him say any death was a blessing. I thought he meant Mother; it would finally lift the load of poor Lock off her mind and back. I nodded. "That's why I didn't tell Mother. I saved it for you."

Dad shook his head and waved me off; I'd misunderstood. What came next was the hardest thing he ever told me. "I've waited for this through long years now." He looked inward past me and stepped on forward to take the lead for maybe five yards. Then he recalled he didn't know where she'd be. I would need to guide him.

He'd never conceded that job to me, not till that moment; but I stepped forward proudly. As I passed him I touched his arm for an instant. "It's not bad, I told you—not one scratch or bruise."

As we went it suddenly dawned on me some dog might have found Lock and mauled her face. So I moved on faster than he usually walked, to get there soon enough and warm him back if her body was changed. For at least five years, I'd forged alone through these same trees, trying to imagine I was threatened by Indians and vicious beasts, all barely hid an arm's reach off. And I always tried to imagine *bravery*, how to walk toward what might be my death without the hair of my neck rising cold. Finally that dusk—with Dad behind me, trusting my knowledge—I was truly fearless. My blood ran warm and steady and smooth as an August river, and the hundred-yard trip seemed longer than Lewis and Clark's whole cross-country trek.

By the time I reached the edge of the clearing, the evening light could barely get through the circling pines. But right away I felt relief. Lock was still upright on the fallen tree, her eyes were still shut, one hand was holding the small limb for balance. I knew a single gust or a hard footstep might tip her forward in a heap on the ground, so I waited in place till Dad caught up.

Faced with a problem, he mostly reacted speedily. Now though he waited silent on my left.

I looked to his profile, and at first he wouldn't face me.

Then he relented and his gray eyes were calm. He all but whispered "Sarge, you're wrong."

I quickly tried to guess his meaning—what else was this old lady but frozen in *rigor mortis* by now? What had I misunderstood?

Dad reached across the gap between us, took my hand and slowly walked toward her.

In my eyes anyhow Lock seemed to quiver as fast as a hummingbird's wing, a visible blur. I figured the force of our gentle footsteps was reaching her body, but it hurt to see, and I must have pulled back on Dad's hand a little.

Anyhow he turned me loose and went on.

I stayed where I stopped, maybe ten feet back.

Dad slowed his pace but went right to her.

She was dead as ever, to my mind at least. Even the bird's-wing blur was still. For the first time I saw what you see on death masks—whatever fears and pains they knew, the dead faces of famous men, like Napoleon, are smooth as children. Maybe death is that easy. Or more likely maybe, before they can mix the plaster and make your mask, the pull of gravity eases the lines of fear and age, leaving you young and hopeful again. My great-aunt didn't look young or glad; but she did look tranquil, a whole new thing in the years I'd known her. I saw Dad's hand reach out toward her hand; and I thought *Lord God, she'll powder to dust*. I'd read about ancient maidens who powdered when their perfectly lovely corpses were touched. Nothing happened though that I could see. He'd only laid two light fingers on her, and soon I figured he was hunting a pulse.

The fingers rested gently on her wrist for a good long while. Then he seemed to shake his head in sadness. But next he drew back and almost whispered "Dear Lock, it's me."

I'd never heard him say *dear* till now. Mother told me once "He'd die for us both, but he won't say *darling* like everybody else." All I could think was *If he's glad she's gone, why's he trying to wake her?* I thought he was trying to pay his respects, to show he was there and honored her body. Then I knew we would have to call for help, strong men with a stretcher. I stepped on to Dad and quietly said "Before much later, we need to get help."

He waited a moment and said "We may have the help we need." With his hand still on her, he whispered "Dear Lock, now answer me." Then he said "Please. This moment."

And over what felt like the next ten years, Lock came on back. Almost no daylight was reaching us, but I thought I could see the color of blood creep back through her face. I knew I could hear the creak of her breath till finally her eyelids quivered fast, and then she was looking up at Dad.

He didn't speak but offered his other hand.

At first she didn't take it. Her eyes searched round till they located me. She didn't quite frown, she surely didn't smile, she gave a slight nod. Then she took Dad's other hand and gradually stood. He looked and acted like the olden beau she never had or the ideal son she claimed he'd been from the day he was born. They passed right by, touching me nowhere, and walked till they reached the thicket again. Lock stopped there and, facing just the woods, she spoke out plainly "Are you taking me home?"

Dad said "I am." They both moved on and I fell in behind them.

But I stayed close enough to hear that, every few yards, Lock would speak—short phrases about the leaves, the light, the weather. I'd never heard her say so much when she and I walked; her breath was too precious.

It seemed her breath was sufficient now, though she stammered some. We were all the way out the far edge of the woods with the house there before us—the kitchen lights—when Lock stopped once more and said a whole sentence. "It's bound to be time to eat and I'm hungry."

Till then I'd never heard Lock mention hunger; she ate a lot less than a hand-sized bird. So I stood in place and watched Dad lead her on to the house and up the back steps, slow as ever.

I was baffled beyond description of course. But I had the bare minimum of sense to wait and fix their picture deep in my mind—a son and his mother somehow alive and certainly changed. At the time I wasn't thinking I'd need the picture ever again. I didn't plan to store it buried in hopes it would bloom someday with news and hope. But here this instant I could take up a pen and draw them for you—Lock and my father—clear as I saw them, though full dark had very nearly fallen between us. All these years later I bring it up on the screen of my eyes more times than most memories.

Whatever happened, what changed in Lock from that night onward was seen by nobody else but me. All her worrisome traits stayed with her right on—the stammer, the ugly marks of age, the draining worship she paid my father were strong as ever. With all the strangeness of those dim hours in a single day, neither Dad nor Lock ever brought it up in conversation, public or private. It might just have been a long dream I had to punish myself for the vicious maddog kenneled inside me, hot to lunge. Did Lock really suffer some brand of death? I had no medical implements with me of course, but even now I'm ready to swear that she wasn't breathing when I left her upright that afternoon. Or was she merely fooling to curb a boyish tendency in me?

Was it all Lock's idea, or was she truly driven on by an unseen judge? If it was some brand of practical joke, it was the first and only such in a long solemn life. If death truly seized her, the way I saw it, then who brought her back—my dad with a touch and one loving word or the unseen judge maybe changing his mind? Dream or fact, it serves Lock's purpose of punishing me, to this minute now when I tell the story; and I've had maybe more occasions than most men to punish myself, again and again for common meanness, by simply calling back to mind the sight of a woman dying for me.

There is one fact I can still bring forward to prove that afternoon's story true, a chain of actions and deeds that happened to sane human creatures other than me. From that time forward, though she'd talk with me as before in public—at meals, in rooms with my parents or sisters—Lock never addressed me in private again, not so much as a *yes* or *no*. Even in public where she often addressed me as before, she never spoke my name, not once. I'd come home every day from school at four, turn on the radio and lie on the rug. Lock would hear the sound and come in from her room—slow and creaky, rolling on her bowlegs like some old sailor—to take her chair and hear our shows with no single word. She'd smile, laugh or frown in accord with the story. She'd meet my eyes as often as ever, always kindly. She'd darn any wornout sock I brought her; she'd still lean down and scratch my scalp as the plots tensed up in our radio shows.

But that was the only way we touched, from then till her second and last departure. I was never again compelled to kiss her powdery whiskers; never smelled her musty neck again, for all our laughter—and we laughed a lot. At first I thought of ways to scare her—to call the firetruck or claim my head had burst into pain like a gasoline fire and would split any instant and scald us both. I held back though and learned to respect her, the way you'd trust a St. Bernard that saved your life but was naturally mute.

That much of my great-aunt was dead to me, shut up and gone. It made me think of a thousand questions only she could answer. They all pertained to my father's youth, things he'd never tell me—what he was weak at, ways he failed before he got so strong and fearless. Finally though I had to believe Lock had told me the last hard thing to know. And she'd told it plainly in real daylight in actual woods the final day I was outright fierce. *You can somehow choose to pay the debts of a needy boy or other grown soul if you have that much to give and are willing.*

Lock died again, for what I assume was the final time, eight quick years later when I was away—my first year of college. Dad's letter said she went in her sleep, no trace of a struggle, ninety-one years old. At first I thought it was the worst kind of death; no living soul could truly mourn her. For years the thought seemed perfectly sound. But then I got my adult life and the ones I cherished, my daughter chiefly.

And the year I was fifty, a business trip took me back to my hometown for several days. The last evening, with time to spare, I found our house. We'd sold it fifteen years before when Mother died. Still it was in better shape than me, fresh-painted though empty—a weathered sign *For Rent* in the yard. I had the good sense not to look in the windows, but I found myself walking straight for the woods.

For whatever reason they were very much changed. Contrary to the general rule of memory, the trees were a good deal taller than before with serious girth way past my reach and a thickness above that shaded out the old thicket and briars and left a clean floor. My legs at least recalled the path; and dead though it seemed those forty years since, Lock's fallen oak was still where she left it the night Dad roused her. Some of the bark had peeled away, but the sturdy trunk was hard as ever. And the small limb that Lock's hand gripped was waiting still. I'm no great keeper of souvenirs; but suddenly there in the quickening dusk, I thought I'd snap off the limb and take it—my great-aunt's anchor in a world she surrendered. And I made two tries, but the limb refused and then I was glad.

Lock Burke blazed up there instantly before me—in my mind, understand—and the sight of her vanishing face and life repeated, clear as the long-gone voice that counseled me, a truth I hold ever close to my heart and mean to enact when my own chance comes.

I've doubted an awful list of things in my long life—the truth of my wife, my friends and God, even my all but flawless daughter. I've doubted that the Earth itself should last or my tragic race, all humankind. But since Aunt Lockie paid all for me—alone in dark woods with night coming down, that she couldn't navigate if we hadn't saved her—I've never since doubted my place in the world or my endless duty to find at last the needful heart for whom one day I lay my own life down and depart.

All Stories Are True

JOHN EDGAR WIDEMAN

And for fear of him the guards trembled
and became like dead men.
Matthew 28:4

My mother is standing on her porch. May 10, 1991. Early morning and the street is quiet now, as peaceful as it gets here, as peaceful as it always stays in other neighborhoods, invisible, not a half mile away behind the tree-topped ridge that separates Tokay, Susquehanna, Dunfermline, Seagirt from their neighbors to the west. The litany of streets always sweet on my tongue. I think I murmur their names, a silence unless you are inside my skull, sing them as a kind of background music that doesn't break the quiet of morning. If I'm not reciting them to myself, I hear the names anyway coming from somewhere else, a place that also knows what lies within the sound of these streets said to oneself again and again. Footsteps, voices, a skein of life dragged bead by bead through a soft needle's eye. And knows the names of streets can open like the gates of a great city, everyone who's ever inhabited the city, walked its streets, suddenly, like a shimmer, like the first notes of a Monk solo, breathing, moving, a world quickens as the gates swing apart. And knows my mother is not alone on her porch this May morning. Knows she hears beneath the stillness enveloping her the sound of street names, what is animated when they are recalled. The presence of other souls as palpable as light playing in the edges of her robe. Her mother and father and children. Her brother and sisters. Grands and great-grands. The man I have become and those whom I've lost becoming him. The song of street names a medium in which we all float, suspended, as if each of us is someone's precious, precious child who must never be allowed to slip from the arms cradling, rocking. And knows my mother is listening to time, time voiced in no manmade measurements of days or minutes or years, time playing as it always must, background or foreground or taking up all the space we have, a tape of the street names chanted that releases every Homewood footstep she's ever heard or dreamed.

I'm afraid for her. Experience one of those moments of missing her intensely, her gone, final good-byes said, though she is here, just ten feet away, through the front door screen, framed by two of the rusty wrought iron columns supporting the roof. A moment where fear of losing her overwhelms me to such an extent that I am bereft, helpless, unconsoled even by her presence, one price I pay for other moments when she's thousands of miles away and I've needed her and she is there, *there* beside me. After nine months of chemo her hair has grown in again, softer, curlier. Many shades of bushy gray and a crown of lighter hair, nearly white, nearly spun to invisibility by morning. I'm aware as I seldom am of her dimensions, how tall, how wide, how much this woman on the porch with her newborn's hair weighs. I need what is tangible, no matter how small she turns out to be, to offset words like frail and vulnerable I can't help saying to myself, words popping up though I try not to think them. I hate words with the power to take her away. *Frail. Old.* The effort of denying them makes her disappear anyway. My eyes cross Tokay, counting cobblestones as they go, remarking the incredible steepness of the street slanting out of my field of vision, the broken curbs and littered gutters, settling on the gigantic tree islanded in the delta where Seagirt and Tokay converge and Bricelyn begins. If the downtown wedge of skyscrapers where three rivers meet is the city's Golden Triangle, this could be its Green Triangle. A massive tree centuries old holds out against the odds here across from my mother's house, one of the biggest trees in Pittsburgh, anchored in a green tangle of weeds and bushes, trunk thick as a Buick, black as night after rain soaks its striated hide. Huge spread of its branches canopies the foot of the hill where the streets come together. Certain times of day in summer it shades my mother's front porch. If it ever tore loose from its moorings, it would crush her house like a sledgehammer. As big as it is, its roots must run under her cellar. The sound of it drinking, lapping nourishment deep underground is part of the quiet when her house is empty. How the tree survived a city growing around it is a mystery. For years no more than a twig, a sapling, a switch someone could have snapped off to beat a balky animal, swat a child's behind. I see a dark fist exploding through the asphalt, thrusting to the sky, the fingers opening, multiplying, fanning outward to form a vast umbrella of foliage. The arm behind it petrifies, other thick limbs burst from knots of hardened flesh, each one duplicating the fan of leaves, the delicate network of branches, thinning, twisting as they climb higher and farther from the source. Full-blown in a matter of seconds, ready to stand here across from my mother's house forever, till its time to be undone in the twinkling of an eye, just the way it arrived.

I didn't say any of this to my mother as I pushed through the screen door with my cup of coffee to join her on the porch. Then it was just one quiet thing after the other, a matter of seconds, the sight of her standing still, her back to me, me thinking thoughts that flashed at warp speed but would take forever to unpack, the door creaking, her turning slowly towards the noise, *You up, Baby,* a quick welcoming smile before she turns back to whatever it was, wherever she was gazing when I saw her first, small, bathed in the soft, remorseless light of morning, when I heard the sound of Homewood street names playing, transforming a commonplace scene into something else, restoring the invisible omnipresence of time, the enabling medium, what brought you to this moment and will carry you away, how things begin and end, always, you about to step out onto your mother's porch, catching her staring off at something, somewhere, home again, morning again, steamy coffee mug in one hand, sure of what you will do next, your fingers press the doorframe, pushing, absolutely unsure, fearing what will happen next, wondering what's in her eyes, behind them this morning in May, and which ghosts crowd the porch, regretting her privacy you are invading with yours. Who will the two of you together summon if you steal her attention, if you are ready and willing to offer yours, if you can break away from the tune playing over and over in your head and maybe in hers of the street names, sorrow and loss in every syllable when you say them to yourself the way you must to locate yourself here, back home in Pittsburgh this morning, Tioga Susquehanna Seagirt Cassina, praying your mother won't move, won't be gone before you reach her.

You hug each other. Not hard, not soft. Briefly. Long enough to remember everything.

I love my flowers.

A guy was selling them in the gas station. At Braddock and Penn. You know. The two big stations across from one another. A white guy in Mickey

Mouse bermudas. He said these hadn't been out in the sun. Too much direct sun's not good for them, he said. These were shoved under a folding table he had set up. Pansies or some other kind, I forget. They just looked pretty to me and I thought you'd like something pretty and growing.

Impatiens. They're beautiful.

And you already have a hook by the door to hang them.

I used to keep a few little plants out here. Then one night just before Easter the flowers grew feet. Woke up one morning and everybody's flowers were gone. I only had a couple nice little plants. Nothing special. But they were gone just like everybody else's up and down both blocks. Flowers grew feet that night and walked away.

You mean somebody ripped off people's flowers.

Should have heard Eva. See the house with the green and white aluminum awning. That's Eva's. You know who I mean, don't you. Small brown-skinned woman always dressed nice. Used to ride the bus to town with me to work. Eva had big-time flowers on her porch. Gone that morning like everybody else's and Eva's fit to be tied. She said she was marching down to the corner and beat the black off him with her own two hands if she caught him with one of her flowers. Said she'd know her flowers if she saw them, pot or no pot or new pot she'd know her own flowers and strangle him with her bare hands if she caught him with her flowers.

Somebody selling flowers on the corner.

Right there on Bennett. Day after the night the flowers walked.

No. You got to be kidding.

Huh uh. Some guy down there big as life selling flowers. Had his stand right on Bennett and Bricelyn. No pots. Dog probably sold people's pots somewhere else. He wasn't completely crazy. A flower sale day after everybody's flowers disappeared off their porches.

He's lucky he didn't get shot.

Eva said she was going down there and look for her flowers. Tear him up if she found any. But how could you know for sure. I kinda looked for mine when I passed by that way, but he had everything tied up in plastic bags of dirt so how you supposed to tell. Flowers are flowers. Eva swore she'd know hers, but I didn't notice any commotion down there. Did his business all day. Gone next morning. Walked away like the flowers walked. Never saw the guy before. Don't care if I ever see him again.

A brazen brother.

That's how they do us. Steal anything and everything. Stained-glass windows out the church. I worry about one of them getting into the house.

Sorry-assed junkies.

Dope turns them crazy. Knock you down as soon as look at you. Kids you've watched grow up around here. I don't believe they intend to hurt anybody, but when that sickness is down on them, my, my, my, they'll do anything. I shudder when I think of your brother crazy that way. Him hurting someone or someone hurting him. Those so-called friends of his he'd bring home. Yes ma'am and no ma'am me and all the time I know their dope eyes counting up what they could come back and steal. Tommy knew it, too. God have mercy on me for saying this about my own son, but I believe now that's why he brought some of them around. To steal from me.

Coffee's not hot. Not cold. I try the porch railing with my hand. It feels solid enough. I remember helping Wade from next door mix concrete for the porch. The good feel of doing hard work with my brothers, the three of us, Dave, Ote and me, Wade's crew sweating into the wet cement, the moment during one cold Iron City break we all felt the presence of the brother missing who should be with us building this porch for our mother. I sit on the rail anchored in our concrete. Ask about Wade.

Poor man had a tough year. Dog died, wife died, he hit that paperboy. Old Wade was way down. Said he wouldn't have made it if it hadn't been for the boy's parents. They didn't blame him. People who witnessed the accident said Wade never had a chance. Going normal speed. The boy rode his bike straight into Wade's car. And thank goodness Wade was on his way to work. So he hadn't been drinking. Wade said if the parents had blamed him for the boy's death, he wouldn't have pulled through.

Dog died. Wife died. That's a rather strange order to put things in, Mother Dear.

You know what I mean. Didn't mean one thing worse than the other or first things first. You know I didn't mean anything like that.

I'm just teasing.

Teasing your fuddle-brained old mother. I know. I know most the time nobody understands what I'm talking about. Half the time don't know my own self. Pay me no mind. I didn't intend any disrespect. Wade loved Nadine dearly and misses her terribly. Loved that raggedy, stump-tailed dog, too. It was just one terrible thing after another falling on the poor man. I don't know how he survived. Thought for awhile he was going to drink himself to death. But he'd clean up every morning and drive off to work. Wade's a strong man. A good man, too, in his way.

Sounds like he was Job last year.

I prayed for him. All alone in his house. I know how that feels, rattling around in a house all by yourself.

The porch is holding up fine, isn't it. A little crack by the glider and one where the steps come up but this porch will be here awhile.

Youall did quite a job.

Wade the only one who knew what he was doing. Me and Dave and Ote supplied the muscle.

It was one hot day. I was worried about youall. None of you used to working out in the broiling sun that way.

Little sweat mixed in the cement makes it stronger, last longer. Why you think the Pyramids been standing all these centuries. Good African blood gluing the stones.

What do you think about this idea going around that Egyptians were black.

Better late than never, Mom. I guess. Most of them a mixture of black Africans and brown Asiatics. Look at what part of the world we're talking about. Look at them today. Not exactly a matter of color, though. More about culture. People migrating and invading and mixing since the dawn of time. Everybody's a mongrel. The wonder is it's taken this long for the obvious to be said out loud. Wonder is it's 1991 and the obvious still resisted in some quarters.

I try to change the faces of the people in the Bible. I can't do it. They still look like the faces I saw in Sunday school, in the little picture books we had to study from. No black faces, except for that one dark wise man with Jesus in the manger. When I close my eyes, I still can't put black faces on the Bible people.

Well, we must of had the same books when I was in Sunday school. Maybe that's one of the reasons you had to drag me. Child abuse every Sunday morning.

Bit more child abuse might not have been a bad idea. I felt terrible knowing I was raising a bunch of little heathens.

Anyway, what I started to say is we used those same jive comic books, but the Bible people never were white to me. They never had a color, really. The funny-looking robes and beards and turbans stuck in my mind. But as far as color, well it's Reverend Felder I think of when I think of Bible days and Bible stories. Him up on the pulpit of A.M.E. Zion shouting and strutting and banging his big fist. Old Frank Felder black as coal and that's the color of everything he preached. Like his voice tar-brushed the Bible. If the faces in the books weren't black it didn't matter cause black was in charge, telling the story.

I did think of Job more than once when I prayed for Wade. And I guess Job surely did have Wade's face and Wade's face, God bless him, surely isn't white. Poor man bent down under all his burdens. I needed the story of Job to understand how Wade could handle it. Strength to bear up to the worst, no matter what, has to come from somewhere. I needed God and Job. Needed them both to understand how Wade survived what he did.

You know, Mom, people look at you and what you've had to deal with and you're just as much a miracle to them as you say Wade is to you.

God doesn't give you more than you can handle.

Not everybody has that kind of god.

I worry about your brother. Where will he turn now. He's still a Muslim, isn't he. He still goes by his Muslim name.

Told me not long ago he's not as active in the group as he once was. But he does pray. Not as regular as he once did, he says, but he keeps the faith.

I hope he has something. Because this last blow. The pardons board turning him down again without a hearing. He believed they'd almost have to let him go. Didn't see how they could say no.

They say whatever they want to say.

Other times he held something back. In his heart he hoped they'd give him a chance, believed he'd earned a chance, but like you say. He knows they don't have to answer to anybody. Do what they want to do. Every time but this he'd held something back to fight the no.

He's in danger now. Like when he was first locked up and wild and determined to tear the prison apart with his bare hands. Worse now because he's on his own. No crew of young wild ones like him fighting back. All he has is us. And we're out here. All he has really is the chance anybody has. To keep pushing on and try to make something of a life, whatever.

Don't think I can go with you today. I'm too shaky today to face that evil prison. Tell him I'll come next week with Denise and Chance.

Don't want to leave you if you're feeling badly.

I'll be all right here. You go talk to your brother. It's just one of those days. I'll take my pills and sit myself down awhile. I'll get it together, Babe.

Is something specific hurting.

Just one of those not so good days. I'm shaky. I have bad days every now and then. Hug him for me. Tell him I love him. I'll be fine here.

I rise with her. The porch one of those quiet, extrawide, featureless elevators in the hospital where she goes Tuesdays for treatments. Below us the map of streets, veins, arteries. We wait on this floor, at this height. The porch rocks like a Ferris wheel car stopped at the apex of the ride. Perhaps the huge motor's broken. Cable snapped. Gears stripped. We wait and listen for music to drift up from the streets.

My brother's arms are prison arms. The kind you see in the street that clue you where a young brother's been spending his time. Bulging biceps, the rippled look of ropy sinews and cords of muscle snaking around the bones. Skinned. Excess flesh boiled away in this cauldron. Must be noisy as a construction site where the weightlifters hang out in the prison yard. Metal clanking. Grunts and groans. Iron pumped till shoulders and chests swell to the bursting point. Men fashioning arms thick enough to wrestle fate, hold off the pressure of walls and bars always bearing down. Large. Big. Nothing else to do all day. Size one measure of time served. Serious time. Bodies honed to stop-time perfection, beyond vulnerability and pain. I see them in their sun-scoured playground sprawled like dazed children.

Hot today in the visiting area, fiery heat like the day we paddled round in Wade's cement. Row row row your concrete boat. It ain't heavy, it's your brother.

Hey, bro, I'd be the last one to deny I'm fucked up. We both know good and well I've had problems all my life doing what I been supposed to do. Here I sit in this godforsaken hole if anybody needs proof I couldn't handle. Something's wrong wit me, man, but the people who runs this joint, something's real wrong wit them, too.

Pressure in my face muscles from the permanent squint I'm wearing to keep sun out of my eyes. A mask of age. Forehead furrowed, cheeks tensed and hollow, eyes narrow, tiny creases incised at their corners, vision dimmed by the hazy porch of lashes and brow pouting to shade the eyes. Sun cooks my right side. I look past my brother to avoid the direct glare, beyond him to the bricks of the visiting room wall, the glass doors opening to this roofless enclosure where we sit. I listen closely but he's a blur in the center of the space across the round table where my eyes would naturally focus if I wasn't hiding from the sun. I don't need to see him. He will be wearing the same face I am. Pinched and sweaty. Older than it should be. Glazed eyes seeking something other than me to fix on, so what I say is a voice-over, as his is to me, listening while I tour the stones stacked forty feet high that surround us, the glass doors black as water, reflecting scraps of the yard.

Motherfuckers don't say shit for three months. Know I'm on pins and needles every minute of every day since I filed my commutation papers, but don't nobody say one god-blessed single solitary word good or bad for three months. I'm going crazy wit the waiting. And too scared to ask anybody what's happening cause you know how that works. Ask a question and they say *no* just to spite you, just to get you out their face. Limbo, man, for three months. Then last week I'm by the desk in the visiting room waiting for Denise and Chance and the guard at the desk hands me the phone, call for you. Lieutenant's on the line and he says to me Board turned you down. Tells me I can cancel my visit and speak to him now or check by his office later. That's it. Boom. Turned down.

Like getting hit in the chest wit a hammer. Couldn't breathe, man. Couldn't catch my breath for three days. Still can't breathe right. Felt like somebody had taken a hammer and whammed me in the heart.

No warning. No explanation. I'm standing in the visiting room trying to catch my breath and Denise and the baby be in here in a minute. Dying, man, and ready to die. My life was over soon's the lieutenant said Board turned you down.

Weird thing is the night before I had a dream. Woke me up. Couldn't go back to sleep. Dreamed I was in one the offices around here and my papers was on the desk. My papers. What I'd been waiting for all these months and finally there they sat. On top the desk and nobody else around. All I had to do was peep at the last sheet, right. There it'd be in black and white. Yes or no. Couldn't believe it be this easy. So much waiting and praying and begging and cursing boneheads out cause they wouldn't give me a clue. Wouldn't tell me nothing, nothing, and now alls I had to do was turn to the last page and I'd know.

Awful thing was I already knew the answer. Couldn't peep at the bottom sheet cause I already knew. Knew in my heart so I kept standing, staring, too scared to read what I knew I'd find.

Right when the dream ended I did look. Couldn't hold out. Looked and saw *denied* stamped on the last page. Whole dream came back to me soon as I put down that phone in the visiting room. Been *denied* all along. And all along I guess I knowed.

Nothing for three months then I'm waiting for a visit from my old lady and son and I get a phone call. Turned you down. Bam. Take that. Like a hammer in my chest. Tell me that ain't evil, man. Saying no is bad enough. They don't have to treat people like dirt saying it.

My own fault I'm in here. I know I done some bad things. I'm in here, man, doing my time. Uh huh. Hard time. Lots of time for doing wrong. But they treat us like dog shit in here and that's wrong too. Guys get killed in here. Go crazy. But nobody cares. Long as they keep us locked up they can do us anyway they want. Figure we in here, so they don't owe us nothing. But wrong is wrong, ain't it. Just cause we down, is it right to keep on kicking us. Guys get meaner and crazier in here. Every day you see the ones can't take it slipping further and further off. Distance in their eyes, b.o. Ain't nobody home in them eyes. They shuffle around here like ghosts. Stop speaking to people. Stop keeping theyselves clean. Gone, man. If you been around here any length of time you seen it happen to a lot of guys. You understand how easy it is to tune out and drop off the edge into your own little world. Another planet. You see why guys go off. Why they so cold and mean if they ever hit the street again.

Now our eyes are meeting. The sun's part of the meeting. A sting, a rawness you try to blink away but only make worse as sweat drips and irritates. Only one other table occupied when you sat down at yours. Now no free ones. The visiting room wall forms one end of the outdoor enclosure. Its other three walls rise forty feet at least, smooth blocks of stone topped by razor wire, a walkway, a guard tower in the far corner. At the base of the sheer stone walls fresh plantings, shrubbery dense and spiky bordering the concrete pavement. A few trees, also recently planted, have been spaced along the inside of the walls, each in a square collar of earth the size of a missing section of paving. You register these details for later. You think it will be crucial at some point to remember this yard exactly. You are uncertain why. Then, still listening to what he's saying, you realize how little of your brother's life you can share. This yard, detail by detail, is part of what you do share. You would be compromised if you come away with only a vague recollection. To fight this place, to force it to disappear, you must not miss anything. The map of it in your head makes its horror real, but also is what you must depend upon to plan an escape.

I think I'm finally beginning to understand why they so evil to us. They're scared of the black man. Really scared. More scared than I ever knew. More scared than they know themselves. When I first come in the joint I knew something about the fear. Knew we had something on them. Wild as we was we didn't give them no chance to run game on us. We had learned the hard way coming up running the streets what they thought of us. Crazy killers. Animals. Dope fiends. Niggers you got to lock up or kill before they kill you. That was the deal. So we played the hand dealed us. We was stone outlaws. Fuck wit us you better be prepared to take us down cause if you don't we coming down on you. I was young and hot-blooded and that cowboy and indian gangster shit okay wit me. Bring it on. Let's git down and dirty. Rock and roll.

We saw fear in their eyes. We fucked with them to keep it there. But they didn't kill me and, all praises to Allah, I didn't kill a guard. I changed. Wasn't really me in the first place. I was just playing the outlaw role I thought I needed to play to survive the joint. I changed but they stayed scared of me. And they hate me for keeping them scared. My buddy Rick. You remember Ricky from up the hill on Tokay. Took him dying to make me really understand what I'm telling you now. You know he got sick in here. Come in when I did, one of our wild bunch. Take no shit from nobody, none of us. But Rick changed, too. Wised up. Then he got sick, real sick, like I said. They wouldn't treat him. Wouldn't try to find out what was wrong. Why should they. If you scared of somebody, why you gon try and help them, fix them up, make them well so they can jump in your chest again. Huh uh. Ricky just rotted. Chased him away from the clinic. Or handed him a aspirin. You know the story. He shrunk down to nothing. Ninety-three goddamn pounds. Finally they had to stick him in the clinic. Let him rot in the clinic till his mother got to somebody and they transferred Ricky out of here and chained him to a bed in a locked ward in a real hospital and diagnosed stomach cancer. By that time Ricky too far gone to help. Drugged him up so he just nodded away. Didn't know people when they came to see him his mother said. Said he was so weak they unchained him. A cop in the room when she visited, but Ricky just laying there. A pitiful sight, plugged up to machines, not even recognizing his own mama. She was in a chair beside his bed on a Sunday she said it must have been Sunday cause she'd been there a couple hours that afternoon and she works six days a week so it must of been Sunday and Rick been sleeping like he always did the whole time so she was just sitting half sleep herself when Ricky's hand reached over and patted hers where she'd laid it on the blanket. She couldn't believe it she said. Tears started rolling down her cheeks she told me because what his touching her meant she thought was that he was ready to die. Too far gone to get better so she just knew Rick using his last strength to say good-bye.

The cop in the room had a different idea. See, he was still scared of Ricky so Ricky moving that hand meant Ricky was dangerous again. Cop jumped up and started refastening the chains.

None of it makes any goddamn sense. Who they keep. Who they let go. Never give you any reasons. They don't have to give reasons for what they do. They just do it. Denied. They stamp your papers *denied* and that's all the reason they got to give. Denied.

One the dudes they didn't deny, a white boy, he busted out of here not too long ago. Busted out and stayed out till he got tired of running and turned hisself in. Escaped the joint, man, and now they granted him a hearing with the full parole board. What kind of sense do it make.

Maybe you ought to arrange a little vacation for yourself before you apply next time.

Don't think I ain't thought about it. Been keeping my eye on that tree over there. Shimmy up, leap over the wall. Gone.

Not much of a tree yet.

Yeah, well, it's still pretty scraggly. But I been watching it.

Long time before those branches grow as high as the wall. And you'd still have a pretty good leap.

Guys in here would try. Plenty of them. Scoot up that tree in a minute. Do a super monkey jump.

Branches awful skinny at the top. Even for a monkey.

Right. Right. Skinny enough so you get up there it'll bend to the wall. Ride it like a surfboard.

You got it all figured out, bro.

Told you I've been keeping my eye on that little tree.

This is where you and Denise were when the leaf got out.

At the table closest to the wall. In the shade. Uh huh. We was sitting there but by the time that leaf blew up near the top of the wall both of us on our feet cheering. Other people had got into it, too. Saw what we was watching and that leaf had a whole lot of fans when it sailed over the wall. Would have thought people cheering for the Steelers or somebody's lottery number hit. Wasn't nothing but a leaf me and Denise noticed that had started blowing higher and higher. Each time the wind would grab it, it would circle up higher. Over in that corner like it was riding a draft or a whirlwind or some damn something keeping it up. You know how something dumb catch your attention and you can't let it go. Leaf kept spinning round and round and rising each time it spinned. Like on a yo-yo. After watching it a while you know that leaf has flying out of here on its mind. Every little whip and twist and bounce starts to matter. Before you know it you're blowing with your breath to help it over the wall and you know something inside you will be hurt if that silly leaf can't finish what it started. Whole visiting yard whooping and hollering when it finally blew over the wall.

Denise cried. And damn. It was everything I could do to keep the tears out of my eyes. Everybody in here needed that leaf to go free.

Kind of magic, man, if you was here in the yard and seen it. Know I sound dumb trying to tell you how it was. But that's how it was. Specially for Denise and me cause earlier in the visit she told me she was carrying my baby. We'd already picked names: Jazz Melody for a girl, Chance Mandela if it was a boy. Couldn't help taking the leaf as a sign.

Chance because the odds were stacked against him ever being conceived, let alone born.

Million to one, bro. And Mandela cause Mandela's my man. You know. In the joint like me but still taking care of business.

Chance Mandela. When Mom called and told me he was born the day after Mandela walked out of prison, I couldn't believe it.

Little day late rascal. But my little guy was close. Real close. Bust out right behind Nelson.

The leaf, the day, the name. Pretty amazing, little brother. Has to be a sign. Gives you something special to fight for. A son, a family. You've come too far to let this denial turn you around.

I think a lot about it. Everything I mean. When I'm alone at night in my cell. Ain't never really alone no more since they double-bunking everybody, but you know what I mean. When I think about giving up, truth is, nothing but me can pull me back from the edge. I got to do it for me. No matter how much I love Chance and Denise and Mom and youall, nothing, not all the love in the world can fill the hole that opens up when I get down, really down. Only way to save myself is to do it for me. I got to be the reason. I got to be worth saving. Can't live a life for nobody else. Nobody can live one for me. You understand what I'm saying.

I'm trying.

The leaf. I told you how it finally blowed free overtop the wall. Couldn't see it no more. Denise grabbed my hand. She was crying and we was bouncing up and down. People shouting. Some even clapped. But you know something. I'm gonna tell you something I don't tell nobody when I tell about the leaf. The dumb thing blew back in here again.

EVIL

The sad truth of the matter is that most evil is done by people who never made up their minds to be or do either evil or good.

Hannah Arendt, *The Life of the Mind*

Evil when we are in its power is not felt as evil but as a necessity, or even a duty.

Simone Weil, *Gravity and Grace*

When the people of the world all know beauty as beauty, there arises the recognition of ugliness. When they all know the good as good, there arises the recognition of evil.

Lao Tzu, *The Way of Lao Tzu*

Stupidity always accompanies evil. Or evil, stupidity.

Louise Bogan (1935),
in Ruth Limmer, ed.,
Journey Around My Room

Obasan

JOY KOGAWA

To him that overcometh
will I give to eat
of the hidden manna
and will give him
a white stone
and in the stone
a new name written . . .
The Bible

The ball I found under the cot that day was never lost again. Obasan keeps it in a box with Stephen's toy cars on the bottom shelf in the bathroom. The rubber is cracked and scored with a black lacy design, and the colours are dull, but it still bounces a little.

Sick Bay, I learned eventually, was not a beach at all. And the place they called the Pool was not a pool of water, but a prison at the exhibition grounds called Hastings Park in Vancouver. Men, women and children outside Vancouver, from the "protected area"—a hundred-mile strip along the coast—were herded into the grounds and kept there like animals until they were shipped off to road-work camps and concentration camps in the interior of the province. From our family, it was only Grandma and Grandpa Nakane who were imprisoned at the Pool.

Some families were able to leave on their own and found homes in British Columbia's interior and elsewhere in Canada. Ghost towns such as Slocan—those old mining settlements, sometimes abandoned, sometimes with a remnant community—were reopened, and row upon row of two-family wooden huts were erected. Eventually the whole coast was cleared and everyone of the Japanese race in Vancouver was sent away.

The tension everywhere was not clear to me then and is not much clearer today. Time has solved few mysteries. Wars and rumours of wars, racial hatreds and fears are with us still.

The reality of today is that Uncle is dead and Obasan is left alone. Weariness has invaded her and settled in her bones. Is it possible that her hearing could deteriorate so rapidly in just one month? The phone is ringing but she does not respond at all.

Aunt Emily is calling from the airport in Calgary where she's waiting for Stephen's flight from Montreal. They'll rent a car and drive down together this afternoon.

"Did you get my parcel?" she asks.

The airport sounds in the background are so loud she can hardly hear me. I shout into the receiver but it's obvious she doesn't know what I'm saying.

"Is Obasan all right? Did she sleep last night?" she asks.

It's such a relief to feel her sharing my concern.

Obasan has gone into the bathroom and is sweeping behind the toilet with a whisk made from a toy broom.

"Would you like to take a bath?" I ask.

She continues sweeping the imaginary dust.

"Ofuro?" I repeat. "Bath?"

"Orai," she replies at last, in a meek voice. "All right."

I run the water the way she prefers it, straight from the hot-water tap. It's been a while since we bathed together. After this, perhaps she'll rest. Piece by piece she removes her layers of underclothes, rags held together with safety pins. The new ones I've bought for her are left unused in boxes under her bed. She is small and naked and bent in the bathroom, the skin of her buttocks loose and drooping in a fold.

"Aah," she exhales deeply in a half-groan as she sinks into the hot water and closes her eyes.

I rub the washcloth over her legs and feet, the thin purple veins a scribbled maze, a skin map, her thick toenails, ancient rock formations. I am reminded of long-extinct volcanoes, the crust and rivulets of lava scars, criss-crossing down the bony hillside. Naked as prehistory, we lie together, the steam from the bath heavily misting the room.

"Any day now is all right," she says. "The work is finished." She is falling asleep in the water.

"It will be good to lie down," I shout, rousing her and draining the tub. I help her to stand and she moves to her room, her feet barely leaving the floor. Almost before I pull the covers over her, she is asleep.

I am feeling a bit dizzy from the heat myself.

❖

I am sometimes not certain whether it is a cluttered attic in which I sit, a waiting room, a tunnel, a train. There is no beginning and no end to the forest, or the dust storm, no edge from which to know where the clearing begins. Here, in this familiar density, beneath this cloak, within this carapace, is the longing within the darkness.

1942.

We are leaving the BC coast—rain, cloud, mist—an air overladen with weeping. Behind us lies a salty sea within which swim our drowning specks of memory—our small waterlogged eulogies. We are going down to the middle of the earth with pick-axe eyes, tunnelling by train to the Interior, carried along by the momentum of the expulsion into the waiting wilderness.

We are hammers and chisels in the hands of would-be sculptors, battering the spirit of the sleeping mountain. We are the chips and sand, the fragments of fragments that fly like arrows from the heart of the rock. We are the silences that speak from stone. We are the despised rendered voiceless, stripped of car, radio, camera and every means of communication, a trainload of eyes covered with mud and spittle. We are the man in the Gospel of John, born into the world for the sake of the light. We are sent to Siloam, the pool called "Sent." We are sent to the sending, that we may bring sight. We are the scholarly and the illiterate, the envied and the ugly, the fierce and the docile. We are those pioneers who cleared the bush and the forest with our hands, the gardeners tending and attending the soil with our tenderness, the fishermen who are flung from the sea to flounder in the dust of the prairies.

We are the Issei and the Nisei and the Sansei, the Japanese Canadians. We disappear into the future undemanding as dew.

❖

The memories are dream images. A pile of luggage in a large hall. Missionaries at the railway station handing out packages of toys. Stephen being carried on board the train, a white cast up to his thigh.

It is three decades ago and I am a small child resting my head in Obasan's lap. I am wearing a wine-coloured dirndl skirt with straps that criss-cross at the back. My white silk blouse has a Peter Pan collar dotted with tiny red flowers. I have a wine-coloured sweater with ivory duck buttons.

Stephen sits sideways on a seat by himself opposite us, his huge white leg like a cocoon.

The train is full of strangers. But even strangers are addressed as "ojisan" or "obasan," meaning uncle or aunt. Not one uncle or aunt, grandfather or grandmother, brother or sister, not one of us on this journey returns home again.

The train smells of oil and soot and orange peels and lurches groggily as we rock our way inland. Along the window-ledge, the black soot leaps and settles like insects. Underfoot and in the aisles and beside us on the seats we are surrounded by odd bits of luggage—bags, lunch baskets, blankets, pillows. My red umbrella with its knobby clear red handle sticks out of a box like the head of an exotic bird. In the seat behind us is a boy in short grey pants and jacket carrying a wooden slatted box with a tabby kitten inside. He is trying to distract the kitten with his finger but the kitten mews and mews, its mouth opening and closing. I can barely hear its high steady cry in the clackity-clack and steamy hiss of the train.

A few seats in front, one young woman is sitting with her narrow shoulders hunched over a tiny red-faced baby. Her short black hair falls into her bird-like face. She is so young, I would call her "onesan," older sister.

The woman in the aisle seat opposite us leans over and whispers to Obasan with a solemn nodding of her head and a flicker of her eyes indicating the young woman.

Obasan moves her head slowly and gravely in a nod as she listens. "Kawaiso," she says under her breath. The word is used whenever there is hurt and a need for tenderness.

The young woman, Kuniko-san, came from Saltspring Island, the woman says. Kuniko-san was rushed on to the train from Hastings Park, a few days after giving birth prematurely to her baby.

"She has nothing," the woman whispers. "Not even diapers."

Aya Obasan does not respond as she looks steadily at the dirt-covered floor. I lean out into the aisle and I can see the baby's tiny fist curled tight against its wrinkled face. Its eyes are closed and its mouth is squinched small as a button. Kuniko-san does not lift her eyes at all.

"Kawai," I whisper to Obasan, meaning that the baby is cute.

Obasan hands me an orange from a wicker basket and gestures towards Kuniko-san, indicating that I should take her the gift. But I pull back.

"For the baby," Obasan says urging me.

I withdraw further into my seat. She shakes open a furoshiki—a square cloth that is used to carry things by tying the corners together—and places a towel and some apples and oranges in it. I watch her lurching from side to side as she walks towards Kuniko-san.

Clutching the top of Kuniko-san's seat with one hand, Obasan bows and holds the furoshiki out to her. Kuniko-san clutches the baby against her breast and bows forward twice while accepting Obasan's gift without looking up.

As Obasan returns towards us, the old woman in the seat diagonal to ours beckons to me, nodding her head, urging me to come to her, her hand gesturing downwards in a digging waving motion. I lean towards her.

"A baby was born," the old woman says. "Is this not so?"

I nod.

The old woman bumps herself forward and off the seat. Her back is as round as a church bell. She is so short that when she is standing, she is lower than when she was sitting. She braces herself against the seat and bends forward.

"There is nothing to offer," she says as Obasan reaches her. She lifts her skirt and begins to remove a white flannel underskirt, her hand gathering the undergarment in pleats.

"Ah, no no Grandmother," Obasan says.

"Last night it was washed. It is nothing, but it is clean."

Obasan supports her in the rock rock of the train and they sway together back and forth. The old woman steps out of the garment, being careful not to let it touch the floor.

"Please—if it is acceptable. For a diaper. There is nothing to offer," the old woman says as she hoists herself on to the seat again. She folds the undergarment into a neat square, the fingers of her hand stiff and curled as driftwood.

❖

I have gathered all the stained cups and dishes, the serving bowls and the teapot, and am cleaning them, removing the stains and grease, soaking them in a sink full of hot sudsy water. When I am half-way through I hear the sounds of two cars entering the driveway. The car doors close and there are voices in the yard. In a moment, there is a slow light rapping on the living-room door and Nakayama-sensei's voice calls "Gomen-nasai," announcing his arrival. He opens the door and calls "Gomen-nasai" again in a loud but gentle voice.

"O," Obasan says and begins to rise, holding the blue pages and the magnifying glass in her hands.

"Please, please." He comes into the room, removing his black felt hat and waving his hand in the rapid patting movement indicating that she should not get up. His thin hair is so white it is almost luminous against his prairie-darkened face. Over the years, Nakayama-sensei has managed to visit Granton about once a month or so, when he is not travelling elsewhere.

Aunt Emily and Stephen are directly behind Nakayama-sensei. I am surprised at the amount of grey hair Stephen has. There is not so much that it streaks but the white is definitely visible as a light spray. He seems also to be slightly heavier than he was before, his face more full.

"Stee-bu san?" Obasan says. She puts the papers and magnifying glass on the chesterfield and stands up tottering. With her two hands outstretched, she steps unsteadily towards him.

Steve bends over and holds her hands with one hand as he removes his shoes with the other. He has just come in the door, and he already looks as if he would like to run out. His light black coat is pocked by large raindrops.

Aunt Emily also removes her shoes, then puts one arm around Obasan's shoulders. Obasan touches Steve's coat where it is wet. "Is it raining?" she asks. Then she chuckles. "Even if there is rain or thunder, these ears cannot hear."

I take Aunt Emily's and Nakayama-sensei's wet coats and hang them on the hooks beside the kitchen, then pour water into the heavy kettle for green tea.

Stephen, still wearing his wet coat, is sitting in the armchair with his legs splayed out like splints.

"Everyone someday dies," Obasan is saying to him.

"What happened, Naomi?" he asks with his back to me.

"I don't know really," I answer. I am slicing the stone bread to serve with the green tea. "I haven't got the details from Dr. Brace."

Aunt Emily puts her bag down behind the armchair and comes into the kitchen. She looks for a dish towel to wipe the teacups.

"The Barkers were here just a while ago."

"Yeah?" Stephen sits up and takes off his coat jerkily. He grunts as Obasan tries to help him with it. Stephen has made himself altogether unfamiliar with speaking Japanese.

Nakayama-sensei has picked up the magnifying glass and paper that Obasan left on the chesterfield and is glancing at the top page when Aunt Emily goes into the living room with the tray of teacups.

She stops short when she sees what Sensei is holding. All the rest of her papers are piled up on one edge of the coffee table.

"Everyone someday dies," Obasan is saying again, softly to herself.

Nakayama-sensei puts the papers and magnifying glass on the coffee table, then leaning back and with his mouth close to Obasan's ear, he says, "Should there be prayer?"

Obasan replies by bending forward in a prolonged bow.

I come into the room with the plate of buttered bread and kneel beside the coffee table. Everyone's head is bowed and we sit together in the stillness for a long time.

At last Nakayama-sensei stands up. He begins a long prayer of thanks in Japanese.

Stephen has his elbows on his knees and is feeling his chin lightly with his fingertips as he listens with his eyes fixed on the floor. I also have my eyes open. At one point, Stephen takes a corner of bread and breaks it off, then changing his mind, he sticks it back on the slice. At the end of the prayer, Aunt Emily says "Amen," and we sit together in the silence once more.

When Nakayama-sensei sits down, Aunt Emily opens her eyes, but Obasan's head remains bowed.

"It is good you are here," Nakayama-sensei says to Aunt Emily and Stephen. "You have come well."

Aunt Emily nods and takes her papers off the coffee table, making room for the teacups. Sensei leans forward to help and removes the blue papers and magnifying glass.

"Letters from a long time ago," Aunt Emily says to Sensei.

"Is that so," Nakayama-sensei says, glancing down through the bottom of his bifocals. His lips gradually become pursed in concentration as he reads the top page. When he comes to the end of the page, he stops.

"About this, I had no knowledge," he says in a low voice.

"What is it, Sensei?" I ask.

He puts the first page aside and reads the next and the next groaning quietly. When he is finished he puts the papers down and addresses Aunt Emily.

"Has there been no telling?"

"No," Aunt Emily says quietly.

"It is better to speak, is it not? They are not children any longer."

Aunt Emily nods slowly. "Yes," she says softly. "We ought to tell them. I always thought we should. But . . . Kodomo no tame—." She fingers the buttons on her sweater and looks at me apologetically. "There was so much sad news. Mark was dead. Father was ill. The first time I came to Granton I brought the letters thinking we should tell them everything, but we decided to respect Nesan's wishes."

"Please, Aunt Emily," I whisper as she turns aside. "Tell us."

Aunt Emily takes the letters and reads the pages, handing them back to Sensei when she is finished.

"What is written?" I ask again.

"A matter of a long time time ago," Sensei says.

"What matter?"

Nakayama-sensei clears his throat. "Senso no toki—in the time of the war—your mother. Your grandmother. That there is suffering and their deep love." He reads the letters in silence once more, then begins reading aloud. The letter is addressed to Grandpa Kato. It is clear as he reads that the letters were never intended for Stephen and me. There were written by Grandma Kato.

The sound of rain beats against the windows and the roof. The rain is collecting in the eaves and pouring in a thin stream into the rain barrel at the corner near the kitchen door. Tomorrow I will fill the plastic bucket and bring the soft frothy water in—use it to water the houseplants and wash my hair.

Sensei's faltering voice is almost drowned out by the splattering gusts against the window. I stare at the gauze-curtained windows and imagine the raindrops sliding down the glass, black on black. In the sound of the howling outside, I hear other howling.

Sensei pauses as he reads. "Naomi," he says softly, "Stephen, your mother is speaking. Listen carefully to her voice."

Many of the Japanese words sound strange and the language is formal.

❖

There are only two letters in the grey cardboard folder. The first is a brief and emotionless statement that Grandma Kato, her niece's daughter, and my mother are the only ones in the immediate family to have survived. The second letter is an outpouring.

I remember Grandma Kato as thin and tough, not given to melodrama or overstatement of any kind. She was unbreakable. I felt she could endure all things and would survive any catastrophe. But I did not then understand what catastrophes were possible in human affairs.

Here, the ordinary Granton rain slides down wet and clean along the glass leaving a trail on the window like the Japanese writing on the thin blue-lined paper—straight down like a bead curtain of asterisks. The rain she describes is black, oily, thick, and strange.

"In the heat of the August sun," Grandma writes, "however much the effort to forget, there is no forgetfulness. As in a dream, I can still see the maggots crawling in the sockets of my niece's eyes. Her strong intelligent young son helped me move a bonsai tree that very morning. There is no forgetfulness."

When Nakayama-sensei reaches the end of the page, he stops reading and folds the letter as if he has decided to read no more. Aunt Emily begins to speak quietly, telling of a final letter from the Canadian missionary, Miss Best.

How often, I am wondering, did Grandma and Mother waken in those years with the unthinkable memories alive in their minds, the visible evidence of horror written on their skin, in their blood, carved in every mirror they passed, felt in every step they took. As a child I was told only that Mother and Grandma Kato were safe in Tokyo, visiting Grandma Kato's ailing mother.

"Someday, surely, they will return," Obasan used to say.

The two letters that reached us in Vancouver before all communication ceased due to the war told us that Mother and Grandma Kato had arrived safely in Japan and were staying with Grandma Kato's sister and her husband in their home near the Tokyo Gas Company. My great-grandmother was then seventy-nine and was not expected to live to be eighty but, happily, she had become so well that she had returned home from the hospital and was even able on occasion to leave the house.

Nakayama-sensei opens the letter again and holds it, reading silently. Then looking over to Stephen, he says, "It is better to speak, is it not?"

"They're dead now," Stephen says.

Sensei nods.

"Please read, Sensei," I whisper.

"Yes," Aunt Emily says. "They should know."

Sensei starts again at the beginning. The letter is dated simply 1949. It was sent, Sensei says, from somewhere in Nagasaki. There was no return address.

"Though it was a time of war," Grandma writes, "what happiness that January 1945, to hear from my niece Setsuko, in Nagasaki." Setsuko's second child was due to be born within the month. In February, just as American air raids in Tokyo were intensifying, Mother went to help her cousin in Nagasaki. The baby was born three days after she arrived. Early in March, air raids and alarms were constant day and night in Tokyo. In spite of all the dangers of travel, Grandma Kato went to Nagasaki to be with my mother and to help with the care of the new baby. The last day she spent with her mother and sister in Tokyo, she said they sat on the tatami and talked, remembering their childhood and the days they went chestnut-picking together. They parted with laughter. The following night, Grandma Kato's sister, their mother and her sister's husband died in the B-29 bombings of 9 March 1945.

From this point on, Grandma's letter becomes increasingly chaotic, the details interspersed without chronological consistency. She and my mother, she writes, were unable to talk of all the things that happened. The horror would surely die sooner, they felt, if they refused to speak. But the silence and the constancy of the nightmare had become unbearable for Grandma and she hoped that by sharing them with her husband, she could be helped to extricate herself from the grip of the past.

"If these matters are sent away in this letter, perhaps they will depart a little from our souls," she writes. "For the burden of these words, forgive me."

Mother, for her part, continued her vigil of silence. She spoke with no one about her torment. She specifically requested that Stephen and I be spared the truth.

In all my high-school days, until we heard from Sensei that her grave had been found in Tokyo, I pictured her trapped in Japan by government regulations, or by an ailing grandmother. The letters I sent to the address in Tokyo were never answered or returned. I could not know that she and Grandma Kato had gone to Nagasaki to stay with Setsuko, her husband who was a dentist, and their two children, four-year-old Tomio and the new baby, Chieko.

The baby, Grandma writes, looked so much like me that she and my mother marvelled and often caught themselves calling her Naomi. With her widow's peak, her fat cheeks and pointed chin, she had a heart-shaped face like mine. Tomio, however, was not like Stephen at all. He was a sturdy child, extremely healthy and athletic, with a strong will like his father. He was fascinated by his new baby sister, sitting and watching her for hours as she slept or nursed. He made dolls for her. He helped to dress her. He loved to hold her in the bath, feeling her fingers holding his fingers tightly. He rocked her to sleep in his arms.

The weather was hot and humid that morning of 9 August. The air-raid alerts had ended. Tomio and some neighbourhood children had gone to the irrigation ditch to play and cool off as they sometimes did.

Shortly after eleven o'clock, Grandma Kato was preparing to make lunch. The baby was strapped to her back. She was bending over a bucket of water beside a large earthenware storage bin when a child in the street was heard shouting, "Look at the parachute!" A few seconds later there was a sudden white flash, brighter than a bolt of lightning. She had no idea what could have exploded. It was as if the entire sky were swallowed up. A moment later she was hurled sideways by a blast. She had a sensation of floating tranquilly in a cool whiteness high above the earth. When she regained consciousness she was slumped forward in a sitting position in the water bin. She gradually became aware of the moisture, an intolerable heat, blood, a mountain of debris and her niece's weak voice sounding at first distant, calling the names of her children. Then she could hear the other sounds—the far-away shouting. Around her, a thick dust made breathing difficult. Chieko was still strapped to her back, but made no sound. She was alive but unconscious.

It took Grandma a long time to claw her way out of the wreckage. When she emerged, it was into an eerie twilight formed of heavy dust and smoke that blotted out the sun. What she saw was incomprehensible. Almost all the buildings were flattened or in flames as far as she could see. The landmarks were gone. Tall columns of fire rose through the haze and everywhere the dying and the wounded crawled, fled, stumbled like ghosts among the ruins. Voices screamed, calling the names of children, fathers, mothers, calling for help, calling for water.

Beneath some wreckage, she saw first the broken arm, then the writhing body of her niece, her head bent back, her hair singed, both her eye sockets blown out. In a weak and delirious voice, she was calling Tomio. Grandma Kato touched her niece's leg and the skin peeled off and stuck to the palm of her hand.

It isn't clear from the letter but at some point she came across Tomio, his legs pumping steadily up and down as he stood in one spot not knowing where to go. She gathered him in her arms. He was remarkably intact, his skin unburned.

She had no idea where Mother was, but with the two children, she began making her way towards the air-raid shelter. All around her people one after another collapsed and died, crying for water. One old man no longer able to keep moving lay on the ground holding up a dead baby and crying, "Save the children. Leave the old." No one took the dead child from his outstretched hands. Men, women, in many cases indistinguishable by sex, hairless, half-clothed, hobbled past. Skin hung from their bodies like tattered rags. One man held his bowels in with the stump of one hand. A child whom Grandma Kato recognized lay on the ground asking for help. She stopped and told him she would return as soon as she could. A woman she knew was begging for someone to help her lift the burning beam beneath which her children were trapped. The woman's children were friends of Tomio's. Grandma was loath to walk past, but with the two children, she could do no more and kept going. At no point does Grandma Kato mention the injuries she herself must have sustained.

Nearing the shelter, Grandma could see through the greyness that the entrance was clogged with dead bodies. She remembered then that her niece's father-in-law lived on a farm on the hillside, and she began making her way back through the burning city towards the river she would have to cross. The water, red with blood, was a raft of corpses. Further upstream, the bridge was twisted like noodles. Eventually she came to a spot where she was able to cross and, still carrying the two children, Grandma Kato made her way up the hillside.

After wandering for some time, she found a wooden water pipe dribbling a steady stream. She held Tomio's mouth to it and allowed him to drink as much as he wished though she had heard that too much water was not good. She unstrapped the still unconscious baby from her back. Exhausted, she drank from the pipe, and gathering the two children in her arms, she looked out at the burning city and lapsed into a sleep so deep she believed she was unconscious.

When she awakened, she was in the home of her niece's relatives and the baby was being fed barley water. The little boy was nowhere.

Almost immediately, Grandma set off to look for the child. Next day she returned to the area of her niece's home and every day thereafter she looked for Mother and the lost boy, checking the lists of the dead, looking over the unclaimed corpses. She discovered that her niece's husband was among the dead.

One evening when she had given up the search for the day, she sat down beside a naked woman she'd seen earlier who was aimlessly chipping wood to make a pyre on which to cremate a dead baby. The woman was utterly disfigured. Her nose and one cheek were almost gone. Great wounds and pustules covered her entire face and body. She was completely bald. She sat in a cloud of flies and maggots wriggled among her wounds. As Grandma watched her, the woman gave her a vacant gaze, then let out a cry. It was my mother.

The little boy was never found. Mother was taken to a hospital and was expected to die, but she survived. During one night she vomited yellow fluid and passed a great deal of blood. For a long time—Grandma does not say how long—Mother wore bandages on her face. When they were removed, Mother felt her face with her fingers, then asked for a cloth mask. Thereafter she would not take off her mask from morning to night.

"At this moment," Grandma writes, "we are preparing to visit Chieko-chan in the hospital." Chieko, four years old in 1949, waited daily for their visit, standing in the hospital corridor, tubes from her wrist attached to a bottle that was hung above her. A small bald-headed girl. She was dying of leukaemia.

"There may not be many more days," Grandma concludes.

After this, what could have happened? Did they leave the relatives in Nagasaki? Where and how did they survive?

When Sensei is finished reading, he folds and unfolds the letter, nodding his head slowly.

I put my hands around the teapot, feeling its round warmth against my palms. My skin feels hungry for warmth, for flesh. Grandma mentioned in her letter that she saw one woman cradling a hot-water bottle as if it were a baby.

Sensei places the letter back in the cardboard folder and closes it with the short red string around the tab.

"That there is brokenness," he says quietly. "That this world is brokenness. But within brokenness is the unbreakable name. How the whole earth groans till Love returns."

I stand up abruptly and leave the room, going into the kitchen for some more hot water. When I return, Sensei is sitting with his face in his hands.

Stephen is staring at the floor, his body hunched forward motionless. He glances up at me then looks away swiftly. I sit on a stool beside him and try to concentrate on what is being said. I can hear Aunt Emily telling us about Mother's grave. Then Nakayama-sensei stands and begins to say the Lord's Prayer under his breath. "And forgive us our trespasses—forgive us our trespasses—" he repeats, sighing deeply, "as we forgive others . . ." He lifts his head, looking upwards. "We are powerless to forgive unless we first are forgiven. It is a high calling my friends—the calling to forgive. But no person, no people is innocent. Therefore we must forgive one another."

I am not thinking of forgiveness. The sound of Sensei's voice grows as indistinct as the hum of distant traffic. Gradually the room grows still and it is as if I am back with Uncle again, listening and listening to the silent earth and the silent sky as I have done all my life.

I close my eyes.

Sweat

ZORA NEALE HURSTON

I

It was eleven o'clock of a Spring night in Florida. It was Sunday. Any other night, Delia Jones would have been in bed for two hours by this time. But she was a washwoman, and Monday morning meant a great deal to her. So she collected the soiled clothes on Saturday when she returned the clean things. Sunday night after church, she sorted and put the white things to soak. It saved her almost a half-day's start. A great hamper in the bedroom held the clothes that she brought home. It was so much neater than a number of bundles lying around.

She squatted on the kitchen floor beside the great pile of clothes, sorting them into small heaps according to color, and humming a song in a mournful key, but wondering through it all where Sykes, her husband, had gone with her horse and buckboard.

Just then something long, round, limp and black fell upon her shoulders and slithered to the floor beside her. A great terror took hold of her. It softened her knees and dried her mouth so that it was a full minute before she could cry out or move. Then she saw that it was the big bull whip her husband liked to carry when he drove.

She lifted her eyes to the door and saw him standing there bent over with laughter at her fright. She screamed at him.

"Sykes, what you throw dat whip on me like dat? You know it would skeer me—looks just like a snake, an' you knows how skeered Ah is of snakes."

"Course Ah knowed it! That's how come Ah done it." He slapped his leg with his hand and almost rolled on the ground in his mirth. "If you such a big fool dat you got to have a fit over a earth worm or a string Ah don't care how bad Ah skeer you."

"You ain't got no business doing it. Gawd knows it's a sin. Some day Ah'm gointuh drop dead from some of yo' foolishness. 'Nother thing, where you been wid mah rig? Ah feeds dat pony. He ain't fuh you to be drivin' wid no bull whip."

"You sho' is one aggravatin' nigger woman!" he declared and stepped into the room. She resumed her work and did not answer him at once. "Ah done tole you time and again to keep them white folks' clothes outa dis house."

He picked up the whip and glared at her. Delia went on with her work. She went out into the yard and returned with a galvanized tub and set it on the washbench. She saw that Sykes had kicked all of the clothes together again, and now stood in her way truculently, his whole manner hoping, *praying*, for an argument. But she walked calmly around him and commenced to re-sort the things.

"Next time, Ah'm gointer kick 'em outdoors," he threatened as he struck a match along the leg of his corduroy breeches.

Delia never looked up from her work, and her thin, stooped shoulders sagged further.

"Ah ain't for no fuss t'night Sykes. Ah just come from taking sacrament at the church house."

He snorted scornfully. "Yeah, you just come from de church house on a Sunday night, but heah you is gone to work on them clothes. You ain't nothing but a hypocrite. One of them amen-corner Christians—sing, whoop, and shout, then come home and wash white folks' clothes on the Sabbath."

He stepped roughly upon the whitest pile of things, kicking them helter-skelter as he crossed the room. His wife gave a little scream of dismay, and quickly gathered them together again.

"Sykes, you quit grindin' dirt into these clothes! How can Ah git through by Sat'day if Ah don't start on Sunday?"

"Ah don't keer if you never git through. Anyhow, Ah done promised Gawd and a couple of other men, Ah ain't gointer have it in mah house. Don't gimme no lip neither, else Ah'll throw 'em out and put mah fist up side yo' head to boot."

Delia's habitual meekness seemed to slip from her shoulders like a blown scarf. She was on her feet; her poor little body, her bare knuckly hands bravely defying the strapping hulk before her.

"Looka heah, Sykes, you done gone too fur. Ah been married to you fur fifteen years, and Ah been takin' in washin' fur fifteen years. Sweat, sweat, sweat! Work and sweat, cry and sweat, pray and sweat!"

"What's that got to do with me?" he asked brutally.

"What's it got to do with you, Sykes? Mah tub of suds is filled yo' belly with vittles more times than yo' hands is filled it. Mah sweat is done paid for this house and Ah reckon Ah kin keep on sweatin' in it."

She seized the iron skillet from the stove and struck a defensive pose, which act surprised him greatly, coming from her. It cowed him and he did not strike her as he usually did.

"Naw you won't," she panted, "that ole snaggle-toothed black woman you runnin' with ain't comin' heah to pile up on *mah* sweat and blood. You ain't paid for nothin' on this place, and Ah'm gointer stay right heah till Ah'm toted out foot foremost."

"Well, you better quit gittin' me riled up, else they'll be totin' you out sooner than you expect. Ah'm so tired of you Ah don't know whut to do. Gawd! How Ah hates skinny wimmen!"

A little awed by this new Delia, he sidled out of the door and slammed the back gate after him. He did not say where he had gone, but she knew too well. She knew very well that he would not return until nearly daybreak also. Her work over, she went on to bed but not to sleep at once. Things had come to a pretty pass!

She lay awake, gazing upon the debris that cluttered their matrimonial trail. Not an image left standing along the way. Anything like flowers had long ago been drowned in the salty stream that had been pressed from her heart. Her tears, her sweat, her blood. She had brought love to the union and he had brought a longing after the flesh. Two months after the wedding, he had given her the first brutal beating. She had the memory of his numerous trips to Orlando with all of his wages when he had returned to her penniless, even before the first year had passed. She was young and soft then, but now she thought of her knotty, muscled limbs, her harsh knuckly hands, and drew herself up into an unhappy little ball in the middle of the big feather bed. Too late now to hope for love, even if it were not Bertha it would be someone else. This case differed from the others only in that she was bolder than the others. Too late for everything except her little home. She had built it for her old days, and planted one by one the trees and flowers there. It was lovely to her, lovely.

Somehow, before sleep came, she found herself saying aloud: "Oh well, whatever goes over the Devil's back, is got to come under his belly. Sometime or ruther, Sykes, like everybody else, is gointer reap his sowing." After that she was able to build a spiritual earthworks against her husband. His shells could no longer reach her. AMEN. She went to sleep and slept until he announced his presence in bed by kicking her feet and rudely snatching the covers away.

"Gimme some kivah heah, an' git yo' damn foots over on yo' own side! Ah oughter mash you in yo' mouf fuh drawing dat skillet on me."

Delia went clear to the rail without answering him. A triumphant indifference to all that he was or did.

II

The week was as full of work for Delia as all other weeks, and Saturday found her behind her little pony, collecting and delivering clothes.

It was a hot, hot day near the end of July. The village men on Joe Clarke's porch even chewed cane listlessly. They did not hurl the cane-knots as usual. They let them dribble over the edge of the porch. Even conversation had collapsed under the heat.

"Heah come Delia Jones," Jim Merchant said, as the shaggy pony came 'round the bend of the road toward them. The rusty buckboard was heaped with baskets of crisp, clean laundry.

"Yep," Joe Lindsay agreed. "Hot or col', rain or shine, jes'ez reg'lar ez de weeks roll roun' Delia carries 'em an' fetches 'em on Sat'day."

"She better if she wanter eat," said Moss. "Syke Jones ain't wuth de shot an' powder hit would tek tuh kill 'em. Not to *huh* he ain't."

"He sho' ain't," Walter Thomas chimed in. "It's too bad, too, cause she wuz a right pretty li'l trick when he got huh. Ah'd uh mah'ied huh mahself if he hadnter beat me to it."

Delia nodded briefly at the men as she drove past.

"Too much knockin' will ruin *any* 'oman. He done beat huh 'nough tuh kill three women, let 'lone change they looks," said Elijah Moseley. "How Syke kin stommuck dat big black greasy Mogul he's layin' roun' wid, gits me. Ah swear dat eight-rock couldn't kiss a sardine can Ah done thowed out de back do' 'way las' yeah."

"Aw, she's fat, thass how come. He's allus been crazy 'bout fat women," put in Merchant. "He'd a' been tied up wid one long time ago if he could a' found one tuh have him. Did Ah tell yuh 'bout him come sidlin' round *mah* wife—bringin' her a basket uh peecans outa his yard fuh a present? Yessir, mah wife! She tol' him tuh take 'em right straight back home, 'cause Delia works so hard ovah dat washtub she reckon everything on de place taste lak sweat an' soapsuds. Ah jus' wisht Ah'd a' caught 'im 'roun' dere! Ah'd a' made his hips ketch on fiah down dat shell road."

"Ah know he done it, too. Ah sees 'im grinnin' at every 'oman dat passes," Walter Thomas said. "But even so, he useter eat some mighty big hunks uh humble pie tuh git dat li'l 'oman he got. She wuz ez pritty ez a speckled pup! Dat wuz fifteen years ago. He useter be so skeered uh losin' huh, she could make him do some parts of a husband's duty. Dey never wuz de same in de mind."

"There oughter be a law about him," said Lindsay. "He ain't fit tuh carry guts tuh a bear."

Clarke spoke for the first time. "Tain't no law on earth dat kin make a man be decent if it ain't in 'im. There's plenty men dat takes a wife lak dey do a joint uh sugar-cane. It's round, juicy an' sweet when dey gits it. But dey squeeze an' grind, squeeze an' grind an' wring tell dey wring every drop uh pleasure dat's in 'em out. When dey's satisfied dat dey is wrung dry, dey treats 'em jes' lak dey do a cane-chew. Dey throws 'em away. Dey knows whut dey is doin' while dey is at it, an' hates theirselves fuh it but they keeps on hangin' after huh tell she's empty. Den dey hates huh fuh bein' a cane-chew an' in de way."

"We oughter take Syke an' dat stray 'oman uh his'n down in Lake Howell swamp an' lay on de rawhide till they cain't say Lawd a' mussy. He allus wuz uh ovahbearin niggah, but since dat white 'oman from up north done teached 'im how to run a automobile, he done got too beggety to live—an' we oughter kill 'im," Old Man Anderson advised.

A grunt of approval went around the porch. But the heat was melting their civic virtue and Elijah Moseley began to bait Joe Clarke.

"Come on, Joe, git a melon outa dere an' slice it up for yo' customers. We'se all sufferin' wid de heat. De bear's done got *me*!"

"Thass right, Joe, a watermelon is jes' whut Ah needs tuh cure de eppizudicks," Walter Thomas joined forces with Moseley. "Come on dere, Joe. We all is steady customers an' you ain't set us up in a long time. Ah chooses dat long, bowlegged Floridy favorite."

"A god, an' be dough. You all gimme twenty cents and slice away," Clarke retorted. "Ah needs a col' slice m'self. Heah, everybody chip in. Ah'll lend y'all mah meat knife."

The money was all quickly subscribed and the huge melon brought forth. At that moment, Sykes and Bertha arrived. A determined silence fell on the porch and the melon was put away again.

Merchant snapped down the blade of his jackknife and moved toward the store door.

"Come on in, Joe, an' gimme a slab uh sow belly an' uh pound uh coffee—almost fuhgot 'twas Sat'day. Got to git on home." Most of the men left also.

Just then Delia drove past on her way home, as Sykes was ordering magnificently for Bertha. It pleased him for Delia to see.

"Git whutsoever yo' heart desires, Honey. Wait a minute, Joe. Give huh two bottles uh strawberry soda-water, uh quart parched ground-peas, an' a block uh chewin' gum."

With all this they left the store, with Sykes reminding Bertha that this was his town and she could have it if she wanted it.

The men returned soon after they left, and held their watermelon feast.

"Where did Syke Jones git da 'oman from nohow?" Lindsay asked.

"Ovah Apopka. Guess dey musta been cleanin' out de town when she lef'. She don't look lak a thing but a hunk uh liver wid hair on it."

"Well, she sho' kin squall," Dave Carter contributed. "When she gits ready tuh laff, she jes' opens huh mouf an' latches it back tuh de las' notch. No ole granpa alligator down in Lake Bell ain't got nothin' on huh."

III

Bertha had been in town three months now. Sykes was still paying her room-rent at Della Lewis's—the only house in town that would have taken her in. Sykes took her frequently to Winter Park to "stomps." He still assured her that he was the swellest man in the state.

"Sho' you kin have dat li'l ole house soon's Ah git dat 'oman outa dere. Everything b'longs tuh me an' you sho' kin have it. Ah sho' 'bominates uh skinny 'oman. Lawdy, you sho' is got one portly shape on you! You kin git *anything* you wants. Dis is *mah* town an' you sho' kin have it."

Delia's work-worn knees crawled over the earth in Gethsemane and up the rocks of Calvary many, many times during these months. She avoided the villagers and meeting places in her efforts to be blind and deaf. But Bertha nullified this to a degree, by coming to Delia's house to call Sykes out to her at the gate.

Delia and Sykes fought all the time now with no peaceful interludes. They slept and ate in silence. Two or three times Delia had attempted a timid friendliness, but she was repulsed each time. It was plain that the breaches must remain agape.

The sun had burned July to August. The heat streamed down like a million hot arrows, smiting all things living upon the earth. Grass withered, leaves browned, snakes went blind in shedding and men and dogs went mad. Dog days!

Delia came home one day and found Sykes there before her. She wondered, but started to go on into the house without speaking, even though he was standing in the kitchen door and she must either stoop under his arm or ask him to move. He made no room for her. She noticed a soap box beside the steps, but paid no particular attention to it. knowing that he must have brought it there. As she was stooping to pass under his outstretched arm, he suddenly pushed her backward, laughingly.

"Look in de box dere Delia, Ah done brung yuh somethin'!"

She nearly fell upon the box in her stumbling, and when she saw what it held, she all but fainted outright.

"Syke! Syke, mah Gawd! You take dat rattlesnake 'way from heah! You *gottuh*. Oh, Jesus, have mussy!"

"Ah ain't got tuh do nuthin' uh de kin'—fact is Ah ain't got tuh do nothin' but die. Tain't no use uh you puttin' on airs makin' out lak you skeered uh dat snake—he's gointer stay right heah tell he die. He wouldn't bite me cause Ah knows how tuh handle 'im. Nohow he wouldn't risk breakin' out his fangs 'gin *yo* skinny laigs."

"Naw, now Syke, don't keep dat thing 'round trying' tuh skeer me tuh death. You knows Ah'm even feared uh earth worms. Thass de biggest snake Ah evah did see. Kill 'im Syke, please."

"Doan ast me tuh do nothin' fuh yuh. Goin' 'round tryin' tuh be so damn asterperious. Naw, Ah ain't gonna kill it. Ah think uh damn sight mo' uh him dan you! Dat's a nice snake an' anybody doan lak 'im kin jes' hit de grit."

The village soon heard that Sykes had the snake, and came to see and ask questions.

"How de hen-fire did you ketch dat six-foot rattler, Syke?" Thomas asked.

"He's full uh frogs so he cain't hardly move, thass how Ah eased up on 'm. But Ah'm a snake charmer an' knows how tuh handle 'em. Shux, dat ain't nothin'. Ah could ketch one eve'y day if Ah so wanted tuh."

"Whut he needs is a heavy hick'ry club leaned real heavy on his head. Dat's de bes' way tuh charm a rattlesnake."

"Naw, Walt, y'all jes' don't understand dese diamon' backs lak Ah do," said Sykes in a superior tone of voice.

The village agreed with Walter, but the snake stayed on. His box remained by the kitchen door with its screen wire covering. Two or three days later it had digested its meal of frogs and literally came to life. It rattled at every movement in the kitchen or the yard. One day as Delia came down the kitchen steps she saw his chalky-white fangs curved like scimitars hung in the wire meshes. This time she did not run away with averted eyes as usual. She stood for a long time in the doorway in a red fury that grew bloodier for every second that she regarded the creature that was her torment.

That night she broached the subject as soon as Sykes sat down to the table.

"Syke, Ah wants you tuh take dat snake 'way fum heah. You done starved me an' Ah put up widcher, you done beat me an Ah took dat, but you done kilt all mah insides bringin' dat varmint heah."

Sykes poured out a saucer full of coffee and drank it deliberately before he answered her.

"A whole lot Ah keer 'bout how you feels inside uh out. Dat snake ain't goin' no damn wheah till Ah gits ready fuh 'im tuh go. So fur as beatin' is concerned, yuh ain't took near all dat you gointer take ef yuh stay 'round *me*."

Delia pushed back her plate and got up from the table. "Ah hates you, Sykes," she said calmly. "Ah hates you tuh de same degree dat Ah useter love yuh. Ah done took an' took till mah belly is full up tuh mah neck. Dat's de reason Ah got mah letter fum de church an' moved mah membership tuh Woodbridge—so Ah don't haftuh take no sacrament wid yuh. Ah don't wantuh see yuh 'round me atall. Lay 'round wid dat 'oman all yuh wants tuh, but gwan 'way fum me an' mah house. Ah hates yuh lak uh suck-egg dog."

Sykes almost let the huge wad of corn bread and collard greens he was chewing fall out of his mouth in amazement. He had a hard time whipping himself up to the proper fury to try to answer Delia.

"Well, Ah'm glad you does hate me. Ah'm sho' tiahed uh you hangin' ontuh me. Ah don't want yuh. Look at yuh stringey ole neck! Yo' rawbony laigs an' arms is enough tuh cut uh man tuh death. You looks jes' lak de devvul's doll-baby tuh *me*. You cain't hate me no worse dan Ah hates you. Ah been hatin' *you* fuh years."

"Yo' ole black hide don't look lak nothin' tuh me, but uh passle uh wrinkled up rubber, wid yo' big ole yeahs flapping' on each side lak uh paih uh buzzard wings. Don't think Ah'm gointuh be run 'way fum mah house neither. Ah'm goin' tuh de white folks 'bout *you*, mah young man, de very nex' time you lay yo' han's on me. Mah cup is done run ovah." Delia said this with no signs of fear and Sykes departed from the house, threatening her, but made not the slightest move to carry out any of them.

That night he did not return at all, and the next day being Sunday, Delia was glad she did not have to quarrel before she hitched up her pony and drove the four miles to Woodbridge.

She stayed to the night service—"love feast"—which was very warm and full of spirit. In the emotional winds her domestic trials were borne far and wide so that she sang as she drove homeward,

Jurden water, black an' col
Chills de body, not de soul
An' Ah wantah cross Jurden in uh calm time.

She came from the barn to the kitchen door and stopped.

"Whut's de mattah, ol' Satan, you ain't kickin' up yo' racket?" She addressed the snake's box. Complete silence. She went on into the house with a new hope in its birth struggles. Perhaps her threat to go to the white folks had frightened Sykes! Perhaps he was sorry! Fifteen years of misery and suppression had brought Delia to the place where she would hope *anything* that looked towards a way over or through her wall of inhibitions.

She felt in the match-safe behind the stove at once for a match. There was only one there.

"Dat niggah wouldn't fetch nothin' heah tuh save his rotten neck, but he kin run threw whut Ah brings quick enough. Now he done toted off nigh on tuh haff uh box uh matches. He done had dat 'oman heah in mah house, too."

Nobody but a woman could tell how she knew this even before she struck the match. But she did and it put her into a new fury.

Presently she brought in the tubs to put the white things to soak. This time she decided she need not bring the hamper out of the bedroom; she would go in there and do the sorting. She picked up the pot-bellied lamp and went in. The room was small and the hamper stood hard by the foot of the white iron bed. She could sit and reach through the bedposts—resting as she worked.

"Ah wantah cross Jurden in uh calm time." She was singing again. The mood of the "love feast" had returned. She threw back the lid of the basket almost gaily. Then, moved by both horror and terror, she sprang back toward the door. *There lay the snake in the basket*! He moved sluggishly at first, but even as she turned round and round, jumped up and down in an insanity of fear, he began to stir vigorously. She saw him pouring his awful beauty from the basket upon the bed, then she seized the lamp and ran as fast as she could to the kitchen. The wind from the open door blew out the light and the dark-

ness added to her terror. She sped to the darkness of the yard, slamming the door after her before she thought to set down the lamp. She did not feel safe even on the ground, so she climbed up in the hay barn.

There for an hour or more she lay sprawled upon the hay a gibbering wreck.

Finally she grew quiet, and after that came coherent thought. With this stalked through her a cold, bloody rage. Hours of this. A period of introspection, a space of retrospection, then a mixture of both. Out of this an awful calm.

"Well, Ah done de bes' Ah could. If things ain't right, Gawd knows tain't mah fault."

She went to sleep—a twitch sleep—and woke up to a faint gray sky. There was a loud hollow sound below. She peered out. Sykes was at the wood-pile, demolishing a wire-covered box.

He hurried to the kitchen door, but hung outside there some minutes before he entered, and stood some minutes more inside before he closed it after him.

The gray in the sky was spreading. Delia descended without fear now, and crouched beneath the low bedroom window. The drawn shade shut out the dawn, shut in the night. But the thin walls held back no sound.

"Dat ol' scratch is woke up now!" She mused at the tremendous whirr inside, which every woodsman knows, is one of the sound illusions. The rattler is a ventriloquist. His whirr sounds to the right, to the left, straight ahead, behind, close under foot—everywhere but where it is. Woe to him who guesses wrong unless he is prepared to hold up his end of the argument! Sometimes he strikes without rattling at all.

Inside, Sykes heard nothing until he knocked a pot lid off the stove while trying to reach the match-safe in the dark. He had emptied his pockets at Bertha's.

The snake seemed to wake up under the stove and Sykes made a quick leap into the bedroom. In spite of the gin he had had, his head was clearing now.

"Mah Gawd!" he chattered, "ef Ah could on'y strack uh light!"

The rattling ceased for a moment as he stood paralyzed. He waited. It seemed that the snake waited also.

"Oh, fuh de light! Ah thought he'd be too sick"—Sykes was muttering to himself when the whirr began again, closer, right underfoot this time. Long before this, Sykes's ability to think had been flattened down to primitive instinct and he leaped—onto the bed.

Outside Delia heard a cry that might have come from a maddened chimpanzee, a stricken gorilla. All the terror, all the horror, all the rage that man possibly could express, without a recognizable human sound.

A tremendous stir inside there, another series of animal screams, the intermittent whirr of the reptile. The shade torn violently down from the window, letting in the red dawn, a huge brown hand seizing the window stick, great dull blows upon the wooden floor punctuating the gibberish of sound long after the rattle of the snake had abruptly subsided. All this Delia could see and hear from her place beneath the window, and it made her ill. She crept over to the four-o'clocks and stretched herself on the cool earth to recover.

She lay there. "Delia, Delia!" She could hear Sykes calling in a most despairing tone as one who expected no answer. The sun crept on up, and he called. Delia could not move—her legs had gone flabby. She never moved, he called, and the sun kept rising.

"Mah Gawd!" She heard him moan, "Mah Gawd fum Heben!" She heard him stumbling about and got up from her flower-bed. The sun was growing warm. As she approached the door she heard him call out hopefully, "Delia, is dat you Ah heah?"

She saw him on his hands and knees as soon as she reached the door. He crept an inch or two toward her—all that he was able, and she saw his horribly swollen neck and his one open eye shining with hope. A surge of pity too strong to support bore her away from that eye that must, could not, fail to see the tubs. He would see the lamp. Orlando with its doctors was too far. She could scarcely reach the chinaberry tree, where she waited in the growing heat while inside she knew the cold river was creeping up and up to extinguish that eye which must know by now that she knew.

God's World

NAJIB MAHFUZ
Translated by Akef Abadir and Roger Allen

Activity began in the secretarial department when "Uncle" Ibrahim, the office boy, came in. He opened the windows one after another and started sweeping the big floor with an air of almost total disinterest. He shook his head with a slow regularity, and his lips kept moving as though he were chewing something. This movement made the white hairs on his chin and cheeks stand up; his head, on the other hand, didn't have a single hair on top. He brushed the dust off the desk tops and arranged the dossiers and instruments. After all that, he took a comprehensive look at the entire room—the department—and moved from one desk to another as though he could see the people who worked at them. At one moment, he seemed to be satisfied and then he looked exasperated; he smiled once and then went away. Now it's time to go and get their breakfast, he told himself.

Mr. Ahmad, the archive clerk, was the first to arrive. He was getting old, about fifty, and his face wore a permanent look of annoyance as though it were a scroll recorded on the bark of time itself. He was followed by Mr. Mustafa, the clerk at the typewriter who laughed a lot; but it was just a nervous laugh which simply covered up his everyday worries. Then came Samir, or the mystery man as he was known in the department; the soldier whose smiling features showed clearly that he had yet to emerge from the joys of childhood. Mr. Lutfi came swaggering in, well dressed and wearing a ring, watch, and tiepin all made of gold. Close behind him came Hammam, slightly built and self-centered. Finally in came the departmental director, Professor Kamil, enveloped in a personal halo of dignity and carrying a rosary.

The office buzzed with the sound of voices and rustling papers, but no one started working. Even the director started talking on the telephone. Immediately newspapers were hoisted into the air like so many flags. Lutfi was following the news:

"The end of the world will be this year," he said. The director raised his voice over the telephone. "How can you deny the obvious?" he asked in delight.

"Why do we all put up with the miseries of marriage and children?" Samir asked. "Here's a young man killing his father with his mother watching!"

"What's the point of writing a prescription?" asked Ahmad with a croaking voice, "if the medicine isn't on the market?"

From where he was sitting, the soldier kept looking through the window at a doctor's clinic in the opposite building; he was waiting for the blonde German nurse to appear at the window.

"Believe me," Lutfi continued confidently, "the end of the world's nearer than you think. . . ."

The director put his hand over the mouthpiece and gave Hammam an order. "Prepare file 1-3/130 this year. . . ." he said. He then resumed his love chat on the phone. Hammam didn't look up from his paper but merely muttered between his teeth: "Son of a bitch!"

Ibrahim came back with a full tray and started handing out *ful*, *ta'miyya'* cheese sandwiches and crushed *tahini* sweets. They began to munch the food and the sound of lips smacking reverberated round the room; their eyes meanwhile remained glued to the news. Ibrahim stood at the entrance to the department watching them eating with a strange bewildered look in his eye.

" 'Uncle' Ibrahim, get our salaries," Ahmad yelled at him with his mouth full of food.

He went away. An hour later, a tie and perfume salesman who visited the department regularly at the beginning of each month came in and went around the desks showing his wares. The civil servants started looking at them and some of them took what they needed. The salesman went away on the understanding that he would come back when they got their salaries. After another hour, the butter seller came to collect the amounts he was owed, but Mustafa laughingly explained to him that he should wait till "Uncle" Ibrahim came back.

The man waited at the door, his lips moving in a nonstop recitation. The typewriter was clacking away busily, and Samir went into the director's office to show him some important papers. For the first time, the sun came in through the window which looked out on the square. The soldier kept on stealing glances in the direction of the clinic window. The director yelled for "Uncle" to do something for him, but Mustafa reminded him that he had not returned from the cashier's office yet. At this point, Ahmad looked up from the files. "The man's late!" he said. "Why is he so late?"

The butter seller went to the other offices, then he would be back. Ahmad went outside the room, looked left and right along the passageway and then came back. "There's no sign of him," he said. "What's holding him up, the old windbag!?"

When the third hour went by, Ahmad lost patience. He got up and announced in a loud voice that he was going to the cashier's office to look for him. He came back looking very angry. "He took the money a full hour ago," he said. "Where's the fool gone?"

"Did he take his own salary?" Lutfi asked. "Yes," was the angry reply. "That's what they told me at the pay window for seasonal workers. . . ."

"Maybe he's gone to do some shopping!"

"Before giving us our salaries?!"

"That's not out of the question. He does something new every day. . . ."

They all looked furious. The director—an old fourth-grader—frowned, and a short silence prevailed until Mustafa broke it with one of his laughs. "Just think," he said, "he might have been robbed in the street!"

Everyone laughed weakly, very weakly in fact; they sounded more like sighs of disapproval.

"Maybe he's had an accident!" Lutfi said. They all looked furious again, and so he corrected himself.

"Whatever happens to 'Uncle' Ibrahim involves the entire department . . ."

"Unless he's got a private cashier's office behind him!" said Ahmad angrily, hinting at Mustafa's rich wife.

Everyone gloated at that remark, but the director tapped on his desk with his Parker pen which he had been given on a happy occasion. He told the department to control itself, although he was really just covering up his own increasing anxiety.

"What happens to money in such circumstances?" the soldier asked in spite of everything.

"Exactly the same as in cases of theft." Nobody laughed.

"What would happen in case of an accident?" the soldier continued.

"Maybe he's been robbed in a crowd, or perhaps the police station is holding the money till things become clear. We'll all be dead and gone before you get it back!"

However, it was obvious that the reserves of laughter had dried up altogether. They all looked gloomy, and the passage of time seemed to weigh more heavily on them than illness itself. Someone asked what on earth had happened to make the day start so badly, and Ahmad started to look for "Uncle" Ibrahim in the entire inspectorate. When he came back, his face made it clear that his efforts had failed.

The director thought about the strange problem which had never occurred to anyone; he refused to believe it. The stupid fool will appear at the door suddenly, he told himself, and will be greeted by a hail of abuse. He'll have all manner of excuses to offer. But . . . If not, what could be done? Lutfi had a rich wife, and Samir was known to be a rogue. But what about the other poor devils like Ahmad who might be finished by this disaster? The butter seller came back again, but did not have time even to open his mouth. "Wait!" the director yelled at him. "It's not the day of judgement yet; we're in a government department, not a sidewalk market. . . ."

The man staggered back in confusion. Some of the civil servants from the inspectorate came to visit the department and look at the situation. Some of them thought about cracking a joke, but they found the atmosphere very melancholy and the jokes faded away before they even left their mouths. There was an air of anxiety and everyone stopped working.

"My heart tells me," said Ahmad with a sigh, "that it's already happened! We're doomed, friends! . . ." Then he got up. "I'll go and ask the doorman of the ministry about him," he said.

He disappeared in a rush. After a while he came back. "The doorman confirms," he yelled angrily, "that he saw him leaving the ministry around nine o'clock this morning!" He carried on in a strangled tone of voice. "What an utter calamity! He can't sell his whole life for a hundred and fifty or two hundred pounds! Could be an accident! Who knows?! Lord in heaven above, this month will never end!"

Lutfi sensed that some of them were looking at him from time to time. "A terrible catastrophe," he said in distress. "Some of you may be wondering how it concerns me! The truth is that my rich wife doesn't pay out a single millieme of her own money."

Ten curses were heaped upon him in secret, but none looked at him.

"Can you believe it, for heaven's sake?" said Ahmad with a sigh. "By the one and only God, I swear to you that after the second day of each month I come and go without a single millieme in my pocket. No coffee, no tea, no cigarettes. I have to walk; there's no way I can use any kind of transportation. Children at secondary school, children at university; and heavy debt because of medicine. God in heaven, what can I do?!"

When it passed one o'clock, the director stood up with a worried look on his face and left his desk. "I must report this to the general supervisor," he said.

The general supervisor listened to the story with evident annoyance. "Isn't it possible he'll come back," he asked, "whatever you may be thinking?"

"I've really completely despaired of that. It's getting on toward two o'clock. . . ."

"You know of course," said the general supervisor in a critical tone, "that your conduct is at fault and contrary to instructions. . . ."

The director cowered in a despairing silence. "All the departments do it. . . ." he muttered.

"So what! Two wrongs don't make a right. Write me a memorandum so that I can submit it to the deputy minister. . . ."

The director cringed. "Everyone needs his salary badly," he said. "We've never had anything like this happen before. . . ."

"What do you want me to do?"

"We haven't received our salaries and haven't signed the list. . . ."

The silence thickened. The director looked like a lost man. The general supervisor lost patience with him and started busying himself with the papers on his desk. The director now relinquished his position and proceeded towards the door with very heavy footsteps. Before reaching the door, he heard the supervisor's voice. "Inform the police. . . ." he was told harshly.

The secretarial department went down to the police station, and made their way to the officer's room between a lot of women sitting cross-legged on the floor. In front of them was a group of brawling men with bloodstained clothes being led along by a policeman. Behind a locked door screams of pain and cries for help could be heard. Mr. Kamil told the officer the story from beginning to end. He told him that "Uncle" Ibrahim was the office boy; he was fifty-five years old and had started in the printing house, but had been made an office boy when he was rude to his boss. His basic salary was six pounds. The civil servants told the officer that he was a good man although he was eccentric and would seem a little distracted at times; he would talk to you, join in a conversation which had nothing whatever to do with him, or volunteer some general observations about politics totally out of context. All they could say about his home was that he lived in house 111 in Darb al-Halla. He had never stolen before or done anything which would lead you to doubt his integrity. After completing the report, the officer said that the station would first make sure that he was not an accident victim, and then the investigation would take its course. The civil servants saw there was nothing to do but to leave. As they came out of the station, they looked almost drunk in their confusion. They were all talking at once, and kept trading complaints and questions about what they could do about the awful responsibility waiting for them at home. They were all united by a corporate desire to remain together till they could find a solution to their problem but in the end they were forced to separate and go to their own homes. The director returned home with no hope of anything but a poker game. Mustafa, who worked on the typewriter, made for the loan places in Bab ash-Sha'riyya where he used to go in times of crisis to borrow money at exorbitant rates. Lutfi's wife used to take charge of the household expenses but he had to devise some way of getting his monthly pocket money out of her. The soldier—who was a young bachelor living under his father's wing—decided to tell his father to accept him for this month as though he were still a schoolboy. Hammam's wife was a part of a savings association with her neighbors, and he would have to convince her to ask for her share which had been set aside for clothes so that he could spend it on household matters, regardless of the cursing, argument, and tears which would inevitably be involved. Things were relatively easy for Samir; as soon as he was left on his own, he thought, he would really be in a fix with no way out, if it were not for bribery. There remained Ahmad the archive clerk. His friends really wondered if he'd be able to survive. He wandered along the road without paying the slightest attention to the people or vehicles around him. He went into his house with a sigh; he looked very ashen as the threw himself down on the first chair and closed his eyes. His wife came in bringing the kitchen smells with her. "What's the matter with you?" she asked in consternation.

"We won't be getting any salary this month!" he said without any preliminaries.

"Why not, for God's sake?!" she asked in amazement. " 'Uncle' Ibrahim brought your salary round early this morning!"

He leapt to his feet like a drowning man who finds that he is breathing at long last. Meanwhile, his wife went out and came back with a wad of notes, his complete monthly salary! He was so happy, he felt almost crazy. He stretched out his hands. "God be good to you, 'Uncle' Ibrahim . . . may He comfort you, 'Uncle' Ibrahim. . . ."

The police raided "Uncle" Ibrahim's house in Darb al-Halla. It consisted of a ground-floor room on the courtyard of an old house with walls almost in a state of collapse. All there was in the room was a shabby mattress, a mat, a stove, a cooking pot, a teak tray, and a one-eyed old woman who was obviously his wife. When she was questioned about her husband, she replied that he was at the ministry. She then declared that she knew nothing about his disappearance; he had no clothes except for a *gallabiyya*, so they searched it and found a small piece of *hashish*. They took the woman to the police station. She said she knew nothing about his running away, nor about the theft of which he was being accused. She wept and cursed for a long time and then started talking about their life together. At first, she said, he had been a good husband and they had had children. One of them was working in the Canal area, and they had lost touch with him for some years; another had been killed in a tram accident when he was ten; and their daughter had married a building worker who had taken her to live in the limits of Upper Egypt, and so she had vanished from their lives just like her brother at the Canal. She admitted that "Uncle" Ibrahim had changed noticeably in recent months after reaching the age of discretion. She had heard rumours that he had become attached to a lottery-ticket seller at Fuad's cafe, and these rumours had caused a serious row between them in the full view of the neighborhood of Darb al-Halla.

The detectives raided Fuad's cafe and came back with a strange collection of children and adolescent cigarette-butt collectors and some shoe cleaners. They all remembered "Uncle" Ibrahim when he was described to them. They said that in recent months he had sat on the furthest chair in the passage which branched off from the main street sipping coffee and staring at the English girl! It emerged that by English girl they meant the lottery-ticket seller, who was seventeen years old with blonde hair and blue eyes; she had been a cigarette-butt collector originally too, and nearly all of them admitted having some personal relationship with her and that the same had been the case with some of the good and modest folk who visited the cafe!! "Uncle" Ibrahim cared a great deal for her. He had seen her once as he was crossing the street, and, when he found out that she was one of the regular features of Fuad's cafe, he had started sitting on a chair at the end of the passageway every evening so that he could see her. He would call her over quite openly to buy a lottery-ticket from her and, if the truth were told, to keep her there as long as possible. From the very first, the girl realized that he was infatuated with her and told them all about it. They started spying on him day after day and regarded him as an enormous joke; he meanwhile was so infatuated with her that he was totally unaware of them. One day, she told them all that he wanted to marry her! He would give her a happy life, she claimed, without all the worries of hard work and vagrancy. They laughed for ages; they looked on the whole thing as a joke, on the one hand because the thought of marriage had never occurred to them, and on the other because the man in question seemed the least likely of all to fit the picture of the bridegroom as they conceived him.

"He looks like one of us!" one of them said with a scoff.

"He's a rich man. . . ." she replied proudly.

They all laughed once more. However, the girl stopped coming to the cafe and vanished from their thoughts altogether!

Generally speaking, the police were convinced they had a lead, but they didn't know that the other end of it was in Abuqir, the suburb of Alexandria. Yes, "Uncle" Ibrahim was in Abuqir. He was sitting relaxed on the beach looking alternately at the sea and at Yasmina whose golden hair was flying in the breeze. He had shaved, and his bald head was covered by a skullcap as white as milk which reflected his blooming complexion. Yasmina was wearing an elegant dress, and her fresh complexion gleamed like distilled water. It was a happy, contented, peaceful family scene, even though there was a cold nip in the April wind. The place was almost empty; none of the summer visitors had arrived yet. The Greek house owners were far from the beach. Love was hovering and dancing round the beautiful scene; Ibrahim's eyes had a look of anticipation and amazement about them, as though he were seeing the world for the first time with all the innocence of childhood. He'd never seen any sea before; in fact, he'd never been out of Cairo all his life. So the roaring sea, the expanse of shore and the blue sky dotted with white clouds, all this delighted him as it wafted through his mind. He began listening to the intermittent roar of the sea with a happy smile which never left his lips. It seemed that he was rid of the snares of anxiety and floating around in a kind of dream; he was obviously enjoying the touching melodies of love which his besotted heart was playing over and over again.

The girl was stretched out in front of him. She seemed relaxed, but a somnolent silence encompassed her and weighed down her eyelids in a way which suggested that she was bored. It was Mr. Lutfi in the secretarial department who had told him about Abuqir quite by chance. Lutfi would spend the summer at this resort every year, and, before he went and when he came back, he would tell his colleagues how beautiful and peaceful it was and what marvellous fish there were there. "Uncle" Ibrahim's imagination was full of the idea of a summer resort, and finally he had worked out a way to get there.

He had come equipped with clothes, make-up implements, presents and things for all kinds of mood, such as *hashish* which would be needed on a honeymoon. The whole day was spent between the furnished room he had taken and the sea shore. His only preoccupations were to love, look around him, smoke, eat, drink, and talk. In one week, he managed to spend more than he had ever spent in a whole year. His sweetheart never stopped asking for things, and he was always ready to answer as quick as a flash. She had eccentric tastes, even wine and drugs; she was very blatant about it almost to the point of being a nuisance. "Where do you get the money?" she asked him once.

"I'm a local dignitary! . . ." he replied with a laugh. The wine could be seen in the coloring of her face.

"I understand. . . ." she said suspiciously. "God forgive you! . . ."

"You've only got four teeth," she said laughing simply. "One on top and three below! . . ."

He laughed indulgently. Sometimes he felt worried, but he was determined to be happy; and he knew more than anyone how fleeting that happiness could be. All he hoped for was to preserve the happiness he had got up till now and not be arrested till the pillars of this happiness collapsed naturally when he had spent the last millieme he had. This was why he decided to be happy even though his sweetheart seemed to be grumbling a lot. She was dying to see Alexandria, but he refused adamantly.

"I told you I understood!" she said with a cunning which she inherited from the pavements.

His answer was to buy her a lovely bracelet and put in front of her fruit, drink, and the forbidden cigarettes. He kissed her rosy cheek and smiled lovingly at her. "Look at the sea and the sky," he said. "Be happy with what you've got, and have a good time!"

He wanted her to be happy like himself. Before he had left, he had gone round with his head lowered; all he had seen of the world was dirt and dust, or else his own preoccupations and worries. But now here he was seeing things he had never seen before; the dawn as it rose magically, the sunset with its incredible colors pouring out at twilight, the ever-watchful stars, the gleaming moon and the horizon stretching away to infinity. All this he saw through the creative power of love till he wondered whether there could be any hardship after all this. . . .

At the beginning of June, the first family which had come for an early summer holiday appeared on the beach. "Uncle" Ibrahim's heart leapt and he felt that adversity was approaching like Fate; soon his happiness would vanish, and forever. This made him even more determined to enjoy the happiness he had been given and so he started chain-smoking *hashish*. One day, he was at the grocer's and spotted Mr. Lutfi, the civil servant in the secretarial department, at the end of the street with a real estate agent. "Uncle" Ibrahim panicked, dashed over to a side alley and then slunk away back to his room. Lutfi had come to hire a house for the two months of July and August as he usually did for the summer. It would be just a few weeks before he would be wandering far and wide along the seashore and then there would be no place left for "Uncle" Ibrahim. The hand of fate was rapping on his door and he could not find any place for himself. His lovely dream would vanish just like those scudding clouds. His sweetheart would desert him just like his own sighs; he still loved her in spite of her moans, her temper, and her peppery tongue. Yes, he loved her and thanked her for the happiness she had given him and the spirit of youth she had breathed into him. So God forgive her and make her happy! He found himself alone in his room. He began counting the money he had left and then wrapped it around his chest. He heard a movement at the door. He turned around and saw her coming towards him. He asked himself whether she had seen him and read a cunning look in her eyes. For that very reason, he could not get to sleep when he threw himself down beside her in bed. He spent the night wide awake thinking. From deep down inside him, he heard a tender voice telling him to give her the money and set her free. I've still got some time left, he said, to which the voice replied that he should give her the money and let her go. The lovely, homeless little girl. Who had her father been . . . and her mother?

"I haven't got anyone in the world. . . ." she'd said once candidly.

That's the way it was with him too. He felt something like a snake touching him in the dark. He focused his attention on her thieving little hand; she was trying to rob him. Was that why the cunning little devil had tried to exhaust him so that he would be fast asleep! The devil. He grabbed her hand and she let out a groan in the darkness. Then there was silence.

"Why?" he asked bitterly. "When did I ever refuse to give you anything?"

She pounced on his hand and bit it viciously till he yelled and pushed her away forcefully. It was the first harsh gesture he had ever made towards her. He leapt for the light and put it on. He looked first at his wrist which was splattered with blood. "How can a little girl like you be so wicked!" he asked.

For a moment she looked ashamed and then turned her back on him.

"How could you try to steal your own money?" She frowned furiously but did not say a word. "I didn't want any more than I had. . . ." he resumed, and then with a bitter laugh "God forgive you!"

Next morning, he gave her most of the money that was left, packed up her things and took her to the station.

From then on Abuqir seemed bleak. Things changed slowly and the summer holiday-makers came up in throngs. He moved to Alexandria where he could wander unconcerned on his own. Once he found himself in front of the Abu al-Abbas mosque and went in. He prayed two prayers as a salute to the mosque and then sat with his face turned towards the wall. He was feeling desperately sad and despondent. He prayed to his Lord in a whisper. "You can't be happy with what has happened to me or with what is happening everywhere. A girl so small, lovely, and evil; does that please you?! Where are my children? Does that please you? The world is after me merely because I love you; does that please you? Among millions of people, I feel so alone, it almost kills me; does that please you?" He burst into tears. As he was leaving the mosque, a voice startled him. " 'Uncle' Ibrahim!" it shouted. He turned round in astonishment without any will to resist, and saw a huge man coming towards him with a look of triumphant satisfaction on his face. From his appearance, he realized he was a detective. He stayed where he was in resignation. The man grabbed him by the shoulder. "You've worn us all out looking for you, damn you. . . ."

The detective noticed that "Uncle" Ibrahim had resigned himself to his fate as he was leading him along and looked red about the eyes. "Can you tell me what made you do all that at your age?!" he asked.

"God. . . ." he muttered with a smile, and then raised his finger up to the sky.

The word escaped from him like a sigh. . . .

Good Country People

FLANNERY O'CONNOR

Besides the neutral expression that she wore when she was alone, Mrs. Freeman had two others, forward and reverse, that she used for all her human dealings. Her forward expression was steady and driving like the advance of a heavy truck. Her eyes never swerved to left or right but turned as the story turned as if they followed a yellow line down the center of it. She seldom used the other expression because it was not often necessary for her to retract a statement, but when she did, her face came to a complete stop, there was an almost imperceptible movement of her black eyes, during which they seemed to be receding, and then the observer would see that Mrs. Freeman, though she might stand there as real as several grain sacks thrown on top of each other, was no longer there in spirit. As for getting anything across to her when this was the case, Mrs. Hopewell had given it up. She might talk her head off. Mrs. Freeman could never be brought to admit herself wrong on any point. She would stand there and if she could be brought to say anything, it was something like, "Well, I wouldn't of said it was and I wouldn't of said it wasn't," or letting her gaze range over the top kitchen shelf where there was an assortment of dusty bottles, she might remark, "I see you ain't ate many of them figs you put up last summer."

They carried on their most important business in the kitchen at breakfast. Every morning Mrs. Hopewell got up at seven o'clock and lit her gas heater and Joy's. Joy was her daughter, a large blonde girl who had an artificial leg.

Mrs. Hopewell thought of her as a child though she was thirty-two years old and highly educated. Joy would get up while her mother was eating and lumber into the bathroom and slam the door, and before long, Mrs. Freeman would arrive at the back door. Joy would hear her mother call, "Come on in," and then they would talk for a while in low voices that were indistinguishable in the bathroom. By the time Joy came in, they had usually finished the weather report and were on one or the other of Mrs. Freeman's daughters, Glynese or Carramae. Joy called them Glycerin and Caramel. Glynese, a redhead, was eighteen and had many admirers; Carramae, a blonde, was only fifteen but already married and pregnant. She could not keep anything on her stomach. Every morning Mrs. Freeman told Mrs. Hopewell how many times she had vomited since the last report.

Mrs. Hopewell liked to tell people that Glynese and Carramae were two of the finest girls she knew and that Mrs. Freeman was a *lady* and that she was never ashamed to take her anywhere or introduce her to anybody they might meet. Then she would tell how she had happened to hire the Freemans in the first place and how they were a godsend to her and how she had had them four years. The reason for her keeping them so long was that they were not trash. They were good country people. She had telephoned the man whose name they had given as a reference and he had told her that Mr. Freeman was a good farmer but that his wife was the nosiest woman ever to walk the earth. "She's got to be into everything," the man said. "If she don't get there before the dust settles, you can bet she's dead, that's all. She'll want to know all your business. I can stand him real good," he had said, "but me nor my wife neither could have stood that woman one more minute on this place." That had put Mrs. Hopewell off for a few days.

She had hired them in the end because there were no other applicants but she had made up her mind beforehand exactly how she would handle the woman. Since she was the type who had to be into everything, then, Mrs. Hopewell had decided, she would not only let her be into everything, she would *see to it* that she was into everything—she would give her the responsibility of everything, she would put her in charge. Mrs. Hopewell had no bad qualities of her own but she was able to use other people's in such a constructive way that she never felt the lack. She had hired the Freemans and she had kept them four years.

Nothing is perfect. This was one of Mrs. Hopewell's favorite sayings. Another was: that is life! And still another, the most important, was: well, other people have their opinions too. She would make these statements, usually at the table, in a tone of gentle insistence as if no one held them but her, and the large hulking Joy, whose constant outrage had obliterated every expression from her face, would stare just a little to the side of her, her eyes icy blue, with the look of someone who has achieved blindness by an act of will and means to keep it.

When Mrs. Hopewell said to Mrs. Freeman that life was like that, Mrs. Freeman would say, "I always said so myself." Nothing had been arrived at by anyone that had not first been arrived at by her. She was quicker than Mr. Freeman. When Mrs. Hopewell said to her after they had been on the place a while, "You know, you're the wheel behind the wheel," and winked, Mrs. Freeman had said, "I know it. I've always been quick. It's some that are quicker than others."

"Everybody is different," Mrs. Hopewell said.

"Yes, most people is," Mrs. Freeman said.

"It takes all kinds to make the world."

"I always said it did myself."

The girl was used to this kind of dialogue for breakfast and more of it for dinner; sometimes they had it for supper too. When they had no guest they ate in the kitchen because that was easier. Mrs. Freeman always managed to arrive at some point during the meal and to watch them finish it. She would stand in the doorway if it were summer but in the winter she would stand with one elbow on top of the refrigerator and look down on them, or she would stand by the gas heater, lifting the back of her skirt slightly. Occasionally she would stand against the wall and roll her head from side to side. At no time was she in any hurry to leave. All this was very trying on Mrs. Hopewell but she was a woman of great patience. She realized that nothing is perfect and that in the Freemans she had good country people and that if, in this day and age, you get good country people, you had better hang onto them.

She had had plenty of experience with trash. Before the Freemans she had averaged one tenant family a year. The wives of these farmers were not the kind you would want to be around you for very long. Mrs. Hopewell, who had divorced her husband long ago, needed someone to walk over the fields with her; and when Joy had to be impressed for these services, her remarks were usually so ugly and her face so glum that Mrs. Hopewell would say, "If you can't come pleasantly, I don't want you at all," to which the girl, standing square and rigid-shouldered with her neck thrust slightly forward, would reply, "If you want me, here I am—LIKE I AM."

Mrs. Hopewell excused this attitude because of the leg (which had been shot off in a hunting accident when Joy was ten). It was hard for Mrs. Hopewell to realize that her child was thirty-two now and that for more than twenty years she had had only one leg. She thought of her still as a child because it tore her heart to think instead of the poor stout girl in her thirties who had never danced a step or had any *normal* good times. Her name was really Joy but as soon as she was twenty-one and away from home, she had had it legally changed. Mrs. Hopewell was certain that she had thought and thought until she had hit upon the ugliest name in any language. Then she had gone and had the beautiful name, Joy, changed without telling her mother until after she had done it. Her legal name was Hulga.

When Mrs. Hopewell thought the name, Hulga, she thought of the broad blank hull of a battleship. She would not use it. She continued to call her Joy to which the girl responded but in a purely mechanical way.

Hulga had learned to tolerate Mrs. Freeman who saved her from taking walks with her mother. Even Glynese and Carramae were useful when they occupied attention that might otherwise have been directed at her. At first she had thought she could not stand Mrs. Freeman for she had found that it was not possible to be rude to her. Mrs. Freeman would take on strange resentments and for days together she would be sullen but the source of her displeasure was always obscure; a direct attack, a positive leer, blatant ugliness to her face—these never touched her. And without warning one day, she began calling her Hulga.

She did not call her that in front of Mrs. Hopewell who would have been incensed but when she and the girl happened to be out of the house together, she would say something and add the name Hulga to the end of it, and the big spectacled Joy-Hulga would scowl and redden as if her privacy had been intruded upon. She considered the name her personal affair. She had arrived at it first purely on the basis of its ugly sound and then the full genius of its fitness had struck her. She had a vision of the name working like the ugly sweating Vulcan who stayed in the furnace and to whom, presumably, the goddess had to come when called. She saw it as the name of her highest creative act. One of her major triumphs was that her mother had not been able to turn her dust into Joy, but the greater one was that she had been able to turn it herself into Hulga. However, Mrs. Freeman's relish for using the name only irritated her. It was as if Mrs. Freeman's beady steel-pointed eyes had penetrated far enough behind her face to reach some secret fact. Something about her seemed to fascinate Mrs. Freeman and then one day Hulga realized that it was the artificial leg. Mrs. Freeman had a special fondness for the details of secret infections, hidden deformities, assaults upon children. Of diseases, she preferred the lingering or incurable. Hulga had heard Mrs. Hopewell give her the details of the hunting accident, how the leg had been literally blasted off, how she had never lost consciousness. Mrs. Freeman could listen to it any time as if it had happened an hour ago.

When Hulga stumped into the kitchen in the morning (she could walk without making the awful noise but she made it—Mrs. Hopewell was certain—because it was ugly-sounding), she glanced at them and did not speak. Mrs. Hopewell would be in her red kimono with her hair tied around her head in rags. She would be sitting at the table, finishing her breakfast and Mrs. Freeman would be hanging by her elbow outward from the refrigerator, looking down at the table. Hulga always put her eggs on the stove to boil and then stood over them with her arms folded, and Mrs. Hopewell would look at her—a kind of indirect gaze divided between her and Mrs. Freeman—and would think that if she would only keep herself up a little, she wouldn't be so bad looking. There was nothing wrong with her face that a pleasant expression wouldn't help. Mrs. Hopewell said that people who looked on the bright side of things would be beautiful even if they were not.

Whenever she looked at Joy this way, she could not help but feel that it would have been better if the child had not taken the Ph.D. It had certainly not brought her out any and now that she had it, there was no more excuse for her to go to school again. Mrs. Hopewell thought it was nice for girls to go to school to have a good time but Joy had "gone through." Anyhow, she would not have been strong enough to go again. The doctors had told Mrs. Hopewell that with the best of care, Joy might see forty-five. She had a weak heart. Joy had made it plain that if it had not been for this condition, she would be far from these red hills and good country people. She would be in a university lecturing to people who knew what she was talking about. And Mrs. Hopewell could very well picture her there, looking like a scarecrow and lecturing to more of the same. Here she went about all day in a six-year-old skirt and a yellow sweat shirt with a faded cowboy on a horse embossed on it. She thought this was funny; Mrs. Hopewell thought it was idiotic and showed simply that she was still a child. She was brilliant but she didn't have a grain of sense. It seemed to Mrs. Hopewell that every year she grew less like other people and more like herself—bloated, rude, and squint-eyed. And she said such strange things! To her own mother she had said—without warning, without excuse, standing up in the middle of a meal with her face purple and her mouth half full—"Woman! do you ever look inside? Do you ever look inside and see what you are *not*? God!" she had cried sinking down again and staring at her plate, "Malebranche was right: we are not our own light.

We are not our own light!" Mrs. Hopewell had no idea to this day what brought that on. She had only made the remark, hoping Joy would take it in, that a smile never hurt anyone.

The girl had taken the Ph.D. in philosophy and this left Mrs. Hopewell at a complete loss. You could say, "My daughter is a nurse," or "My daughter is a schoolteacher," or even, "My daughter is a chemical engineer." You could not say, "My daughter is a philosopher." That was something that had ended with the Greeks and Romans. All day Joy sat on her neck in a deep chair, reading. Sometimes she went for walks but she didn't like dogs or cats or birds or flowers or nature or nice young men. She looked at nice young men as if she could smell their stupidity.

One day Mrs. Hopewell had picked up one of the books the girl had just put down and opening it at random, she read, "Science, on the other hand, has to assert its soberness and seriousness afresh and declare that it is concerned solely with what-is. Nothing—how can it be for science anything but a horror and a phantasm? If science is right, then one thing stands firm: science wishes to know nothing of nothing. Such is after all the strictly scientific approach to Nothing. We know it by wishing to know nothing of Nothing." These words had been underlined with a blue pencil and they worked on Mrs. Hopewell like some evil incantation in gibberish. She shut the book quickly and went out of the room as if she were having a chill.

This morning when the girl came in, Mrs. Freeman was on Carramae. "She thrown up four times after supper," she said, "and was up twict in the night after three o'clock. Yesterday she didn't do nothing but ramble in the bureau drawer. All she did. Stand up there and see what she could run up on."

"She's got to eat," Mrs. Hopewell muttered, sipping her coffee, while she watched Joy's back at the stove. She was wondering what the child had said to the Bible salesman. She could not imagine what kind of a conversation she could possibly have had with him.

He was a tall gaunt hatless youth who had called yesterday to sell them a Bible. He had appeared at the door, carrying a large black suitcase that weighted him so heavily on one side that he had to brace himself against the door facing. He seemed on the point of collapse but he said in a cheerful voice, "Good morning, Mrs. Cedars!" and set the suitcase down on the mat. He was not a bad-looking young man though he had on a bright blue suit and yellow socks that were not pulled up far enough. He had prominent face bones and a streak of sticky-looking brown hair falling across his forehead.

"I'm Mrs. Hopewell," she said.

"Oh!" he said, pretending to look puzzled but with his eyes sparkling, "I saw it said 'The Cedars,' on the mailbox so I thought you was Mrs. Cedars!" and he burst out in a pleasant laugh. He picked up the satchel and under cover of a pant, he fell forward into her hall. It was rather as if the suitcase had moved first, jerking him after it. "Mrs. Hopewell!" he said and grabbed her hand. "I hope you are well!" and he laughed again and then all at once his face sobered completely. He paused and gave her a straight earnest look and said, "Lady, I've come to speak of serious things."

"Well, come in," she muttered, none too pleased because her dinner was almost ready. He came into the parlor and sat down on the edge of a straight chair and put the suitcase between his feet and glanced around the room as if he were sizing her up by it. Her silver gleamed on the two sideboards; she decided he had never been in a room as elegant as this.

"Mrs. Hopewell," he began, using her name in a way that sounded almost intimate, "I know you believe in Chrustian service."

"Well, yes," she murmured.

"I know," he said and paused, looking very wise with his head cocked on one side, "that you're a good woman. Friends have told me."

Mrs. Hopewell never liked to be taken for a fool. "What are you selling?" she asked.

"Bibles," the young man said and his eye raced around the room before he added, "I see you have no family Bible in your parlor, I see that is the one lack you got!"

Mrs. Hopewell could not say, "My daughter is an atheist and won't let me keep the Bible in the parlor." She said, stiffening slightly, "I keep my Bible by my bedside." This was not the truth. It was in the attic somewhere.

"Lady," he said, "the word of God ought to be in the parlor."

"Well, I think that's a matter of taste," she began. "I think . . ."

"Lady," he said, "for a Chrustian, the word of God ought to be in every room in the house besides in his heart. I know you're a Chrustian because I can see it in every line of your face."

She stood up and said, "Well, young man, I don't want to buy a Bible and I smell my dinner burning."

He didn't get up. He began to twist his hands and looking down at them, he said softly, "Well lady, I'll tell you the truth—not many people want to buy one nowadays and besides, I know I'm real simple. I don't know how to say a thing but to say it. I'm just a country boy." He glanced up into her unfriendly face. "People like you don't like to fool with country people like me!"

"Why!" she cried, "good country people are the salt of the earth! Besides, we all have different ways of doing, it takes all kinds to make the world go 'round. That's life!"

"You said a mouthful," he said.

"Why, I think there aren't enough good country people in the world!" she said, stirred. "I think that's what's wrong with it!"

His face had brightened. "I didn't inraduce myself," he said. "I'm Manley Pointer from out in the country around Willohobie, not even from a place, just from near a place."

"You wait a minute," she said. "I have to see about my dinner." She went out to the kitchen and found Joy standing near the door where she had been listening.

"Get rid of the salt of the earth," she said, "and let's eat."

Mrs. Hopewell gave her a pained look and turned the heat down under the vegetables. "*I* can't be rude to anybody," she murmured and went back into the parlor.

He had opened the suitcase and was sitting with a Bible on each knee.

"You might as well put those up," she told him. "I don't want one."

"I appreciate your honesty," he said. "You don't see any more real honest people unless you go way out in the country."

"I know," she said, "real genuine folks!" Through the crack in the door she heard a groan.

"I guess a lot of boys come telling you they're working their way through college," he said, "but I'm not going to tell you that. Somehow," he said, "I don't want to go to college. I want to devote my life to Chrustian service. See," he said, lowering his voice, "I got this heart condition. I may not live long. When you know it's something wrong with you and you may not live long, well then, lady . . ." He paused, with his mouth open, and stared at her.

He and Joy had the same condition! She knew that her eyes were filling with tears but she collected herself quickly and murmured, "Won't you stay for dinner? We'd love to have you!" and was sorry the instant she heard herself say it.

"Yes mam," he said in an abashed voice, "I would sher love to do that!"

Joy had given him one look on being introduced to him and then throughout the meal had not glanced at him again. He had addressed several remarks to her, which she had pretended not to hear. Mrs. Hopewell could not understand deliberate rudeness, although she lived with it, and she felt she had always to overflow with hospitality to make up for Joy's lack of courtesy. She urged him to talk about himself and he did. He said he was the seventh child of twelve and that his father had been crushed under a tree when he himself was eight year old. He had been crushed very badly, in fact, almost cut in two and was practically not recognizable. His mother had got along the best she could by hard working and she had always seen that her children went to Sunday School and that they read the Bible every evening. He was now nineteen year old and he had been selling Bibles for four months. In that time he had sold seventy-seven Bibles and had the promise of two more sales. He wanted to become a missionary because he thought that was the way you could do most for people. "He who losest his life shall find it," he said simply and he was so sincere, so genuine and earnest that Mrs. Hopewell would not for the world have smiled. He prevented his peas from sliding onto the table by blocking them with a piece of bread which he later cleaned his plate with. She could see Joy observing sidewise how he handled his knife and fork and she saw too that every few minutes, the boy would dart a keen appraising glance at the girl as if he were trying to attract her attention.

After dinner Joy cleared the dishes off the table and disappeared and Mrs. Hopewell was left to talk with him. He told her again about his childhood and his father's accident and about various things that had happened to him. Every five minutes or so she would stifle a yawn. He sat for two hours until finally she told him she must go because she had an appointment in town. He packed his Bibles and thanked her and prepared to leave, but in the doorway he stopped and wrung her hand and said that not on any of his trips had he met a lady as nice as her and he asked if he could come again. She had said she would always be happy to see him.

Joy had been standing in the road, apparently looking at something in the distance, when he came down the steps toward her, bent to the side with his heavy valise. He stopped where she was standing and confronted her directly. Mrs. Hopewell could not hear what he said but she trembled to think what Joy would say to him. She could see that after a minute Joy said something and that then the boy began to speak again, making an excited gesture with his free hand. After a minute Joy said something else at which the boy began to speak once more. Then to her amazement, Mrs. Hopewell saw the two of them walk off together, toward the gate. Joy had walked all the way to the gate with him and Mrs. Hopewell could not imagine what they had said to each other, and she had not yet dared to ask.

Mrs. Freeman was insisting upon her attention. She had moved from the refrigerator to the heater so that Mrs. Hopewell had to turn and face her in order to seem to be listening. "Glynese gone out with Harvey Hill again last night," she said. "She had this sty."

"Hill," Mrs. Hopewell said absently, "is that the one who works in the garage?"

"Nome, he's the one that goes to chiropractor school," Mrs. Freeman said. "She had this sty. Been had it two days. So she says when he brought her in the other night he says, 'Lemme get rid of that sty for you,' and she says, 'How?' and he says, 'You just lay yourself down acrost the seat of that car and I'll show you.' So she done it and he popped her neck. Kept on a-popping it several times until she made him quit. This morning," Mrs. Freeman said, "she ain't got no sty. She ain't got no traces of a sty."

"I never heard of that before," Mrs. Hopewell said.

"He ast her to marry him before the Ordinary," Mrs. Freeman went on, "and she told him she wasn't going to be married in no *office*."

"Well, Glynese is a fine girl," Mrs. Hopewell said. "Glynese and Carramae are both fine girls."

"Carramae said when her and Lyman was married Lyman said it sure felt sacred to him. She said he said he wouldn't take five hundred dollars for being married by a preacher."

"How much would he take?" the girl asked from the stove.

"He said he wouldn't take five hundred dollars," Mrs. Freeman repeated.

"Well we all have work to do," Mrs. Hopewell said.

"Lyman said it just felt more sacred to him," Mrs. Freeman said. "The doctor wants Carramae to eat prunes. Says instead of medicine. Says them cramps is coming from pressure. You know where I think it is?"

"She'll be better in a few weeks," Mrs. Hopewell said.

"In the tube," Mrs. Freeman said. "Else she wouldn't be as sick as she is."

Hulga had cracked her two eggs into a saucer and was bringing them to the table along with a cup of coffee that she had filled too full. She sat down carefully and began to eat, meaning to keep Mrs. Freeman there by questions if for any reason she showed an inclination to leave. She could perceive her mother's eye on her. The first roundabout question would be about the Bible salesman and she did not wish to bring it on. "How did he pop her neck?" she asked.

Mrs. Freeman went into a description of how he had popped her neck. She said he owned a '55 Mercury but that Glynese said she would rather marry a man with only a '36 Plymouth who would be married by a preacher. The girl asked what if he had a '32 Plymouth and Mrs. Freeman said what Glynese had said was a '36 Plymouth.

Mrs. Hopewell said there were not many girls with Glynese's common sense. She said what she admired in those girls was their common sense. She said that reminded her that they had had a nice visitor yesterday, a young man selling Bibles. "Lord," she said, "he bored me to death but he was so sincere and genuine I couldn't be rude to him. He was just good country people, you know," she said, "—just the salt of the earth."

"I seen him walk up," Mrs. Freeman said, "and then later—I seen him walk off," and Hulga could feel the slight shift in her voice, the slight insinuation, that he had not walked off alone, had he? Her face remained expressionless but the color rose into her neck and she seemed to swallow it down with the next spoonful of egg. Mrs. Freeman was looking at her as if they had a secret together.

"Well, it takes all kinds of people to make the world go 'round," Mrs. Hopewell said. "It's very good we aren't all alike."

"Some people are more alike than others," Mrs. Freeman said.

Hulga got up and stumped, with about twice the noise that was necessary, into her room and locked the door. She was to meet the Bible salesman at ten o'clock at the gate. She had thought about it half the night. She had started thinking of it as a great joke and then she had begun to see profound implications in it. She had lain in bed imagining dialogues for them that were insane on the surface but that reached below to depths that no Bible salesman would be aware of. Their conversation yesterday had been of this kind.

He had stopped in front of her and had simply stood there. His face was bony and sweaty and bright, with a little pointed nose in the center of it, and his look was different from what it had been at the dinner table. He was gazing at her with open curiosity, with fascination, like a child watching a new fantastic animal at the zoo, and he was breathing as if he had run a great distance to reach her. His gaze seemed somehow familiar but she could not think where she had been regarded with it before. For almost a minute he didn't say anything. Then on what seemed an insuck of breath, he whispered, "You ever ate a chicken that was two days old?"

The girl looked at him stonily. He might have just put this question up for consideration at the meeting of a philosophical association. "Yes," she presently replied as if she had considered it from all angles.

"It must have been mighty small!" he said triumphantly and shook all over with little nervous giggles, getting very red in the face, and subsiding finally into his gaze of complete admiration, while the girl's expression remained exactly the same.

"How old are you?" he asked softly.

She waited some time before she answered. Then in a flat voice she said, "Seventeen."

His smiles came in succession like waves breaking on the surface of a little lake. "I see you got a wooden leg," he said. "I think you're real brave. I think you're real sweet."

The girl stood blank and solid and silent.

"Walk to the gate with me," he said. "You're a brave sweet little thing and I liked you the minute I seen you walk in the door."

Hulga began to move forward.

"What's your name?" he asked, smiling down on the top of her head.

"Hulga," she said.

"Hulga," he murmured, "Hulga. Hulga. I never heard of anybody name Hulga before. You're shy, aren't you, Hulga?" he asked.

She nodded, watching his large red hand on the handle of the giant valise.

"I like girls that wear glasses," he said. "I think a lot. I'm not like these people that a serious thought don't ever enter their heads. It's because I may die."

"I may die too," she said suddenly and looked up at him. His eyes were very small and brown, glittering feverishly.

"Listen," he said, "don't you think some people was meant to meet on account of what all they got in common and all? Like they both think serious thoughts and all?" He shifted the valise to his other hand so that the hand nearest her was free. He caught hold of her elbow and shook it a little. "I don't work on Saturday," he said. "I like to walk in the woods and see what Mother Nature is wearing. O'er the hills and far away. Pic-nics and things. Couldn't we go on a pic-nic tomorrow? Say yes, Hulga," he said and gave her a dying look as if he felt his insides about to drop out of him. He had even seemed to sway slightly toward her.

During the night she had imagined that she seduced him. She imagined that the two of them walked on the place until they came to the storage barn beyond the two back fields and there, she imagined, that things came to such a pass that she very easily seduced him and that then, of course, she had to reckon with his remorse. True genius can get an idea across even to an inferior mind. She imagined that she took his remorse in hand and changed it into a deeper understanding of life. She took all his shame away and turned it into something useful.

She set off for the gate at exactly ten o'clock, escaping without drawing Mrs. Hopewell's attention. She didn't take anything to eat, forgetting that food is usually taken on a picnic. She wore a pair of slacks and a dirty white shirt, and as an afterthought, she had put some Vapex on the collar of it since she did not own any perfume. When she reached the gate no one was there.

She looked up and down the empty highway and had the furious feeling that she had been tricked, that he had only meant to make her walk to the gate after the idea of him. Then suddenly he stood up, very tall, from behind a bush on the opposite embankment. Smiling, he lifted his hat which was new and wide-brimmed. He had not worn it yesterday and she wondered if he had bought it for the occasion. It was toast-colored with a red and white band around it and was slightly too large for him. He stepped from behind the bush still carrying the black valise. He had on the same suit and the same yellow socks sucked down in his shoes from walking. He crossed the highway and said, "I knew you'd come!"

The girl wondered acidly how he had known this. She pointed to the valise and asked, "Why did you bring your Bibles?"

He took her elbow, smiling down on her as if he could not stop. "You can never tell when you'll need the word of God, Hulga," he said. She had a moment in which she doubted that this was actually happening and then they began to climb the embankment. They went down into the pasture toward the woods. The boy walked lightly by her side, bouncing on his toes. The valise did not seem to be heavy today; he even swung it. They crossed half the pasture without saying anything and then, putting his hand easily on the small of her back, he asked softly, "Where does your wooden leg join on?"

She turned an ugly red and glared at him and for an instant the boy looked abashed. "I didn't mean you no harm," he said. "I only meant you're so brave and all. I guess God takes care of you."

"No," she said, looking forward and walking fast, "I don't even believe in God."

At this he stopped and whistled. "No!" he exclaimed as if he were too astonished to say anything else.

She walked on and in a second he was bouncing at her side, fanning with his hat. "That's very unusual for a girl," he remarked, watching her out of the corner of his eye. When they reached the edge of the wood, he put his hand on her back again and drew her against him without a word and kissed her heavily.

The kiss, which had more pressure than feeling behind it, produced that extra surge of adrenaline in the girl that enables one to carry a packed trunk out of a burning house, but in her, the power went at once to the brain. Even before he released her, her mind, clear and detached and ironic anyway, was regarding him from a great distance, with amusement but with pity. She had never been kissed before and she was pleased to discover that it was an unexceptional experience and all a matter of the mind's control. Some people might enjoy drain water if they were told it was vodka. When the boy, looking expectant but uncertain, pushed her gently away, she turned and walked on, saying nothing as if such business, for her, were common enough.

He came along panting at her side, trying to help her when he saw a root that she might trip over. He caught and held back the long swaying blades of thorn vine until she had passed beyond them. She led the way and he came breathing heavily behind her. Then they came out on a sunlit hillside, sloping softly into another one a little smaller. Beyond, they could see the rusted top of the old barn where the extra hay was stored.

The hill was sprinkled with small pink weeds. "Then you ain't saved?" he asked suddenly, stopping.

The girl smiled. It was the first time she had smiled at him at all. "In my economy," she said, "I'm saved and you are damned but I told you I didn't believe in God."

Nothing seemed to destroy the boy's look of admiration. He gazed at her now as if the fantastic animal at the zoo had put its paw through the bars and given him a loving poke. She thought he looked as if he wanted to kiss her again and she walked on before he had the chance.

"Ain't there somewheres we can sit down sometime?" he murmured, his voice softening toward the end of the sentence.

"In that barn," she said.

They made for it rapidly as if it might slide away like a train. It was a large two-story barn, cool and dark inside. The boy pointed up the ladder that led into the loft and said, "It's too bad we can't go up there."

"Why can't we?" she asked.

"Yer leg," he said reverently.

The girl gave him a contemptuous look and putting both hands on the ladder, she climbed it while he stood below, apparently awestruck. She pulled herself expertly through the opening and then looked down at him and said, "Well, come on if you're coming," and he began to climb the ladder, awkwardly bringing the suitcase with him.

"We won't need the Bible," she observed.

"You never can tell," he said, panting. After he had got into the loft, he was a few seconds catching his breath. She had sat down in a pile of straw. A wide sheath of sunlight, filled with dust particles, slanted over her. She lay back against a bale, her face turned away, looking out the front opening of the barn where hay was thrown from a wagon into the loft. The two pink-speckled hillsides lay back against a dark ridge of woods. The sky was cloudless and cold blue. The boy dropped down by her side and put one arm under her and the other over her and began methodically kissing her face, making little noises like a fish. He did not remove his hat but it was pushed far enough back not to interfere. When her glasses got in his way, he took them off of her and slipped them into his pocket.

The girl at first did not return any of the kisses but presently she began to and after she had put several on his cheek, she reached his lips and remained there, kissing him again and again as if she were trying to draw all the breath out of him. His breath was clear and sweet like a child's and the kisses were sticky like a child's. He mumbled about loving her and about knowing when he first seen her that he loved her, but the mumbling was like the sleepy fretting of a child being put to sleep by his mother. Her mind, throughout this, never stopped or lost itself for a second to her feelings. "You ain't said you loved me none," he whispered finally, pulling back from her. "You got to say that."

She looked away from him off into the hollow sky and then down at a black ridge and then down farther into what appeared to be two green swelling lakes. She didn't realize he had taken her glasses but this landscape could not seem exceptional to her for she seldom paid any close attention to her surroundings.

"You got to say it," he repeated. "You got to say you love me."

She was always careful how she committed herself. "In a sense," she began, "if you use the word loosely, you might say that. But it's not a word I use. I don't have illusions. I'm one of those people who see *through* to nothing."

The boy was frowning. "You got to say it. I said it and you got to say it," he said.

The girl looked at him almost tenderly. "You poor baby," she murmured. "It's just as well you don't understand," and she pulled him by the neck, face-down, against her. "We are all damned," she said, "but some of us have taken off our blindfolds and see that there's nothing to see. It's a kind of salvation."

The boy's astonished eyes looked blankly through the ends of her hair. "Okay," he almost whined, "but do you love me or don'tcher?"

"Yes," she said and added, "in a sense. But I must tell you something. There mustn't be anything dishonest between us." She lifted his head and looked him in the eye. "I am thirty years old," she said. "I have a number of degrees."

The boy's look was irritated but dogged. "I don't care," he said. "I don't care a thing about what all you done. I just want to know if you love me or don'tcher?" and he caught her to him and wildly planted her face with kisses until she said, "Yes, yes."

"Okay then," he said, letting her go. "Prove it."

She smiled, looking dreamily out on the shifty landscape. She had seduced him without even making up her mind to try. "How?" she asked, feeling that he should be delayed a little.

He leaned over and put his lips to her ear. "Show me where your wooden leg joins on," he whispered.

The girl uttered a sharp little cry and her face instantly drained of color. The obscenity of the suggestion was not what shocked her. As a child she had sometimes been subject to feelings of shame but education had removed the last traces of that as a good surgeon scrapes for cancer; she would no more have felt it over what he was asking than she would have believed in his Bible. But she was as sensitive about the artificial leg as a peacock about his tail. No one ever touched it but her. She took care of it as someone else would his soul, in private and almost with her own eyes turned away. "No," she said.

"I known it," he muttered, sitting up. "You're just playing me for a sucker."

"Oh no no!" she cried. "It joins on at the knee. Only at the knee. Why do you want to see it?"

The boy gave her a long penetrating look. "Because," he said, "it's what makes you different. You ain't like anybody else."

She sat staring at him. There was nothing about her face or her round freezing-blue eyes to indicate that this had moved her; but she felt as if her heart had stopped and left her mind to pump her blood. She decided that for the first time in her life she was face to face with real innocence. This boy, with an instinct that came from beyond wisdom, had touched the truth about her. When after a minute, she said in a hoarse high voice, "All right," it was like surrendering to him completely. It was like losing her own life and finding it again, miraculously, in his.

Very gently he began to roll the slack leg up. The artificial limb, in a white sock and brown flat shoe, was bound in a heavy material like canvas and ended in an ugly jointure where it was attached to the stump. The boy's face and his voice were entirely reverent as he uncovered it and said, "Now show me how to take it off and on."

She took it off for him and put it back on again and then he took it off himself, handling it as tenderly as if it were a real one. "See!" he said with a delighted child's face. "Now I can do it myself!"

"Put it back on," she said. She was thinking that she would run away with him and that every night he would take the leg off and every morning put it back on again. "Put it back on," she said.

"Not yet," he murmured, setting it on its foot out of her reach. "Leave it off for a while. You got me instead."

She gave a little cry of alarm but he pushed her down and began to kiss her again. Without the leg she felt entirely dependent on him. Her brain seemed to have stopped thinking altogether and to be about some other function that it was not very good at. Different expressions raced back and forth over her face. Every now and then the boy, his eyes like two steel spikes, would glance behind him where the leg stood. Finally she pushed him off and said, "Put it back on me now."

"Wait," he said. He leaned the other way and pulled the valise toward him and opened it. It had a pale blue spotted lining and there were only two Bibles in it. He took one of these out and opened the cover of it. It was hollow and contained a pocket flask of whiskey, a pack of cards, and a small blue box with printing on it. He laid these out in front of her one at a time in an evenly-spaced row, like one presenting offerings at the shrine of a goddess. He put the blue box in her hand. THIS PRODUCT TO BE USED ONLY FOR THE PREVENTION OF DISEASE, she read, and dropped it. The boy was unscrewing the top of the flask. He stopped and pointed, with a smile, to the deck of cards. It was not an ordinary deck but one with an obscene picture on the back of each card. "Take a swig," he said, offering her the bottle first. He held it in front of her, but like one mesmerized, she did not move.

Her voice when she spoke had an almost pleading sound. "Aren't you," she murmured, "aren't you just good country people?"

The boy cocked his head. He looked as if he were just beginning to understand that she might be trying to insult him. "Yeah," he said, curling his lip slightly, "but it ain't held me back none. I'm as good as you any day in the week."

"Give me my leg," she said.

He pushed it farther away with his foot. "Come on now, let's begin to have us a good time," he said coaxingly. "We ain't got to know one another good yet."

"Give me my leg!" she screamed and tried to lunge for it but he pushed her down easily.

"What's the matter with you all of a sudden?" he asked, frowning as he screwed the top on the flask and put it quickly back inside the Bible. "You just a while ago said you didn't believe in nothing. I thought you was some girl!"

Her face was almost purple. "You're a Christian!" she hissed. "You're a fine Christian! You're just like them all—say one thing and do another. You're a perfect Christian, you're . . ."

The boy's mouth was set angrily. "I hope you don't think," he said in a lofty indignant tone, "that I believe in that crap! I may sell Bibles but I know which end is up and I wasn't born yesterday and I know where I'm going!"

"Give me my leg!" she screeched. He jumped up so quickly that she barely saw him sweep the cards and the blue box back into the Bible and throw the Bible into the valise. She saw him grab the leg and then she saw it for an instant slanted forlornly across the inside of the suitcase with a Bible at either side of its opposite ends. He slammed the lid shut and snatched up the valise and swung it down the hole and then stepped through himself.

When all of him had passed but his head, he turned and regarded her with a look that no longer had any admiration in it. "I've gotten a lot of interesting things," he said. "One time I got a woman's glass eye this way. And you needn't to think you'll catch me because Pointer ain't really my name. I use a different name at every house I call at and don't stay nowhere long. And I'll tell you another thing, Hulga," he said, using the name as if he didn't think much of it, "you ain't so smart. I been believing in nothing ever since I was born!" and then the toast-colored hat disappeared down the hole and the girl was left, sitting on the straw in the dusty sunlight. When she turned her churning face toward the opening, she saw his blue figure struggling successfully over the green speckled lake.

Mrs. Hopewell and Mrs. Freeman, who were in the back pasture, digging up onions, saw him emerge a little later from the woods and head across the meadow toward the highway. "Why, that looks like that nice dull young man that tried to sell me a Bible yesterday," Mrs. Hopewell said, squinting. "He must have been selling them to the Negroes back in there. He was so simple," she said, "but I guess the world would be better off if we were all that simple."

Mrs. Freeman's gaze drove forward and just touched him before he disappeared under the hill. Then she returned her attention to the evil-smelling onion shoot she was lifting from the ground. "Some can't be that simple," she said. "I know I never could."

Act of Faith

IRWIN SHAW

"Present it to him in a pitiful light," Olson was saying as they picked their way through the almost frozen mud toward the orderly-room tent. "Three combat-scarred veterans, who fought their way from Omaha Beach to . . . What was the name of the town we fought our way to?"

"Königstein," Seeger said.

"Königstein." Olson lifted his right foot heavily out of a puddle and stared admiringly at the three pounds of mud clinging to his overshoe. "The backbone of the Army. The noncommissioned officer. We deserve better of our country. Mention our decorations, in passing."

"What decorations should I mention?" Seeger asked. "The Marksman's Medal?"

"Never quite made it," Olson said. "I had a cross-eyed scorer at the butts. Mention the Bronze Star, the Silver Star, the Croix de Guerre with palms, the Unit Citation, the Congressional Medal of Honor."

"I'll mention them all." Seeger grinned. "You don't think the C.O.'ll notice that we haven't won most of them, do you?"

"Gad, sir," Olson said with dignity, "do you think that one Southern military gentleman will dare doubt the word of another Southern military gentleman in the hour of victory?"

"I come from Ohio," Seeger said.

"Welch comes from Kansas," Olson said, coolly staring down a second lieutenant who was passing. The lieutenant made a nervous little jerk with his hand, as though he expected a salute, then kept it rigid, as a slight, superior smile of scorn twisted at the corner of Olson's mouth. The lieutenant dropped his eyes and splashed on through the mud. "You've heard of Kansas," Olson said. "Magnolia-scented Kansas."

"Of course," said Seeger. "I'm no fool."

"Do your duty by your men, Sergeant." Olson stopped to wipe the cold rain off his face and lectured him. "Highest-ranking noncom present took the initiative and saved his comrades, at great personal risk, above and beyond the call of you-know-what, in the best traditions of the American Army."

"I will throw myself in the breach," Seeger said.

"Welch and I can't ask more," said Olson.

They walked heavily through the mud on the streets between the rows of tents. The camp stretched drearily over the Reims plain, with the rain beating on the sagging tents. The division had been there over three weeks, waiting to be shipped home, and all the meager diversions of the neighborhood had been sampled and exhausted, and there was an air of watchful suspicion and impatience with the military life hanging over the camp now, and there was even reputed to be a staff sergeant in C Company who was laying odds they would not get back to America before July 4th.

"I'm redeployable," Olson sang. "It's so enjoyable." It was a jingle he had composed, to no recognizable melody, in the early days after the victory in Europe, when he had added up his points and found they came to only sixty-three, but he persisted in singing it. He was a short, round boy who had been flunked out of air cadets' school and transferred to the infantry but whose spirits had not been damaged in the process. He had a high, childish voice and a pretty, baby face. He was very good-natured, and had a girl waiting for him at the University of California, where he intended to finish his course at government expense when he got out of the Army, and he was just the type who is killed off early and predictably and sadly in moving pictures about the war, but he had gone through four campaigns and six major battles without a scratch.

Seeger was a large, lanky boy, with a big nose, who had been wounded at St.-Lô but had come back to his outfit in the Siegfried Line quite unchanged. He was cheerful and dependable and he knew his business. He had broken in five or six second lieutenants, who had later been killed or wounded, and the C.O. had tried to get him commissioned in the field, but the war had ended while the paperwork was being fumbled over at headquarters.

They reached the door of the orderly tent and stopped. "Be brave, Sergeant," Olson said. "Welch and I are depending on you."

"O.K.," Seeger said, and went in.

The tent had the dank, Army-canvas smell that had been so much a part of Seeger's life in the past three years. The company clerk was reading an October, 1945, issue of the Buffalo *Courier-Express,* which had just reached him, and Captain Taney, the company C.O., was seated at a sawbuck table which he used as a desk, writing a letter to his wife, his lips pursed with effort. He was a small, fussy man, with sandy hair that was falling out. While the fighting had been going on, he had been lean and tense and his small voice had been cold and full of authority. But now he had relaxed, and a little pot belly was creeping up under his belt and he kept the top button of his trousers open when he could do it without too public loss of dignity. During the war, Seeger had thought of him as a natural soldier—tireless, fanatic about detail, aggressive, severely anxious to kill Germans. But in the last few months, Seeger had seen him relapsing gradually and pleasantly into the small-town hardware merchant he had been before the war, sedentary and a little shy, and, as he had once told Seeger, worried, here in the bleak champagne fields of France, about his daughter, who had just turned twelve and had a tendency to go after the boys and had been caught by her mother kissing a fifteen-year-old neighbor in the hammock after school.

"Hello, Seeger," he said, returning the salute with a mild, offhand gesture. "What's on your mind?"

"Am I disturbing you, sir?"

"Oh, no. Just writing a letter to my wife. You married, Seeger?" He peered at the tall boy standing before him.

"No, sir."

"It's very difficult," Taney sighed, pushing dissatisfiedly at the letter before him. "My wife complains I don't tell her I love her often enough. Been married fifteen years. You'd think she'd know by now." He smiled at Seeger. "I thought you were going to Paris," he said. "I signed the passes yesterday."

"That's what I came to see you about, sir."

"I suppose something's wrong with the passes." Taney spoke resignedly, like a man who has never quite got the hang of Army regulations and has had requisitions, furloughs, and requests for courts-martial returned for correction in a baffling flood.

"No, sir," Seeger said. "The passes're fine. They start tomorrow. Well, it's just—" He looked around at the company clerk, who was on the sports page.

"This confidential?" Taney asked.

"If you don't mind, sir."

"Johnny," Taney said to the clerk, "go stand in the rain someplace."

"Yes, sir," the clerk said, and slowly got up and walked out.

Taney looked shrewdly at Seeger and spoke in a secret whisper. "You pick up anything?" he asked.

Seeger grinned. "No, sir, haven't had my hands on a girl since Strasbourg."

"Ah, that's good." Taney leaned back, relieved, happy that he didn't have to cope with the disapproval of the Medical Corps.

"It's—well," said Seeger, embarrassed, "it's hard to say—but it's money."

Taney shook his head sadly. "I know."

"We haven't been paid for three months, sir, and—"

"Damn it!" Taney stood up and shouted furiously. "I would like to take every bloody, chair-warming old lady in the Finance Department and wring their necks."

The clerk stuck his head into the tent. "Anything wrong? You call for me, sir?"

"No!" Taney shouted. "Get out of here!"

The clerk ducked out.

Taney sat down again. "I suppose," he said, in a more normal voice, "they have their problems. Outfits being broken up, being moved all over the place. But it's rugged."

"It wouldn't be so bad," Seeger said, "but we're going to Paris tomorrow. Olson, Welch, and myself. And you need money in Paris."

"Don't I know it?" Taney wagged his head. "Do you know what I paid for a bottle of champagne on the Place Pigalle in September?" He paused significantly. "I won't tell you. You wouldn't have any respect for me the rest of your life."

Seeger laughed. "Hanging is too good for the guy who thought up the rate of exchange," he said.

"I don't care if I never see another franc as long as I live." Taney waved his letter in the air, although it had been dry for a long time.

There was silence in the tent, and Seeger swallowed a little embarrassedly. "Sir," he said, "the truth is, I've come to borrow some money for Welch, Olson, and myself. We'll pay it back out of the first pay we get, and that can't be too long from now. If you don't want to give it to us, just tell me and I'll understand and get the hell out of here. We don't like to ask, but you might just as well be dead as in Paris broke."

Taney stopped waving his letter and put it down thoughtfully. He peered at it, wrinkling his brow, looking like an aged bookkeeper in the single, gloomy light that hung in the middle of the tent.

"Just say the word, Captain," Seeger said, "and I'll blow."

"Stay where you are, son," said Taney. He dug in his shirt pocket and took out a worn, sweat-stained wallet. He looked at it for a moment. "Alligator," he said, with automatic, absent pride. "My wife sent it to me when we were in England. Pounds don't fit in it. However . . ." He opened it and took out all the contents. There was a small pile of francs on the table in front of him when he finished. He counted them. "Four hundred francs," he said. "Eight bucks."

"Excuse me," Seeger said humbly. "I shouldn't've asked."

"Delighted," Taney said vigorously. "Absolutely delighted." He started dividing the francs into two piles. "Truth is, Seeger, most of my money goes home in allotments. And the truth is, I lost eleven hundred francs in a poker game three nights ago, and I ought to be ashamed of myself. Here." He shoved one pile toward Seeger. "Two hundred francs."

Seeger looked down at the frayed, meretricious paper, which always seemed to him like stage money anyway. "No, sir," he said. "I can't take it."

"Take it," Taney said. "That's a direct order."

Seeger slowly picked up the money, not looking at Taney. "Sometime, sir," he said, "after we get out, you have to come over to my house, and you and my father and my brother and I'll go on a real drunk."

"I regard that," Taney said gravely, "as a solemn commitment."

They smiled at each other, and Seeger started out.

"Have a drink for me," said Taney, "at the Café de la Paix. A small drink." He was sitting down to tell his wife he loved her when Seeger went out of the tent.

Olson fell into step with Seeger and they walked silently through the mud between the tents.

"Well, *mon vieux?*" Olson said finally.

"Two hundred francs," said Seeger.

Olson groaned. "Two hundred francs! We won't be able to pinch a whore's behind on the Boulevard des Capucines for two hundred francs. That miserable, penny-loving Yankee!"

"He only had four hundred," Seeger said.

"I revise my opinion," said Olson.

They walked disconsolately and heavily back toward their tent.

Olson spoke only once before they got there. "These raincoats," he said, patting his. "Most ingenious invention of the war. Highest saturation point of any modern fabric. Collect more water per square inch, and hold it, than any material known to man. All hail the quartermaster!"

Welch was waiting at the entrance of their tent. He was standing there peering excitedly and shortsightedly out at the rain through his glasses, looking angry and tough, like a big-city hack driver, individual and incorruptible even in the ten-million colored uniform. Every time Seeger came upon Welch unexpectedly, he couldn't help smiling at the belligerent stance, the harsh stare through the steel-rimmed G.I. glasses, which had nothing at all to do with the way Welch really was. "It's a family inheritance," Welch had once explained. "My whole family stands as though we were getting ready to rap a drunk with a beer glass. Even my old lady." Welch had six brothers, all devout, according to Welch, and Seeger from time to time idly pictured them standing in a row, on Sunday mornings in church, seemingly on the verge of general violence, amid the hushed Latin and the Sabbath millinery.

"How much?" Welch asked loudly.

"Don't make us laugh," Olson said, pushing past him into the tent.

"What do you think I could get from the French for my combat jacket?" Seeger said. He went into the tent and lay down on his cot.

Welch followed them in and stood between the two of them. "Boys," he said, "on a man's errand."

"I can just see us now," Olson murmured, lying on his cot with his hands clasped behind his head, "painting Montmartre red. Please bring on the naked dancing girls. Four bucks' worth."

"I am not worried," Welch announced.

"Get out of here." Olson turned over on his stomach.

"I know where we can put our hands on sixty-five bucks." Welch looked triumphantly first at Olson, then at Seeger.

Olson turned over slowly and sat up. "I'll kill you," he said, "if you're kidding."

"While you guys are wasting your time fooling around with the infantry," Welch said, "I used my head. I went into Reems and used my head."

"Rance," Olson said automatically. He had had two years of French in college and he felt, now that the war was over, that he had to introduce his friends to some of his culture.

"I got to talking to a captain in the Air Force," Welch said eagerly. "A little, fat old paddle-footed captain that never got higher off the ground than the second floor of Com Z headquarters, and he told me that what he would ad-mire to do more than anything else is take home a nice shiny German Luger pistol with him to show to the boys back in Pacific Grove, California."

Silence fell on the tent, and Welch and Olson looked at Seeger.

"Sixty-five bucks for a Luger, these days," Olson said, "is a very good figure."

"They've been sellin' for as low as thirty-five," said Welch hesitantly.

"I'll bet," he said to Seeger, "you could sell yours now and buy another one back when you got some dough, and make a clear twenty-five on the deal."

Seeger didn't say anything. He had killed the owner of the Luger, an enormous S.S. major, in Coblenz, behind some bales of paper in a warehouse, and the major had fired at Seeger three times with it, once nicking his helmet, before Seeger hit him in the face at twenty feet. Seeger had kept the Luger, a heavy, well-balanced gun, lugging it with him, hiding it at the bottom of his bedroll, oiling it three times a week, avoiding all opportunities of selling it, although he had once been offered a hundred dollars for it and several times eighty and ninety, while the war was still on, before German weapons became a glut on the market.

"Well," said Welch, "there's no hurry. I told the captain I'd see him tonight around eight o'clock in front of the Lion d'Or Hotel. You got five hours to make up your mind. Plenty of time."

"Me," said Olson, after a pause, "I won't say anything."

Seeger looked reflectively at his feet, and the two other men avoided looking at him.

Welch dug in his pocket. "I forgot," he said. "I picked up a letter for you." He handed it to Seeger.

"Thanks," Seeger said. He opened it absently, thinking about the Luger.

"Me," said Olson. "I won't say a bloody word. I'm just going to lie here and think about that nice, fat Air Force captain."

Seeger grinned a little at him and went to the tent opening to read the letter in the light. The letter was from his father, and even from one glance at the handwriting, scrawly and hurried and spotted, so different from his father's usual steady, handsome, professorial script, he knew that something was wrong.

"Dear Norman," it read, "sometime in the future, you must forgive me for writing this letter. But I have been holding this in so long, and there is no one here I can talk to, and because of your brother's condition I must pretend to be cheerful and optimistic all the time at home, both with him and your mother, who has never been the same since Leonard was killed. You're the oldest now, and although I know we've never talked very seriously about anything before, you have been through a great deal by now, and I imagine you must have matured considerably, and you've seen so many different places and people. Norman, I need help. While the war was on and you were fighting, I kept this to myself. It wouldn't have been fair to burden you with this. But now the war is over, and I no longer feel I can stand up under this alone. And you will have to face it sometime when you get home, if you haven't faced it already, and perhaps we can help each other by facing it together."

"I'm redeployable. It's so enjoyable," Olson was singing softly, on his cot. He fell silent after his burst of song.

Seeger blinked his eyes in the gray, wintry, rainy light, and went on reading his father's letter, on the stiff white stationery with the university letterhead in polite engraving at the top of each page.

"I've been feeling this coming on for a long time," the letter continued, "but it wasn't until last Sunday morning that something happened to make me feel it in its full force. I don't know how much you've guessed about the reason for Jacob's discharge from the Army. It's true he was pretty badly wounded in the leg at Metz, but I've asked around, and I know that men with worse wounds were returned to duty after hospitalization. Jacob got a medical discharge, but I don't think it was for the shrapnel wound in his thigh. He is suffering now from what I suppose you call combat fatigue, and he is subject to fits of depression and hallucinations. Your mother and I thought that as time went by and the war and the Army receded, he would grow better. Instead, he is growing worse. Last Sunday morning when I came down into the living room from upstairs he was crouched in his old uniform, next to the window, peering out."

"What the hell," Olson was saying. "If we don't get the sixty-five bucks we can always go to the Louvre. I understand the Mona Lisa is back."

"I asked Jacob what he was doing," the letter went on. "He didn't turn around. 'I'm observing,' he said. 'V-1s and V-2s. Buzz bombs and rockets. They're coming in by the hundred.' I tried to reason with him and he told me to crouch and save myself from flying glass. To humor him I got down on the floor beside him and tried to tell him the war was over, that we were in Ohio, 4,000 miles away from the nearest spot where bombs had fallen, that America had never been touched. He wouldn't listen. 'These're the new rocket bombs,' he said, 'for the Jews.'"

"Did you ever hear of the Panthéon?" Olson asked loudly.

"No," said Welch.

"It's free."

"I'll go," said Welch.

Seeger shook his head a little and blinked his eyes before he went back to the letter.

"After that," his father went on, "Jacob seemed to forget about the bombs from time to time, but he kept saying that the mobs were coming up the street armed with bazookas and Browning automatic rifles. He mumbled incoherently a good deal of the time and kept walking back and forth saying, 'What's the situation? Do you know what the situation is?' And once he told me he wasn't worried about himself, he was a soldier and he expected to be killed, but he was worried about Mother and myself and Leonard and you. He seemed to forget that Leonard was dead. I tried to calm him and get him back to bed before your mother came down, but he refused and wanted to set out immediately to rejoin his division. It was all terribly disjointed, and at one time he took the ribbon he got for winning the Bronze Star and threw it in the fireplace, then he got down on his hands and knees and picked it out of the ashes and made me pin it on him again, and he kept repeating, 'This is when they are coming for the Jews.' "

"The next war I'm in," said Olson, "they don't get me under the rank of colonel."

It had stopped raining by now, and Seeger folded the unfinished letter and went outside. He walked slowly down to the end of the company street, and, facing out across the empty, soaked French fields, scarred and neglected by various armies, he stopped and opened the letter again.

"I don't know what Jacob went through in the Army," his father wrote, "that has done this to him. He never talks to me about the war and he refuses to go to a psychoanalyst, and from time to time he is his own bouncing, cheerful self, playing handball in the afternoons and going around with a large group of girls. But he has devoured all the concentration-camp reports, and I found him weeping when the newspapers reported that a hundred Jews were killed in Tripoli some time ago.

"The terrible thing is, Norman, that I find myself coming to believe that it is not neurotic for a Jew to behave like this today. Perhaps Jacob is the normal one, and I, going about my business, teaching economics in a quiet classroom, pretending to understand that the world is comprehensible and orderly, am really the mad one. I ask you once more to forgive me for writing you a letter like this, so different from any letter or any conversation I've ever had with you. But it is crowding me, too. I do not see rockets and bombs, but I see other things.

"Wherever you go these days—restaurants, hotels, clubs, trains—you seem to hear talk about the Jews, mean, hateful, murderous talk. Whatever page you turn to in the newspapers, you seem to find an article about Jews being killed somewhere on the face of the globe. And there are large, influential newspapers and well-known columnists who each day are growing more and more outspoken and more popular. The day that Roosevelt died I heard a drunken man yelling outside a bar, 'Finally they got the Jew out of the White House.' And some of the people who heard him merely laughed, and nobody stopped him. And on V-J Day, in celebration, hoodlums in Los Angeles savagely beat a Jewish writer. It's difficult to know what to do, whom to fight, where to look for allies.

"Three months ago, for example, I stopped my Thursday-night poker game, after playing with the same men for over ten years. John Reilly happened to say that the Jews got rich out of the war, and when I demanded an apology, he refused, and when I looked around at the faces of the men who had been my friends for so long, I could see they were not with me. And when I left the house, no one said good night to me. I know the poison was spreading from Germany before the war and during it, but I had not realized it had come so close.

"And in my economics class, I find myself idiotically hedging in my lectures. I discover that I am loath to praise any liberal writer or any liberal act, and find myself somehow annoyed and frightened to see an article of criticism of existing abuses signed by a Jewish name. And I hate to see Jewish names on important committees, and hate to read of Jews fighting for the poor, the oppressed, the cheated and hungry. Somehow, even in a country where my family has lived a hundred years, the enemy has won this subtle victory over me—he has made me disfranchise myself from honest causes by calling them foreign, Communist, using Jewish names connected with them as ammunition against them.

"Most hateful of all, I found myself looking for Jewish names in the casualty lists and secretly being glad when I saw them there, to prove that there, at least, among the dead and wounded, we belonged. Three times, thanks to you and your brothers, I found our name there, and, may God forgive me, at the expense of your blood and your brother's life, through my tears, I felt that same twitch of satisfaction.

"When I read the newspapers and see another story that Jews are still being killed in Poland, or Jews are requesting that they be given back their homes in France or that they be allowed to enter some country where they will not be murdered, I am annoyed with them. I feel that they are boring the rest of the world with their problems, that they are making demands upon the rest of the world by being killed, that they are disturbing everyone by being hungry and asking for the return of their property. If we could all fall in through the crust of the earth and vanish in one hour, with our heroes and poets and prophets and martyrs, perhaps we would be doing the memory of the Jewish race a service.

"This is how I feel today, son. I need some help. You've been to the war, you've fought and killed men, you've seen the people of other countries. Maybe you understand things that I don't understand. Maybe you see some hope somewhere. Help me. Your loving Father."

Seeger folded the letter slowly, not seeing what he was doing, because the tears were burning his eyes. He walked slowly and aimlessly across the dead, sodden grass of the empty field, away from the camp. He tried to wipe away his tears, because, with his eyes full and dark, he kept seeing his father and brother crouched in the old-fashioned living room in Ohio, and hearing his brother, dressed in the old, discarded uniform, saying, "These're the new rocket bombs. For the Jews."

He sighed, looking out over the bleak, wasted land. Now, he thought, now I have to think about it. He felt a slight, unreasonable twinge of anger at his father for presenting him with the necessity of thinking about it. The Army was good about serious problems. While you were fighting, you were too busy and frightened and weary to think about anything, and at other times you were relaxing, putting your brain on a shelf, postponing everything to that impossible time of clarity and beauty after the war. Well, now, here was the impossible, clear, beautiful time, and here was his father, demanding that he think. There are all sorts of Jews, he thought: there are the sort whose every waking moment is ridden by the knowledge of Jewishness; who see signs against the Jew in every smile on a streetcar, every whisper; who see pogroms in every newspaper article, threats in every change of the weather, scorn in every handshake, death behind each closed door. He had not been like that. He was young, he was big and healthy and easygoing, and people of all kinds had liked him all his life, in the Army and out. In America, especially, what was going on in Europe had been remote, unreal, unrelated to him. The chanting, bearded old men burning in the Nazi furnaces, and the dark-eyed women screaming prayers in Polish and Russian and German as they were pushed naked into the gas chambers, had seemed as shadowy and almost as unrelated to him, as he trotted out onto the stadium field for a football game, as they must have been to the men named O'Dwyer and Wickersham and Poole who played in the line beside him.

These tortured people had seemed more related to him in Europe. Again and again, in the towns that had been taken back from the Germans, gaunt, gray-faced men had stopped him humbly, looking searchingly at him, and had asked, peering at his long, lined, grimy face under the anonymous helmet, "Are you a Jew?" Sometimes they asked it in English, sometimes French, sometimes Yiddish. He didn't know French or Yiddish, but he learned to recognize that question. He had never understood exactly why they asked the question, since they never demanded anything of him, rarely even could speak to him. Then, one day in Strasbourg, a little, bent old man and a small, shapeless woman had stopped him and asked, in English, if he was Jewish. "Yes," he'd said, smiling at them. The two old people had smiled widely, like children. "Look," the old man had said to his wife. "A young American soldier. A Jew. And so large and strong." He had touched Seeger's arm reverently with the tips of his fingers, then had touched the Garand Seeger was carrying. "And such a beautiful rifle."

And there, for a moment, although he was not particularly sensitive, Seeger had got an inkling of why he had been stopped and questioned by so many before. Here, to these bent, exhausted old people, ravaged of their families, familiar with flight and death for so many years, was a symbol of continuing life. A large young man in the uniform of the liberator, blood, as they thought, of their blood, but not in hiding, not quivering in fear and helplessness, but striding secure and victorious down the street, armed and capable of inflicting terrible destruction on his enemies.

Seeger had kissed the old lady on the cheek and she had wept, and the old man had scolded her for it while shaking Seeger's hand fervently and thankfully before saying goodbye.

Thinking back on it, he knew that it was silly to pretend that, even before his father's letter, he had been like any other American soldier going through the war. When he had stood over the huge, dead S.S. major with the face blown in by his bullets in the warehouse in Coblenz, and taken the pistol from the dead hand, he had tasted a strange little extra flavor of triumph. How many Jews, he'd thought, has this man killed? How fitting it is that I've killed him. Neither Olson nor Welch, who were like his brothers, would have felt that in picking up the Luger, its barrel still hot from the last shots its owner had fired before dying. And he had resolved that he was going to make sure to take his gun back with him to America, and plug it and keep it on his desk at home, as a kind of vague, half-understood sign to himself that justice had once been done and he had been its instrument.

Maybe, he thought, maybe I'd better take it back with me, but not as a memento. Not plugged, but loaded. America by now was a strange country for him. He had been away a long time and he wasn't sure what was waiting for him when he got home. If the mobs were coming down the street toward his house, he was not going to die singing and praying.

When he had been taking basic training, he'd heard a scrawny, clerkish soldier from Boston talking at the other end of the PX bar, over the watered beer. "The boys at the office," the scratchy voice was saying, "gave me a party before I left. And they told me one thing. 'Charlie,' they said, 'hold onto your bayonet. We're going to be able to use it when you get back. On the Yids.' "

He hadn't said anything then, because he'd felt it was neither possible nor desirable to fight against every random overheard voice raised against the Jews from one end of the world to the other. But again and again, at odd moments, lying on a barracks cot, or stretched out trying to sleep on the floor of a ruined French farmhouse, he had heard that voice, harsh, satisfied, heavy with hate and ignorance, saying above the beery grumble of apprentice soldiers at the bar, "Hold onto your bayonet."

And the other stories. Jews collected stories of hatred and injustice and inklings of doom like a special, lunatic kind of miser. The story of the Navy officer, commander of a small vessel off the Aleutians, who in the officers' wardroom had complained that he hated the Jews because it was the Jews who had demanded that the Germans be beaten first, and the forces in the Pacific had been starved in consequence. And when one of his junior officers, who had just come aboard, had objected and told the commander that he was a Jew, the commander had risen from the table and said, "Mister, the Constitution of the United States says I have to serve in the same Navy with Jews, but it doesn't say I have to eat at the same table with them." In the fogs and the cold, swelling Arctic seas off the Aleutians, in a small boat, subject to sudden, mortal attack at any moment. . . . And the million other stories. Jews, even the most normal and best adjusted, became living treasuries of them, scraps of malice and bloodthirstiness, clever and confusing and cunningly twisted so that every act by every Jew became suspect and blameworthy and hateful. Seeger had heard the stories and had made an almost conscious effort to forget them. Now, holding his father's letter in his hand, he remembered them all.

He stared unseeingly out in front of him. Maybe, he thought, maybe it would've been better to have been killed in the war, like Leonard. Simpler. Leonard would never have to face a crowd coming for his mother and father. Leonard would not have to listen and collect these hideous, fascinating little stories that made of every Jew a stranger in any town, on any field, on the face of the earth. He had come so close to being killed so many times; it would have been so easy, so neat and final. Seeger shook his head. It was ridiculous to feel like that, and he was ashamed of himself for the weak moment. At the age of twenty-one, death was not an answer.

"Seeger!" It was Olson's voice. He and Welch had sloshed silently up behind Seeger, standing in the open field. "Seeger, *mon vieux,* what're you doing—grazing?"

Seeger turned slowly to them. "I wanted to read my letter," he said.

Olson looked closely at him. They had been together so long, through so many things, that flickers and hints of expression on each other's faces were recognized and acted upon. "Anything wrong?" Olson asked.

"No," said Seeger. "Nothing much."

"Norman," Welch said, his voice young and solemn. "Norman, we've been talking, Olson and me. We decided—you're pretty attached to that Luger, and maybe, if you—well—"

"What he's trying to say," said Olson, "is we withdraw the request. If you want to sell it, O.K. If you don't, don't do it for our sake. Honest."

Seeger looked at them standing there, disreputable and tough and familiar. "I haven't made up my mind yet," he said.

"Anything you decide," Welch said oratorically, "is perfectly all right with us. Perfectly."

The three of them walked aimlessly and silently across the field, away from camp. As they walked, their shoes making a wet, sliding sound in the damp, dead grass, Seeger thought of the time Olson had covered him in the little town outside Cherbourg, when Seeger had been caught, going down the side of a street, by four Germans with a machine gun in the second story of a house on the corner and Olson had had to stand out in the middle of the street with no cover at all for more than a minute, firing continuously, so that Seeger could get away alive. And he thought of the time outside St.-Lô when he had been wounded and had lain in a minefield for three hours and Welch and Captain Taney had come looking for him in the darkness and had found him and picked him up and run for it, all of them expecting to get blown up any second. And he thought of all the drinks they'd had together, and the long marches and the cold winter together, and all the girls they'd gone out with together, and he thought of his father and brother crouching behind the window in Ohio waiting for the rockets and the crowds armed with Browning automatic rifles.

"Say." He stopped and stood facing them. "Say, what do you guys think of the Jews?"

Welch and Olson looked at each other, and Olson glanced down at the letter in Seeger's hand.

"Jews?" Olson said finally. "What're they? Welch, you ever hear of the Jews?"

Welch looked thoughtfully at the gray sky. "No," he said. "But remember, I'm an uneducated fellow."

"Sorry, bud," Olson said, turning to Seeger. "We can't help you. Ask us another question. Maybe we'll do better."

Seeger peered at the faces of his friends. He would have to rely upon them, later on, out of uniform, on their native streets, more than he had ever relied on them on the bullet-swept street and in the dark minefield in France. Welch and Olson stared back at him, troubled, their faces candid and tough and dependable.

"What time," Seeger asked, "did you tell that captain you'd meet him?"

"Eight o'clock," Welch said. "But we don't have to go. If you have any feeling about that gun—"

"We'll meet him," Seeger said. "We can use that sixty-five bucks."

"Listen," Olson said, "I know how much you like that gun, and I'll feel like a heel if you sell it."

"Forget it," Seeger said, starting to walk again. "What could I use it for in America?"

THE SUPERNATURAL

The supernatural is only the natural of which the laws are not yet understood.

Agatha Christie, title story,
The Hound of Death

I knew in some marvelous way I had touched the hem of the unknown. And being me, I wanted to lift that hemline a little bit more.

Mae West,
Goodness Had Nothing to Do with It!

The age of Miracles is forever here!

Thomas Carlyle,
Heroes and Hero-Worship

They say miracles are past.

William Shakespeare,
All's Well That Ends Well

Love Medicine

LOUISE ERDRICH

Lipsha Morrissey

I never really done much with my life, I suppose. I never had a television. Grandma Kashpaw had one inside her apartment at the Senior Citizens, so I used to go there and watch my favorite shows. For a while she used to call me the biggest waste on the reservation and hark back to how she saved me from my own mother, who wanted to tie me in a potato sack and throw me in a slough. Sure, I was grateful to Grandma Kashpaw for saving me like that, for raising me, but gratitude gets old. After a while, stale. I had to stop thanking her. One day I told her I had paid her back in full by staying at her beck and call. I'd do anything for Grandma. She knew that. Besides, I took care of Grandpa like nobody else could, on account of what a handful he'd gotten to be.

But that was nothing. I know the tricks of mind and body inside out without ever having trained for it, because I got the touch. It's a thing you got to be born with. I got secrets in my hands that nobody ever knew to ask. Take Grandma Kashpaw with her tired veins all knotted up in her legs like clumps of blue snails. I take my fingers and I snap them on the knots. The medicine flows out of me. The touch. I run my fingers up the maps of those rivers of veins or I knock very gentle above their hearts or I make a circling motion on their stomachs, and it helps them. They feel much better. Some women pay me five dollars.

I couldn't do the touch for Grandpa, though. He was a hard nut. You know, some people fall right through the hole in their lives. It's invisible, but they come to it after time, never knowing where. There is this woman here, Lulu Lamartine, who always had a thing for Grandpa. She loved him since she was a girl and always said he was a genius. Now she says that his mind got so full it exploded.

How can I doubt that? I know the feeling when your mental power builds up too far. I always used to say that's why the Indians got drunk. Even statistically we're the smartest people on the earth. Anyhow with Grandpa I couldn't hardly believe it, because all my youth he stood out as a hero to me. When he started getting toward second childhood he went through different moods. He would stand in the woods and cry at the top of his shirt. It scared me, scared everyone, Grandma worst of all.

Yet he was so smart—do you believe it?—that he *knew* he was getting foolish.

He said so. He told me that December I failed school and come back on the train to Hoopdance. I didn't have nowhere else to go. He picked me up there and he said it straight out: "I'm getting into my second childhood." And then he said something else I still remember: "I been chosen for it. I couldn't say no." So I figure that a man so smart all his life—tribal chairman and the star of movies and even pictured in the statehouse and on cans of snuff—would know what he's doing by saying yes. I think he was called to second childhood like anybody else gets a call for the priesthood or the army or whatever. So I really did not listen too hard when the doctor said this was some kind of disease old people got eating too much sugar. You just can't tell me that a man who went to Washington and gave them bureaucrats what for could lose his mind from eating too much Milky Way. No, he put second childhood on himself.

Behind those songs he sings out in the middle of Mass, and back of those stories that everybody knows by heart, Grandpa is thinking hard about life. I know the feeling. Sometimes I'll throw up a smokescreen to think behind. I'll hitch up to Winnipeg and play the Space Invaders for six hours, but all the time there and back I will be thinking some fairly deep thoughts that surprise even me, and I'm used to it. As for him, if it was just the thoughts there wouldn't be no problem. Smokescreen is what irritates the social structure, see, and Grandpa has done things that just distract people to the point they want to throw him in the cookie jar where they keep the mentally insane.

He's far from that, I know for sure, but even Grandma had trouble keeping her patience once he started sneaking off to Lamartine's place. He's not supposed to have his candy, and Lulu feeds it to him. That's *one* of the reasons why he goes.

Grandma tried to get me to put the touch on Grandpa soon after he began stepping out. I didn't want to, but before Grandma started telling me again what a bad state my bare behind was in when she first took me home, I thought I should at least pretend.

I put my hands on either side of Grandpa's head. You wouldn't look at him and say he was crazy. He's a fine figure of a man; as Lamartine would say, with all his hair and half his teeth, a beak like a hawk, and cheeks like the blades of a hatchet. They put his picture on all the tourist guides to North Dakota and even copied his face for artistic paintings. I guess you could call him a monument all of himself. He started grinning when I put my hands on his templates, and I knew right then he knew how come I touched him. I knew the smokescreen was going to fall.

And I was right: just for a moment it fell.

"Let's pitch whoopee," he said across my shoulder to Grandma.

They don't use that expression much around here anymore, but for damn sure it must have meant something. It got her goat right quick.

She threw my hands off his head herself and stood in front of him, overmatching him pound for pound, and taller too, for she had a growth spurt in middle age while he had shrunk, so now the length and breadth of her surpassed him. She glared and spoke her piece into his face about how he was off at all hours tomcatting and chasing Lamartine again and making a damn old fool of himself.

"And you got no more whoopee to pitch anymore anyhow!" she yelled at last, surprising me so my jaw just dropped, for us kids all had pretended for so long that those rustling sounds we heard from their side of the room at night never happened. She sure had pretended it, up till now, anyway. I saw that tears were in her eyes. And that's when I saw how much grief and love she felt for him. And it gave me a real shock to the system. You see I thought love got easier over the years so it didn't hurt so bad when it hurt, or feel so good when it felt good. I thought it smoothed out and old people hardly noticed it. I thought it curled up and died, I guess. Now I saw it rear up like a whip and lash.

She loved him. She was jealous. She mourned him like the dead.

And he just smiled into the air, trapped in the seams of his mind.

So I didn't know what to do. I was in a laundry then. They was like parents to me, the way they had took me home and reared me. I could see her point for wanting to get him back the way he was so at least she could argue with him, sleep with him, not be shamed out by Lamartine. She'd always love him. That hit me like a ton of bricks. For one whole day I felt this odd feeling that cramped my hands. When you have the touch, that's where longing gets you. I never loved like that. It made me feel all inspired to see them fight, and I wanted to go out and find a woman who I would love until one of us died or went crazy. But I'm not like that really. From time to time I heal a person all up good inside, however when it comes to the long shot I doubt that I got staying power.

And you need that, staying power, going out to love somebody. I knew this quality was not going to jump on me with no effort. So I turned my thoughts back to Grandma and Grandpa. I felt her side of it with my hands and my tangled guts, and I felt his side of it within the stretch of my mentality. He had gone out to lunch one day and never come back. He was fishing in the middle of Matchimanito. And there was big thoughts on his line, and he kept throwing them back for even bigger ones that would explain to him, say, the meaning of how we got here and why we have to leave so soon. All in all, I could not see myself treating Grandpa with the touch, bringing him back, when the real part of him had chose to be off thinking somewhere. It was only the rest of him that stayed around causing trouble, after all, and we could handle most of it without any problem.

Besides, it was hard to argue with his reasons for doing some things. Take Holy Mass. I used to go there just every so often, when I got frustrated mostly, because even though I know the Higher Power dwells everyplace, there's something very calming about the cool greenish inside of our mission. Or so I thought, anyway. Grandpa was the one who stripped off my delusions in this matter, for it was he who busted right through what Father calls the sacred serenity of the place.

We filed in that time. Me and Grandpa. We sat down in our pews. Then the rosary got started up pre-Mass and that's when Grandpa filled up his chest and opened his mouth and belted out them words.

HAIL MARIE FULL OF GRACE.

He had a powerful set of lungs.

And he kept on like that. He did not let up. He hollered and he yelled them prayers, and I guess people was used to him by now, because they only muttered theirs and did not quit and gawk like I did. I was getting red-faced, I admit. I give him the elbow once or twice, but that wasn't nothing to him.

He kept on. He shrieked to heaven and he pleaded like a movie actor and he pounded his chest like Tarzan in the Lord I Am Not Worthies. I thought he might hurt himself. Then after a while I guess I got used to it, and that's when I wondered: how come?

So afterwards I out and asked him. "How come? How come you yelled?"

"God don't hear me otherwise," said Grandpa Kashpaw.

I sweat. I broke right into a little cold sweat at my hairline because I knew this was perfectly right and for years not one damn other person had noticed it. God's been going deaf. Since the Old Testament, God's been deafening up on us. I read, see. Besides the dictionary, which I'm constantly in use of, I had this Bible once. I read it. I found there was discrepancies between then and now. It struck me. Here God used to raineth bread from clouds, smite the Phillippines, sling fire down on red-light districts where people got stabbed. He even appeared in person every once in a while. God used to pay attention, is what I'm saying.

Now there's your God in the Old Testament and there is Chippewa Gods as well. Indian Gods, good and bad, like tricky Nanabozho or the water monster, Missepeshu, who lives over in Matchimanito. That water monster was the last God I ever heard to appear. It had a weakness for young girls and grabbed one of the Pillagers off her rowboat. She got to shore all right, but only after this monster had its way with her. She's an old lady now. Old Lady Pillager. She still doesn't like to see her family fish that lake.

Our Gods aren't perfect, is what I'm saying, but at least they come around. They'll do a favor if you ask them right. You don't have to yell. But you do have to know, like I said, how to ask in the right way. That makes problems, because to ask proper was an art that was lost to the Chippewas once the Catholics gained ground. Even now, I have to wonder if Higher Power turned it back, if we got to yell, or if we just don't speak its language.

I looked around me. How else could I explain what all I had seen in my short life—King smashing his fist in things, Gordie drinking himself down to the Bismarck hospitals, or Aunt June left by a white man to wander off in the snow. How else to explain the times my touch don't work, and farther back, to the old-time Indians who was swept away in the outright germ warfare and dirty-dog killing of the whites. In those times, us Indians was so much kindlier than now.

We took them in.

Oh yes, I'm bitter as an old cutworm just thinking of how they done to us and doing still.

So Grandpa Kashpaw just opened my eyes a little there. Was there any sense relying on a God whose ears was stopped? Just like the government? I says then, right off, maybe we got nothing but ourselves. And that's not much, just personally speaking. I know I don't got the cold hard potatoes it takes to understand everything. Still, there's things I'd like to do. For instance, I'd like to help some people like my Grandpa and Grandma Kashpaw get back some happiness within the tail ends of their lives.

I told you once before I couldn't see my way clear to putting the direct touch on Grandpa's mind, and I kept my moral there, but something soon happened to make me think a little bit of mental adjustment wouldn't do him and the rest of us no harm.

It was after we saw him one afternoon in the sunshine courtyard of the Senior Citizens with Lulu Lamartine. Grandpa used to like to dig there. He had his little dandelion fork out, and he was prying up them dandelions right and left while Lamartine watched him.

"He's scratching up the dirt, all right," said Grandma, watching Lamartine watch Grandpa out the window.

Now Lamartine was about half the considerable size of Grandma, but you would never think of sizes anyway. They were different in an even more noticeable way. It was the difference between a house fixed up with paint and picky fence, and a house left to weather away into the soft earth, is what I'm saying. Lamartine was jacked up, latticed, shuttered, and vinyl sided, while Grandma sagged and bulged on her slipped foundations and let her hair go the silver gray of rain-dried lumber. Right now, she eyed the Lamartine's pert flowery dress with such a look it despaired me. I knew what this could lead to with Grandma. Alterating tongue storms and rock-hard silences was hard on a man, even one who didn't notice, like Grandpa. So I went fetching him.

But he was gone when I popped through the little screen door that led out on the courtyard. There was nobody out there either, to point which way they went. Just the dandelion fork quibbling upright in the ground. That gave me an idea. I snookered over to the Lamartine's door and I listened in first, then knocked. But nobody. So I went walking through the lounges and around the card tables. Still nobody. Finally it was my touch that led me to the laundry room. I cracked the door. I went in. There they were. And he was really loving her up good, boy, and she was going hell for leather. Sheets was flapping on the lines above, and washcloths, pillowcases, shirts was also flying through the air, for they was trying to clear out a place for themselves in a high-heaped but shallow laundry cart. The washers and the dryers was all on, chock-full of quarters, shaking and moaning. I couldn't hear what

Grandpa and the Lamartine was billing and cooing, and they couldn't hear me.

I didn't know what to do, so I went inside and shut the door.

The Lamartine wore a big curly light-brown wig. Looked like one of them squeaky little white-people dogs. Poodles they call them. Anyway, that wig is what saved us from the worse. For I could hardly shout and tell them I was in there, no more could I try and grab him. I was trapped where I was. There was nothing I could really do but hold the door shut. I was scared of somebody else upsetting in and really getting an eyeful. Turned out though, in the heat of the clinch, as I was trying to avert my eyes you see, the Lamartine's curly wig jumped off her head. And if you ever been in the midst of something and had a big change like that occur in the someone, you can't help know how it devastates your basic urges. Not only that, but her wig was almost with a life of its own. Grandpa's eyes were bugging at the change already, and swear to God if the thing didn't rear up and pop him in the face like it was going to start something. He scrambled up, Grandpa did, and the Lamartine jumped up after him all addled looking. They just stared at each other, huffing and puffing, with quizzical expression. The surprise seemed to drive all sense completely out of Grandpa's mind.

"The letter was what started the fire," he said. "I never would have done it."

"What letter?" said the Lamartine. She was stiff-necked now, and elegant, even bald, like some alien queen. I gave her back the wig. The Lamartine replaced it on her head, and whenever I saw her after that, I couldn't help thinking of her bald, with special powers, as if from another planet.

"That was a close call," I said to Grandpa after she had left.

But I think he had already forgot the incident. He just stood there all quiet and thoughtful. You really wouldn't think he was crazy. He looked like he was just about to say something important, explaining himself. He said something, all right, but it didn't have nothing to do with anything that made sense.

He wondered where the heck he put his dandelion fork. That's when I decided about the mental adjustment.

Now what was mostly our problem was not so much that he was not all there, but that what was there of him often hankered after Lamartine. If we could put a stop to that, I thought, we might be getting someplace. But here, see, my touch was of no use. For what could I snap my fingers at to make him faithful to Grandma? Like the quality of staying power, this faithfulness was invisible. I know it's something that you got to acquire, but I never known where from. Maybe there's no rhyme or reason to it, like my getting the touch, and then again maybe it's a kind of magic.

It was Grandma Kashpaw who thought of it in the end. She knows things. Although she will not admit she has a scrap of Indian blood in her, there's no doubt in my mind she's got some Chippewa. How else would you explain the way she'll be sitting there, in front of her TV story, rocking in her armchair and suddenly she turns on me, her brown eyes hard as lake-bed flint.

"Lipsha Morrissey," she'll say, "you went out last night and got drunk."

How did she know that? I'll hardly remember it myself. Then she'll say she just had a feeling or ache in the scar of her hand or a creak in her shoulder. She is constantly being told things by little aggravations in her joints or by her household appliances. One time she told Gordie never to ride with a crazy Lamartine boy. She had seen something in the polished-up tin of her bread toaster. So he didn't. Sure enough, the time came we heard how Lyman and Henry went out of control in their car, ending up in the river. Lyman swam to the top, but Henry never made it.

Thanks to Grandma's toaster, Gordie was probably spared.

Someplace in the blood Grandma Kashpaw knows things. She also remembers things, I found. She keeps things filed away. She's got a memory like them video games that don't forget your score. One reason she remembers so many details about the trouble I gave her in early life is so she can flash back her total when she needs to.

Like now. Take the love medicine. I don't know where she remembered that from. It came tumbling from her mind like an asteroid off the corner of the screen.

Of course she starts out by mentioning the time I had this accident in church and did she leave me there with wet overhalls? No she didn't. And ain't I glad? Yes I am. Now what you want now, Grandma?

But when she mentions them love medicines, I feel my back prickle at the danger. These love medicines is something of an old Chippewa specialty. No other tribe has got them down so well. But love medicines is not for the layman to handle. You don't just go out and get one without paying for it. Before you get one, even, you should go through one hell of a lot of mental condensation. You got to think it over. Choose the right one. You could really mess up your life grinding up the wrong little thing.

So anyhow, I said to Grandma I'd give this love medicine some thought. I knew the best thing was to go ask a specialist like Old Lady Pillager, who lives up in a tangle of bush and never shows herself. But the truth is I was afraid of her, like everyone else. She was known for putting the twisted mouth on people, seizing up their hearts. Old Lady Pillager was serious business, and I have always thought it best to steer clear of that whenever I could. That's why I took the powers in my own hands. That's why I did what I could.

I put my whole mentality to it, nothing held back. After a while I started to remember things I'd heard gossiped over.

I heard of this person once who carried a charm of seeds that looked like baby pearls. They was attracted to a metal knife, which made them powerful. But I didn't know where them seeds grew. Another love charm I heard about I couldn't go along with, because how was I suppose to catch frogs in the act, which it required. Them little creatures is slippery and fast. And then the powerfullest of all, the most extreme, involved nail clips and such. I wasn't anywhere near asking Grandma to provide me all the little body bits that this last love recipe called for. I went walking around for days just trying to think up something that would work.

Well I got it. If it hadn't been the early fall of the year, I never would have got it. But I was sitting underneath a tree one day down near the school just watching people's feet go by when something tells me, look up! Look up! So I look up, and I see two honkers, Canada geese, the kind with little masks on their faces, a bird what mates for life. I see them flying right over my head naturally preparing to land in some slough on the reservation, which they certainly won't get off of alive.

It hits me, anyway. Them geese, they mate for life. And I think to myself, just what if I went out and got a pair? And just what if I fed some part—say the goose heart—of the female to Grandma and Grandpa ate the other heart? Wouldn't that work? Maybe it's all invisible, and then maybe again it's magic. Love is a stony road. We know that for sure. If it's true that the higher feelings of devotion get lodged in the heart like people say, then we'd be home free. If not, eating goose heart couldn't harm nobody anyway. I thought it was worth my effort, and Grandma Kashpaw thought so, too. She had always known a good idea when she heard one. She borrowed me Grandpa's gun.

So I went out to this particular slough, maybe the exact same slough I never got thrown in by my mother, thanks to Grandma Kashpaw, and I hunched down in a good comfortable pile of rushes. I got my gun loaded up. I ate a few of these soft baloney sandwiches Grandma made me for lunch. And then I waited. The cattails blown back and forth above my head. Them stringy blue herons was spearing up their prey. The thing I know how to do best in this world, the thing I been training for all my life, is to wait. Sitting there and sitting there was no hardship on me. I got to thinking about some funny things that happened. There was this one time that Lulu Lamartine's little blue tweety bird, a paraclete, I guess you'd call it, flown up inside her dress and got lost within there. I recalled her running out into the hallway trying to yell something, shaking. She was doing a right good jig there, cutting the rug for sure, and the thing is it *never* flown out. To this day people speculate where it went. They fear she might perhaps of crushed it in her corsets. It sure hasn't ever yet been seen alive. I thought of funny things for a while, but then I used them up, and strange things that happened started weaseling their way into my mind.

I got to thinking quite naturally of the Lamartine's cousin named Wristwatch. I never knew what his real name was. They called him Wristwatch because he got his father's broken wristwatch as a young boy when his father passed on. Never in his whole life did Wristwatch take his father's watch off. He didn't care if it worked, although after a while he got sensitive when people asked what time it was, teasing him. He often put it to his ear like he was listening to the tick. But it was broken for good and forever, people said so, at least that's what they thought.

Well I saw Wristwatch smoking in his pickup one afternoon and by nine that evening he was dead.

He died sitting at the Lamartine's table, too. As she told it, Wristwatch had just eaten himself a good-size dinner and she said would he take seconds on the hot dish when he fell over to the floor. They turnt him over. He was gone. But here's the strange thing: when the Senior Citizens' orderly took the pulse he noticed that the wristwatch Wristwatch wore was now working. The moment he died the wristwatch started keeping perfect time. They buried him with the watch still ticking on his arm.

I got to thinking. What if some gravediggers dug up Wristwatch's casket in two hundred years and that watch was still going? I thought what question they would ask and it was this: Whose hand wound it?

I started shaking like a piece of grass at just the thought.

Not to get off the subject or nothing. I was still hunkered in the slough. It was passing late into the afternoon and still no honkers had touched down. Now I don't need to tell you that the waiting did not get to me, it was the chill. The rushes was very soft, but damp. I was getting cold and debating to leave, when they landed. Two geese swimming here and there as big as life, looking deep into each other's little pinhole eyes. Just the ones I was looking for. So I lifted Grandpa's gun to my shoulder and I aimed perfectly, and *blam! Blam!* I delivered two accurate shots. But the thing is, them shots missed. I couldn't hardly believe it. Whether it was that the stock had warped or the barrel got bent someways, I don't quite know, but anyway them geese flown off into the dim sky, and Lipsha Morrissey was left there in the rushes with evening fallen and his two cold hands empty. He had before him just the prospect of another day of bone-cracking chill in them rushes, and the thought of it got him depressed.

Now it isn't my style, in no way, to get depressed.

So I said to myself, Lipsha Morrissey, you're a happy S.O.B. who could be covered up with weeds by now down at the bottom of this slough, but instead you're alive to tell the tale. You might have problems in life, but you still got the touch. You got the power, Lipsha Morrissey. Can't argue that. So put your mind to it and figure out how not to be depressed.

I took my advice. I put my mind to it. But I never saw at the time how my thoughts led me astray toward a tragic outcome none could have known. I ignored all the danger, all the limits, for I was tired of sitting in the slough and my feet were numb. My face was aching. I was chilled, so I played with fire. I told myself love medicine was simple. I told myself the old superstitions was just that—strange beliefs. I told myself to take the ten dollars Mary MacDonald had paid me for putting the touch on her arthritis joint, and the other five I hadn't spent yet from winning bingo last Thursday. I told myself to go down to the Red Owl store.

And here is what I did that made the medicine backfire. I took an evil shortcut. I looked at birds that was dead and froze.

All right. So now I guess you will say, "Slap a malpractice suit on Lipsha Morrissey."

I heard of those suits. I used to think it was a color clothing quack doctors had to wear so you could tell them from the good ones. Now I know better that it's law.

As I walked back from the Red Owl with the rock-hard, heavy turkeys, I argued to myself about malpractice. I thought of faith. I thought to myself that faith could be called belief against the odds and whether or not there's any proof. How does that sound? I thought how we might have to yell to be heard by Higher Power, but that's not saying it's not *there*. And that is faith for you. It's belief even when the goods don't deliver. Higher Power makes promises we all know they can't back up, but anybody ever go and slap an old malpractice suit on God? Or the U.S. government? No they don't. Faith might be stupid, but it gets us through. So what I'm heading at is this. I finally convinced myself that the real actual power to the love medicine was not the goose heart itself but the faith in the cure.

I didn't believe it, I knew it was wrong, but by then I had waded so far into my lie I was stuck there. And then I went one step further.

The next day, I cleaned the hearts away from the paper packages of gizzards inside the turkeys. Then I wrapped them hearts with a clean hankie and brung them both to get blessed up at the mission. I wanted to get official blessings from the priest, but when Father answered the door to the rectory, wiping his hands on a little towel, I could tell he was a busy man.

"Booshoo, Father," I said. "I got a slight request to make of you this afternoon."

"What is it?" he said.

"Would you bless this package?" I held out the hankie with the hearts tied inside it.

He looked at the package, questioning it.

"It's turkey hearts," I honestly had to reply.

A look of annoyance crossed his face.

"Why don't you bring this matter over to Sister Martin," he said. "I have duties."

And so, although the blessing wouldn't be as powerful, I went over to the Sisters with the package.

I rung the bell, and they brought Sister Martin to the door. I had her as a music teacher, but I was always so shy then. I never talked out loud. Now, I had grown taller than Sister Martin. Looking down, I saw that she was not feeling up to snuff. Brown circles hung under her eyes.

"What's the matter?" she said, not noticing who I was.

"Remember me, Sister?"

She squinted up at me.

"Oh yes," she said after a moment. "I'm sorry, you're the youngest of the Kashpaws. Gordie's brother."

Her face warmed up.

"Lipsha," I said, "that's my name."

"Well, Lipsha," she said, smiling broad at me now, "what can I do for you?"

They always said she was the kindest-hearted of the Sisters up the hill, and she was. She brought me back into their own kitchen and made me take a big yellow wedge of cake and a glass of milk.

"Now tell me," she said, nodding at my package. "What have you got wrapped up so carefully in those handkerchiefs?"

Like before, I answered honestly.

"Ah," said Sister Martin. "Turkey hearts." She waited.

"I hoped you could bless them."

She waited some more, smiling with her eyes. Kindhearted though she was, I began to sweat. A person could not pull the wool down over Sister Martin. I stumbled through my mind for an explanation, quick, that wouldn't scare her off.

"They're a present," I said, "for Saint Kateri's statue."

"She's not a saint yet."

"I know," I stuttered on. "In the hopes they will crown her."

"Lipsha," she said, "I never heard of such a thing."

So I told her. "Well the truth is," I said, "it's a kind of medicine."

"For what?"

"Love."

"Oh Lipsha," she said after a moment, "you don't need any medicine. I'm sure any girl would like you exactly the way you are."

I just sat there. I felt miserable, caught in my pack of lies.

"Tell you what," she said, seeing how bad I felt, "my blessing won't make any difference anyway. But there is something you can do."

I looked up at her, hopeless.

"Just be yourself."

I looked down at my plate. I knew I wasn't much to brag about right then, and I shortly became even less. For as I walked out the door I stuck my fingers in the cup of holy water that was sacred from their touches. I put my fingers in and blessed the hearts, quick, with my own hand.

I went back to Grandma and sat down in her little kitchen at the Senior Citizens. I unwrapped them hearts on the table, and her hard agate eyes went soft. She said she wasn't even going to cook those hearts up but eat them raw so their power would go down strong as possible.

I couldn't hardly watch when she munched hers. Now that's true love. I was worried abut how she would get Grandpa to eat his, but she told me she'd think of something and don't worry. So I did not. I was supposed to hide off in her bedroom while she put dinner on a plate for Grandpa and fixed up the heart so he'd eat it. I caught a glint of the plate she was making for him. She put that heart smack on a piece of lettuce like in a restaurant and then attached to it a little heap of boiled peas.

He sat down. I was listening in the next room.

She said, "Why don't you have some mash potato?" So he had some mash potato. Then she gave him a little piece of boiled meat. He ate that. Then she said, "Why you didn't never touch your salad yet. See that heart? I'm feeding you it because the doctor said your blood needs building up."

I couldn't help it, at that point I peeked through a crack in the door.

I saw Grandpa picking at that heart on his plate with a certain look. He didn't look appetized at all, is what I'm saying. I doubted our plan was going to work. Grandma was getting worried, too. She told him one more time, loudly, that he had to eat that heart.

"Swallow it down," she said. "You'll hardly notice it."

He just looked at her straight on. The way he looked at her made me think I was going to see the smokescreen drop a second time, and sure enough it happened.

"What you want me to eat this for so bad?" he asked her uncannily.

Now Grandma knew the jig was up. She knew that he knew she was working medicine. He put his fork down. He rolled the heart around his saucer plate.

"I don't want to eat this," he said to Grandma. "It don't look good."

"Why it's fresh grade-A," she told him. "One hundred percent."

He didn't ask percent what, but his eyes took on an even more warier look.

"Just go on and try it," she said, taking the salt shaker up in her hand. She was getting annoyed. "Not tasty enough? You want me to salt it for you?" She waved the shaker over his plate.

"All right, skinny white girl!" She had got Grandpa mad. Oopsy-daisy, he popped the heart into his mouth. I was about to yawn loudly and come out of the bedroom. I was about ready for this crash of wills to be over, when I saw he was still up to his old tricks. First he rolled it into one side of his cheek. "Mmmmm," he said. Then he rolled it into the other side of his cheek. "Mmmmmmm," again. Then he stuck his tongue out with the heart on it and put it back, and there was no time to react. He had pulled Grandma's leg once too far. Her goat was got. She was so mad she hopped up quick as a wink and slugged him between the shoulderblades to make him swallow.

Only thing is, he choked.

He choked real bad. A person can choke to death. You ever sit down at a restaurant table and up above you there is a list of instructions what to do if something slides down the wrong pipe? It sure makes you chew slow, that's for damn sure. When Grandpa fell off his chair better believe me that little graphic illustrated poster fled into my mind. I jumped out the bedroom. I done everything within my power that I could do to unlodge what was choking him. I squeezed underneath his rib cage. I socked him in the back. I was desperate. But here's the factor of decision: he wasn't choking on the heart alone. There was more to it than that. It was other things that choked him as well. It didn't seem like he wanted to struggle or fight. Death came and tapped his chest, so he went just like that. I'm sorry all through my body at what I done to him with that heart, and there's those who will say Lipsha Morrissey is just excusing himself off the hook by giving song and dance about how Grandpa gave up.

Maybe I can't admit what I did. My touch had gone worthless, that is true. But here is what I seen while he lay in my arms.

You hear a person's life will flash before their eyes when they're in danger. It was him in danger, not me, but it was *his* life come over me. I saw him dying, and it was like someone pulled the shade down in a room. His eyes clouded over and squeezed shut, but just before that I looked in. He was still fishing in the middle of Matchimanito. Big thoughts was on his line and he had half a case of beer in the boat. He waved at me, grinned, and then the bobber went under.

Grandma had gone out of the room crying for help. I bunched my force up in my hands and I held him. I was so wound up I couldn't even breathe. All the moments he had spent with me, all the times he had hoisted me on his shoulders or pointed into the leaves was concentrated in that moment. Time was flashing back and forth like a pinball machine. Lights blinked and balls hopped and rubber bands chirped, until suddenly I realized the last ball had gone down the drain and there was nothing. I felt his force leaving him, flowing out of Grandpa never to return. I felt his mind weakening. The bobber going under in the lake. And I felt the touch retreat back into the darkness inside my body, from where it came.

One time, long ago, both of us were fishing together. We caught a big old snapper what started towing us around like it was a motor. "This here fishline is pretty damn good," Grandpa said. "Let's keep this turtle on and see where he takes us." So we rode along behind that turtle, watching as from time to time it surfaced. The thing was just about the size of a washtub. It took us all around the lake twice, and as it was traveling, Grandpa said something as a joke. "Lipsha," he said, "we are glad your mother didn't want you because we was always looking for a boy like you who would tow us around the lake."

"I ain't no snapper. Snappers is so stupid they stay alive when their head's chopped off," I said.

"That ain't stupidity," said Grandpa. "Their brain's just in their heart, like yours is."

When I looked up, I knew the fuse had blown between my heart and my mind and that a terrible understanding was to be given.

Grandma got back into the room and I saw her stumble. And then she went down too. It was like a house you can't hardly believe has stood so long, through years of record weather, suddenly goes down in the worst yet. It makes sense, is what I'm saying, but you still can't hardly believe it. You think a person you know has got through death and illness and being broke and living on commodity rice will get through anything. Then they fold and you see how fragile were the stones that underpinned them. You see how instantly the ground can shift you thought was solid. You see the stop signs and the yellow dividing markers of roads you traveled and all the instructions you had played according to vanish. You see how all the everyday things you counted on was just a dream you had been having by which you run your whole life. She had been over me, like a sheer overhang of rock dividing Lipsha Morrissey from outer space. And now she went underneath. It was as though the banks gave way on the shores of Matchimanito, and where Grandpa's passing was just the bobber swallowed under by his biggest thought, her fall was the house and the rock under it sliding after, sending half the lake splashing up to the clouds.

Where there was nothing.

You play them games never knowing what you see. When I fell into the dream alongside of both of them I saw that the dominions I had defended myself from anciently was but delusions of the screen. Blips of light. And I was scot-free now, whistling through space.

I don't know how I come back. I don't know from where. They was slapping my face when I arrived back at Senior Citizens and they was oxygenating her. I saw her chest move, almost unwilling. She sighed the way she would when somebody bothered her in the middle of a row of beads she was counting. I think it irritated her to no end that they brought her back. I knew from the way she looked after they took the mask off, she was not going to forgive them disturbing her restful peace. Nor was she forgiving Lipsha Morrissey. She had been stepping out onto the road of death, she told the children later at the funeral. I asked was there any stop signs or dividing markers on that road, but she clamped her lips in a vise the way she always done when she was mad.

Which didn't bother me. I knew when things had cleared out she wouldn't have no choice. I was not going to speculate where the blame was put for Grandpa's death. We was in it together. She had slugged him between the shoulders. My touch had failed him, never to return.

All the blood children and the took-ins, like me, came home from Minneapolis and Chicago, where they had relocated years ago. They stayed with friends on the reservation or with Aurelia or slept on Grandma's floor. They were struck down with grief and bereavement to be sure, every one of them. At the funeral I sat down in the back of the church with Albertine. She had gotten all skinny and ragged haired from cramming all her years of study into two or three. She had decided that to be a nurse was not enough for her so she was going to be a doctor. But the way she was straining her mind didn't look too hopeful. Her eyes were bloodshot from driving and crying. She took my hand. From the back we watched all the children and the mourners as they hunched over their prayers, their hands stuffed full of Kleenex. It was someplace in that long sad service that my vision shifted. I began to see things different, more clear. The family kneeling down turned to rocks in a field. It struck me how strong and reliable grief was, and death. Until the end of time, death would be our rock.

So I had perspective on it all, for death gives you that. All the Kashpaw children had done various things to me in their lives—shared their folks with me, loaned me cash, beat me up in secret—and I decided, because of death, then and there I'd call it quits. If I ever saw King again, I'd shake his hand. Forgiving somebody else made the whole thing easier to bear.

Everybody saw Grandpa off into the next world. And then the Kashpaws had to get back to their jobs, which was numerous and impressive. I had a few beers with them and I went back to Grandma, who had sort of got lost in the shuffle of everybody being sad about Grandpa and glad to see one another.

Zelda had sat beside her the whole time and was sitting with her now. I wanted to talk to Grandma, say how sorry I was, that it wasn't her fault, but only mine. I would have, but Zelda gave me one of her looks of strict warning as if to say, "I'll take care of Grandma. Don't horn in on the women."

If only Zelda knew, I thought, the sad realities would change her. But of course I couldn't tell the dark truth.

It was evening, late. Grandma's light was on underneath a crack in the door. About a week had passed since we buried Grandpa. I knocked first but there wasn't no answer, so I went right in. The door was unlocked. She was there but she didn't notice me at first. Her hands were tied up in her rosary, and her gaze was fully absorbed in the easy chair opposite her, the one that had always been Grandpa's favorite. I stood there, staring with her, at the little green nubs in the cloth and plastic armrest covers and the sad little hair-tonic stain he had made on the white doily where he laid his head. For the life of me I couldn't figure what she was staring at. Thin space. Then she turned.

"He ain't gone yet," she said.

Remember that chill I luckily didn't get from waiting in the slough? I got it now. I felt it start from the very center of me, where fear hides, waiting to attack. It spiraled outward so that in minutes my fingers and teeth were shaking and clattering. I knew she told the truth. She seen Grandpa. Whether or not he had been there is not the point. She had *seen* him, and that meant anybody else could see him, too. Not only that but, as is usually the case with these here ghosts, he had a certain uneasy reason to come back. And of course Grandma Kashpaw had scanned it out.

I sat down. We sat together on the couch watching his chair out of the corner of our eyes. She had found him sitting in his chair when she walked in the door.

"It's the love medicine, my Lipsha," she said. "It was stronger than we thought. He came back even after death to claim me to his side."

I was afraid. "We shouldn't have tampered with it," I said. She agreed. For a while we sat still. I don't know what she thought, but my head felt screwed on backward. I couldn't accurately consider the situation, so I told Grandma to go to bed. I would sleep on the couch keeping my eye on Grandpa's chair. Maybe he would come back and maybe he wouldn't. I guess I feared the one as much as the other, but I got to thinking, see, as I lay there in darkness, that perhaps even through my terrible mistakes some good might come. If Grandpa did come back, I thought he'd return in his right mind. I could talk with him. I could tell him it was all my fault for playing with power I did not understand. Maybe he'd forgive me and rest I peace. I hoped this. I calmed myself and waited for him all night.

He fooled me though. He knew what I was waiting for, and it wasn't what he was looking to hear. Come dawn I heard a blood-splitting cry from the bedroom and I rushed in there. Grandma turnt the lights on. She was sitting on the edge of the bed and her face looked harsh, pinched-up, gray.

"He was here," she said. "He came and laid down next to me in bed. And he touched me."

Her heart broke down. She cried. His touch was so cold. She laid back in bed after a while, as it was morning, and I went to the couch. As I lay there, falling asleep, I suddenly felt Grandpa's presence and the barrier between us like a swollen river. I felt how I had wronged him. How awful was the place where I had sent him. Behind the wall of death, he'd watched the living eat and cry and get drunk. He was lonesome, but I understood he meant no harm.

"Go back," I said to the dark, afraid and yet full of pity. "You got to be with your own kind now," I said. I felt him retreating, like a sigh, growing less. I felt his spirit as it shrunk back through the walls, the blinds, the brick courtyard of Senior Citizens. "Look up Aunt June," I whispered as he left.

I slept late the next morning, a good hard sleep allowing the sun to rise and warm the earth. It was past noon when I awoke. There is nothing, to my mind, like a long sleep to make those hard decisions that you neglect under stress of wakefulness. Soon as I woke up that morning, I saw exactly what I'd say to Grandma. I had gotten humble in the past week, not just losing the touch but getting jolted into the understanding that would prey on me from here on out. Your life feels different on you, once you greet death and understand your heart's position. You wear your life like a garment from the mission bundle sale ever after—lightly because you realize you never paid nothing for it, cherishing because you know you won't ever come by such a bargain again. Also you have the feeling someone wore it before you and someone will after. I can't explain that, not yet, but I'm putting my mind to it.

"Grandma," I said, "I got to be honest about the love medicine."

She listened. I knew from then on she would be listening to me the way I had listened to her before. I told her about the turkey hearts and how I had them blessed. I told her what I used as love medicine was purely a fake, and then I said to her what my understanding brought me.

"Love medicine ain't what brings him back to you, Grandma. No, it's something else. He loved you over time and distance, but he went off so quick he never got the chance to tell you how he loves you, how he doesn't blame you, how he understands. It's true feeling, not no magic. No supermarket heart could have brung him back."

She looked at me. She was seeing the years and days I had no way of knowing, and she didn't believe me. I could tell this. Yet a look came on her face. It was like the look of mothers drinking sweetness from their children's eyes. It was tenderness.

"Lipsha," she said, "you was always my favorite."

She took the beads off the bedpost, where she kept them to say at night, and she told me to put out my hand. When I did this, she shut the beads inside of my fist and held them there a long minute, tight, so my hand hurt. I almost cried when she did this. I don't really know why. Tears shot up behind my eyelids, and yet it was nothing. I didn't understand, except her hand was so strong, squeezing mine.

The earth was full of life and there were dandelions growing out the window, thick as thieves, already seeded, fat as big yellow plungers. She let my hand go. I got up. "I'll go out and dig a few dandelions," I told her.

Outside, the sun was hot and heavy as a hand on my back. I felt it flow down my arms, out my fingers, arrowing through the ends of the fork into the earth. With every root I prized up there was return, as if I was kin to its secret lesson. The touch got stronger as I worked through the grassy afternoon. Uncurling from me like a seed out of the blackness where I was lost, the touch spread. The spiked leaves full of bitter mother's milk. A buried root. A nuisance people dig up and throw in the sun to wither. A globe of frail seeds that's indestructible.

The Celestial Omnibus

E. M. FORSTER

I

The boy who resided at Agathox Lodge, 28, Buckingham Park Road, Surbiton, had often been puzzled by the old sign-post that stood almost opposite. He asked his mother about it, and she replied that it was a joke, and not a very nice one, which had been made many years back by some naughty young men, and that the police ought to remove it. For there were two strange things about this sign-post: firstly, it pointed up a blank alley, and, secondly, it had painted on it, in faded characters, the words, "To Heaven."

"What kind of young men were they?" he asked.

"I think your father told me that one of them wrote verses, and was expelled from the University and came to grief in other ways. Still, it was a long time ago. You must ask your father about it. He will say the same as I do, that it was put up as a joke."

"So it doesn't mean anything at all?"

She sent him up-stairs to put on his best things, for the Bonses were coming to tea, and he was to hand the cake-stand.

It struck him, as he wrenched on his tightening trousers, that he might do worse than ask Mr. Bons about the sign-post. His father, though very kind, always laughed at him—shrieked with laughter whenever he or any other child asked a question or spoke. But Mr. Bons was serious as well as kind. He had a beautiful house and lent one books, he was a churchwarden, and a candidate for the County Council; he had donated to the Free Library enormously, he presided over the Literary Society, and had Members of Parliament to stop with him—in short, he was probably the wisest person alive.

Yet even Mr. Bons could only say that the sign-post was a joke—the joke of a person named Shelley.

"Of course!" cried the mother; "I told you so, dear. That was the name."

"Had you never heard of Shelley?" asked Mr. Bons.

"No," said the boy, and hung his head.

"But is there no Shelley in the house?"

"Why, yes!" exclaimed the lady, in much agitation. "Dear Mr. Bons, we aren't such Philistines as that. Two at the least. One a wedding present, and the other, smaller print, in one of the spare rooms."

"I believe we have seven Shelleys," said Mr. Bons, with a slow smile. Then he brushed the cake crumbs off his stomach, and, together with his daughter, rose to go.

The boy, obeying a wink from his mother, saw them all the way to the garden gate, and when they had gone he did not at once return to the house, but gazed for a little up and down Buckingham Park Road.

His parents lived at the right end of it. After No. 39 the quality of the houses dropped very suddenly, and 64 had not even a separate servants' entrance. But at the present moment the whole road looked rather pretty, for the sun had just set in splendour, and the inequalities of rent were drowned in a saffron afterglow. Small birds twittered, and the breadwinners' train shrieked musically down through the cutting—that wonderful cutting which has drawn to itself the whole beauty out of Surbiton, and clad itself, like any Alpine valley, with the glory of the fir and the silver birch and the primrose. It was this cutting that had first stirred desires within the boy—desires for something just a little different, he knew not what, desires that would return whenever things were sunlit, as they were this evening, running up and down inside him, up and down, up and down, till he would feel quite unusual all over, and as likely as not would want to cry. This evening he was even sillier, for he slipped across the road towards the sign-post and began to run up the blank alley.

The alley runs between high walls—the walls of the gardens of "Ivanhoe" and "Belle Vista" respectively. It smells a little all the way, and is scarcely twenty yards long, including the turn at the end. So not unnaturally the boy soon came to a standstill. "I'd like to kick that Shelley," he exclaimed, and glanced idly at a piece of paper which was pasted on the wall. Rather an odd piece of paper, and he read it carefully before he turned back. This is what he read:

S. AND C. R. C. C.

Alteration in Service

Owing to lack of patronage the Company are regretfully compelled to suspend the hourly service, and to retain only the

Sunrise and Sunset Omnibuses,

which will run as usual. It is to be hoped that the public will patronize an arrangement which is intended for their convenience. As an extra inducement, the Company will, for the first time, now issue

Return Tickets!

(available one day only), which may be obtained of the driver. Passengers are again reminded that *no tickets are issued at the other end*, and that no complaints in this connection will receive consideration from the Company. Nor will the Company be responsible for any negligence or stupidity on the part of Passengers, nor for Hailstorms, Lightning, Loss of Tickets, nor for any Act of God.

For the Direction

Now he had never seen this notice before, nor could he imagine where the omnibus went to. S. of course was for Surbiton, and R.C.C. meant Road Car Company. But what was the meaning of the other C.? Coombe and Malden, perhaps, or possibly "City." Yet it could not hope to compete with the South-Western. The whole thing, the boy reflected, was run on hopelessly unbusiness-like lines. Why no tickets from the other end? And what an hour to start! Then he realized that unless the notice was a hoax, an omnibus must have been starting just as he was wishing the Bonses good-bye. He peered at the ground through the gathering dusk, and there he saw what might or might not be the marks of wheels. Yet nothing had come out of the alley. And he had never seen an omnibus at any time in the Buckingham Park Road. No: it must be a hoax, like the sign-posts, like the fairy tales, like the dreams upon which he would wake suddenly in the night. And with a sigh he stepped from the alley—right into the arms of his father.

Oh, how his father laughed! "Poor, poor Popsey!" he cried. "Diddums! Diddums! Diddums think he'd walky-palky up to Evvink!" And his mother, also convulsed with laughter, appeared on the steps of Agathox Lodge. "Don't Bob!" she gasped. "Don't be so naughty! Oh, you'll kill me! Oh, leave the boy alone!"

But all the evening the joke was kept up. The father implored to be taken too. Was it a very tiring walk? Need one wipe one's shoes on the door-mat? And the boy went to bed feeling faint and sore, and thankful for only one thing—that he had not said a word about the omnibus. It was a hoax, yet through his dreams it grew more and more real, and the streets of Surbiton, through which he saw it driving, seemed instead to become hoaxes and shadows. And very early in the morning he woke with a cry, for he had had a glimpse of its destination.

He struck a match, and its light fell not only on his watch but also on his calendar, so that he knew it to be half-an-hour to sunrise. It was pitch dark, for the fog had come down from London in the night, and all Surbiton was wrapped in its embraces. Yet he sprang out and dressed himself, for he was determined to settle once for all which was real: the omnibus or the streets. "I shall be a fool one way or the other," he thought, "until I know." Soon he was shivering in the road under the gas lamp that guarded the entrance to the alley.

To enter the alley itself required some courage. Not only was it horribly dark, but he now realized that it was an impossible terminus for an omnibus. If it had not been for a policeman, whom he heard approaching through the fog, he would never have made the attempt. The next moment he had made the attempt and failed. Nothing. Nothing but a blank alley and a very silly boy gaping at its dirty floor. It *was* a hoax. "I'll tell papa and mamma," he decided. "I deserve it. I deserve that they should know. I am too silly to be alive." And he went back to the gate of Agathox Lodge.

There he remembered that his watch was fast. The sun was not risen; it would not rise for two minutes. "Give the bus every chance," he thought cynically, and returned into the alley.

But the omnibus was there.

II

It had two horses, whose sides were still smoking from their journey, and its two great lamps shone through the fog against the alley's walls, changing their cobwebs and moss into tissues of fairyland. The driver was huddled up in a cape. He faced the blank wall, and how he had managed to drive in so neatly and so silently was one of the many things that the boy never discovered. Nor could he imagine how ever he would drive out.

"Please," his voice quavered through the foul brown air, "Please, is that an omnibus?"

"Omnibus est," said the driver, without turning round. There was a moment's silence. The policeman passed, coughing, by the entrance of the alley. The boy crouched in the shadow, for he did not want to be found out. He was pretty sure, too, that it was a Pirate; nothing else, he reasoned, would go from such odd places and at such odd hours.

"About when do you start?" He tried to sound nonchalant.

"At sunrise."

"How far do you go?"

"The whole way."

"And can I have a return ticket which will bring me all the way back?"

"You can."

"Do you know, I half think I'll come." The driver made no answer. The sun must have risen, for he unhitched the brake. And scarcely had the boy jumped in before the omnibus was off.

How? Did it turn? There was no room. Did it go forward? There was a blank wall. Yet it was moving—moving at a stately pace through the fog, which had turned from brown to yellow. The thought of warm bed and warmer breakfast made the boy feel faint. He wished he had not come. His parents would not have approved. He would have gone back to them if the weather had not made it impossible. The solitude was terrible; he was the only passenger. And the omnibus, though well-built, was cold and somewhat musty. He drew his coat round him, and in so doing chanced to feel his pocket. It was empty. He had forgotten his purse.

"Stop!" he shouted. "Stop!" And then, being of a polite disposition, he glanced up at the painted notice-board so that he might call the driver by name. "Mr. Browne! stop; O, do please stop!"

Mr. Browne did not stop, but he opened a little window, and looked in at the boy. His face was a surprise, so kind it was and modest.

"Mr. Browne, I've left my purse behind. I've not got a penny. I can't pay for the ticket. Will you take my watch, please? I am in the most awful hole."

"Tickets on this line," said the driver, "whether single or return, can be purchased by coinage from no terrene mint. And a chronometer, though it had solaced the vigils of Charlemagne, or measured the slumbers of Laura, can acquire by no mutation the double-cake that charms the fangless Cerberus of Heaven!" So saying, he handed in the necessary ticket, and, while the boy said "Thank you," continued: "Titular pretensions, I know it well, are vanity. Yet they merit no censure when uttered on a laughing lip, and in an homonymous world are in some sort useful, since they do serve to distinguish one Jack from his fellow. Remember me, therefore, as Sir Thomas Browne."

"Are you a Sir? Oh, sorry!" He had heard of these gentlemen drivers. "It *is* good of you about the ticket. But if you go on at this rate, however does your bus pay?

"It does not pay. It was not intended to pay. Many are the faults of my equipage; it is compounded too curiously of foreign woods; its cushions tickle erudition rather than promote repose; and my horses are nourished not on the evergreen pastures of the moment, but on the dried bents and clovers of Latinity. But that it pays!—that error at all events was never intended and never attained."

"Sorry again," said the boy rather hopelessly. Sir Thomas looked sad, fearing that, even for a moment, he had been the cause of sadness. He invited the boy to come up and sit beside him on the box, and together they journeyed on through the fog, which was now changing from yellow to white. There were no houses by the road; so it must be either Putney Heath or Wimbledon Common.

"Have you been a driver always?"

"I was a physician once."

"But why did you stop? Weren't you good?"

"As a healer of bodies I had scant success, and several score of my patients preceded me. But as a healer of the spirit I have succeeded beyond my hopes and my deserts. For though my draughts were not better nor subtler than those of other men, yet, by reason of the cunning goblets wherein I offered them, the queasy soul was ofttimes tempted to sip and be refreshed."

"The queasy soul," he murmured; "if the sun sets with trees in front of it, and you suddenly come strange all over, is that a queasy soul?"

"Have you felt that?"

"Why yes."

After a pause he told the boy a little, a very little, about the journey's end. But they did not chatter much, for the boy, when he liked a person, would as soon sit silent in his company as speak, and this, he discovered, was also the mind of Sir Thomas Browne and of many others with whom he was to be acquainted. He heard, however, about the young man Shelley, who was now quite a famous person, with a carriage of his own, and about some of the other drivers who are in the service of the Company. Meanwhile the light grew stronger, though the fog did not disperse. It was now more like mist than fog, and at times would travel quickly across them, as if it was part of a cloud. They had been ascending, too, in a most puzzling way; for over two hours the horses had been pulling against the collar, and even if it were Richmond Hill they ought to have been at the top long ago. Perhaps it was Epsom, or even the North Downs; yet the air seemed keener than that which blows on either. And as to the name of their destination, Sir Thomas Browne was silent.

Crash!

"Thunder, by Jove!" said the boy, "and not so far off either. Listen to the echoes! It's more like mountains."

He thought, not very vividly, of his father and mother. He saw them sitting down to sausages and listening to the storm. He saw his own empty place. Then there would be questions, alarms, theories, jokes, consolations. They would expect him back at lunch. To lunch he would not come, nor tea, but he would be in for dinner, and so his day's truancy would be over. If he had had his purse he would have bought them presents—not that he should have known what to get them.

Crash!

The peal and the lightning came together. The cloud quivered as if it were alive, and torn streamers of mist rushed past. "Are you afraid?" asked Sir Thomas Browne.

"What is there to be afraid of? Is it much farther?"

The horses of the omnibus stopped just as a ball of fire burst up and exploded with a ringing noise that was deafening but clear, like the noise of a blacksmith's forge. All the cloud was shattered.

"Oh, listen, Sir Thomas Browne! No, I mean look; we shall get a view at last. No, I mean listen; that sounds like a rainbow!"

The noise had died into the faintest murmur, beneath which another murmur grew, spreading stealthily, steadily, in a curve that widened but did not vary. And in widening curves a rainbow was spreading from the horses' feet into the dissolving mists.

"But how beautiful! What colours! Where will it stop? It is more like the rainbows you can tread on. More like dreams."

The colour and the sound grew together. The rainbow spanned an enormous gulf. Clouds rushed under it and were pierced by it, and still it grew, reaching forward, conquering the darkness, until it touched something that seemed more solid than a cloud.

The boy stood up. "What is that out there?" he called. "What does it rest on, out at that other end?"

In the morning sunshine a precipice shone forth beyond the gulf. A precipice—or was it a castle? The horses moved. They set their feet upon the rainbow.

"Oh, look!" the boy shouted. "Oh, listen! Those caves—or are they gateways? Oh, look between those cliffs at those ledges. I see people! I see trees!"

"Look also below," whispered Sir Thomas. "Neglect not the diviner Acheron."

The boy looked below, past the flames of the rainbow that licked against their wheels. The gulf also had cleared, and in its depths there flowed an everlasting river. One sunbeam entered and struck a green pool, and as they passed over he saw three maidens rise to the surface of the pool, singing, and playing with something that glistened like a ring.

"You down in the water———" he called.

They answered, "You up on the bridge———" There was a burst of music. "You up on the bridge, good luck to you. Truth in the depth, truth on the height."

"You down in the water, what are you doing?"

Sir Thomas Browne replied: "They sport in the mancipiary possession of their gold"; and the omnibus arrived.

III

The boy was in disgrace. He sat locked up in the nursery of Agathox Lodge, learning poetry for a punishment. His father had said, "My boy! I can pardon anything but untruthfulness," and had caned him, saying at each stroke, "There is *no* omnibus, *no* driver, *no* bridge, *no* mountain; you are a *truant*, a *gutter snipe*, a *liar*." His father could be very stern at times. His mother had begged him to say he was sorry. But he could not say that. It was the greatest day of his life, in spite of the caning and the poetry at the end of it.

He had returned punctually at sunset—driven not by Sir Thomas Browne, but by a maiden lady who was full of quiet fun. They had talked of omnibuses and also of barouche landaus. How far away her gentle voice seemed now! Yet it was scarcely three hours since he had left her up the alley.

His mother called through the door. "Dear, you are to come down and to bring your poetry with you."

He came down, and found that Mr. Bons was in the smoking-room with his father. It had been a dinner party.

"Here is the great traveller!" said his father grimly. "Here is the young gentleman who drives in an omnibus over rainbows, while young ladies sing to him." Pleased with his wit, he laughed.

"After all," said Mr. Bons, smiling, "there is something a little like it in Wagner. It is odd how, in quite illiterate minds, you will find glimmers of Artistic Truth. The case interests me. Let me plead for the culprit. We have all romanced in our time, haven't we?"

"Hear how kind Mr. Bons is," said his mother, while his father said, "Very well. Let him say his Poem, and that will do. He is going away to my sister on Tuesday, and *she* will cure him of this alley-slopering." (Laughter.) "Say your Poem."

The boy began. " 'Standing aloof in giant ignorance.' "

His father laughed again—roared. "One for you, my son! 'Standing aloof in giant ignorance!' I never knew these poets talked sense. Just describes you. Here, Bons, you go in for poetry. Put him through it, will you, while I fetch up the whisky?"

"Yes, give me the Keats," said Mr. Bons. "Let him say his Keats to me."

So for a few moments the wise man and the ignorant boy were left alone in the smoking-room.

" 'Standing aloof in giant ignorance, of thee I dream and of the Cyclades, as one who sits ashore and longs perchance to visit——' "

"Quite right. To visit what?"

" 'To visit dolphin coral in deep seas,' " said the boy, and burst into tears.

"Come, come! why do you cry?"

"Because—because all these words that only rhymed before, now that I've come back they're me."

Mr. Bons laid the Keats down. The case was more interesting than he had expected. "*You?*" he exclaimed. "This sonnet, *you?*"

"Yes—and look further on: 'Aye, on the shores of darkness there is light, and precipices show untrodden green.' It *is* so, sir. All these things are true."

"I never doubted it," said Mr. Bons, with closed eyes.

"You—then you believe me? You believe in the omnibus and the driver and the storm and that return ticket I got for nothing and——"

"Tut, tut! No more of your yarns, my boy. I meant that I never doubted the essential truth of Poetry. Some day, when you have read more, you will understand what I mean."

"But Mr. Bons, it *is* so. There *is* light upon the shores of darkness. I have seen it coming. Light and a wind."

"Nonsense," said Mr. Bons.

"If I had stopped! They tempted me. They told me to give up my ticket—for you cannot come back if you lose your ticket. They called from the river for it, and indeed I was tempted, for I have never been so happy as among those precipices. But I thought of my mother and father, and that I must fetch them. Yet they will not come, though the road starts opposite our house. It has all happened as the people up there warned me, and Mr. Bons has disbelieved me like every one else. I have been caned. I shall never see that mountain again."

"What's that about me?" said Mr. Bons, sitting up in his chair very suddenly.

"I told them about you, and how clever you were, and how many books you had, and they said, 'Mr. Bons will certainly disbelieve you.' "

"Stuff and nonsense, my young friend. You grow impertinent. I—well—I will settle the matter. Not a word to your father. I will cure you. To-morrow evening I will myself call here to take you for a walk, and at sunset we will go up this alley opposite and hunt for your omnibus, you silly little boy."

His face grew serious, for the boy was not disconcerted, but leapt about the room singing, "Joy! Joy! I told them you would believe me. We will drive together over the rainbow. I told them that you would come." After all, could there be anything in the story? Wagner? Keats? Shelley? Sir Thomas Browne? Certainly the case was interesting.

And on the morrow evening, though it was pouring with rain, Mr. Bons did not omit to call at Agathox Lodge.

The boy was ready, bubbling with excitement, and skipping about in a way that rather vexed the President of the Literary Society. They took a turn down Buckingham Park Road, and then—having seen that no one was watching them—slipped up the alley. Naturally enough (for the sun was setting) they ran straight against the omnibus.

"Good heavens!" exclaimed Mr. Bons. "Good gracious heavens!"

It was not the omnibus in which the boy had driven first, nor yet that in which he had returned. There were three horses—black, gray, and white, the gray being the finest. The driver, who turned round at the mention of goodness and of heaven, was a sallow man with terrifying jaws and sunken eyes. Mr. Bons, on seeing him, gave a cry as if of recognition, and began to tremble violently.

The boy jumped in.

"Is it possible?" cried Mr. Bons. "Is the impossible possible?"

"Sir; come in, sir. It is such a fine omnibus. Oh, here is his name—Dan some one."

Mr. Bons sprang in too. A blast of wind immediately slammed the omnibus door, and the shock jerked down all the omnibus blinds, which were very weak on their springs.

"Dan . . . Show me. Good gracious heavens! We're moving."

"Hooray!" said the boy.

Mr. Bons became flustered. He had not intended to be kidnapped. He could not find the door-handle, nor push up the blinds. The omnibus was quite dark, and by the time he had struck a match, night had come on outside also. They were moving rapidly.

"A strange, a memorable adventure," he said, surveying the interior of the omnibus, which was large, roomy, and constructed with extreme regularity, every part exactly answering to every other part. Over the door (the handle of which was outside) was written, "Lasciate ogni baldanza voi che entrate"—at least, that was what was written, but Mr. Bons said that it was Lashy arty something, and that baldanza was a mistake for speranza. His voice sounded as if he was in church. Meanwhile, the boy called to the cadaverous driver for two return tickets. They were handed in without a word. Mr. Bons covered his face with his hands and again trembled. "Do you know who that is!" he whispered, when the little window had shut upon them. "It is the impossible."

"Well, I don't like him as much as Sir Thomas Browne, though I shouldn't be surprised if he had even more in him."

"More in him?" He stamped irritably. "By accident you have made the greatest discovery of the century, and all you can say is that there is more in this man. Do you remember those vellum books in my library, stamped with red lilies, This—sit still, I bring you stupendous news!—*this is the man who wrote them.*"

The boy sat quite still. "I wonder if we shall see Mrs. Gamp?" he asked, after a civil pause.

"Mrs.———?"

"Mrs. Gamp and Mrs. Harris. I like Mrs. Harris. I came upon them quite suddenly. Mrs. Gamp's bandboxes have moved over the rainbow so badly. All the bottoms have fallen out, and two of the pippins off her bedstead tumbled into the stream."

"Out there sits the man who wrote my vellum books!" thundered Mr. Bons, "and you talk to me of Dickens and of Mrs. Gamp?"

"I know Mrs. Gamp so well," he apologized. "I could not help being glad to see her. I recognized her voice. She was telling Mrs. Harris about Mrs. Prig."

"Did you spend the whole day in her elevating company?"

"Oh, no. I raced. I met a man who took me out beyond to a race-course. You run, and there are dolphins out at sea."

"Indeed. Do you remember the man's name?"

"Achilles. No; he was later. Tom Jones."

Mr. Bons sighed heavily. "Well, my lad, you have made a miserable mess of it. Think of a cultured person with your opportunities! A cultured person would have known all these characters and known what to have said to each. He would not have wasted his time with a Mrs. Gamp or a Tom Jones. The creations of Homer, of Shakespeare, and of Him who drives us now, would alone have contented him. He would not have raced. He would have asked intelligent questions."

"But, Mr. Bons," said the boy humbly, "you will be a cultured person. I told them so."

"True, true, and I beg you not to disgrace me when we arrive. No gossiping. No running. Keep close to my side, and never speak to these Immortals unless they speak to you. Yes, and give me the return tickets. You will be losing them."

The boy surrendered the tickets, but felt a little sore. After all, he had found the way to this place. It was hard first to be disbelieved and then to be lectured. Meanwhile, the rain had stopped, and moonlight crept into the omnibus through the cracks in the blinds.

"But how is there to be a rainbow?" cried the boy.

"You distract me," snapped Mr. Bons. "I wish to meditate on beauty. I wish to goodness I was with a reverent and sympathetic person."

The lad bit his lip. He made a hundred good resolutions. He would imitate Mr. Bons all the visit. He would not laugh, or run, or sing, or do any of the vulgar things that must have disgusted his new friends last time. He would be very careful to pronounce their names properly, and to remember who knew whom. Achilles did not know Tom Jones—at least, so Mr. Bons said. The Duchess of Malfi was older than Mrs. Gamp—at least, so Mr. Bons said. He would be self-conscious, reticent, and prim. He would never say he liked any one. Yet, when the blind flew up at a chance touch of his head, all these good resolutions went to the winds, for the omnibus had reached the summit of a moonlit hill, and there was the chasm, and there, across it, stood the old precipices, dreaming, with their feet in the everlasting river. He exclaimed, "The mountain! Listen to the new tune in the water! Look at the camp fires in the ravines," and Mr. Bons, after a hasty glance, retorted, "Water? Camp fires? Ridiculous rubbish. Hold your tongue. There is nothing at all."

Yet, under his eyes, a rainbow formed, compounded not of sunlight and storm, but of moonlight and the spray of the river. The three horses put their feet upon it. He thought it the finest rainbow he had seen, but did not dare say so, since Mr. Bons said that nothing was there. He leant out—the window had opened—and sang the tune that rose from the sleeping waters.

"The prelude to Rhinegold?" said Mr. Bons suddenly. "Who taught you these *leit motifs?*" He, too, looked out of the window. Then he behaved very oddly. He gave a choking cry, and fell back on to the omnibus floor. He writhed and kicked. His face was green.

"Does the bridge make you dizzy?" the boy asked.

"Dizzy!" gasped Mr. Bons. "I want to go back. Tell the driver."

But the driver shook his head.

"We are nearly there," said the boy. "They are asleep. Shall I call? They will be so pleased to see you, for I have prepared them."

Mr. Bons moaned. They moved over the lunar rainbow, which ever and ever broke away behind their wheels. How still the night was! Who would be sentry at the Gate?

"I am coming," he shouted, again forgetting the hundred resolutions. "I am returning—I, the boy."

"The boy is returning," cried a voice to other voices, who repeated, "The boy is returning."

"I am bringing Mr. Bons with me."

Silence.

"I should have said Mr. Bons is bringing me with him."

Profound silence.

"Who stands sentry?"

"Achilles."

And on the rocky causeway, close to the springing of the rainbow bridge, he saw a young man who carried a wonderful shield.

"Mr. Bons, it is Achilles, armed."

"I want to go back," said Mr. Bons.

The last fragment of the rainbow melted, the wheels sang upon the living rock, the door of the omnibus burst open. Out leapt the boy—he could not resist—and sprang to meet the warrior, who, stooping suddenly, caught him on his shield.

"Achilles!" he cried, "let me get down, for I am ignorant and vulgar, and I must wait for that Mr. Bons of whom I told you yesterday."

But Achilles raised him aloft. He crouched on the wonderful shield, on heroes and burning cities, on vineyards graven in gold, on every dear passion, every joy, on the entire image of the Mountain that he had discovered, encircled, like it, with an everlasting stream. "No, no," he protested, "I am not worthy. It is Mr. Bons who must be up here."

But Mr. Bons was whimpering, and Achilles trumpeted and cried, "Stand upright upon my shield!"

"Sir, I did not mean to stand! Something made me stand. Sir, why do you delay? Here is only the great Achilles, whom you knew."

Mr. Bons screamed, "I see no one. I see nothing. I want to go back." Then he cried to the driver, "Save me! Let me stop in your chariot. I have honoured you. I have quoted you. I have bound you in vellum. Take me back to my world."

The driver replied, "I am the means and not the end. I am the food and not the life. Stand by yourself, as that boy has stood. I cannot save you. For poetry is a spirit; and they that would worship it must worship in spirit and in truth."

Mr. Bons—he could not resist—crawled out of the beautiful omnibus. His face appeared, gaping horribly. His hands followed, one gripping the step, the other beating the air. Now his shoulders emerged, his chest, his stomach. With a shriek of "I see London," he fell—fell against the hard, moonlit rock, fell into it as if it were water, fell though it, vanished, and was seen by the boy no more.

"Where have you fallen to, Mr. Bons? Here is a procession arriving to honour you with music and torches. Here come the men and women whose names you know. The mountain is awake, the river is awake, over the racecourse the sea is awaking those dolphins, and it is all for you. They want you——"

There was the touch of fresh leaves on his forehead. Some one had crowned him.

ΤΕΛΟΣ

From the *Kingston Gazette,*
Surbiton Times,
and *Raynes Park Observer.*

The body of Mr. Septimus Bons has been found in a shockingly mutilated condition in the vicinity of the Bermondsey gas-works. The deceased's pockets contained a sovereign-purse, a silver cigar-case, a bijou pronouncing dictionary, and a couple of omnibus tickets. The unfortunate gentleman had apparently been hurled from a considerable height. Foul play is suspected, and a thorough investigation is pending by the authorities.

[1908]

On Mortality

MAXINE HONG KINGSTON

As you know, any plain person you chance to meet can prove to be a powerful immortal in disguise come to test you.

Li Fu-yen told a story about Tu Tzu-chun, who lived from A.D. 558 to 618, during the Northern Chou and Sui dynasties. Tu's examiner was a Taoist monk, who made him rich twice, and twice Tu squandered his fortune though it took him two lifetimes to do so. The third time the Taoist gave him money, he bought a thousand li of good land, plowed it himself, seeded it, built houses, roads, and bridges, then welcomed widows and orphans to live on it. With the leftover money, he found a husband for each spinster and a wife for every bachelor in his family, and also paid for the weddings. When he met the Taoist again, he said, "I've used up all your money on the unfortunates I've come across."

"You'll have to repay me by working for me," said the Taoist monk. "I need your help on an important difficult task." He gave Tu three white pills. "Swallow these," he said, pouring him a cup of wine." All that you'll see and feel will be illusions. No matter what happens, don't speak; don't scream. Remember the saying, 'Hide your broken arms in your sleeves.' "

"How easy," said Tu as he swallowed the pills in three gulps of wine. "Why should I scream if I know they're illusions?"

Level by level he descended into the nine hells. At first he saw oxheads, horsefaces, and the heads of generals decapitated in war. Illusions. Only illusions, harmless. He laughed at the heads. He had seen heads before. Soon fewer heads whizzed through the dark until he saw no more of them.

Suddenly his wife was being tortured. Demons were cutting her up into pieces, starting with her toes. He heard her scream; he heard her bones crack. He reminded himself that she was an illusion. *Illusion*, he thought. She was ground into bloodmeal.

Then the tortures on his own body began. Demons poured bronze down his throat and beat him with iron clubs and chains. They mortar-and-pestled and packed him into a pill.

He had to walk over mountains of knives and through fields of knives and forests of swords. He was killed, his head chopped off, rolling into other people's nightmares.

He heard gods and goddesses talking about him, "This man is too wicked to be reborn a man. Let him be born a woman." He saw the entrance of a black tunnel and felt tired. He would have to squeeze his head and shoulders down into the enclosure and travel a long distance. He pushed head first through the entrance, only the beginning. A god kicked him in the butt to give him a move on. (This kick is the reason many Chinese babies have a blue-gray spot on their butts or lower backs, the "Mongolian spot.") Sometimes stuck in the tunnel, sometimes shooting helplessly through it, he emerged again into light with many urgent things to do, many messages to deliver, but his hands were useless baby's hands, his legs wobbly baby's legs, his voice a wordless baby's cries. Years had to pass before he could regain adult powers; he howled as he began to forget the cosmos, his attention taken up with mastering how to crawl, how to stand, how to walk, how to control his bowel movements.

He discovered that he had been reborn a deaf-mute female named Tu. When she became a woman, her parents married her to a man named Lu, who at first did not mind. "Why does she need to talk," said Lu, "to be a good wife? Let her set an example for women." They had a child. But years later, Lu tired of Tu's dumbness. "You're just being stubborn," he said, and lifted their child by the feet. "Talk, or I'll dash its head against the rocks." The poor mother held her hand to her mouth. Lu swung the child, broke its head against the wall.

Tu shouted out, "Oh! Oh!"—and he was back with the Taoist, who sadly told him that at the moment when she said, "Oh! Oh!" the Taoist was about to complete the last step in making the elixir for immortality. Now that Tu had broken his silence, the formula was spoiled, no immortality for the human race. "You overcame joy and sorrow, anger, fear, and evil desire, but not love," said the Taoist, and went on his way.

The Silver Crown

BERNARD MALAMUD

Gans, the father, lay dying in a hospital bed. Different doctors said different things, held different theories. There was talk of an exploratory operation but they thought it might kill him. One doctor said cancer.

"Of the heart," the old man said bitterly.

"It wouldn't be impossible."

The young Gans, Albert, a high school biology teacher, in the afternoons walked the streets in sorrow. What can anybody do about cancer? His soles wore thin with walking. He was easily irritated; angered by the war, atom bomb, pollution, death, obviously the strain of worrying about his father's illness. To be able to do nothing for him made him frantic. He had done nothing for him all his life.

A female colleague, an English teacher he had slept with once, a girl who was visibly aging, advised, "If the doctors don't know, Albert, try a faith healer. Different people know different things; nobody knows everything. You can't tell about the human body."

Albert laughed mirthlessly but listened. If specialists disagree who do you agree with? If you've tried everything what else can you try?

One afternoon after a long walk alone, as he was about to descend the subway stairs somewhere in the Bronx, still burdened by his worries, uneasy that nothing had changed, he was accosted by a fat girl with bare meaty arms who thrust a soiled card at him that he tried to avoid. She was a stupefying sight, retarded at the very least. Fifteen, he'd say, though she looks thirty and probably has the mentality of age ten. Her skin glowed, face wet, fleshy, the small mouth open and would be forever; eyes set wide apart on the broad unfocused face, either washed-out green or brown, or one of each—he wasn't sure. She seemed not to mind his appraisal, gurgled faintly. Her thick hair was braided in two ropelike strands; she wore bulging cloth slippers, bursting at seams and soles; a faded red skirt down to massive ankles; and a heavy brown sweater vest, buttoned over blown breasts, though the weather was still hot September.

The teacher's impulse was to pass by her outthrust plump baby hand. Instead he took the card from her. Simple curiosity—once you had learned to read you read anything? Charitable impulse?

Albert recognized Yiddish and Hebrew but read in English: "Heal The Sick. Save The Dying. Make A Silver Crown."

"What kind of silver crown would that be?"

She uttered impossible noises. Depressed, he looked away. When his eyes turned to hers she ran off.

He studied the card. "Make A Silver Crown." It gave a rabbi's name and address no less: Jonas Lifschitz, close by in the neighborhood. The silver crown mystified him. He had no idea what it had to do with saving the dying but felt he ought to know. Although at first repelled by the thought, he made up his mind to visit the rabbi and felt, in a way, relieved.

The teacher hastened along the street a few blocks until he came to the address on the card, a battered synagogue in a store, Congregation Theodor Herzl, painted in large uneven white letters on the plate-glass window. The rabbi's name, in smaller, gold letters, was A. Marcus. In the doorway to the left of the store the number of the house was repeated in tin numerals, and on a card under the vacant name plate under the mezuzah, appeared in pencil, "Rabbi J. Lifschitz. Retired. Consultations. Ring The Bell." The bell, when he decided to chance it, did not work—seemed dead to the touch—so Albert, his heartbeat erratic, turned the knob. The door gave easily enough and he hesitantly walked up a dark flight of narrow wooden stairs. Ascending, assailed by doubts, peering up through the gloom, he thought of turning back but at the first-floor landing compelled himself to knock loudly on the door.

"Anybody home here?"

He rapped harder, annoyed with himself for being there, engaging in the act of entrance—who would have predicted it an hour ago? The door opened a crack and that broad, badly formed face appeared. The retarded girl, squinting one bulbous eye, made noises like two eggs frying, and ducked back, slamming the door. The teacher, after momentary reflection, thrust it open in time to see her, bulky as she was, running swiftly along the long tight corridor, her body bumping the walls before she disappeared into a room at the rear.

Albert entered cautiously, with a sense of embarrassment, if not danger, warning himself to depart at once; yet stayed to peek curiously into a front room off the hallway, darkened by lowered green shades through which thread-like rivulets of light streamed. The shades resembled faded maps of ancient lands. An old gray-bearded man with thickened left eyelid, wearing a yarmulke, sat heavily asleep, a book in his lap, on a sagging armchair. Someone in the room gave off a stale odor, unless it was the armchair. As Albert stared, the old man awoke in a hurry. The small thick book on his lap fell with a thump to the floor, but instead of picking it up, he shoved it with a kick of his heel under the chair.

"So where were we?" he inquired pleasantly, a bit breathless.

The teacher removed his hat, remembered whose house he was in, and put it back on his head.

He introduced himself. "I was looking for Rabbi J. Lifschitz. Your—ah—girl let me in."

"Rabbi Lifschitz; this was my daughter Rifkele. She's not perfect, though God who made her in His image is Himself perfection. What this means I don't have to tell you."

His heavy eyelid went down in a wink, apparently involuntarily.

"What does it mean?" Albert asked.

"In her way she is also perfect."

"Anyway she let me in and here I am."

"So what did you decide?"

"Concerning what if I may ask?"

"What did you decide about what we were talking about—the silver crown?"

His eyes roved as he spoke; he rubbed a nervous thumb and forefinger. Crafty type, the teacher decided. Him I have to watch myself with.

"I came here to find out about this crown you advertised," he said, "but actually we haven't talked about it or anything else. When I entered here you were sound asleep."

"At my age—" the rabbi explained with a little laugh.

"I don't mean any criticism. All I'm saying is I am a stranger to you."

"How can we be strangers if we both believe in God?"

Albert made no argument of it.

The rabbi raised the two shades and the last of daylight fell into the spacious high-ceilinged room, crowded with at least a dozen stiff-back and folding chairs, plus a broken sofa. What kind of operation is he running here? Group consultations? He dispensed rabbinic therapy? The teacher felt renewed distaste for himself for having come. On the wall hung a single oval mirror, framed in gold-plated groupings of joined metal circles, large and small; but no pictures. Despite the empty chairs, or perhaps because of them, the room seemed barren.

The teacher observed that the rabbi's trousers were a week from ragged. He was wearing an unpressed worn black suit-coat and a yellowed white shirt without a tie. His wet grayish-blue eyes were restless. Rabbi Lifschitz was a dark-faced man with brown eye pouches and smelled of old age. This was the odor. It was hard to say whether he resembled his daughter; Rifkele resembled her species.

"So sit," said the old rabbi with a light sigh. "Not on the couch, sit on a chair."

"Which in particular?"

"You have a first-class humor." Smiling absently he pointed to two kitchen chairs and seated himself in one.

He offered a thin cigarette.

"I'm off them," the teacher explained.

"I also." The old man put the pack away. "So who is sick?" he inquired.

Albert tightened at the question as he recalled the card he had taken from the girl: "Heal The Sick, Save The Dying."

"To come to the point, my father's in the hospital with a serious ailment. In fact he's dying."

The rabbi, nodding gravely, dug into his pants pocket for a pair of glasses, wiped them with a large soiled handkerchief and put them on, lifting the wire earpieces over each fleshy ear.

"So we will make then a crown for him?"

"That depends. The crown is what I came here to find out about."

"What do you wish to find out?"

"I'll be frank with you." The teacher blew his nose and slowly wiped it. "My cast of mind is naturally empiric and objective—you might say nonmystical. I'm suspicious of faith healing but I've come here, frankly, because I want to do anything possible to help my father recover his former health. To put it otherwise, I don't want anything to go untried."

"You love your father?" the rabbi clucked, a glaze of sentiment veiling his eyes.

"What I feel is obvious. My real concern right now mainly is how does the crown work. Could you be explicit about the mechanism of it all? Who wears it, for instance? Does he? Do you? Or do I have to? In other words, how does it function? And if you wouldn't mind saying, what's the principle, or rationale, behind it? This is terra incognita for me, but I think I might be willing to take a chance if I could justify it to myself. Could I see a sample of the crown, for instance, if you have one on hand?"

The rabbi, with an absent-minded start, seemed to interrupt himself about to pick his nose.

"What is the crown?" he asked, at first haughtily, then again, gently. "It's a crown, nothing else. There are crowns in Mishna, Proverbs, Kabbalah; the holy scrolls of the Torah are often protected by crowns. But this one is different, this you will understand when it does the work. It's a miracle. A sample doesn't exist. The crown has to be made individual for your father. Then his health will be restored. There are two prices—"

"Kindly explain what's supposed to cure the sickness," Albert said. "Does it work like sympathetic magic? I'm not nay-saying, you understand. I just happen to be interested in all kinds of phenomena. Is the crown supposed to draw off the illness like some kind of poultice, or what?"

"The crown is not a medicine, it is the health of your father. We offer the crown to God and God returns to your father his health. But first we got to make it the way it must be made—this I will do with my assistant, a retired jeweler. He has helped me to make a thousand crowns. Believe me, he knows silver—the right amount to the ounce according to the size you wish. Then I will say the blessings. Without the right blessings, exact to each word, the crown don't work. I don't have to tell you why. When the crown is finished your father will get better. This I will guarantee you. Let me read you some words from the mystic book."

"The Kabbalah?" the teacher asked respectfully.

"Like the Kabbalah."

The rabbi rose, went to his armchair, got slowly down on his hands and knees and withdrew the book he had shoved under the misshapen chair, a thick small volume with faded purple covers, not a word imprinted on it. The rabbi kissed the book and murmured a prayer.

"I hid it for a minute," he explained, "when you came in the room. It's a terrible thing nowadays, goyim come in your house in the middle of the day and take away that which belongs to you, if not your life itself."

"I told you right away that your daughter had let me in," Albert said in embarrassment.

"Once you mentioned I knew."

The teacher then asked, "Suppose I am a non-believer? Will the crown work if it's ordered by a person who has his doubts?"

"Doubts we all got. We doubt God and God doubts us. This is natural on account of the nature of existence. Of this kind doubts I am not afraid so long as you love your father."

"You're putting it as sort of a paradox."

"So what's so bad about a paradox?"

"My father wasn't the easiest man in the world to get along with, and neither am I for that matter, but he has been generous to me and I'd like to repay him in some way."

"God respects a grateful son. If you love your father this will go in the crown and help him to recover his health. Do you understand Hebrew?"

"Unfortunately not."

The rabbi flipped a few pages of his thick tome, peered at one closely and read aloud in Hebrew which he then translated into English. " 'The crown is the fruit of God's grace. His grace is love of creation.' These words I will read seven times over the silver crown. This is the most important blessing."

"Fine. But what about those two prices you mentioned a minute ago?"

"This depends how quick you wish the cure."

"I want the cure to be immediate, otherwise there's no sense to the whole deal," Albert said, controlling anger. "If you're questioning my sincerity, I've already told you I'm considering this recourse even though it goes against the grain of some of my strongest convictions. I've gone out of my way to make my pros and cons absolutely clear."

"Who says no?"

The teacher became aware of Rifkele standing at the door, eating a slice of bread with lumps of butter on it. She beheld him in mild stupefaction, as though seeing him for the first time.

"Shpeter, Rifkele," the rabbi said patiently.

The girl shoved the bread into her mouth and ran ponderously down the passageway.

"Anyway, what about those two prices?" Albert asked, annoyed by the interruption. Every time Rifkele appeared his doubts of the enterprise rose before him like warriors with spears.

"We got two kinds crowns," said the rabbi. "One is for 401 and the other is 986."

"Dollars, you mean, for God's sake?—that's fantastic."

"The crown is pure silver. The client pays in silver dollars. So the silver dollars we melt—more for the large-size crown, less for the medium."

"What about the small?"

"There is no small. What good is a small crown?"

"I wouldn't know, but the assumption seems to be the bigger the better. Tell me, please, what can a 986 crown do that a 401 can't? Does the patient get better faster with the larger one? It hastens the reaction?"

The rabbi, five fingers hidden in his limp beard, assented.

"Are there any other costs?"

"Costs?"

"Over and above the quoted prices?"

"The price is the price, there is no extra. The price is for the silver and for the work and for the blessings."

"Now would you kindly tell me, assuming I decide to get involved in this, where am I supposed to lay my hands on 401 silver dollars? Or if I should opt for the 986 job, where can I get a pile of cartwheels of that amount? I don't suppose that any bank in the whole Bronx would keep that many silver dollars on hand nowadays. The Bronx is no longer the Wild West, Rabbi Lifschitz. But what's more to the point, isn't it true the mint isn't making silver dollars all silver any more?"

"So if they are not making we will get wholesale. If you will leave with me the cash I will order the silver from a wholesaler, and we will save you the trouble to go to the bank. It will be the same amount of silver, only in small bars, I will weigh them on a scale in front of your eyes."

"One other question. Would you take my personal check in payment? I could give it to you right away once I've made my final decision."

"I wish I could, Mr. Gans," said the rabbi, his veined hand still nervously exploring his beard, "but it's better cash when the patient is so sick, so I can start to work right away. A check sometimes comes back, or gets lost in the bank, and this interferes with the crown."

Albert did not ask how, suspecting that a bounced check, or a lost one, wasn't the problem. No doubt some customers for crowns had stopped their checks on afterthought.

As the teacher reflected concerning his next move—should he, shouldn't he?—weighing a rational thought against a sentimental, the old rabbi sat in his chair, reading quickly in his small mystic book, his lips hastening along silently.

Albert at last got up.

"I'll decide the question once and for all tonight. If I go ahead and commit myself on the crown I'll bring you the cash after work tomorrow."

"Go in good health," said the rabbi. Removing his glasses he wiped both eyes with his handkerchief.

Wet or dry? thought the teacher.

As he let himself out of the downstairs door, more inclined than not toward trying the crown, he felt relieved, almost euphoric.

But by the next morning, after a difficult night, Albert's mood had about-faced. He fought gloom, irritation, felt flashes of hot and cold anger. It's throwing money away, pure and simple. I'm dealing with a clever confidence man, that's plain to me, but for some reason I am not resisting strongly. Maybe my subconscious is telling me to go along with a blowing wind and have the crown made. After that we'll see what happens—whether it rains, snows, or spring comes. Not much will happen, I suppose, but whatever does, my conscience will be in the clear.

But when he visited Rabbi Lifschitz that afternoon in the same roomful of empty chairs, though the teacher carried the required cash in his wallet, he was still uncomfortable about parting with it.

"Where do the crowns go after they are used and the patient recovers his health?" he cleverly asked the rabbi.

"I'm glad you asked me this question," said the rabbi alertly, his thick lid drooping. "They are melted and the silver we give to the poor. A mitzvah for one makes a mitzvah for another."

"To the poor you say?"

"There are plenty poor people, Mr. Gans. Sometimes they need a crown for a sick wife or a sick child. Where will they get the silver?"

"I see what you mean—recycled, sort of, but can't a crown be re-used as it is? I mean do you permit a period of time to go by before you melt them down? Suppose a dying man who recovers gets seriously ill again at a future date?"

"For a new sickness you will need a new crown. Tomorrow the world is not the same as today, though God listens with the same ear."

"Look, Rabbi Lifschitz," Albert said impatiently, "I'll tell you frankly that I am inching toward ordering the crown, but it would make my decision a whole lot easier all around if you would let me have a quick look at one of them—it wouldn't have to be for more than five seconds—at a crown-in-progress for some other client."

"What will you see in five seconds?"

"Enough—whether the object is believable, worth the fuss and not inconsequential investment."

"Mr. Gans," replied the rabbi, "this is not a showcase business. You are not buying from me a new Chevrolet automobile. Your father lays now dying in the hospital. Do you love him? Do you wish me to make a crown that will cure him?"

The teacher's anger flared. "Don't be stupid, rabbi, I've answered that. Please don't sidetrack the real issue. You're working on my guilt so I'll suspend my perfectly reasonable doubts of the whole freaking business. I won't fall for that."

They glared at each other. The rabbi's beard quivered. Albert ground his teeth.

Rifkele, in a nearby room, moaned.

The rabbi, breathing emotionally, after a moment relented.

"I will show you the crown," he sighed.

"Accept my apologies for losing my temper."

The rabbi accepted. "Now tell me please what kind of sickness your father has got."

"Ah," said Albert, "nobody is certain for sure. One day he got into bed, turned to the wall and said, 'I'm sick.' They suspected leukemia at first but the lab tests didn't confirm it."

"You talked to the doctors?"

"In droves. Till I was blue in the face. A bunch of ignoramuses," said the teacher hoarsely. "Anyway, nobody knows exactly what he has wrong with him. The theories include rare blood diseases, also a possible carcinoma of certain endocrine glands. You name it, I've heard it, with complications suggested, like Parkinson's or Addison's disease, multiple sclerosis, or something similar, alone or in combination with other sicknesses. It's a mysterious case, all in all."

"This means you will need a special crown," said the rabbi.

The teacher bridled. "What do you mean special? What will it cost?"

"The cost will be the same," the rabbi answered dryly, "but the design and the kind of blessings will be different. When you are dealing with such a mystery you got to make another one but it must be bigger."

"How would that work?"

"Like two winds that they meet in the sky. A white and a blue. The blue says, 'Not only I am blue but inside I am also purple and orange.' So the white goes away."

"If you can work it up for the same price, that's up to you."

Rabbi Lifschitz then drew down the two green window shades and shut the door, darkening the room.

"Sit," he said in the heavy dark, "I will show you the crown."

"I'm sitting."

"So sit where you are, but turn your head to the wall where is the mirror."

"But why so dark?"

"You will see light."

He heard the rabbi strike a match and it flared momentarily, casting shadows of candles and chairs amid the empty chairs in the room.

"Look now in the mirror."

"I'm looking."

"What do you see?"

"Nothing."

"Look with your eyes."

A silver candelabrum, first with three, then five, then seven burning bony candlesticks appeared like ghostly hands with flaming fingertips in the oval mirror. The heat of it hit Albert in the face and for a moment he was stunned.

But recalling the games of his childhood, he thought, who's kidding who? It's one of those illusion things I remember from when I was a kid. In that case I'm getting the hell out of here. I can stand maybe mystery but not magic tricks or dealing with a rabbinical magician.

The candelabrum had vanished, although not its light, and he now saw the rabbi's somber face in the glass, his gaze addressing him. Albert glanced quickly around to see if anyone was standing at his shoulder, but nobody was. Where the rabbi was hiding at the moment the teacher did not know; but in the lit glass appeared his old man's lined and shrunken face, his sad eyes, compelling, inquisitive, weary, perhaps even frightened, as though they had seen more than they had cared to but were still looking.

What's this, slides or home movies? Albert sought some source of projection but saw no ray of light from wall or ceiling, nor object or image that might be reflected by the mirror.

The rabbi's eyes glowed like sun-filled clouds. A moon rose in the blue sky. The teacher dared not move, afraid to discover he was unable to. He then beheld a shining crown on the rabbi's head.

It had appeared at first like a braided mother-of-pearl turban, then had luminously become—like an intricate star in the night sky—a silver crown, constructed of bars, triangles, half-moons and crescents, spires, turrets, trees, points of spears; as though a wild storm had swept them up from the earth and flung them together in its vortex, twisted into a single glowing interlocked sculpture, a forest of disparate objects.

The sight in the ghostly mirror, a crown of rare beauty—very impressive, Albert thought—lasted no longer than five short seconds, then the reflecting glass by degrees turned dark and empty.

The shades were up. The single bulb in a frosted lily fixture on the ceiling shone harshly in the room. It was night.

The old rabbi sat, exhausted, on the broken sofa.

"So you saw it?"

"I saw something."

"You believe what you saw—the crown?"

"I believe I saw. Anyway, I'll take it."

The rabbi gazed at him blankly.

"I mean I agree to have the crown made," Albert said, having to clear his throat.

"Which size?"

"Which size was the one I saw?"

"Both sizes. This is the same design for both sizes, but there is more silver and also more blessings for the $986 size."

"But didn't you say that the design for my father's crown, because of the special nature of his illness, would have a different style, plus some special blessings?"

The rabbi nodded. "This comes also in two sizes—the $401 and $986."

The teacher hesitated a split second. "Make it the big one," he said decisively.

He had his wallet in his hand and counted out fifteen new bills—nine one hundreds, four twenties, a five and a single—adding to $986.

Putting on his glasses, the rabbi hastily counted the money, snapping with thumb and forefinger each crisp bill as though to be sure none had stuck together. He folded the stiff paper and thrust the wad into his pants pocket.

"Could I have a receipt?"

"I would like to give you a receipt," said Rabbi Lifschitz earnestly, "but for the crowns there are no receipts. Some things are not a business."

"If money is exchanged, why not?"

"God will not allow. My father did not give receipts and also my grandfather."

"How can I prove I paid you if something goes wrong?"

"You have my word, nothing will go wrong."

"Yes, but suppose something unforeseen did," Albert insisted, "would you return the cash?"

"Here is your cash," said the rabbi, handing the teacher the packet of folded bills.

"Never mind," said Albert hastily. "Could you tell me when the crown will be ready?"

"Tomorrow night before Shabbos, the latest."

"So soon?"

"Your father is dying."

"That's right, but the crown looks like a pretty intricate piece of work to put together out of all those odd pieces."

"We will hurry."

"I wouldn't want you to rush the job in any way that would—let's say—prejudice the potency of the crown, or for that matter, in any way impair the quality of it as I saw it in the mirror—or however I saw it."

Down came the rabbi's eyelid, quickly raised without a sign of self-consciousness.

"Mr. Gans, all my crowns are first-class jobs. About this you got nothing to worry about."

They then shook hands. Albert, still assailed by doubts, stepped into the corridor. He felt he did not, in essence, trust the rabbi; and suspected that Rabbi Lifschitz knew it and did not, in essence, trust him.

Rifkele, panting like a cow for a bull, let him out the front door, perfectly.

In the subway, Albert figured he would call it an investment in experience and see what came of it. Education costs money but how else can you get it? He pictured the crown as he had seen it established on the rabbi's head, and then seemed to remember that as he had stared at the man's shifty face in the mirror the thickened lid of his right eye had slowly dropped into a full wink. Did he recall this in truth, or was he seeing in his mind's eye and transposing into the past something that had happened just before he left the house? What does he mean by his wink?—not only is he a fake but he kids you? Uneasy once more, the teacher clearly remembered, when he was staring into the rabbi's fish eyes in the glass, after which they had lit in visionary light, that he had fought a hunger to sleep; and the next thing there's the sight of the old boy, as though on the television screen, wearing this high-hat magic crown.

Albert, rising, cried, "Hypnosis! The bastard magician hypnotized me! He never did produce a silver crown, it's out of my imagination—I've been suckered!"

He was outraged by the knavery, hypocrisy, fat nerve of Rabbi Jonas Lifschitz. The concept of a curative crown, if he had ever for a moment believed in it, crumbled in his brain and all he could think of were 986 blackbirds flying in the sky. As three curious passengers watched, Albert bolted out of the car at the next stop, rushed up the stairs, hurried across the street, then cooled his impatient heels for twenty-two minutes till the next train clattered into the station, and he rode back to the stop near the rabbi's house. Though he banged with both fists on the door, kicked at it, "rang" the useless bell until his thumb was blistered, the boxlike wooden house, including dilapidated synagogue store, was dark, monumentally starkly still, like a gigantic, slightly tilted tombstone in a vast graveyard; and in the end unable to arouse a soul, the teacher, long past midnight, had to head home.

He awoke next morning cursing the rabbi and his own stupidity for having got involved with a faith healer. This is what happens when a man—even for a minute—surrenders his true beliefs. There are less punishing ways to help the dying. Albert considered calling the cops but had no receipt and did not want to appear that much a fool. He was tempted, for the first time in six years of teaching, to phone in sick; then take a cab to the rabbi's house and demand the return of his cash. The thought agitated him. On the other hand, suppose Rabbi Lifschitz was seriously at work assembling the crown with his helper; on which, let's say, after he had bought the silver and paid the retired jeweler for his work, he made, let's say, a hundred bucks clear profit—not so very much; and there really *was* a silver crown, and the rabbi sincerely and religiously believed it would reverse the course of his father's illness? Although nervously disturbed by his suspicions, Albert felt he had better not get the police into the act too soon because the crown wasn't promised—didn't the old gent say—until before the Sabbath, which gave him till sunset tonight.

If he produces the thing by then, I have no case against him even if it's a piece of junk. So I better wait. But what a dope I was to order the $986 job instead of the $401. On that decision alone I lost $585.

After a distracted day's work Albert taxied to the rabbi's house and tried to rouse him, even hallooing at the blank windows facing the street; but either nobody was home or they were both hiding, the rabbi under the broken sofa, Rifkele trying to shove her bulk under a bathtub. Albert decided to wait them out. Soon the old boy would have to leave the house to step into the shul on Friday night. He would speak to him, warn him to come clean. But the sun set; dusk settled on the earth; and though the autumn stars and a sliver of moon gleamed in the sky, the house was dark, shades drawn; and no Rabbi Lifschitz emerged. Lights had gone on in the little shul, candles were lit. It occurred to Albert, with chagrin, that the rabbi might be already worshipping; he might all this time have been in the synagogue.

The teacher entered the long, brightly lit store. On yellow folding chairs scattered around the room sat a dozen men holding worn prayer books, praying. The Rabbi A. Marcus, a middle-aged man with a high voice and a short reddish beard, was dovening at the Ark, his back to the congregation.

As Albert entered and embarrassedly searched from face to face, the congregants stared at him. The old rabbi was not among them. Disappointed, the teacher withdrew.

A man sitting by the door touched his sleeve.

"Stay awhile and read with us."

"Excuse me, I'd like to but I'm looking for a friend."

"Look," said the man, "maybe you'll find him."

Albert waited across the street under a chestnut tree losing its leaves. He waited patiently—till tomorrow if he had to.

Shortly after nine the lights went out in the synagogue and the last of the worshippers left for home. The red-bearded rabbi then emerged with his key in his hand to lock the store door.

"Excuse me, rabbi," said Albert, approaching. "Are you acquainted with Rabbi Jonas Lifschitz, who lives upstairs with his daughter Rifkele—if she is his daughter?"

"He used to come here," said the rabbi with a small smile, "but since he retired he prefers a big synagogue on Mosholu Parkway, a palace."

"Will he be home soon, do you think?"

"Maybe in an hour. It's Shabbat, he must walk."

"Do you—ah—happen to know anything about his work on silver crowns?"

"What kind of silver crowns?"

"To assist the sick, the dying?"

"No," said the rabbi, locking the shul door, pocketing the key, and hurrying away.

The teacher, eating his heart, waited under the chestnut tree till past midnight, all the while urging himself to give up and go home but unable to unstick the glue of his frustration and rage. Then shortly before 1 A.M. he saw some shadows moving and two people drifting up the shadow-encrusted street. One was the old rabbi, in a new caftan and snappy black Homburg, walking tiredly. Rifkele, in sexy yellow mini, exposing to above the big-bone knees her legs like poles, walked lightly behind him, stopping to strike her ears with her hands. A long white shawl, pulled short on the right shoulder, hung down to her left shoe.

"On my income their glad rags."

Rifkele chanted a long "boooo" and slapped both ears with her pudgy hands to keep from hearing it.

They toiled up the ill-lit narrow staircase, the teacher trailing them.

"I came to see my crown," he told the pale, astonished rabbi, in the front room.

"The crown," the rabbi said haughtily, "is already finished. Go home and wait, your father will soon get better."

"I called the hospital before leaving my apartment, there's been no improvement."

"How can you expect so soon improvement if the doctors themselves don't know what is the sickness? You must give the crown a little more time. God Himself has trouble to understand human sickness."

"I came to see the thing I paid for."

"I showed you already, you saw before you ordered."

"That was an image of a facsimile, maybe, or something of the sort. I insist on seeing the real thing, for which I paid close to one thousand smackers."

"Listen, Mr. Gans," said the rabbi patiently, "there are some things we are allowed to see which He lets us see them. Sometimes I wish He didn't let us. There are other things we are not allowed to see—Moses knew this—and one is God's face, and another is the real crown that He makes and blesses it. A miracle is a miracle, this is God's business."

"Don't you see it?"

"Not with my eyes."

"I don't believe a word of it, you faker, two-bit magician."

"The crown is a real crown. If you think there is magic, it is on account those people that they insist to see it—we try to give them an idea. For those who believe, there is no magic."

"Rifkele," the rabbi said hurriedly, "bring to Papa my book of letters."

She left the room, after a while, a little in fright, her eyes evasive; and returned in ten minutes, after flushing the toilet, in a shapeless long flannel nightgown, carrying a large yellowed notebook whose loose pages were thickly interleaved with old correspondence.

"Testimonials," said the rabbi.

Turning several loose pages, with trembling hand he extracted a letter and read it aloud, his voice husky with emotion.

" 'Dear Rabbi Lifschitz: Since the miraculous recovery of my mother, Mrs. Max Cohen, from her recent illness, my impulse is to cover your bare feet with kisses. Your crown worked wonders and I am recommending it to all my friends. Yours truly and sincerely, (Mrs.) Esther Polatnik.' "

"This is a college teacher."

He read another. " 'Dear Rabbi Lifschitz, Your $986 crown totally and completely cured my father of cancer of the pancreas, with serious complications of the lungs, after nothing else had worked. Never before have I believed in miraculous occurrences, but from now on I will have less doubts. My thanks to you and God. Most sincerely, Daniel Schwartz.' "

"A lawyer," said the rabbi.

He offered the book to Albert. "Look yourself, Mr. Gans, hundreds of letters."

Albert wouldn't touch it.

"There's only one thing I want to look at, Rabbi Lifschitz, and it's not a book of useless testimonials. I want to see my father's silver crown."

"This is impossible. I already explained to you why I can't do this. God's word is God's law."

"So if it's the law you're citing, either I see the crown in the next five minutes, or the first thing tomorrow morning I'm reporting you and your activities to the Bronx County District Attorney."

"Booo-ooo," sang Rifkele, banging her ears.

"Shut up!" Albert said.

"Have respect," cried the rabbi. "Grubber yung!"

"I will swear out a complaint and the D.A. will shut you down, the whole freaking plant, if you don't at once return the $986 you swindled me out of."

The rabbi wavered in his tracks. "Is this the way to talk to a rabbi of God?"

"A thief is a thief."

Rifkele blubbered, squealed.

"Sha," the rabbi thickly whispered to Albert, clasping and unclasping his gray hands. "You'll frighten the neighbors. Listen to me, Mr. Gans, you saw with your eyes what it looks like the real crown. I give you my word that nobody of my whole clientele ever saw this before. I showed you for your father's sake so you would tell me to make the crown which will save him. Don't spoil now the miracle."

"Miracle," Albert bellowed, "it's a freaking fake magic, with an idiot girl for a come-on and hypnotic mirrors. I was mesmerized, suckered by you."

"Be kind," begged the rabbi, tottering as he wandered amid empty chairs. "Be merciful to an old man. Think of my poor child. Think of your father who loves you."

"He hates me, the son-of-a-bitch, I hope he croaks."

In an explosion of silence the girl slobbered in fright.

"Aha," cried the wild-eyed rabbi, pointing a finger at God in heaven.

"Murderer," he cried, aghast.

Moaning, father and daughter rushed into each other's arms, as Albert, wearing a massive, spike-laden headache, rushed down the booming stairs.

An hour later the elder Gans shut his eyes and expired.

The Man in the Black Suit

STEPHEN KING

I am now a very old man and this is something that happened to me when I was very young—only nine years old. It was 1914, the summer after my brother, Dan, died in the west field and not long before America got into the First World War. I've never told anyone about what happened at the fork in the stream that day, and I never will. I've decided to write it down, though, in this book, which I will leave on the table beside my bed. I can't write long, because my hands shake so these days and I have next to no strength, but I don't think it will take long.

Later, someone may find what I have written. That seems likely to me, as it is pretty much human nature to look in a book marked "Diary" after its owner has passed along. So, yes—my words will probably be read. A better question is whether anyone will believe them. Almost certainly not, but that doesn't matter. It's not belief I'm interested in but freedom. Writing can give that, I've found. For twenty years I wrote a column called "Long Ago and Far Away" for the Castle Rock *Call*, and I know that sometimes it works that way—what you write down sometimes leaves you forever, like old photographs left in the bright sun, fading to nothing but white.

I pray for that sort of release.

A man in his eighties should be well past the terrors of childhood, but as my infirmities slowly creep up on me, like waves licking closer and closer to some indifferently built castle of sand, that terrible face grows clearer and clearer in my mind's eye. It glows like a dark star in the constellations of my childhood. What I might have done yesterday, who I might have seen here in my room at the nursing home, what I might have said to them or they to me—those things are gone, but the face of the man in the black suit grows ever clearer, ever closer, and I remember every word he said. I don't want to think of him but I can't help it, and sometimes at night my old heart beats so hard and so fast I think it will tear itself right clear of my chest. So I uncap my fountain pen and force my trembling old hand to write this pointless anecdote in the diary one of my great-grandchildren—I can't remember her name for sure, at least not right now, but I know it starts with an "S"—gave to me last Christmas, and which I have never written in until now. Now I will write in it. I will write the story of how I met the man in the black suit on the bank of Castle Stream one afternoon in the summer of 1914.

The town of Motton was a different world in those days—more different than I could ever tell you. That was a world without airplanes droning overhead, a world almost without cars and trucks, a world where the skies were not cut into lanes and slices by overhead power lines. There was not a single paved road in the whole town, and the business district consisted of nothing but Corson's General Store, Thut's Livery & Hardware, the Methodist church at Christ's Corner, the school, the town hall, and half a mile down from there, Harry's Restaurant, which my mother called, with unfailing disdain, "the liquor house."

Mostly, though, the difference was in how people lived—how *apart* they were. I'm not sure people born after the middle of the century could quite credit that, although they might say they could, to be polite to old folks like me. There were no phones in western Maine back then, for one thing. The first one wouldn't be installed for another five years, and by the time there was a phone in our house, I was nineteen and going to college at the University of Maine in Orono.

But that is only the roof of the thing. There was no doctor closer than Casco, and there were no more than a dozen houses in what you would call town. There were no neighborhoods (I'm not even sure we knew the word, although we had a verb—"neighboring"—that described church functions and barn dances), and open fields were the exception rather than the rule. Out of town the houses were farms that stood far apart from each other, and from December until the middle of March we mostly hunkered down in the little pockets of stove warmth we called families. We hunkered and listened to the wind in the chimney and hoped no one would get sick or break a leg or get a headful of bad ideas, like the farmer over in Castle Rock who had chopped up his wife and kids three winters before and then said in court that the ghosts made him do it. In those days before the Great War, most of Motton was woods and bog—dark long places full of moose and mosquitoes, snakes and secrets. In those days there were ghosts everywhere.

This thing I'm telling about happened on a Saturday. My father gave me a whole list of chores to do, including some that would have been Dan's, if he'd still been alive. He was my only brother, and he'd died of a bee sting. A year had gone by, and still my mother wouldn't hear that. She said it was something else, *had* to have been, that no one ever died of being stung by a bee. When Mama Sweet, the oldest lady in the Methodist Ladies' Aid, tried to tell her—at the church supper the previous winter, this was—that the same thing had happened to her favorite uncle back in '73, my mother clapped her hands over her ears, got up, and walked out of the church basement. She'd never been back since, and nothing my father could say to her would change her mind. She claimed she was done with church, and that if she ever had to see Helen Robichaud again (that was Mama Sweet's real name) she would slap her eyes out. She wouldn't be able to help herself, she said.

That day Dad wanted me to lug wood for the cookstove, weed the beans and the cukes, pitch hay out of the loft, get two jugs of water to put in the cold pantry, and scrape as much old paint off the cellar bulkhead as I could. Then, he said, I could go fishing, if I didn't mind going by myself—he had to go over and see Bill Eversham about some cows. I said I sure didn't mind going by myself, and my dad smiled as if that didn't surprise him so very much. He'd given me a bamboo pole the week before—not because it was my birthday or anything but just because he liked to give me things sometimes—and I was wild to try it in Castle Stream, which was by far the troutiest brook I'd ever fished.

"But don't you go too far in the woods," he told me. "Not beyond where the water splits."

"No, sir."

"Promise me."

"Yessir, I promise."

"Now promise your mother."

We were standing on the back stoop; I had been bound for the springhouse with the water jugs when my dad stopped me. Now he turned me around to face my mother, who was standing at the marble counter in a flood of strong morning sunshine falling through the double windows over the sink. There was a curl of hair lying across the side of her forehead and touching her eyebrow—you see how well I remember it all? The bright light turned that little curl to filaments of gold and made me want to run to her and put my arms around her. In that instant I saw her as a woman, saw her as my father must have seen her. She was wearing a housedress with little red roses all over it, I remember, and she was kneading bread. Candy Bill, our little black Scottie dog, was standing alertly beside her feet, looking up, waiting for anything that might drop. My mother was looking at me.

"I promise," I said.

She smiled, but it was the worried kind of smile she always seemed to make since my father brought Dan back from the west field in his arms. My father had come sobbing and bare-chested. He had taken off his shirt and draped it over Dan's face, which had swelled and turned color. *My boy!* he had been crying. *Oh, look at my boy! Jesus, look at my boy!* I remember that as if it were yesterday. It was the only time I ever heard my dad take the Saviour's name in vain.

"What do you promise, Gary?" she asked.

"Promise not to go no further than where the stream forks, Ma'am."

"Any further."

"Any."

She gave me a patient look, saying nothing as her hands went on working in the dough, which now had a smooth, silky look.

"I promise not to go any further than where the stream forks, Ma'am."

"Thank you, Gary," she said. "And try to remember that grammar is for the world as well as for school."

"Yes, Ma'am."

Candy Bill followed me as I did my chores, and sat between my feet as I bolted my lunch, looking up at me with the same attentiveness he had shown my mother while she was kneading her bread, but when I got my new bamboo pole and my old, splintery creel and started out of the dooryard, he stopped and only stood in the dust by an old roll of snow fence, watching. I called him but he wouldn't come. He yapped a time or two, as if telling me to come back, but that was all.

"Stay, then," I said, trying to sound as if I didn't care. I did, though, at least a little. Candy Bill *always* went fishing with me.

My mother came to the door and looked out at me with her left hand held up to shade her eyes. I can see her that way still, and it's like looking at a photograph of someone who later became unhappy, or died suddenly. "You mind your dad now, Gary!"

"Yes, Ma'am, I will."

She waved. I waved, too. Then I turned my back on her and walked away.

The sun beat down on my neck, hard and hot, for the first quarter-mile or so, but then I entered the woods, where double shadow fell over the road and it was cool and fir-smelling and you could hear the wind hissing through the deep, needled groves. I walked with my pole on my shoulder the way boys did back then, holding my creel in my other hand like a valise or a salesman's sample case. About two miles into the woods along a road that was really nothing but a double rut with a grassy strip growing up the center hump, I began to hear the hurried, eager gossip of Castle Stream. I thought of trout with bright speckled backs and pure-white bellies, and my heart went up in my chest.

The stream flowed under a little wooden bridge, and the banks leading down to the water were steep and brushy. I worked my way down carefully, holding on where I could and digging my heels in. I went down out of summer and back into mid-spring, or so it felt. The cool rose gently off the water, and there was a green smell like moss. When I got to the edge of the water I only stood there for a little while, breathing deep of that mossy smell and watching the dragonflies circle and the skitterbugs skate. Then, further down, I saw a trout leap at a butterfly—a good big brookie, maybe fourteen inches long—and remembered I hadn't come here just to sightsee.

I walked along the bank, following the current, and wet my line for the first time, with the bridge still in sight upstream. Something jerked the tip of my pole down once or twice and ate half my worm, but whatever it was was too sly for my nine-year-old hands—or maybe just not hungry enough to be careless—so I quit that place.

I stopped at two or three other places before I got to the place where Castle Stream forks, going southwest into Castle Rock and southeast into Kashwakamak Township, and at one of them I caught the biggest trout I have ever caught in my life, a beauty that measured nineteen inches from tip to tail on the little ruler I kept in my creel. That was a monster of a brook trout, even for those days.

If I had accepted this as gift enough for one day and gone back, I would not be writing now (and this is going to turn out longer than I thought it would, I see that already), but I didn't. Instead I saw to my catch right then and there as my father had shown me—cleaning it, placing it on dry grass at the bottom of the creel, then laying damp grass on top of it—and went on. I did not, at age nine, think that catching a nineteen-inch brook trout was particularly remarkable, although I do remember being amazed that my line had not broken when I, netless as well as artless, had hauled it out and swung it toward me in a clumsy tail-flapping arc.

Ten minutes later, I came to the place where the stream split in those days (it is long gone now; there is a settlement of duplex homes where Castle Stream once went its course, and a district grammar school as well, and if there is a stream it goes in darkness), dividing around a huge gray rock nearly the size of our outhouse. There was a pleasant flat space here, grassy and soft, overlooking what my dad and I called South Branch. I squatted on my heels, dropped my line into the water, and almost immediately snagged a fine rainbow trout. He wasn't the size of my brookie—only a foot or so—but a good fish, just the same. I had it cleaned out before the gills had stopped flexing, stored it in my creel, and dropped my line back into the water.

This time there was no immediate bite, so I leaned back, looking up at the blue stripe of sky I could see along the stream's course. Clouds floated by, west to east, and I tried to think what they looked like. I saw a unicorn, then a rooster, then a dog that looked like Candy Bill. I was looking for the next one when I drowsed off.

Or maybe slept. I don't know for sure. All I know is that a tug on my line so strong it almost pulled the bamboo pole out of my hand was what brought me back into the afternoon. I sat up, clutched the pole, and suddenly became aware that something was sitting on the tip of my nose: I crossed my eyes and saw a bee. My heart seemed to fall dead in my chest, and for a horrible second I was sure I was going to wet my pants.

The tug on my line came again, stronger this time, but although I maintained my grip on the end of the pole so it wouldn't be pulled into the stream and perhaps carried away (I think I even had the presence of mind to snub the line with my forefinger), I made no effort to pull in my catch. All my horrified attention was fixed on the fat black-and-yellow thing that was using my nose as a rest stop.

I slowly poked out my lower lip and blew upward. The bee ruffled a little but kept its place. I blew again and it ruffled again—but this time it also seemed to shift impatiently, and I didn't dare blow anymore, for fear it would lose its temper completely and give me a shot. It was too close for me to focus on what it was doing, but it was easy to imagine it ramming its stinger into one of my nostrils and shooting its poison up toward my eyes. And my brain.

A terrible idea came to me: that this was the very bee that had killed my brother. I knew it wasn't true, and not only because honeybees probably didn't live longer than a single year (except maybe for the queens; about them I was not so sure). It couldn't be true, because honeybees died when they stung, and even at nine I knew it. Their stingers were barbed, and when they tried to fly away after doing the deed, they tore themselves apart. Still, the idea stayed. This was a special bee, a devil-bee, and it had come back to finish the other of Albion and Loretta's two boys.

And here is something else: I had been stung by bees before, and although the stings had swelled more than is perhaps usual (I can't really say for sure), I had never died of them. That was only for my brother, a terrible trap that had been laid for him in his very making—a trap that I had somehow escaped. But as I crossed my eyes until they hurt, in an effort to focus on the bee, logic did not exist. It was the *bee* that existed, only that—the bee that had killed my brother, killed him so cruelly that my father had slipped down the straps of his overalls so he could take off his shirt and cover Dan's swollen, engorged face. Even in the depths of his grief he had done that, because he didn't want his wife to see what had become of her firstborn. Now the bee had returned, and now it would kill me. I would die in convulsions on the bank, flopping just as a brookie flops after you take the hook out of its mouth.

As I sat there trembling on the edge of panic—ready to bolt to my feet and then bolt anywhere—there came a report from behind me. It was as sharp and peremptory as a pistol shot, but I knew it wasn't a pistol shot; it was someone clapping his hands. One single clap. At that moment, the bee tumbled off my nose and fell into my lap. It lay there on my pants with its legs sticking up and its stinger a threatless black thread against the old scuffed brown of the corduroy. It was dead as a doornail, I saw that at once. At the same moment, the pole gave another tug—the hardest yet—and I almost lost it again.

I grabbed it with both hands and gave it a big stupid yank that would have made my father clutch his head with both hands, if he had been there to see. A rainbow trout, a good bit larger than either of the ones I had already caught, rose out of the water in a wet flash, spraying fine drops of water from its tail—it looked like one of those fishing pictures they used to put on the covers of men's magazines like *True* and *Man's Adventure* back in the forties and fifties. At that moment hauling in a big one was about the last thing on my mind, however, and when the line snapped and the fish fell back into the stream, I barely noticed. I looked over my shoulder to see who had clapped. A man was standing above me, at the edge of the trees. His face was very long and pale. His black hair was combed tight against his skull and parted with rigorous care on the left side of his narrow head. He was very tall. He was wearing a black three-piece suit, and I knew right away that he was not a human being, because his eyes were the orangey red of flames in a woodstove. I don't mean just the irises, because he *had* no irises, and no pupils, and certainly no whites. His eyes were completely orange—an orange that shifted and flickered. And it's really too late not to say exactly what I mean, isn't it? He was on fire inside, and his eyes were like the little isinglass portholes you sometimes see in stove doors.

My bladder let go, and the scuffed brown the dead bee was lying on went a darker brown. I was hardly aware of what had happened, and I couldn't take my eyes off the man standing on top of the bank and looking down at me—the man who had apparently walked out of thirty miles of trackless western Maine woods in a fine black suit and narrow shoes of gleaming leather. I could see the watch chain looped across his vest glittering in the summer sunshine. There was not so much as a single pine needle on him. And he was smiling at me.

"Why, it's a fisherboy!" he cried in a mellow, pleasing voice. "Imagine that! Are we well met, fisherboy?"

"Hello, sir," I said. The voice that came out of me did not tremble, but it didn't sound like my voice, either. It sounded older. Like Dan's voice, maybe. Or my father's, even. And all I could think was that maybe he would let me go if I pretended not to see what he was. If I pretended I didn't see there were flames glowing and dancing where his eyes should have been.

"I've saved you a nasty sting, perhaps," he said, and then, to my horror, he came down the bank to where I sat with a dead bee in my wet lap and a bamboo fishing pole in my nerveless hands. His slick-soled city shoes should have slipped on the low, grassy weeds dressing the steep bank, but they didn't; nor did they leave tracks, I saw. Where his feet had touched—or seemed to touch—there was not a single broken twig, crushed leaf, or trampled shoe-shape.

Even before he reached me, I recognized the aroma baking up from the skin under the suit—the smell of burned matches. The smell of sulfur. The man in the black suit was the Devil. He had walked out of the deep woods between Motton and Kashwakamak, and now he was standing here beside me. From the corner of one eye I could see a hand as pale as the hand of a store-window dummy. The fingers were hideously long.

He hunkered beside me on his hams, his knees popping just as the knees of any normal man might, but when he moved his hands so they dangled between his knees, I saw that each of those long fingers ended in not a fingernail but a long yellow claw.

"You didn't answer my question, fisherboy," he said in his mellow voice. It was, now that I think of it, like the voice of one of those radio announcers on the big-band shows years later, the ones that would sell Geritol and Serutan and Ovaltine and Dr. Grabow pipes. "Are we well met?"

"Please don't hurt me," I whispered, in a voice so low I could barely hear it. I was more afraid than I could ever write down, more afraid than I want to remember. But I do. I do. It never crossed my mind to hope I was having a dream, although it might have, I suppose, if I had been older. But I was nine, and I knew the truth when it squatted down beside me. I knew a hawk from a handsaw, as my father would have said. The man who had come out of the woods on that Saturday afternoon in midsummer was the Devil, and inside the empty holes of his eyes his brains were burning.

"Oh, do I smell something?" he asked, as if he hadn't heard me, although I knew he had. "Do I smell something . . . wet?"

He leaned toward me with his nose stuck out, like someone who means to smell a flower. And I noticed an awful thing; as the shadow of his head travelled over the bank, the grass beneath it turned yellow and died. He lowered his head toward my pants and sniffed. His glaring eyes half closed, as if he had inhaled some sublime aroma and wanted to concentrate on nothing but that.

"Oh, bad!" he cried. "Lovely-bad!" And then he chanted: "Opal! Diamond! Sapphire! Jade! I smell Gary's lemonade!" He threw himself on his back in the little flat place and laughed.

I thought about running, but my legs seemed two counties away from my brain. I wasn't crying, though; I had wet my pants, but I wasn't crying. I was too scared to cry. I suddenly knew that I was going to die, and probably painfully, but the worst of it was that that might not be the worst of it. The worst might come later. *After* I was dead.

He sat up suddenly, the smell of burnt matches fluffing out from his suit and making me feel gaggy in my throat. He looked at me solemnly from his narrow white face and burning eyes, but there was a sense of laughter about him, too. There was always that sense of laughter about him.

"Sad news, fisherboy," he said. "I've come with sad news."

I could only look at him—the black suit, the fine black shoes, the long white fingers that ended not in nails but in talons.

"Your mother is dead."

"No!" I cried. I thought of her making bread, of the curl lying across her forehead and just touching her eyebrow, of her standing there in the strong morning sunlight, and the terror swept over me again, but not for myself this time. Then I thought of how she'd looked when I set off with my fishing pole, standing in the kitchen doorway with her hand shading her eyes, and how she had looked to me in that moment like a photograph of someone you expected to see again but never did. "No, you lie!" I screamed.

He smiled—the sadly patient smile of a man who has often been accused falsely. "I'm afraid not," he said. "It was the same thing that happened to your brother, Gary. It was a bee."

"No, that's not true," I said, and now I *did* begin to cry. "She's old, she's thirty-five—if a bee sting could kill her the way it did Danny she would have died a long time ago, and you're a lying bastard!"

I had called the Devil a lying bastard. I was aware of this, but the entire front of my mind was taken up by the enormity of what he'd said. My mother dead? He might as well have told me that the moon had fallen on Vermont. But I believed him. On some level I believed him completely, as we always believe, on some level, the worst thing our hearts can imagine.

"I understand your grief, little fisherboy, but that particular argument just doesn't hold water, I'm afraid." He spoke in a tone of bogus comfort that was horrible, maddening, without remorse or pity. "A man can go his whole life without seeing a mockingbird, you know, but does that mean mockingbirds don't exist? Your mother—"

A fish jumped below us. The man in the black suit frowned, then pointed a finger at it. The trout convulsed in the air, its body bending so strenuously that for a split second it appeared to be snapping at its own tail, and when it fell back into Castle Stream it was floating lifelessly. It struck the big gray rock where the waters divided, spun around twice in the whirlpool eddy that formed there, and then floated away in the direction of Castle Rock. Meanwhile, the terrible stranger turned his burning eyes on me again, his thin lips pulled back from tiny rows of sharp teeth in a cannibal smile.

"Your mother simply went through her entire life without being stung by a bee," he said. "But then—less than an hour ago, actually—one flew in through the kitchen window while she was taking the bread out of the oven and putting it on the counter to cool."

I raised my hands and clapped them over my ears. He pursed his lips as if to whistle and blew at me gently. It was only a little breath, but the stench was foul beyond belief—clogged sewers, outhouses that have never known a single sprinkle of lime, dead chickens after a flood.

My hands fell away from the sides of my face.

"Good," he said. "You need to hear this, Gary; you need to hear this, my little fisherboy. It was your mother who passed that fatal weakness on to your brother. You got some of it, but you also got a protection from your father that poor Dan somehow missed." He pursed his lips again, only this time he made a cruelly comic little *tsk-tsk* sound instead of blowing his nasty breath at me. "So although I don't like to speak ill of the dead, it's almost a case of poetic justice, isn't it? After all, she killed your brother Dan as surely as if she had put a gun to his head and pulled the trigger."

"No," I whispered. "No, it isn't true."

"I assure you it is," he said. "The bee flew in the window and lit on her neck. She slapped at it before she even knew what she was doing—*you* were wiser than that, weren't you, Gary?—and the bee stung her. She felt her throat start to close up at once. That's what happens, you know, to people who can't tolerate bee venom. Their throats close and they drown in the open air. That's why Dan's face was so swollen and purple. That's why your father covered it with his shirt."

I stared at him, now incapable of speech. Tears streamed down my cheeks. I didn't want to believe him, and knew from my church schooling that the Devil is the father of lies, but I *did* believe him just the same.

"She made the most wonderfully awful noises," the man in the black suit said reflectively, "and she scratched her face quite badly, I'm afraid. Her eyes bulged out like a frog's eyes. She wept." He paused, then added: "She wept as she died, isn't that sweet? And here's the most beautiful thing of all. After she was dead, after she had been lying on the floor for fifteen minutes or so with no sound but the stove ticking and with that little thread of a bee stinger still poking out of the side of her neck—so small, so small—do you know what Candy Bill did? That little rascal licked away her tears. First on one side, and then on the other."

He looked out at the stream for a moment, his face sad and thoughtful. Then he turned back to me and his expression of bereavement disappeared like a dream. His face was as slack and as avid as the face of a corpse that has died hungry. His eyes blazed. I could see his sharp little teeth between his pale lips.

"I'm starving," he said abruptly. "I'm going to kill you and eat your guts, little fisherboy. What do you think about that?"

No, I tried to say, *please no*, but no sound came out. He meant to do it, I saw. He really meant to do it.

"I'm just so *hungry*," he said, both petulant and teasing. "And you won't want to live without your precious mommy, anyhow, take my word for it. Because your father's the sort of man who'll have to have some warm hole to stick it in, believe me, and if you're the only one available, you're the one who'll have to serve. I'll save you all that discomfort and unpleasantness. Also, you'll go to Heaven, think of that. Murdered souls *always* go to Heaven. So we'll both be serving God this afternoon, Gary. Isn't that nice?"

He reached for me again with his long, pale hands, and without thinking what I was doing, I flipped open the top of my creel, pawed all the way down to the bottom, and brought out the monster brookie I'd caught earlier—the one I should have been satisfied with. I held it out to him blindly, my fingers in the red slit of its belly, from which I had removed its insides as the man in the black suit had threatened to remove mine. The fish's glazed eye stared dreamily at me, the gold ring around the black center reminding me of my mother's wedding ring. And in that moment I saw her lying in her coffin with the sun shining off the wedding band and knew it was true—she had been stung by a bee, she had drowned in the warm, bread-smelling kitchen air, and Candy Bill had licked her dying tears from her swollen cheeks.

"Big fish!" the man in the black suit cried in a guttural, greedy voice. "Oh, *biiig fiiish!*"

He snatched it away from me and crammed it into a mouth that opened wider than any human mouth ever could. Many years later, when I was sixty-five (I know it was sixty-five, because that was the summer I retired from teaching), I went to the aquarium in Boston and finally saw a shark. The mouth of the man in the black suit was like that shark's mouth when it opened, only his gullet was blazing orange, the same color as his eyes, and I felt heat bake out of it and into my face, the way you feel a sudden wave of heat come pushing out of a fireplace when a dry piece of wood catches alight. And I didn't imagine that heat, either—I know I didn't—because just before he slid the head of my nineteen-inch brook trout between his gaping jaws, I saw the scales along the sides of the fish rise up and begin to curl like bits of paper floating over an open incinerator.

He slid the fish in like a man in a travelling show swallowing a sword. He didn't chew, and his blazing eyes bulged out, as if in effort. The fish went in and went in, his throat bulged as it slid down his gullet, and now he began to cry tears of his own—except his tears were blood, scarlet and thick.

I think it was the sight of those bloody tears that gave me my body back. I don't know why that should have been, but I think it was. I bolted to my feet like a Jack released from its box, turned with my bamboo pole still in one hand, and fled up the bank, bending over and tearing tough bunches of weeds out with my free hand in an effort to get up the slope more quickly.

He made a strangled, furious noise—the sound of any man with his mouth too full—and I looked back just as I got to the top. He was coming after me, the back of his suit coat flapping and his thin gold watch chain flashing and winking in the sun. The tail of the fish was still protruding from his mouth and I could smell the rest of it, roasting in the oven of his throat.

He reached for me, groping with his talons, and I fled along the top of the bank. After a hundred yards or so I found my voice and went to screaming—screaming in fear, of course, but also screaming in grief for my beautiful dead mother.

He was coming after me. I could hear snapping branches and whipping bushes, but I didn't look back again. I lowered my head, slitted my eyes against the bushes and low-hanging branches along the stream's bank, and ran as fast as I could. And at every step I expected to feel his hands descending on my shoulders, pulling me back into a final burning hug.

That didn't happen. Some unknown length of time later—it couldn't have been longer than five or ten minutes, I suppose, but it seemed like forever—I saw the bridge through layerings of leaves and firs. Still screaming, but breathlessly now, sounding like a teakettle that has almost boiled dry, I reached this second, steeper bank and charged up.

Halfway to the top, I slipped to my knees, looked over my shoulder, and saw the man in the black suit almost at my heels, his white face pulled into a convulsion of fury and greed. His cheeks were splattered with his bloody tears and his shark's mouth hung open like a hinge.

"*Fisherboy!*" he snarled, and started up the bank after me, grasping at my foot with one long hand. I tore free, turned, and threw my fishing pole at him. He batted it down easily, but it tangled his feet up somehow and he went to his knees. I didn't wait to see any more; I turned and bolted to the top of the slope. I almost slipped at the very top, but managed to grab one of the support struts running beneath the bridge and save myself.

"You can't get away, fisherboy!" he cried from behind me. He sounded furious, but he also sounded as if he were laughing. "It takes more than a mouthful of trout to fill *me* up!"

"Leave me alone!" I screamed back at him. I grabbed the bridge's railing and threw myself over it in a clumsy somersault, filling my hands with splinters and bumping my head so hard on the boards when I came down that I saw stars. I rolled over on my belly and began crawling. I lurched to my feet just before I got to the end of the bridge, stumbled once, found my rhythm, and then began to run. I ran as only nine-year-old boys can run, which is like the wind. It felt as if my feet only touched the ground with every third or fourth stride, and, for all I know, that may be true. I ran straight up the right-hand wheel rut in the road, ran until my temples pounded and my eyes pulsed in their sockets, ran until I had a hot stitch in my left side from the bottom of my ribs to my armpit, ran until I could taste blood and something like metal shavings in the back of my throat. When I couldn't run anymore I stumbled to a stop and looked back over my shoulder, puffing and blowing like a wind-broken horse. I was convinced I would see him standing right there behind me in his natty black suit, the watch chain a glittering loop across his vest and not a hair out of place.

But he was gone. The road stretching back toward Castle Stream between the darkly massed pines and spruces was empty. And yet I sensed him somewhere near in those woods, watching me with his grassfire eyes, smelling of burned matches and roasted fish.

I turned and began walking as fast as I could, limping a little—I'd pulled muscles in both legs, and when I got out of bed the next morning I was so sore I could barely walk. I kept looking over my shoulder, needing again and again to verify that the road behind me was still empty. It was each time I looked, but those backward glances seemed to increase my fear rather than lessen it. The firs looked darker, massier, and I kept imagining what lay behind the trees that marched beside the road—long, tangled corridors of forest, leg-breaking deadfalls, ravines where anything might live. Until that Saturday in 1914, I had thought that bears were the worst thing the forest could hold.

A mile or so farther up the road, just beyond the place where it came out of the woods and joined the Geegan Flat Road, I saw my father walking toward me and whistling "The Old Oaken Bucket." He was carrying his own rod, the one with the fancy spinning reel from Monkey Ward. In his other hand he had his creel, the one with the ribbon my mother had woven through the handle back when Dan was still alive. "Dedicated to Jesus" that ribbon said. I had been walking, but when I saw him I started to run again, screaming *Dad! Dad! Dad!* at the top of my lungs and staggering from side to side on my tired, sprung legs like a drunken sailor. The expression of surprise on his face when he recognized me might have been comical under other circumstances. He dropped his rod and creel into the road without so much as a downward glance at them and ran to me. It was the fastest I ever saw my dad run in his life; when we came together it was a wonder the impact didn't knock us both senseless, and I struck my face on his belt buckle hard enough to start a little nosebleed. I didn't notice that until later, though. Right then I only reached out my arms and clutched him as hard as I could. I held on and rubbed my hot face back and forth against his belly, covering his old blue workshirt with blood and tears and snot.

"Gary, what is it? What happened? Are you all right?"

"Ma's dead!" I sobbed. "I met a man in the woods and he told me! Ma's dead! She got stung by a bee and it swelled her all up just like what happened to Dan, and she's dead! She's on the kitchen floor and Candy Bill . . . licked the t-t-tears . . . off her . . . off her . . ."

Face was the last word I had to say, but by then my chest was hitching so bad I couldn't get it out. My own tears were flowing again, and my dad's startled, frightened face had blurred into three overlapping images. I began to howl—not like a little kid who's skinned his knee but like a dog that's seen something bad by moonlight—and my father pressed my head against his hard flat stomach again. I slipped out from under his hand, though, and looked back over my shoulder. I wanted to make sure the man in the black suit wasn't coming. There was no sign of him; the road winding back into the woods was completely empty. I promised myself I would never go back down that road again, not ever, no matter what, and I suppose now that God's greatest blessing to His creatures below is that they can't see the future. It might have broken my mind if I had known I *would* be going back down that road, and not two hours later. For that moment, though, I was only relieved to see we were still alone. Then I thought of my mother—my beautiful dead mother—and laid my face back against my father's stomach and bawled some more.

"Gary, listen to me," he said a moment or two later. I went on bawling. He gave me a little longer to do that, then reached down and lifted my chin so he could look down into my face and I could look up into his. "Your mom's fine," he said.

I could only look at him with tears streaming down my cheeks. I didn't believe him.

"I don't know who told you different, or what kind of dirty dog would want to put a scare like that into a little boy, but I swear to God your mother's fine."

"But . . . but he said . . ."

"I don't care *what* he said. I got back from Eversham's earlier than I expected—he doesn't want to sell any cows, it's all just talk—and decided I had time to catch up with you. I got my pole and my creel and your mother made us a couple of jelly fold-overs. Her new bread. Still warm. So she was fine half an hour ago, Gary, and there's nobody knows any different that's come from this direction, I guarantee you. Not in just half an hour's time." He looked over my shoulder. "Who was this man? And where was he? I'm going to find him and thrash him within an inch of his life."

I thought a thousand things in just two seconds—that's what it seemed like, anyway—but the last thing I thought was the most powerful: if my Dad met up with the man in the black suit, I didn't think my Dad would be the one to do the thrashing. Or the walking away.

I kept remembering those long white fingers, and the talons at the ends of them.

"Gary?"

"I don't know that I remember," I said.

"Were you where the stream splits? The big rock?"

I could never lie to my father when he asked a direct question—not to save his life or mine. "Yes, but don't go down there." I seized his arm with both hands and tugged it hard. "Please don't. He was a scary man." Inspiration struck like an illuminating lightning bolt. "I think he had a gun."

He looked at me thoughtfully. "Maybe there wasn't a man," he said, lifting his voice a little on the last word and turning it into something that was almost but not quite a question. "Maybe you fell asleep while you were fishing, son, and had a bad dream. Like the ones you had about Danny last winter."

I *had* had a lot of bad dreams about Dan last winter, dreams where I would open the door to our closet or to the dark, fruity interior of the cider shed and see him standing there and looking at me out of his purple strangulated face; from many of these dreams I had awakened screaming, and awakened my parents as well. I had fallen asleep on the bank of the stream for a little while, too—dozed off, anyway—but I hadn't dreamed, and I was sure I had awakened just before the man in the black suit clapped the bee dead, sending it tumbling off my nose and into my lap. I hadn't dreamed him the way I had dreamed Dan, I was quite sure of that, although my meeting with him had already attained a dreamlike quality in my mind, as I suppose supernatural occurrences always must. But if my Dad thought that the man had only existed in my own head, that might be better. Better for him.

"It might have been, I guess," I said.

"Well, we ought to go back and find your rod and your creel."

He actually started in that direction, and I had to tug frantically at his arm to stop him again and turn him back toward me.

"Later," I said. "Please, Dad? I want to see Mother. I've got to see her with my own eyes."

He thought that over, then nodded. "Yes, I suppose you do. We'll go home first, and get your rod and creel later."

So we walked back to the farm together, my father with his fish pole propped on his shoulder just like one of my friends, me carrying his creel, both of us eating folded-over slices of my mother's bread smeared with black-currant jam.

"Did you catch anything?" he asked as we came in sight of the barn.

"Yes, sir," I said. "A rainbow. Pretty good-sized." *And a brookie that was a lot bigger*, I thought but didn't say.

"That's all? Nothing else?"

"After I caught it I fell asleep." This was not really an answer but not really a lie, either.

"Lucky you didn't lose your pole. You didn't, did you, Gary?"

"No, sir," I said, very reluctantly. Lying about that would do no good even if I'd been able to think up a whopper—not if he was set on going back to get my creel anyway, and I could see by his face that he was.

Up ahead, Candy Bill came racing out of the back door, barking his shrill bark and wagging his whole rear end back and forth the way Scotties do when they're excited. I couldn't wait any longer. I broke away from my father and ran to the house, still lugging his creel and still convinced, in my heart of hearts, that I was going to find my mother dead on the kitchen floor with her face swollen and purple, as Dan's had been when my father carried him in from the west field, crying and calling the name of Jesus.

But she was standing at the counter, just as well and fine as when I had left her, humming a song as she shelled peas into a bowl. She looked around at me, first in surprise and then in fright as she took in my wide eyes and pale cheeks.

"Gary, what is it? What's the matter?"

I didn't answer, only ran to her and covered her with kisses. At some point my father came in and said, "Don't worry, Lo—he's all right. He just had one of his bad dreams, down there by the brook."

"Pray God it's the last of them," she said, and hugged me tighter while Candy Bill danced around our feet, barking his shrill bark.

"You don't have to come with me if you don't want to, Gary," my father said, although he had already made it clear that he thought I should—that I should go back, that I should face my fear, as I suppose folks would say nowadays.

That's very well for fearful things that are make-believe, but two hours hadn't done much to change my conviction that the man in the black suit had been real. I wouldn't be able to convince my father of that, though. I don't think there was a nine-year-old who ever lived would have been able to convince his father he'd seen the Devil walking out of the woods in a black suit.

"I'll come," I said. I had come out of the house to join him before he left, mustering all my courage to get my feet moving, and now we were standing by the chopping block in the side yard, not far from the woodpile.

"What you got behind your back?" he asked.

I brought it out slowly. I would go with him, and I would hope the man in the black suit with the arrow-straight part down the left side of his head was gone. But if he wasn't, I wanted to be prepared. As prepared as I could be, anyway. I had the family Bible in the hand I had brought out from behind my back. I'd set out just to bring my New Testament, which I had won for memorizing the most psalms in the Thursday-night Youth Fellowship competition (I managed eight, although most of them except the Twenty-third had floated out of my mind in a week's time), but the little red Testament didn't seem like enough when you were maybe going to face the Devil himself, not even when the words of Jesus were marked out in red ink.

My father looked at the old Bible, swollen with family documents and pictures, and I thought he'd tell me to put it back, but he didn't. A look of mixed grief and sympathy crossed his face, and he nodded. "All right," he said. "Does your mother know you took that?"

"No, sir."

He nodded again. "Then we'll hope she doesn't spot it gone before we get back. Come on. And don't drop it."

Half an hour or so later, the two of us stood on the bank at the place where Castle Stream forked, and at the flat place where I'd had my encounter with the man with the red-orange eyes. I had my bamboo rod in my hand—I'd picked it up below the bridge—and my creel lay down below, on the flat place. Its wicker top was flipped back. We stood looking down, my father and I, for a long time, and neither of us said anything.

Opal! Diamond! Sapphire! Jade! I smell Gary's lemonade! That had been his unpleasant little poem, and once he had recited it, he had thrown himself on his back, laughing like a child who has just discovered he has enough courage to say bathroom words like shit or piss. The flat place down there was as green and lush as any place in Maine that the sun can get to in early July. Except where the stranger had lain. There the grass was dead and yellow in the shape of a man.

I was holding our lumpy old family Bible straight out in front of me with both thumbs pressing so hard on the cover that they were white. It was the way Mama Sweet's husband, Norville, held a willow fork when he was trying to dowse somebody a well.

"Stay here," my father said at last, and skidded sideways down the bank, digging his shoes into the rich soft soil and holding his arms out for balance. I stood where I was, holding the Bible stiffly out at the ends of my arms, my heart thumping. I don't know if I had a sense of being watched that time or not; I was too scared to have a sense of anything, except for a sense of wanting to be far away from that place and those woods.

My dad bent down, sniffed at where the grass was dead, and grimaced. I knew what he was smelling: something like burnt matches. Then he grabbed my creel and came on back up the bank, hurrying. He snagged one fast look over his shoulder to make sure nothing was coming along behind. Nothing was. When he handed me the creel, the lid was still hanging back on its cunning little leather hinges. I looked inside and saw nothing but two handfuls of grass.

"Thought you said you caught a rainbow," my father said, "but maybe you dreamed that, too."

Something in his voice stung me. "No, sir," I said. "I caught one."

"Well, it sure as hell didn't flop out, not if it was gutted and cleaned. And you wouldn't put a catch into your fisherbox without doing that, would you, Gary? I taught you better than that."

"Yes, sir, you did, but—"

"So if you didn't dream catching it and if it was dead in the box, something must have come along and eaten it," my father said, and then he grabbed another quick glance over his shoulder, eyes wide, as if he had heard something move in the woods. I wasn't exactly surprised to see drops of sweat standing out on his forehead like big clear jewels. "Come on," he said. "Let's get the hell out of here."

I was for that, and we went back along the bank to the bridge, walking quick without speaking. When we got there, my dad dropped to one knee and examined the place where we'd found my rod. There was another patch of dead grass there, and the lady's slipper was all brown and curled in on itself, as if a blast of heat had charred it. I looked in my empty creel again. "He must have gone back and eaten my other fish, too," I said.

My father looked up at me. "*Other* fish!"

"Yes, sir. I didn't tell you, but I caught a brookie, too. A big one. He was awful hungry, that fella." I wanted to say more, and the words trembled just behind my lips, but in the end I didn't.

We climbed up to the bridge and helped each other over the railing. My father took my creel, looked into it, then went to the railing and threw it over. I came up beside him in time to see it splash down and float away like a boat, riding lower and lower in the stream as the water poured in between the wicker weavings.

"It smelled bad," my father said, but he didn't look at me when he said it, and his voice sounded oddly defensive. It was the only time I ever heard him speak just that way.

"Yes, sir."

"We'll tell your mother we couldn't find it. If she asks. If she doesn't ask, we won't tell her anything."

"No, sir, we won't."

And she didn't and we didn't, and that's the way it was.

That day in the woods is eighty years gone, and for many of the years in between I have never even thought of it—not awake, at least. Like any other man or woman who ever lived, I can't say about my dreams, not for sure. But now I'm old, and I dream awake, it seems. My infirmities have crept up like waves that will soon take a child's abandoned sand castle, and my memories have also crept up, making me think of some old rhyme that went, in part, "Just leave them alone / And they'll come home / Wagging their tails behind them." I remember meals I ate, games I played, girls I kissed in the school cloakroom when we played post office, boys I chummed with, the first drink I ever took, the first cigarette I ever smoked (cornshuck behind Dicky Hamner's pig shed, and I threw up). Yet of all the memories the one of the man in the black suit is the strongest, and glows with its own spectral, haunted light. He was real, he was the Devil, and that day I was either his errand or his luck. I feel more and more strongly that escaping him was my luck—*just* luck, and not the intercession of the God I have worshipped and sung hymns to all my life.

As I lie here in my nursing-home room, and in the ruined sand castle that is my body, I tell myself that I need not fear the Devil—that I have lived a good, kindly life, and I need not fear the Devil. Sometimes I remind myself that it was I, not my father, who finally coaxed my mother back to church later on that summer. In the dark, however, these thoughts have no power to ease or comfort. In the dark comes a voice that whispers that the nine-year-old fisherboy I was had done nothing for which he might legitimately fear the Devil, either, and yet the Devil came—to him. And in the dark I sometimes hear that voice drop even lower, into ranges that are inhuman. *Big fish!* it whispers in tones of hushed greed, and all the truths of the moral world fall to ruin before its hunger.

RECONCILIATION

Who understands much, forgives much.

Madame de Staël, *Corinne*

How can God direct our steps if we're not taking any?

Sarah Leah Grafstein,
in Sherry Ruth Anderson and
Patricia Hopkins,
The Feminine Face of God

Everything in life that we really accept undergoes a change.

Katherine Mansfield,
Journal of Katherine Mansfield

Nothing worth doing is completed in our lifetime; therefore, we must be saved by hope. Nothing true or beautiful or good makes complete sense in any immediate context of history; therefore, we must be saved by faith. Nothing we do, however virtuous, can be accomplished alone; therefore, we are saved by love. No virtuous act is quite as virtuous from the standpoint of our friend or foe as from our standpoint. Therefore, we must be saved by the final form of love which is forgiveness.

Reinhold Niebuhr,
The Irony of American History

Cathedral

RAYMOND CARVER

This blind man, an old friend of my wife's, he was on his way to spend the night. His wife had died. So he was visiting the dead wife's relatives in Connecticut. He called my wife from his in-laws'. Arrangements were made. He would come by train, a five-hour trip, and my wife would meet him at the station. She hadn't seen him since she worked for him one summer in Seattle ten years ago. But she and the blind man had kept in touch. They made tapes and mailed them back and forth. I wasn't enthusiastic about his visit. He was no one I knew. And his being blind bothered me. My idea of blindness came from the movies. In the movies, the blind moved slowly and never laughed. Sometimes they were led by seeing-eye dogs. A blind man in my house was not something I looked forward to.

That summer in Seattle she had needed a job. She didn't have any money. The man she was going to marry at the end of the summer was in officers' training school. He didn't have any money, either. But she was in love with the guy, and he was in love with her, etc. She'd seen something in the paper: HELP WANTED—*Reading to Blind Man*, and a telephone number. She phoned and went over, was hired on the spot. She'd worked with this blind man all summer. She read stuff to him, case studies, reports, that sort of thing. She helped him organize his little office in the county social-service department. They'd become good friends, my wife and the blind man. How do I know these things? She told me. And she told me something else. On her last day in the office, the blind man asked if he could touch her face. She agreed to this. She told me he touched his fingers to every part of her face, her nose—even her neck! She never forgot it. She even tried to write a poem about it. She was always trying to write a poem. She wrote a poem or two every year, usually after something really important had happened to her.

When we first started going out together, she showed me the poem. In the poem, she recalled his fingers and the way they had moved around over her face. In the poem, she talked about what she had felt at the time, about what went through her mind when the blind man touched her nose and lips. I can remember I didn't think much of the poem. Of course, I didn't tell her that. Maybe I just don't understand poetry. I admit it's not the first thing I reach for when I pick up something to read.

Anyway, this man who'd first enjoyed her favors, the officer-to-be, he'd been her childhood sweetheart. So okay. I'm saying that at the end of the summer she let the blind man run his hands over her face, said good-bye to him, married her childhood etc., who was now a commissioned officer, and she moved away from Seattle. But they'd kept in touch, she and the blind man. She made the first contact after a year or so. She called him up one night from an Air Force base in Alabama. She wanted to talk. They talked. He asked her to send him a tape and tell him about her life. She did this. She sent the tape. On the tape, she told the blind man about her husband and about their life together in the military. She told the blind man she loved her husband but she didn't like it where they lived and she didn't like it that he was a part of the military-industrial thing. She told the blind man she'd written a poem and he was in it. She told him that she was writing a poem about what it was like to be an Air Force officer's wife. The poem wasn't finished yet. She was still writing it. The blind man made a tape. He sent her the tape. She made a tape. This went on for years. My wife's officer was posted to one base and then another. She sent tapes from Moody AFB, McGuire, McConnell, and finally Travis, near Sacramento, where one night she got to feeling lonely and cut off from people she kept losing in that moving-around life. She got to feeling she couldn't go it another step. She went in and swallowed all the pills and capsules in the medicine chest and washed them down with a bottle of gin. Then she got into a hot bath and passed out.

But instead of dying, she got sick. She threw up. Her officer—why should he have a name? he was the childhood sweetheart, and what more does he want?—came home from somewhere, found her, and called the ambulance. In time, she put it all on a tape and sent the tape to the blind man. Over the years, she put all kinds of stuff on tapes and sent the tapes off lickety-split. Next to writing a poem every year, I think it was her chief means of recreation. On one tape, she told the blind man she'd decided to live away from her officer for a time. On another tape, she told him about her divorce. She and I began going out, and of course she told her blind man about it. She told him everything, or so it seemed to me. Once she asked me if I'd like to hear the latest tape from the blind man. This was a year ago. I was on the tape, she said. So I said okay, I'd listen to it. I got us drinks and we settled down in the living room. We made ready to listen. First she inserted the tape into the player and adjusted a couple of dials. Then she pushed a lever. The tape squeaked and someone began to talk in this loud voice. She lowered the volume. After a few minutes of harmless chitchat, I heard my own name in the mouth of this stranger, this blind man I didn't even know! And then this: "From all you've said about him, I can only conclude—" But we were interrupted, a knock at the door, something, and we didn't ever get back to the tape. Maybe it was just as well. I'd heard all I wanted to.

Now this same blind man was coming to sleep in my house.

"Maybe I could take him bowling," I said to my wife. She was at the draining board doing scalloped potatoes. She put down the knife she was using and turned around.

"If you love me," she said, "you can do this for me. If you don't love me, okay. But if you had a friend, any friend, and the friend came to visit, I'd make him feel comfortable." She wiped her hands with the dish towel.

"I don't have any blind friends," I said.

"You don't have *any* friends," she said. "Period. Besides," she said, "goddamn it, his wife's just died! Don't you understand that? The man's lost his wife!"

I didn't answer. She'd told me a little about the blind man's wife. Her name was Beulah. Beulah! That's a name for a colored woman.

"Was his wife a Negro?" I asked.

"Are you crazy?" my wife said. "Have you just flipped or something?" She picked up a potato. I saw it hit the floor, then roll under the stove. "What's wrong with you?" she said. "Are you drunk?"

"I'm just asking," I said.

Right then my wife filled me in with more detail than I cared to know. I made a drink and sat at the kitchen table to listen. Pieces of the story began to fall into place.

Beulah had gone to work for the blind man the summer after my wife had stopped working for him. Pretty soon Beulah and the blind man had themselves a church wedding. It was a little wedding—who'd want to go to such a wedding in the first place?—just the two of them, plus the minister and the minister's wife. But it was a church wedding just the same. It was what Beulah had wanted, he'd said. But even then Beulah must have been carrying the cancer in her glands. After they had been inseparable for eight years—my wife's word, *inseparable*—Beulah's health went into a rapid decline. She died in a Seattle hospital room, the blind man sitting beside the bed and holding on to her hand. They'd married, lived and worked together, slept together—had sex, sure—and then the blind man had to bury her. All this without his having ever seen what the goddamned woman looked like. It was beyond my understanding. Hearing this, I felt sorry for the blind man for a little bit. And then I found myself thinking what a pitiful life this woman must have led. Imagine a woman who could never see herself as she was seen in the eyes of her loved one. A woman who could go on day after day and never receive the smallest compliment from her beloved. A woman whose husband could never read the expression on her face, be it misery or something better. Someone who could wear makeup or not—what difference to him? She could, if she wanted, wear green eye-shadow around one eye, a straight pin in her nostril, yellow slacks, and purple shoes, no matter. And then to slip off into death, the blind man's hand on her hand, his blind eyes streaming tears—I'm imagining now—her last thought maybe this: that he never even knew what she looked like, and she on an express to the grave. Robert was left with a small insurance policy and half of a twenty-peso Mexican coin. The other half of the coin went into the box with her. Pathetic.

So when the time rolled around, my wife went to the depot to pick him up. With nothing to do but wait—sure, I blamed him for that—I was having a drink and watching the TV when I heard the car pull into the drive. I got up from the sofa with my drink and went to the window to have a look.

I saw my wife laughing as she parked the car. I saw her get out of the car and shut the door. She was still wearing a smile. Just amazing. She went around to the other side of the car to where the blind man was already starting to get out. This blind man, feature this, he was wearing a full beard! A beard on a blind man! Too much, I say. The blind man reached into the backseat and dragged out a suitcase. My wife took his arm, shut the car door, and, talking all the way, moved him down the drive and then up the steps to the front porch. I turned off the TV. I finished my drink, rinsed the glass, dried my hands. Then I went to the door.

My wife said, "I want you to meet Robert. Robert, this is my husband. I've told you all about him." She was beaming. She had this blind man by his coat sleeve.

The blind man let go of his suitcase and up came his hand.

I took it. He squeezed hard, held my hand, and then he let it go.

"I feel like we've already met," he boomed.

"Likewise," I said. I didn't know what else to say. Then I said, "Welcome. I've heard a lot about you." We began to move then, a little group, from the porch into the living room, my wife guiding him by the arm. The blind man was carrying his suitcase in his other hand. My wife said things like, "To your left here, Robert. That's right. Now watch it, there's a chair. That's it. Sit down right here. This is the sofa. We just bought this sofa two weeks ago."

I started to say something about the old sofa. I'd liked that old sofa. But I didn't say anything. Then I wanted to say something else, small-talk, about the scenic ride along the Hudson. How going *to* New York, you should sit on the right-hand side of the train, and coming *from* New York, the left-hand side.

"Did you have a good train ride?" I said. "Which side of the train did you sit on, by the way?"

"What a question, which side!" my wife said. "What's it matter which side?" she said.

"I just asked," I said.

"Right side," the blind man said. "I hadn't been on a train in nearly forty years. Not since I was a kid. With my folks. That's been a long time. I'd nearly forgotten the sensation. I have winter in my beard now," he said. "So I've been told, anyway. Do I look distinguished, my dear?" the blind man said to my wife.

"You look distinguished, Robert," she said. "Robert," she said. "Robert, it's just so good to see you."

My wife finally took her eyes off the blind man and looked at me. I had the feeling she didn't like what she saw. I shrugged.

I've never met, or personally known, anyone who was blind. This blind man was late forties, a heavy-set, balding man with stooped shoulders, as if he carried a great weight there. He wore brown slacks, brown shoes, a light-brown shirt, a tie, a sports coat. Spiffy. He also had this full beard. But he didn't use a cane and he didn't wear dark glasses. I'd always thought dark glasses were a must for the blind. Fact was, I wished he had a pair. At first glance, his eyes looked like anyone else's eyes. But if you looked close, there was something different about them. Too much white in the iris, for one thing, and the pupils seemed to move around in the sockets without his knowing it or being able to stop it. Creepy. As I stared at his face, I saw the left pupil turn in toward his nose while the other made an effort to keep in one place. But it was only an effort, for that eye was on the roam without his knowing it or wanting it to be.

I said, "Let me get you a drink. What's your pleasure? We have a little of everything. It's one of our pastimes."

"Bub, I'm a Scotch man myself," he said fast enough in this big voice.

"Right," I said. Bub! "Sure you are. I knew it."

He let his fingers touch his suitcase, which was sitting alongside the sofa. He was taking his bearings. I didn't blame him for that.

"I'll move that up to your room," my wife said.

"No, that's fine," the blind man said loudly. "It can go up when I go up."

"A little water with the Scotch?" I said.

"Very little," he said.

"I knew it," I said.

He said, "Just a tad. The Irish actor, Barry Fitzgerald? I'm like that fellow. When I drink water, Fitzgerald said, I drink water. When I drink whiskey, I drink whiskey." My wife laughed. The blind man brought his hand up under his beard. He lifted his beard slowly and let it drop.

I did the drinks, three big glasses of Scotch with a splash of water in each. Then we made ourselves comfortable and talked about Robert's travels. First the long flight from the West Coast to Connecticut, we covered that. Then from Connecticut up here by train. We had another drink concerning that leg of the trip.

I remembered having read somewhere that the blind didn't smoke because, as speculation had it, they couldn't see the smoke they exhaled. I thought I knew that much and that much only about blind people. But this blind man smoked his cigarette down to the nubbin and then lit another one. This blind man filled his ashtray and my wife emptied it.

When we sat down at the table for dinner, we had another drink. My wife heaped Robert's plate with cube steak, scalloped potatoes, green beans. I buttered him up two slices of bread. I said, "Here's bread and butter for you." I swallowed some of my drink. "Now let us pray," I said, and the blind man lowered his head. My wife looked at me, her mouth agape. "Pray the phone won't ring and the food doesn't get cold," I said.

We dug in. We ate everything there was to eat on the table. We ate like there was no tomorrow. We didn't talk. We ate. We scarfed. We grazed that table. We were into serious eating. The blind man had right away located his foods, he knew just where everything was on his plate. I watched with admiration as he used his knife and fork on the meat. He'd cut two pieces of meat, fork the meat into his mouth, and then go all out for the scalloped potatoes, the beans next, and then he'd tear off a hunk of buttered bread and eat that. He'd follow this up with a big drink of milk. It didn't seem to bother him to use his fingers once in a while, either.

We finished everything, including half a strawberry pie. For a few moments, we sat as if stunned. Sweat beaded on our faces. Finally, we got up from the table and left the dirty plates. We didn't look back. We took ourselves into the living room and sank into our places again. Robert and my wife sat on the sofa. I took the big chair. We had us two or three more drinks while they talked about the major things that had come to pass for them in the past ten years. For the most part, I just listened. Now and then I joined in. I didn't want him to think I'd left the room, and I didn't want her to think I was feeling left out. They talked of things that had happened to them—to them!—these past ten years. I waited in vain to hear my name on my wife's sweet lips: "And then my dear husband came into my life"—something like that. But I heard nothing of the sort. More talk of Robert. Robert had done a little of everything, it seemed, a regular blind jack-of-all-trades. But most recently he and his wife had had an Amway distributorship, from which, I gathered, they'd earned their living, such as it was. The blind man was also a ham radio operator. He talked in his loud voice about conversations he'd had with fellow operators in Guam, in the Philippines, in Alaska, and even in Tahiti. He said he'd have a lot of friends there if he ever wanted to go visit those places. From time to time, He'd turn his blind face toward me, put his hand under his beard, ask me something. How long had I been in my present position? (Three years.) Did I like my work? (I didn't.) Was I going to stay with it? (What were the options?) Finally, when I thought he was beginning to run down, I got up and turned on the TV.

My wife looked at me with irritation. She was heading toward a boil. Then she looked at the blind man and said, "Robert, do you have a TV?"

The blind man said, "My dear, I have two TVs. I have a color set and a black-and-white thing, an old relic. It's funny, but if I turn the TV on, and I'm always turning it on, I turn on the color set. It's funny, don't you think?"

I didn't know what to say to that. I had absolutely nothing to say to that. No opinion. So I watched the news program and tried to listen to what the announcer was saying.

"This is a color TV," the blind man said. "Don't ask me how, but I can tell."

"We traded up a while ago," I said.

The blind man had another taste of his drink. He lifted his beard, sniffed it, and let it fall. He leaned forward on the sofa. He positioned his ashtray on the coffee table, then put the lighter to his cigarette. He leaned back on the sofa and crossed his legs at the ankles.

My wife covered her mouth, and then she yawned. She stretched. She said, "I think I'll go upstairs and put on my robe. I think I'll change into something else. Robert, you make yourself comfortable," she said.

"I'm comfortable," the blind man said.

"I want you to feel comfortable in this house," she said.

"I am comfortable," the blind man said.

After she'd left the room, he and I listened to the weather report and then to the sports roundup. By that time, she'd been gone so long I didn't know if she was going to come back. I thought she might have gone to bed. I wished she'd come back downstairs. I didn't want to be left alone with a blind man. I asked him if he wanted another drink, and he said sure. Then I asked if he wanted to smoke some dope with me. I said I'd just rolled a number. I hadn't, but I planned to do so in about two shakes.

"I'll try some with you," he said.

"Damn right," I said. "That's the stuff."

I got our drinks and sat down on the sofa with him. Then I rolled us two fat numbers. I lit one and passed it. I brought it to his fingers. He took it and inhaled.

"Hold it as long as you can," I said. I could tell he didn't know the first thing.

My wife came back downstairs wearing her pink robe and her pink slippers.

"What do I smell?" she said.

"We thought we'd have us some cannabis," I said.

My wife gave me a savage look. Then she looked at the blind man and said, "Robert, I didn't know you smoked."

He said, "I do now, my dear. There's a first time for everything. But I don't feel anything yet."

"This stuff is pretty mellow," I said. "This stuff is mild. It's dope you can reason with," I said. "It doesn't mess you up."

"Not much it doesn't, bub," he said, and laughed.

My wife sat on the sofa between the blind man and me. I passed her the number. She took it and toked and then passed it back to me. "Which way is this going?" she said. Then she said, "I shouldn't be smoking this. I can hardly keep my eyes open as it is. That dinner did me in. I shouldn't have eaten so much."

"It was the strawberry pie," the blind man said. "That's what did it," he said, and he laughed his big laugh. Then he shook his head.

"There's more strawberry pie," I said.

"Do you want some more, Robert?" my wife said.

"Maybe in a little while," he said.

We gave our attention to the TV. My wife yawned again. She said, "Your bed is made up when you feel like going to bed, Robert. I know you must have had a long day. When you're ready to go to bed, say so." She pulled his arm. "Robert?"

He came to and said, "I've had a real nice time. This beats tapes, doesn't it?"

I said, "Coming at you," and I put the number between his fingers. He inhaled, held the smoke, and then let it go. It was like he'd been doing it since he was nine years old.

"Thanks, bub," he said. "But I think this is all for me. I think I'm beginning to feel it," he said. He held the burning roach out for my wife.

"Same here," she said. "Ditto. Me, too." She took the roach and passed it to me. "I may just sit here for a while between you two guys with my eyes closed. But don't let me bother you, okay? Either one of you. If it bothers you, say so. Otherwise, I may just sit here with my eyes closed until you're ready to go to bed," she said. "Your bed's made up, Robert, when you're ready. It's right next to our room at the top of the stairs. We'll show you up when you're ready. You wake me up now, you guys, if I fall asleep." She said that and then she closed her eyes and went to sleep.

The news program ended. I got up and changed the channel. I sat back down on the sofa. I wished my wife hadn't pooped out. Her head lay across the back of the sofa, her mouth open. She'd turned so that her robe had slipped away from her legs, exposing a juicy thigh. I reached to draw her robe back over her, and it was then that I glanced at the blind man. What the hell! I flipped the robe open again.

"You say when you want some strawberry pie," I said.

"I will," he said.

I said, "Are you tired? Do you want me to take you up to your bed? Are you ready to hit the hay?"

"Not yet," he said. "No, I'll stay up with you, bub. If that's all right. I'll stay up until you're ready to turn in. We haven't had a chance to talk. Know what

I mean? I feel like me and her monopolized the evening." He lifted his beard and he let if fall. He picked up his cigarettes and his lighter.

"That's all right," I said. Then I said, "I'm glad for the company."

And I guess I was. Every night I smoked dope and stayed up as long as I could before I fell asleep. My wife and I hardly ever went to bed at the same time. When I did go to sleep, I had these dreams. Sometimes I'd wake up from one of them, my heart going crazy.

Something about the church and the Middle Ages was on the TV. Not your run-of-the-mill TV fare. I wanted to watch something else. I turned to the other channels. But there was nothing on them, either. So I turned back to the first channel and apologized.

"Bub, it's all right," the blind man said. "It's fine with me. Whatever you want to watch is okay. I'm always learning something. Learning never ends. It won't hurt me to learn something tonight. I got ears," he said.

We didn't say anything for a time. He was leaning forward with his head turned at me, his right ear aimed in the direction of the set. Very disconcerting. Now and then his eyelids drooped and then they snapped open again. Now and then he put his fingers into his beard and tugged, like he was thinking about something he was hearing on the television.

On the screen, a group of men wearing cowls was being set upon and tormented by men dressed in skeleton costumes and men dressed as devils. The men dressed as devils wore devil masks, horns, and long tails. This pageant was part of a procession. The Englishman who was narrating the thing said it took place in Spain once a year. I tried to explain to the blind man what was happening.

"Skeletons," he said. "I know about skeletons," he said, and he nodded.

The TV showed this one cathedral. Then there was a long, slow look at another one. Finally, the picture switched to the famous one in Paris, with its flying buttresses and its spires reaching up to the clouds. The camera pulled away to show the whole of the cathedral rising above the skyline.

There were times when the Englishman who was telling the thing would shut up, would simply let the camera move around over the cathedrals. Or else the camera would tour the countryside, men in fields walking behind oxen. I waited as long as I could. Then I felt I had to say something. I said, "They're showing the outside of this cathedral now. Gargoyles. Little statues carved to look like monsters. Now I guess they're in Italy. Yeah, they're in Italy. There's paintings on the walls of this one church."

"Are those fresco paintings, bub?" he asked, and he sipped from his drink.

I reached for my glass. But it was empty. I tried to remember what I could remember. "You're asking me are those frescoes?" I said. "That's a good question. I don't know."

The camera moved to a cathedral outside Lisbon. The differences in the Portuguese cathedral compared with the French and Italian were not that great. But they were there. Mostly the interior stuff. Then something occurred to me, and I said, "Something has occurred to me. Do you have any idea what a cathedral is? What they look like, that is? Do you follow me? If somebody says cathedral to you, do you have any notion what they're talking about? Do you know the difference between that and a Baptist church, say?"

He let the smoke dribble from his mouth. "I know they took hundreds of workers fifty or a hundred years to build," he said. "I just heard the man say that, of course. I know generations of the same families worked on a cathedral. I heard him say that, too. The men who began their life's work on them, they never lived to see the completion of their work. In that wise, bub, they're no different from the rest of us, right?" He laughed. Then his eyelids drooped again. His head nodded. He seemed to be snoozing. Maybe he was imagining himself in Portugal. The TV was showing another cathedral now. This one was in Germany. The Englishman's voice droned on. "Cathedrals," the blind man said. He sat up and rolled his head back and forth. "If you want the truth, bub, that's about all I know. What I just said. What I heard him say. But maybe you could describe one to me? I wish you'd do it. I'd like that. If you want to know, I really don't have a good idea."

I stared hard at the shot of the cathedral on the TV. How could I even begin to describe it? But say my life depended on it. Say my life was being threatened by an insane guy who said I had to do it or else.

I stared some more at the cathedral before the picture flipped off into the countryside. There was no use. I turned to the blind man and said, "To begin with, they're very tall." I was looking around the room for clues. "They reach way up. Up and up. Toward the sky. They're so big, some of them, they have to have these supports. To help hold them up, so to speak. These supports are called buttresses. They remind me of viaducts, for some reason. But maybe you don't know viaducts, either? Sometimes the cathedrals have devils and such carved into the front. Sometimes lords and ladies. Don't ask me why this is," I said.

He was nodding. The whole upper part of his body seemed to be moving back and forth.

"I'm not doing so good, am I?" I said.

He stopped nodding and leaned forward on the edge of the sofa. As he listened to me, he was running his fingers through his beard. I wasn't getting through to him, I could see that. But he waited for me to go on just the same. He nodded, like he was trying to encourage me. I tried to think what else to say. "They're really big," I said. "They're massive. They're built of stone. Marble, too, sometimes. In those olden days, when they built cathedrals, men wanted to be close to God. In those olden days, God was an important part of everyone's life. You could tell this from their cathedral-building. I'm sorry," I said, "but it looks like that's the best I can do for you. I'm just no good at it."

"That's all right, bub," the blind man said. "Hey, listen. I hope you don't mind my asking you. Can I ask you something? Let me ask you a simple question, yes or no. I'm just curious and there's no offense. You're my host. But let me ask if you are in any way religious? You don't mind my asking?"

I shook my head. He couldn't see that, though. A wink is the same as a nod to a blind man. "I guess I don't believe in it. In anything. Sometimes it's hard. You know what I'm saying?"

"Sure, I do," he said.

"Right," I said.

The Englishman was still holding forth. My wife sighed in her sleep. She drew a long breath and went on with her sleeping.

"You'll have to forgive me," I said. "But I can't tell you what a cathedral looks like. It just isn't in me to do it. I can't do any more than I've done."

The blind man sat very still, his head down, as he listened to me.

I said, "The truth is, cathedrals don't mean anything special to me. Nothing. Cathedrals. They're something to look at on late-night TV. That's all they are."

It was then that the blind man cleared his throat. He brought something up. He took a handkerchief from his back pocket. Then he said, "I get it, bub. It's okay. It happens. Don't worry about it," he said. "Hey, listen to me. Will you do me a favor? I got an idea. Why don't you find us some heavy paper? And a pen. We'll do something. We'll draw one together. Get us a pen and some heavy paper. Go on, bub, get the stuff," he said.

So I went upstairs. My legs felt like they didn't have any strength in them. They felt like they did after I'd done some running. In my wife's room, I looked around. I found some ballpoints in a little basket on her table. And then I tried to think where to look for the kind of paper he was talking about.

Downstairs, in the kitchen, I found a shopping bag with onion skins in the bottom of the bag. I emptied the bag and shook it. I brought it into the living room and sat down with it near his legs. I moved some things, smoothed the wrinkles from the bag, spread it out on the coffee table.

The blind man got down from the sofa and sat next to me on the carpet.

He ran his fingers over the paper. He went up and down the sides of the paper. The edges, even the edges. He fingered the corners.

"Al right," he said. "All right, let's do her."

He found my hand, the hand with the pen. He closed his hand over my hand. "Go ahead, bub, draw," he said. "Draw. You'll see. I'll follow along with you. It'll be okay. Just begin now like I'm telling you. You'll see. Draw," the blind man said.

So I began. First I drew a box that looked like a house. It could have been the house I lived in. Then I put a roof on it. At either end of the roof, I drew spires. Crazy.

"Swell," he said. "Terrific. You're doing fine," he said. "Never thought anything like this could happen in your lifetime, did you, bub? Well, it's a strange life, we all know that. Go on now. Keep it up."

I put in windows with arches. I drew flying buttresses. I hung great doors. I couldn't stop. The TV station went off the air. I put down the pen and closed and opened my fingers. The blind man felt around over the paper. He moved the tips of his fingers over the paper, all over what I had drawn, and he nodded.

"Doing fine," the blind man said.

I took up the pen again, and he found my hand. I kept at it. I'm no artist. But I kept drawing just the same.

My wife opened up her eyes and gazed at us. She sat up on the sofa, her robe hanging open. She said, "What are you doing? Tell me, I want to know."

I didn't answer her.

The blind man said, "We're drawing a cathedral. Me and him are working on it. Press hard," he said to me. "That's right. That's good," he said. "Sure. You got it, bub. I can tell. You didn't think you could. But you can, can't you? You're cooking with gas now. You know what I'm saying? We're going to really have us something here in a minute. How's the old arm?" he said. "Put some people in there now. What's a cathedral without people?"

My wife said, "What's going on? Robert, what are you doing? What's going on?"

"It's all right," he said to her. "Close your eyes now," the blind man said to me.

I did it. I closed them just like he said.

"Are they closed?" he said. "Don't fudge."

"They're closed," I said.

"Keep them that way," he said. He said, "Don't stop now. Draw."

So we kept on with it. His fingers rode my fingers as my hand went over the paper. It was like nothing else in my life up to now.

Then he said, "I think that's it. I think you got it," he said. "Take a look. What do you think?"

But I had my eyes closed. I thought I'd keep them that way for a little longer. I thought it was something I ought to do.

"Well?" he said. "Are you looking?"

My eyes were still closed. I was in my house. I knew that. But I didn't feel like I was inside anything.

"It's really something," I said.

Zoo Animal Keeper 1, REC-SVC-ZK

MARTHA GIES

2 APRIL

I was quite amazed to see an ad for Animal Keeper in the *Maui News*. The zoo is run by Maui County Recreation Services, a division of our local third-world county government, which is made up of haggling factions—Japanese, Chinese, and Portuguese. I thought you couldn't get a job with the County unless your brother or uncle worked there. But since the savings I brought from the mainland are nearly gone, I have decided to apply.

Disadvantaged by being a male—worse, a *haole* male—and having no relatives working for the County—or anywhere else—I also wrote my old boss at the Seattle Zoo for a letter of introduction. I have now moved to Ka'ili'ili Road, where I serve as caretaker for the house of my tea master while he is in Kyoto. The old Sensei wished to visit Daitoku-ji Monastery once again, and to be a pilgrim at the many Buddhist shrines. I love this secluded tropical farm, where Sensei has electricity, hot and cold running water, a telephone, and many rooms.

But I miss the Sensei, and especially our tea lessons. In his absence, I study the seven secrets of the way of tea: *prepare an umbrella even if no rain falls, attune your heart to the guests*, and so forth. They appear obvious, but there is much to be mastered.

3 APRIL

At eight this morning, I was in the County office building, filling out a job application. I submitted my application along with a humble cover letter. About one hundred people applied. We shall see.

Afterwards, I went to have a look at the little zoo, which has twenty goats, eight ducks, some chickens, a pair of ostriches, and a water buffalo. A real zoo I could not handle, what with gardening for the Sensei and studying tea, but this is perfect.

I met Luke Santos, the supervisor. He is an upcountry Portuguese, an energetic little man with a shock of white hair and much zoo experience. Together we "talked story" while walking through the zoo, which is set in a little jungle valley. Though I did not mention it to Luke, I did note that the viewing platform over the *koi* pond might be replaced and expanded. We visited the water buffalo, a lumbering creature, and I saw something of the Sensei himself in those tremendous sorrowing eyes. I scratched the animal's forelock fearlessly.

For two years, Luke was saying, he has been trying to get the pair of ostriches to breed. They lay, but won't tend the eggs. I told him of Seattle and my many attempts to get the ostriches separated from the springbok, whose sudden leaps made them jumpy. Sadly, Luke told me he had nothing to do with the hiring, though he said he respected my credentials. He offered me a small cigarillo, which I wrapped in a handkerchief and placed in my pocket.

It was during this visit with Luke that I began low level political lobbying in earnest: I volunteered to help him set up for ZOOFEST!, a local event sponsored by the zoo's primary patron, the Maui County Philharmonic Society. An amphitheater is needed in a grassy hollow adjacent to the zoo, and many citizens are planning to help construct it.

Back at home, I made a bowl of tea. With the Sensei absent, the sound of soft evening rain fills the house.

Tonight I am reading about the remarkable sixteenth-century tea master, Sen Rikyu, who was also a zen monk: Alone in his tea house, meditating, Sen Rikyu senses someone creeping up behind him. Without turning around, he raises the bamboo water ladle up over his right shoulder and strikes the assassin's sword. The bamboo shatters steel.

10 APRIL

It is still another two months before the Sensei returns from Japan. From the Hundred Rules of Sen Rikyu: *If anyone wishes to enter the way of tea he must be his own teacher.*

Today I received a reply from Winston Donnelly, my old boss at the Seattle Zoo. He sent a "To Whom It May Concern" letter to the Maui Department of Personnel Services on my behalf. He also gave me a bit of news: It seems the female European brown bear killed one of her cubs in a dispute over an orange thrown into the enclosure by a visitor. In the ensuing scuffle, the cub bit its mother, and she turned and cuffed it. After eating the orange, the mother turned to lick the heavily bleeding wound of the cub, then proceeded to kill and eat it. All of this occurred at six o'clock on a warm spring evening, in front of many parents and children.

Reading this letter, I was saddened at the zoo's harsh and reactionary decision to suspend public feeding. I was also reminded of the many arguments and controversies stemming from the contradictory purposes of the zoo, and how relieved I was to finally leave it. *Fame and profit are both dispensed with*, was my thought in resigning. This is the exact phrase from which Sen Rikyu took his tea name.

The good news in Donnelly's letter is that they've put the patient, ox-like eland on display with the ostriches and they are getting along so well that the entire group beds down together at night. A welcome change from the flighty springbok. Could the little Maui zoo invest in an eland, I wonder?

15 APRIL

One of Sen Rikyu's sayings: *If you wish to follow the way of Buddha it is only this: lead a life of leisure and don't take things seriously.* Clearly, Sen Rikyu did not have to contend with Maui County bureaucracy.

ZOOFEST! brought to the attention of the Maui County Council the use of volunteer labor and donations to construct the amphitheater without approval of the Council. The Council has attacked Bud Hokoana, the director of Recreation Services, for being sloppy and unprofessional. Hokoana is a rare native Hawaiian in a position of power. The Council's attack on this man was intense, though many citizens supported him through letters to the editor in the *Maui News*.

Today I begin clearing an old taro terrace, the site of my newest project, a low altitude garden, in accordance with the poet Soji: *A glimpse of the sea through the trees and the flash of the stream at my feet.*

21 APRIL

It's 4:30 A.M., dark and damp. The dew creeps into the Sensei's screened-in back porch where I have set up my old typewriter. Trying to write letters is not an easy task in the jungle, which is dripping around me.

The writing paper is soggy, the stamps stick together, and the envelope glues itself shut. I've filtered a cup of dark roast Kona coffee and have three kerosene lamps gathered around my table. Outside the screen are many gardenia bushes, heavy with buds soon to go off.

I have decided to offer my support to Bud Hokoana, the director of Recreation Services, with the following letter:

> Dear Mr. Hokoana:
>
> The "amphitheater controversy," with its thorny birth in Council budget scrutiny, reveals a very positive picture of the hard work of County Recreation employees and the inspiring initiative of volunteers. Especially to be admired is your department's flexibility in using whatever is at hand, and in not being bound to useless rules. As famous tea master Sen Rikyu noted: *Only a stupid person will glue the bridges of a harp in place.*
>
> I myself helped Luke Santos with ZOOFEST!, and I was amazed by the sheer volume of volunteers, from many diverse factions, all working together. Your notion of the community "accepting responsibility for their own leisure pursuits" seems especially fundamental in these low budget times.
>
> The extraordinary and inappropriate assault of Council members Cordova and Tsutakawa strikes me as an attempt to cover up for their own deficit in attention regarding the workings of your department. Though I respect the vast scope of information and data that must be assimilated by these elected officials, your position aroused much empathy from this County resident.
>
> This letter also serves to introduce myself as a potential County of Maui, Recreation Services employee. I worked as an animal keeper at the Woodland Park Zoo in Seattle, Washington, from July 1987 to June 1992. There my primary responsibility was the bird collection. Animal care and feeding, exhibit cleaning and maintenance, medication and breeding programs, recordkeeping and dealing with the public are among my capabilities.

I hope I may put these skills at your service as a Maui County employee.

My sincere aloha,
William Rivers

P.S. I append a well-known *haiku* which I thought might be of use to you in this (I hope brief) time of political strife:

Wind comes to bamboo
Wind passed by
Bamboo retains not wind.

28 APRIL

Today I received a reply from Bud Hokoana, thanking me for my letter of support. He reminded me that the County Personnel Department handles the hiring process, but says "your empathy for our cause is welcome."

I also learned that I survived the first screening of applications, and have been given a date for the exam—6:00 P.M., the day after tomorrow.

29 APRIL

This morning I perused data previously checked out from the library. I began by taking a sample federal civil service exam for janitors and custodians, but found I could not focus on the many multiple choice questions involving the virtues of single rotor and double rotor floor buffers. I moved on to the almanac, reading all sections having to do with animal gestation periods, what the young of animals are called, what groupings of different animals are called, etc. From there, I went right into GED sample math tests. Though I can answer quickly, I am wrong ninety percent of the time. Fortunately, the answer section states the specific data necessary to solve the problems, so I am still at it.

Among the Hundred Rules of Sen Rikyu we read: *One who is ashamed to show ignorance will never be any good.*

30 APRIL

Tonight, approximately one hundred people appeared in the Kahului School cafeteria to be tested. Most were taking carpenter tests. Only five were taking the zoo animal keeper exam, which indicates some severe pruning. Although we had two hours, I finished in eighteen minutes. I sat waiting for a local to finish so I wouldn't have to turn in my exam first. A young Japanese man finished, and I turned in my paper and left. We shall see.

2 MAY

Though it's still a month away, I am already thinking about a party to welcome the Sensei's return from Kyoto. I am guided by the spirit of a famous story about Sen Rikyu:

Once he invited the famous General Hideyoshi to tea. The night before the general was expected, snow began to fall. Sen Rikyu went into the garden and set cushions on each of the stepping stones which led to the tea house. At dawn he took them up again. When the great general arrived, the entire garden was covered with snow and only the stepping stones were smooth and bare.

Of course, we have no snow here in the jungle, but it is hoped that I can prepare in a way that will show my eagerness to honor the old Sensei without being merely clever.

9 MAY

They sent me the test results: I got the highest score, and a number one civil service rating in my category.

12 MAY

I was called in for an interview today. I expected it to be with the Personnel Department, but it was with Bud Hokoana and the zoo supervisor, Luke. Hokoana is a large man, perhaps fifty, with a sweet round face. When I admired his native shirt, a black-and-white palm-leaf print, he told me with a smile that he bought it at The Gap in San Francisco. I was relaxed and the interview was brief. When asked to expound my zoo philosophy, I quickly made one up: *Each animal is a guest; we must attune our hearts to the guest.*

I waited at the zoo for Luke to get back from the other interviews. He told me I had his vote for sure, and he thought I had Hokoana's vote also. However, Luke did warn me that the other applicant has strong family connections in County government. He gave me another cigarillo, which I graciously accepted and put in my shirt pocket.

13 MAY

Today I am hacking back the tangle of guava trees which encroach on the hibiscus hedge I planted last year along the south property line. I alternated varieties, planting a lavender-pink species mixed in with a hybrid double-blossom orange. Among them are a few of the Oahu white hibiscus with its six-inch petal. They will bloom soon if the guava jungle doesn't take over. The sun is completely up, and it's extraordinarily beautiful.

14 MAY

A letter arrived from the County Personnel Department saying June Tsutakawa has been hired to fill Zoo Animal Keeper I, REC-SVC-ZK. It was a cordial letter, reminding me that many qualified persons applied.

I phoned Luke Santos at the zoo. He seemed uneasy, and grumbled a bit about so much training required for the new employee, yet I raised the point with him that this woman (who turns out to be Councilman Tsutakawa's niece) will have "the humble but eager heart of the beginner." It is this quality which the great tea masters remind us to preserve in ourselves.

As we talked a bit, I thought Luke relaxed. I thanked him for his support. Then I described the eland, with its backward flying horns, and mentioned the possibility of his acquiring one as a way of increasing the comfort of the ostrich family. Luke chuckled and said next they'd be asking him to breed eland. That is probably true.

I invited Luke to come to Ka'ili'ili Road after work to have a bowl of tea, and he said he just might do that, which sounded to me like he would not. We shall see. I have placed two of the cigarillos which he likes in the Sensei's humidor, just in case he drops by some day.

I only wish the Sensei could be here to drink a bowl of tea with me now. He has written a long letter describing his visit to the monastery of Daitoku-ji. There is a postscript, which I recognize as Sen Rikyu: *If even one guest is missing, then the haunting and lasting flavor of the tea must take his place.*

First Confession

FRANK O'CONNOR

All the trouble began when my grandfather died and my grandmother—my father's mother—came to live with us. Relations in the one house are a strain at the best of times, but, to make matters worse, my grandmother was a real old countrywoman and quite unsuited to the life in town. She had a fat, wrinkled old face, and, to Mother's great indignation, went round the house in bare feet—the boots had her crippled, she said. For dinner she had a jug of porter and a pot of potatoes with—sometimes—a bit of salt fish, and she poured out the potatoes on the table and ate them slowly, with great relish, using her fingers by way of a fork.

Now, girls are supposed to be fastidious, but I was the one who suffered most from this. Nora, my sister, just sucked up to the old woman for the penny she got every Friday out of the old-age pension, a thing I could not do. I was too honest, that was my trouble; and when I was playing with Bill Connell, the sergeant-major's son, and saw my grandmother steering up the path with the jug of porter sticking out from beneath her shawl I was mortified. I made excuses not to let him come into the house, because I could never be sure what she would be up to when we went in.

When Mother was at work and my grandmother made the dinner I wouldn't touch it. Nora once tried to make me, but I hid under the table from her and took the bread-knife with me for protection. Nora let on to be very indignant (she wasn't, of course, but she knew Mother saw through her, so she sided with Gran) and came after me. I lashed out at her with the bread-knife, and after that she left me alone. I stayed there till Mother came in from work and made my dinner, but when Father came in later Nora said in a shocked voice: "Oh, Dadda, do you know what Jackie did at dinnertime?" Then, of course, it all came out; Father gave me a flaking; Mother interfered, and for days after that he didn't speak to me and Mother barely spoke to Nora. And all because of that old woman! God knows, I was heart-scalded.

Then, to crown my misfortune, I had to make my first confession and communion. It was an old woman called Ryan who prepared us for these. She was about the one age with Gran; she was well-to-do, lived in a big house on Montenotte, wore a black cloak and bonnet, and came every day to school at three o'clock when we should have been going home, and talked to us of hell. She may have mentioned the other place as well, but that could only have been by accident, for hell had the first place in her heart.

She lit a candle, took out a new half-crown, and offered it to the first boy who would hold one finger—only one finger!—in the flame for five minutes by the school clock. Being always very ambitious I was tempted to volunteer, but I thought it might look greedy. Then she asked were we afraid of holding one finger—only one finger!—in a little candle flame for five minutes and not afraid of burning all over in roasting hot furnaces for all eternity. "All eternity! Just think of that! A whole lifetime goes by and it's nothing, not even a drop in the ocean of your sufferings." The woman was really interesting about hell, but my attention was all fixed on the half-crown. At the end of the lesson she put it back in her purse. It was a great disappointment; a religious woman like that, you wouldn't think she'd bother about a thing like a half-crown.

Another day she said she knew a priest who woke one night to find a fellow he didn't recognize leaning over the end of his bed. The priest was a bit frightened—naturally enough—but he asked the fellow what he wanted, and the fellow said in a deep, husky voice that he wanted to go to confession. The priest said it was an awkward time and wouldn't it do in the morning, but the fellow said that last time he went to confession, there was one sin he kept back, being ashamed to mention it, and now it was always on his mind. Then the priest knew it was a bad case, because the fellow was after making a bad confession and committing a mortal sin. He got up to dress, and just then the cock crew in the yard outside, and—lo and behold!—when the priest looked round there was no sign of the fellow, only a smell of burning timber, and when the priest looked at his bed didn't he see the print of two hands burned in it? That was because the fellow had made a bad confession. This story made a shocking impression on me.

But the worst of all was when she showed us how to examine our conscience. Did we take the name of the Lord, our God, in vain? Did we honour our father and our mother? (I asked her did this include grandmothers and she said it did.) Did we love our neighbours as ourselves? Did we covet our neighbour's goods? (I thought of the way I felt about the penny that Nora got every Friday.) I decided that, between one thing and another, I must have broken the whole ten commandments, all on account of that old woman, and so far as I could see, so long as she remained in the house I had no hope of ever doing anything else.

I was scared to death of confession. The day the whole class went I let on to have a toothache, hoping my absence wouldn't be noticed; but at three o'clock, just as I was feeling safe, along comes a chap with a message from Mrs. Ryan that I was to go to confession myself on Saturday and be at the chapel for communion with the rest. To make it worse, Mother couldn't come with me and sent Nora instead.

Now, that girl had ways of tormenting me that Mother never knew of. She held my hand as we went down the hill, smiling sadly and saying how sorry she was for me, as if she were bringing me to the hospital for an operation.

"Oh, God help us!" she moaned. "Isn't it a terrible pity you weren't a good boy? Oh, Jackie, my heart bleeds for you! How will you ever think of all your sins? Don't forget you have to tell him about the time you kicked Gran on the shin."

"Lemme go!" I said, trying to drag myself free of her. "I don't want to go to confession at all."

"But sure, you'll have to go to confession, Jackie," she replied in the same regretful tone. "Sure, if you didn't, the parish priest would be up to the house, looking for you. T'isn't, God knows, that I'm not sorry for you. Do you remember the time you tried to kill me with the bread-knife under the table? And the language you used to me? I don't know what he'll do with you at all, Jackie. He might have to send you up to the bishop."

I remember thinking bitterly that she didn't know the half of what I had to tell—if I told it. I knew I couldn't tell it, and understood perfectly why the fellow in Mrs. Ryan's story made a bad confession; it seemed to me a great shame that people wouldn't stop criticizing him. I remember that steep hill down to the church, and the sunlit hillsides beyond the valley of the river, which I saw in the gaps between the houses like Adam's last glimpse of Paradise.

Then, when she had maneuvered me down the long flight of steps to the chapel yard, Nora suddenly changed her tone. She became the raging malicious devil she really was.

"There you are!" she said with a yelp of triumph, hurling me through the church door. "And I hope he'll give you the penitential psalms, you dirty little caffler."

I knew then I was lost, given up to eternal justice. The door with the coloured-glass panels swung shut behind me, the sunlight went out and gave place to deep shadow, and the wind whistled outside so that the silence within seemed to crackle like ice under my feet. Nora sat in front of me by the confession box. There were a couple of old women ahead of her, and then a miserable-looking poor devil came and wedged me in at the other side, so that I couldn't escape even if I had the courage. He joined his hands and rolled his eyes in the direction of the roof, muttering aspirations in an anguished tone, and I wondered had he a grandmother too. Only a grandmother could account for a fellow behaving in that heartbroken way, but he was better off than I, for he at least could go and confess his sins; while I would make a bad confession and then die in the night and be continually coming back and burning people's furniture.

Nora's turn came, and I heard the sound of something slamming, and then her voice as if butter wouldn't melt in her mouth, and then another slam, and out she came. God, the hypocrisy of women! Her eyes were lowered, her head was bowed, and her hands were joined very low down on her stomach, and she walked up the aisle to the side altar looking like a saint. You never saw such an exhibition of devotion, and I remembered the devilish malice with which she had tormented me all the way from our door, and wondered were all religious people like that, really. It was my turn now. With the fear of damnation in my soul I went in, and the confessional door closed of itself behind me.

It was pitch-dark and I couldn't see priest or anything else. Then I really began to be frightened. In the darkness it was a matter between God and me, and He had all the odds. He knew what my intentions were before I even started; I had no chance. All I had ever been told about confession got mixed up in my mind, and I knelt to one wall and said: "Bless me, father, for I have sinned; this is my first confession." I waited for a few minutes, but nothing happened, so I tried it on the other wall. Nothing happened there either. He had me spotted all right.

It must have been then that I noticed the shelf at about one height with my head. It was really a place for grown-up people to rest their elbows, but in my distracted state I thought it was probably the place you were supposed to kneel. Of course, it was on the high side and not very deep, but I was always good at climbing and managed to get up all right. Staying up was the trouble. There was room only for my knees, and nothing you could get a grip on but a sort of wooden moulding, a bit above it. I held on to the moulding and repeated the words a little louder, and this time something happened all right. A slide was slammed back; a little light entered the box, and a man's voice said: "Who's there?"

" 'Tis me, father," I said for fear he mightn't see me and go away again. I couldn't see him at all. The place the voice came from was under the moulding, about level with my knees, so I took a good grip of the moulding and swung myself down till I saw the astonished face of a young priest looking up at me. He had to put his head on one side to see me, and I had to put mine on one side to see him, so we were more or less talking to one another upside-down. It struck me as a queer way of hearing confessions, but I didn't feel it my place to criticize.

"Bless me father, for I have sinned; this is my first confession," I rattled off all in one breath, and swung myself down the least shade more to make it easier for him.

"What are you doing up there?" he shouted in an angry voice, and the strain the politeness was putting on my hold of the moulding, and the shock of being addressed in such an uncivil tone, were too much for me. I lost my grip, tumbled, and hit the door an unmerciful wallop before I found myself flat on my back in the middle of the aisle. The people who had been waiting stood up with their mouths open. The priest opened the door of the middle box and came out, pushing his biretta back from his forehead; he looked something terrible. Then Nora came scampering down the aisle.

"Oh, you dirty little caffler!" she said. "I might have known you'd do it. I might have known you'd disgrace me. I can't leave you out of my sight for one minute."

Before I could even get to my feet to defend myself she bent down and gave me a clip across the ear. This reminded me that I was so stunned I had even forgotten to cry, so that people might think I wasn't hurt at all, when in fact I was probably maimed for life. I gave a roar out of me.

"What's all this about?" the priest hissed, getting angrier than ever and pushing Nora off me. "How dare you hit the child like that, you little vixen?"

"But I can't do my penance with him, father," Nora cried, cocking an outraged eye up to him.

"Well, go and do it, or I'll give you some more to do," he said, giving me a hand up. "Was it coming to confession you were, my poor man?" he asked me.

" 'Twas, father," said I with a sob.

"Oh," he said respectfully, "a big hefty fellow like you must have terrible sins. Is this your first?"

" 'Tis, father," said I.

"Worse and worse," he said gloomily. "The crimes of a lifetime. I don't know will I get rid of you at all today. You'd better wait now till I'm finished with these old ones. You can see by the looks of them they haven't much to tell."

"I will, father," I said with something approaching joy.

The relief of it was really enormous. Nora stuck out her tongue at me from behind his back, but I couldn't even be bothered retorting. I knew from the very moment that man opened his mouth that he was intelligent above the ordinary. When I had time to think, I saw how right I was. It only stood to reason that a fellow confessing after seven years would have more to tell than people that went every week. The crimes of a lifetime, exactly as he said. It was only what he expected, and the rest was the cackle of old women and girls with their talk of hell, the bishop, and the penitential psalms. That was all they knew. I started to make my examination of conscience, and barring the one bad business of my grandmother it didn't seem so bad.

The next time, the priest steered me into the confession box himself and left the shutter back the way I could see him get in and sit down at the further side of the grille from me.

"Well, now," he said, "what do they call you?"

"Jackie, father," said I.

"And what's a-trouble to you, Jackie?"

"Father," I said, feeling I might as well get it over while I had him in good humour, "I had it all arranged to kill my grandmother."

He seemed a bit shaken by that, all right, because he said nothing for quite a while.

"My goodness," he said at last, "that'd be a shocking thing to do. What put that into your head?"

"Father," I said, feeling very sorry for myself, "she's an awful woman."

"Is she?" he asked. "What way is she awful?"

"She takes porter, father," I said, knowing well from the way Mother talked of it that this was a mortal sin, and hoping it would make the priest take a more favourable view of my case.

"Oh, my!" he said, and I could see he was impressed.

"And snuff, father," said I.

"That's a bad case, sure enough, Jackie," he said.

"And she goes round in her bare feet, father," I went on in a rush of self-pity, "and she knows I don't like her, and she gives pennies to Nora and none to me, and my da sides with her and flakes me, and one night I was so heart-scalded I made up my mind I'd have to kill her."

"And what would you do with the body?" he asked with great interest.

"I was thinking I could chop that up and carry it away in a barrow I have," I said.

"Begor, Jackie," he said, "do you know you're a terrible child?"

"I know, father," I said, for I was just thinking the same thing myself. "I tried to kill Nora too with a bread-knife under the table, only I missed her."

"Is that the little girl that was beating you just now?" he asked.

" 'Tis, father."

"Someone will go for her with a bread-knife one day, and he won't miss her," he said rather cryptically. "You must have great courage. Between ourselves, there's a lot of people I'd like to do the same to but I'd never have the nerve. Hanging is an awful death."

"Is it, father?" I asked with the deepest interest—I was always very keen on hanging. "Did you ever see a fellow hanged?"

"Dozens of them," he said solemnly. "And they all died roaring."

"Jay!" I said.

"Oh, a horrible death!" he said with great satisfaction. "Lots of the fellows I saw killed their grandmothers too, but they all said 'twas never worth it."

He had me there for a full ten minutes talking, and then walked out the chapel yard with me. I was genuinely sorry to part with him, because he was the most entertaining character I'd ever met in the religious line. Outside, after the shadow of the church, the sunlight was like the roaring of waves on a beach; it dazzled me; and when the frozen silence melted and I heard the screech of trams on the road my heart soared. I knew now I wouldn't die in the night and come back, leaving marks on my mother's furniture. It would be a great worry to her, and the poor soul had enough.

Nora was sitting on the railing, waiting for me, and she put on a very sour puss when she saw the priest with me. She was made jealous because a priest had never come out of the church with her.

"Well," she asked coldly, after he left me, "what did he give you?"

"Three Hail Marys," I said.

"Three Hail Marys," she repeated incredulously. "You mustn't have told him anything."

"I told him everything," I said confidently.

"About Gran and all?"

"About Gran and all."

(All she wanted was to be able to go home and say I'd made a bad confession.)

"Did you tell him you went for me with the bread-knife?" she asked with a frown.

"I did to be sure."

"And he only gave you three Hail Marys?"

"That's all."

She slowly got down from the railing with a baffled air. Clearly, this was beyond her. As we mounted the steps back to the main road she looked at me suspiciously.

"What are you sucking?" she asked.

"Bulls'-eyes."

"Was it the priest gave them to you?"

" 'Twas."

"Lord God," she wailed bitterly, "some people have all the luck! 'Tis no advantage to anybody trying to be good. I might just as well be a sinner like you."

Gimpel the Fool

ISAAC BASHEVIS SINGER
Translated by Saul Bellow

I

I am Gimpel the fool. I don't think myself a fool. On the contrary. But that's what folks call me. They gave me the name while I was still in school. I had seven names in all: imbecile, donkey, flax-head, dope, glump, ninny, and fool. The last name stuck. What did my foolishness consist of? I was easy to take in. They said, "Gimpel, you know the rabbi's wife has been brought to childbed?" So I skipped school. Well, it turned out to be a lie. How was I supposed to know? She hadn't had a big belly. But I never looked at her belly. Was that really so foolish? The gang laughed and hee-hawed, stomped and danced and chanted a good-night prayer. And instead of the raisins they give when a woman's lying in, they stuffed my hand full of goat turds. I was no weakling. If I slapped someone he'd see all the way to Cracow. But I'm really not a slugger by nature. I think to myself: Let it pass. So they take advantage of me.

I was coming home from school and heard a dog barking. I'm not afraid of dogs, but of course I never want to start up with them. One of them may be mad, and if he bites there's not a Tartar in the world who can help you. So I made tracks. Then I looked around and saw the whole market-place wild with laughter. It was no dog at all but Wolf-Leib the Thief. How as I supposed to know it was he? It sounded like a howling bitch.

When the pranksters and leg-pullers found that I was easy to fool, every one of them tried his luck with me. "Gimpel, the Czar is coming to Frampol; Gimpel, the moon fell down in Turbeen; Gimpel, little Hodel Furpiece found a treasure behind the bathhouse." And I like a golem believed everyone. In the first place, everything is possible, as it is written in the Wisdom of the Fathers, I've forgotten just how. Second, I had to believe when the whole town came down on me! If I ever dared to say, "Ah, you're kidding!" there was trouble. People got angry. "What do you mean! You want to call everyone a liar?" What was I to do? I believed them, and I hope at least that did them some good.

I was an orphan. My grandfather who brought me up was already bent toward the grave. So they turned me over to a baker, and what a time they gave me there! Every woman or girl who came to bake a batch of noodles had to fool me at least once. "Gimpel, there's a fair in heaven; Gimpel, the rabbi gave birth to a calf in the seventh month; Gimpel, a cow flew over the roof and laid brass eggs." A student from the yeshiva came once to buy a roll, and he said, "You, Gimpel, while you stand here scraping with your baker's shovel the Messiah has come. The dead have arisen." "What do you mean?" I said. "I heard no one blowing the ram's horn!" He said, "Are you deaf?" And all began to cry, "We heard it, we heard!" Then in came Rietze the Candle-dipper and called out in her hoarse voice, "Gimpel, your father and mother have stood up from the grave. They're looking for you."

To tell the truth, I knew very well that nothing of the sort had happened, but all the same, as folks were talking, I threw on my wool vest and went out. Maybe something had happened. What did I stand to lose by looking? Well, what a cat music went up! And then I took a vow to believe nothing more. But that was no go either. They confused me so that I didn't know the big end from the small.

I went to the rabbi to get some advice. He said, "It is written, better to be a fool all your days than for one hour to be evil. You are not a fool. They are the fools. For he who causes his neighbor to feel shame loses Paradise himself." Nevertheless the rabbi's daughter took me in. As I left the rabbinical court she said, "Have you kissed the wall yet?" I said, "No; what for?" She answered, "It's the law; you've got to do it after every visit." Well, there didn't seem to be any harm in it. And she burst out laughing. It was a fine trick. She put one over on me all right.

I wanted to go off to another town, but then everyone got busy matchmaking, and they were after me so they nearly tore my coat tails off. They talked at me and talked until I got water on the ear. She was no chaste maiden, but they told me she was a virgin pure. She had a limp, and they said it was deliberate, from coyness. She had a bastard, and they told me the child was her little brother. I cried, "You're wasting your time. I'll never marry that whore." But they said indignantly, "What a way to talk! Aren't you ashamed of yourself? We can take you to the rabbi and have you fined for giving her a bad name." I saw then that I wouldn't escape them so easily and I thought: They're set on making me their butt. But when you're married the husband's the master, and if that's all right with her it's agreeable to me too. Besides, you can't pass through life unscathed, nor expect to.

I went to her clay house, which was built on the sand, and the whole gang, hollering and chorusing, came after me. They acted like bear-baiters. When we came to the well they stopped all the same. They were afraid to start anything with Elka. Her mouth would open as if it were on a hinge, and she had a fierce tongue. I entered the house. Lines were strung from wall to wall and clothes were drying. Barefoot she stood by the tub, doing the wash. She was dressed in a worn hand-me-down gown of plush. She had her hair up in braids and pinned across her head. It took my breath away, almost, the reek of it all.

Evidently she knew who I was. She took a look at me and said, "Look who's here! He's come, the drip. Grab a seat."

I told her all; I denied nothing. "Tell me the truth," I said, "are you really a virgin, and is that mischievous Yechiel actually your little brother? Don't be deceitful with me, for I'm an orphan."

"I'm an orphan myself," she answered, "and whoever tries to twist you up, may the end of his nose take a twist. But don't let them think they can take advantage of me. I want a dowry of fifty guilders, and let them take up a collection besides. Otherwise they can kiss my you-know-what." She was very plainspoken. I said, "It's the bride and not the groom who gives a dowry." Then she said, "Don't bargain with me. Either a flat 'yes' or a flat 'no'—Go back where you came from."

I thought: No bread will ever be baked from *this* dough. But ours is not a poor town. They consented to everything and proceeded with the wedding. It so happened that there was a dysentery epidemic at the time. The ceremony was held at the cemetery gates, near the little corpse-washing hut. The fellows got drunk. While the marriage contract was being drawn up I heard the most pious high rabbi ask, "Is the bride a widow or a divorced woman?" And the sexton's wife answered for her, "Both a widow and divorced." It was a black moment for me. But what was I to do, run away from under the marriage canopy?

There was singing and dancing. An old granny danced opposite me, hugging a braided white *chalah*. The master of revels made a "God 'a mercy" in memory of the bride's parents. The schoolboys threw burrs, as on Tishe b'Av fast day. There were a lot of gifts after the sermon: a noodle board, a kneading trough, a bucket, brooms, ladles, household articles galore. Then I took a look and saw two strapping young men carrying a crib. "What do we need this for?" I asked. So they said, "Don't rack your brains about it. It's all right, it'll come in handy." I realized I was going to be rooked. Take it another way though, what did I stand to lose? I reflected: I'll see what comes of it. A whole town can't go altogether crazy.

II

At night I came where my wife lay, but she wouldn't let me in. "Say, look here, is this what they married us for?" I said. And she said, "My monthly has come." "But yesterday they took you to the ritual bath, and that's afterward, isn't it supposed to be?" "Today isn't yesterday," said she, "and yesterday's not today. You can beat it if you don't like it." In short, I waited.

Not four months later she was in childbed. The townsfolk hid their laughter with their knuckles. But what could I do? She suffered intolerable pains and clawed at the walls. "Gimpel," she cried, "I'm going. Forgive me!" The house filled with women. They were boiling pans of water. The screams rose to the welkin.

The thing to do was to go to the House of Prayer to repeat Psalms, and that was what I did.

The townsfolk liked that, all right. I stood in a corner saying Psalms and prayers, and they shook their heads at me. "Pray, pray!" they told me. "Prayer never made any woman pregnant." One of the congregation put a straw to my mouth and said, "Hay for the cows." There was something to that too, by God!

She gave birth to a boy. Friday at the synagogue the sexton stood up before the Ark, pounded on the reading table, and announced, "The wealthy Reb Gimpel invites the congregation to a feast in honor of the birth of a son." The whole House of Prayer rang with laughter. My face was flaming. But there was nothing I could do. After all, I *was* the one responsible for the circumcision honors and rituals.

Half the town came running. You couldn't wedge another soul in. Women brought peppered chick-peas, and there was a keg of beer from the tavern. I ate and drank as much as anyone, and they all congratulated me. Then there was a circumcision, and I named the boy after my father, may he rest in peace. When all were gone and I was left with my wife alone, she thrust her head through the bed-curtain and called me to her.

"Gimpel," said she, "why are you silent? Has your ship gone and sunk?"

"What shall I say?" I answered. "A fine thing you've done to me! If my mother had known of it she'd have died a second time."

She said, "Are you crazy, or what?"

"How can you make such a fool," I said, "of one who should be the lord and master?"

"What's the matter with you?" she said. "What have you taken it into your head to imagine?"

I saw that I must speak bluntly and openly. "Do you think this is the way to use an orphan?" I said. "You have borne a bastard."

She answered, "Drive this foolishness out of your head. The child is yours."

"How can he be mine?" I argued. "He was born seventeen weeks after the wedding."

She told me then that he was premature. I said, "Isn't he a little too premature?" She said she had had a grandmother who carried just as short a time and she resembled this grandmother of hers as one drop of water does another. She swore to it with such oaths that you would have believed a peasant at the fair if he had used them. To tell the plain truth, I didn't believe her; but when I talked it over the next day with the schoolmaster he told me that the very same thing had happened to Adam and Eve. Two they went up to bed, and four they descended.

"There isn't a woman in the world who is not the granddaughter of Eve," he said.

That was how it was; they argued me dumb. But then, who really knows how such things are?

I began to forget my sorrow. I loved the child madly, and he loved me too. As soon as he saw me he'd wave his little hands and want me to pick him up, and when he was colicky I was the only one who could pacify him. I bought him a little bone teething ring and a little gilded cap. He was forever catching the evil eye from someone, and then I had to run to get one of those abracadabras for him that would get him out of it. I worked like an ox. You know how expenses go up when there's an infant in the house. I don't want to lie about it; I didn't dislike Elka either, for that matter. She swore at me and cursed, and I couldn't get enough of her. What strength she had! One of her looks could rob you of the power of speech. And her orations! Pitch and sulphur, that's what they were full of, and yet somehow also full of charm. I adored her every word. She gave me bloody wounds though.

In the evening I brought her a white loaf as well as a dark one, and also poppyseed rolls I baked myself. I thieved because of her and swiped everything I could lay hands on: macaroons, raisins, almonds, cakes. I hope I may be forgiven for stealing from the Saturday pots the women left to warm in the baker's oven. I would take out scraps of meat, a chunk of pudding, a chicken leg or head, a piece of tripe, whatever I could nip quickly. She ate and became fat and handsome.

I had to sleep away from home all during the week, at the bakery. On Friday nights when I got home she always made an excuse of some sort. Either she had heartburn, or a stitch in the side, or hiccups, or headaches. You know what women's excuses are. I had a bitter time of it. It was rough. To add to it, this little brother of hers, the bastard, was growing bigger. He'd put lumps on me, and when I wanted to hit back she'd open her mouth and curse so powerfully I saw a green haze floating before my eyes. Ten times a day she threatened to divorce me. Another man in my place would have taken French leave and disappeared. But I'm the type that bears it and says nothing. What's one to do? Shoulders are from God, and burdens too.

One night there was a calamity in the bakery; the oven burst, and we almost had a fire. There was nothing to do but go home, so I went home. Let me, I thought, also taste the joy of sleeping in bed in mid-week. I didn't want to wake the sleeping mite and tiptoed into the house. Coming in, it seemed to me that I heard not the snoring of one but, as it were, a double snore, one a thin enough snore and the other like the snoring of a slaughtered ox. Oh, I didn't like that! I didn't like it at all. I went up to the bed, and things suddenly turned black. Next to Elka lay a man's form. Another in my place would have made an uproar, and enough noise to rouse the whole town, but the thought occurred to me that I might wake the child. A little thing like that—why frighten a little swallow, I thought. All right then, I went back to the bakery and stretched out on a sack of flour and till morning I never shut an eye. I shivered as if I had had malaria. "Enough of being a donkey," I said to myself. "Gimpel isn't going to be a sucker all his life. There's a limit even to the foolishness of a fool like Gimpel."

In the morning I went to the rabbi to get advice, and it made a great commotion in the town. They sent the beadle for Elka right away. She came, carrying the child. And what do you think she did? She denied it, denied everything, bone and stone! "He's out of his head," she said. "I know nothing of dreams or divinations." They yelled at her, warned her, hammered on the table, but she stuck to her guns: it was a false accusation, she said.

The butchers and the horse-traders took her part. One of the lads from the slaughterhouse came by and said to me, "We've got our eye on you, you're a marked man." Meanwhile the child started to bear down and soiled itself. In the rabbinical court there was an Ark of the Covenant, and they couldn't allow that, so they sent Elka away.

I said to the rabbi, "What shall I do?"

"You must divorce her at once," said he.

"And what if she refuses?" I asked.

He said, "You must serve the divorce. That's all you have to do."

I said, "Well, all right, Rabbi. Let me think about."

"There's nothing to think about," said he. "You mustn't remain under the same roof with her."

"And if I want to see the child?" I asked.

"Let her go, the harlot," said he, "and her brood of bastards with her."

The verdict he gave was that I mustn't even cross her threshold—never again, as long as I should live.

During the day it didn't bother me so much. I thought: It was bound to happen, the abscess had to burst. But at night when I stretched out upon the sacks I felt it all very bitterly. A longing took me, for her and for the child. I wanted to be angry, but that's my misfortune exactly, I don't have it in me to be really angry. In the first place—this was how my thoughts went—there's bound to be a slip sometimes. You can't live without errors. Probably that lad who was with her led her on and gave her presents and what not, and women are often long on hair and short on sense, and so he got around her. And then since she denies it so, maybe I was only seeing things? Hallucinations do happen. You see a figure or a mannikin or something, but when you come up closer it's nothing, there's not a thing there. And if that's so, I'm doing her an injustice. And when I got so far in my thoughts I started to weep. I sobbed so that I wet the flour where I lay. In the morning I went to the rabbi and told him that I had made a mistake. The rabbi wrote on with his quill, and he said that if that were so he would have to reconsider the whole case. Until he had finished I wasn't to go near my wife, but I might send her bread and money by messenger.

III

Nine months passed before all the rabbis could come to an agreement. Letters went back and forth. I hadn't realized that there could be so much erudition about a matter like this.

Meanwhile Elka gave birth to still another child, a girl this time. On the Sabbath I went to the synagogue and invoked a blessing on her. They called me up to the Torah, and I named the child for my mother-in-law—may she rest in peace. The louts and loudmouths of the town who came into the bakery gave me a going over. All Frampol refreshed its spirits because of my trouble and grief. However, I resolved that I would always believe what I was told. What's the good of *not* believing? Today it's your wife you don't believe; tomorrow it's God Himself you won't take stock in.

By an apprentice who was her neighbor I sent daily a corn or a wheat loaf, or a piece of pastry, rolls or bagels, or, when I got the chance, a slab of pudding, a slice of honeycake, or wedding strudel—whatever came my way. The apprentice was a goodhearted lad, and more than once he added something on his own. He had formerly annoyed me a lot, plucking my nose and digging me in the ribs, but when he started to be a visitor to my house he became kind and friendly, "Hey, you, Gimpel," he said to me, "you have a very decent little wife and two fine kids. You don't deserve them."

"But the things people say about her," I said.

"Well, they have long tongues," he said, "and nothing to do with them but babble. Ignore it as you ignore the cold of last winter."

One day the rabbi sent for me and said, "Are you certain, Gimpel, that you were wrong about your wife?"

I said, "I'm certain."

"Why, but look here! You yourself saw it."

"It must have been a shadow," I said.

"The shadow of what?"

"Just one of the beams, I think."

"You can go home then. You owe thanks to the Yanover rabbi. He found an obscure reference in Maimonides that favored you."

I seized the rabbi's hand and kissed it.

I wanted to run home immediately. It's no small thing to be separated for so long a time from wife and child. Then I reflected: I'd better go back to work now, and go home in the evening. I said nothing to anyone, although as far as my heart was concerned it was like one of the Holy Days. The women teased and twitted me as they did every day, but my thought was: Go on, with your loose talk. The truth is out, like the oil upon the water. Maimonides says it's right, and therefore it is right!

At night, when I had covered the dough to let it rise, I took my share of bread and a little sack of flour and started homeward. The moon was full and the stars were glistening, something to terrify the soul. I hurried onward, and before me darted a long shadow. It was winter, and a fresh snow had fallen. I had a mind to sing, but it was growing late and I didn't want to wake the householders. Then I felt like whistling, but I remembered that you don't whistle at night because it brings the demons out. So I was silent and walked as fast as I could.

Dogs in the Christian yards barked at me when I passed, but I thought: Bark your teeth out! What are you but mere dogs? Whereas I am a man, the husband of a fine wife, the father of promising children.

As I approached the house my heart started to pound as though it were the heart of a criminal. I felt no fear, but my heart went thump! thump! Well, no drawing back. I quietly lifted the latch and went in. Elka was asleep. I looked at the infant's cradle. The shutter was closed, but the moon forced its way through the cracks. I saw the newborn child's face and loved it as soon as I saw it—immediately—each tiny bone.

Then I came nearer to the bed. And what did I see but the apprentice lying there beside Elka. The moon went out all at once. It was utterly black, and I trembled. My teeth chattered. The bread fell from my hands, and my wife waked and said, "Who is that, ah?"

I muttered, "It's me."

"Gimpel?" she asked. "How come you're here? I thought it was forbidden."

"The rabbi said," I answered and shook as with a fever.

"Listen to me, Gimpel," she said, "go out to the shed and see if the goat's all right. It seems she's been sick." I have forgotten to say that we had a goat. When I heard she was unwell I went into the yard. The nannygoat was a good little creature. I had a nearly human feeling for her.

With hesitant steps I went up to the shed and opened the door. The goat stood there on her four feet. I felt her everywhere, drew her by the horns, examined her udders, and found nothing wrong. She had probably eaten too much bark. "Good night, little goat," I said. "Keep well." And the little beast answered with a "Maa" as though to thank me for the good will.

I went back. The apprentice had vanished.

"Where," I asked, "is the lad?"

"What lad?" my wife answered.

"What do you mean?" I said. "The apprentice. You were sleeping with him."

"The things I have dreamed this night and the night before," she said, "may they come true and lay you low, body and soul! An evil spirit has taken root in you and dazzles your sight." She screamed out, "You hateful creature! You moon calf! You spook! You uncouth man! Get out, or I'll scream all Frampol out of bed!"

Before I could move, her brother sprang out from behind the oven and struck me a blow on the back of the head. I thought he had broken my neck. I felt that something about me was deeply wrong, and I said, "Don't make a scandal. All that's needed now is that people should accuse me of raising spooks and *dybbuks*." For that was what she had meant. "No one will touch bread of my baking."

In short, I somehow calmed her.

"Well," she said, "that's enough. Lie down, and be shattered by wheels."

Next morning I called the apprentice aside. "Listen here, brother!" I said. And so on and so forth. "What do you say?" He stared at me as though I had dropped from the roof or something.

"I swear," he said, "you'd better go to an herb doctor or some healer. I'm afraid you have a screw loose, but I'll hush it up for you." And that's how the thing stood.

To make a long story short, I lived twenty years with my wife. She bore me six children, four daughters and two sons. All kinds of things happened, but I neither saw nor heard. I believed, and that's all. The rabbi recently said to me, "Belief in itself is beneficial. It is written that a good man lives by his faith."

Suddenly my wife took sick. It began with a trifle, a little growth upon the breast. But she evidently was not destined to live long; she had no years. I spent a fortune on her. I have forgotten to say that by this time I had a bakery of my own and in Frampol was considered to be something of a rich man. Daily the healer came, and every witch doctor in the neighborhood was brought. They decided to use leeches, and after that to try cupping. They even called a doctor from Lublin, but it was too late. Before she died she called me to her bed and said, "Forgive me, Gimpel."

I said, "What is there to forgive? You have been a good and faithful wife."

"Woe, Gimpel!" she said. "It was ugly how I deceived you all these years. I want to go clean to my Maker, and so I have to tell you that the children are not yours."

If I had been clouted on the head with a piece of wood it couldn't have bewildered me more.

"Whose are they?" I asked.

"I don't know," she said. "There were a lot . . . but they're not yours." And as she spoke she tossed her head to the side, her eyes turned glassy, and it was all up with Elka. On her whitened lips there remained a smile.

I imagined that, dead as she was, she was saying, "I deceived Gimpel. That was the meaning of my brief life."

IV

One night, when the period of mourning was done, as I lay dreaming on the flour sacks, there came the Spirit of Evil himself and said to me, "Gimpel, why do you sleep?"

I said, "What should I be doing? Eating *kreplach?*"

"The whole world deceives you," he said, "and you ought to deceive the world in your turn."

"How can I deceive all the world?" I asked him.

He answered, "You might accumulate a bucket of urine every day and at night pour it into the dough. Let the sages of Frampol eat filth."

"What about the judgment in the world to come?" I said.

"There is no world to come," he said. "They've sold you a bill of goods and talked you into believing you carried a cat in your belly. What nonsense!"

"Well then," I said, "and is there a God?"

He answered, "There is no God either."

"What," I said, "*is* there, then?"

"A thick mire."

He stood before my eyes with a goatish beard and horn, long-toothed, and with a tail. Hearing such words, I wanted to snatch him by the tail, but I tumbled from the flour sacks and nearly broke a rib. Then it happened that I had to answer the call of nature, and, passing, I saw the risen dough, which seemed to say to me, "Do it." In brief, I let myself be persuaded.

At dawn the apprentice came. We kneaded the bread, scattered caraway seeds on it, and set it to bake. Then the apprentice went away, and I was left sitting in the little trench by the oven on a pile of rags. Well, Gimpel, I thought, you've revenged yourself on them for all the shame they've put on you. Outside the frost glittered, but it was warm beside the oven. The flames heated my face. I bent my head and fell into a doze.

I saw in a dream at once, Elka in her shroud. She called to me, "What have you done, Gimpel?"

I said to her, "It's all your fault," and started to cry.

"You fool!" she said. "You fool! Because I was false is everything false too? I never deceived anyone but myself. I'm paying for it all, Gimpel. They spare you nothing here."

I looked at her face. It was black; I was startled and waked, and remained sitting dumb. I sensed that everything hung in the balance. A false step now and I'd lose Eternal Life. But God gave me His help. I seized the long shovel and took out the loaves, carried them into the yard, and started to dig a hole in the frozen earth.

My apprentice came back as I was doing it. "What are you doing boss?" he said, and grew pale as a corpse.

"I know what I'm doing," I said, and I buried it all before his very eyes.

Then I went home, and took my hoard from its hiding place, and divided it among the children. "I saw your mother tonight," I said. "She's turning black, poor thing."

They were so astounded they couldn't speak a word.

"Be well," I said, "and forget that such a one as Gimpel ever existed." I put on my short coat, a pair of boots, took the bag that held my prayer shawl in one hand, my stock in the other, and kissed the *mezzuzah*. When people saw me in the street they were greatly surprised.

"Where are you going?" they said.

I answered, "Into the world." And so I departed from Frampol.

I wandered over the land, and good people did not neglect me. After many years I became old and white; I heard a great deal, many lies and falsehoods, but the longer I lived the more I understood that there were really no lies. Whatever doesn't really happen is dreamed at night. It happens to one if it doesn't happen to another, tomorrow if not today, or a century hence if not next year. What difference can it make? Often I heard tales of which I said, "Now this is a thing that cannot happen." But before a year had elapsed I heard that it actually had come to pass somewhere.

Going from place to place, eating at strange tables, it often happens that I spin yarns—improbable things that could never have happened—about devils, magicians, windmills, and the like. The children run after me, calling, "Grandfather, tell us a story." Sometimes they ask for particular stories, and I try to please them. A fat young boy once said to me, "Grandfather, it's the same story you told us before." The little rogue, he was right.

So it is with dreams too. It is many years since I left Frampol, but as soon as I shut my eyes I am there again. And whom do you think I see? Elka. She is standing by the washtub, as at our first encounter, but her face is shining and her eyes are as radiant as the eyes of a saint, and she speaks outlandish words to me, strange things. When I wake I have forgotten it all. But while the dream lasts I am comforted. She answers all my queries, and what comes out is that all is right. I weep and implore, "Let me be with you." And she consoles me and tells me to be patient. The time is nearer than it is far. Sometimes she strokes and kisses me and weeps upon my face. When I awaken I feel her lips and taste the salt of her tears.

No doubt the world is entirely an imaginary world, but it is only once removed from the true world. At the door of the hovel where I lie, there stands the plank on which the dead are taken away. The gravedigger Jew has his spade ready. The grave waits and the worms are hungry; the shrouds are prepared—I carry them in my beggar's sack. Another *shnorrer* is waiting to inherit my bed of straw. When the time comes I will go joyfully. Whatever may be there, it will be real, without complication, without ridicule, without deception. God be praised: there even Gimpel cannot be deceived.

Everyday Use

ALICE WALKER

For your grandmama

I will wait for her in the yard that Maggie and I made so clean and wavy yesterday afternoon. A yard like this is more comfortable than most people know. It is not just a yard. It is like an extended living room. When the hard clay is swept clean as a floor and the fine sand around the edges lined with tiny, irregular grooves anyone can come and sit and look up into the elm tree and wait for the breezes that never come inside the house.

Maggie will be nervous until after her sister goes: she will stand hopelessly in corners, homely and ashamed of the burn scars down her arms and legs, eyeing her sister with a mixture of envy and awe. She thinks her sister has held life always in the palm of one hand, that "no" is a word the world never learned to say to her.

You've no doubt seen those TV shows where the child who had "made it" is confronted, as a surprise, by her own mother and father, tottering in weakly from backstage. (A pleasant surprise, of course: What would they do if parent and child came on the show only to curse out and insult each other?) On TV mother and child embrace and smile into each other's faces. Sometimes the mother and father weep, the child wraps them in her arms and leans across the table to tell how she would not have made it without their help. I have seen these programs.

Sometimes I dream a dream in which Dee and I are suddenly brought together on a TV program of this sort. Out of a dark and soft-seated limousine I am ushered into a bright room filled with many people. There I meet a smiling, gray, sporty man like Johnny Carson who shakes my hand and tells me what a fine girl I have. Then we are on the stage and Dee is embracing me with tears in her eyes. She pins on my dress a large orchid, even though she has told me once that she thinks orchids are tacky flowers.

In real life I am a large, big-boned woman with rough, man-working hands. In the winter I wear flannel nightgowns to bed and overalls during the day. I can kill and clean a hog as mercilessly as a man. My fat keeps me hot in zero weather. I can work outside all day, breaking ice to get water for washing. I can eat pork liver cooked over the open fire minutes after it comes steaming from the hog. One winter I knocked a bull calf straight in the brain between the eyes with a sledge hammer and had the meat hung up to chill before nightfall. But of course all this does not show on television. I am the way my daughter would want me to be: a hundred pounds lighter, my skin like an uncooked barley pancake. My hair glistens in the hot bright lights. Johnny Carson has much to do to keep up with my quick and witty tongue.

But that is a mistake. I know even before I wake up. Who ever knew a Johnson with a quick tongue? Who can even imagine me looking a strange white man in the eye? It seems to me I have talked to them always with one foot raised in flight, with my head turned in whichever way is farthest from them. Dee, though. She would always look anyone in the eye. Hesitation was no part of her nature.

"How do I look, Mama?" Maggie says, showing just enough of her thin body enveloped in pink skirt and red blouse for me to know she's there, almost hidden by the door.

"Come out into the yard," I say.

Have you ever seen a lame animal, perhaps a dog run over by some careless person rich enough to own a car, sidle up to someone who is ignorant enough to be kind to him? That is the way my Maggie walks. She has been like this, chin on chest, eyes on ground, feet in shuffle, ever since the fire that burned the other house to the ground.

Dee is lighter than Maggie, with nicer hair and a fuller figure. She's a woman now, though sometimes I forget. How long ago was it that the other house burned? Ten, twelve years? Sometimes I can still hear the flames and feel Maggie's arms sticking to me, her hair smoking and her dress falling off her in little black papery flakes. Her eyes seemed stretched open, blazed open by the flames reflected in them. And Dee. I see her standing off under the sweet gum tree she used to dig gum out of; a look of concentration on her face as she watched the last dingy gray board of the house fall in toward the red-hot brick chimney. Why don't you do a dance around the ashes? I'd wanted to ask her. She had hated the house that much.

I used to think she hated Maggie, too. But that was before we raised the money, the church and me, to send her to Augusta to school. She used to read to us without pity; forcing words, lies, other folks' habits, whole lives upon us two, sitting trapped and ignorant underneath her voice. She washed us in a river of make-believe, burned us with a lot of knowledge we didn't necessarily need to know. Pressed us to her with the serious way she read, to shove us away at just the moment, like dimwits, we seemed about to understand.

Dee wanted nice things. A yellow organdy dress to wear to her graduation from high school; black pumps to match a green suit she'd made from an old suit somebody gave me. She was determined to stare down any disaster in her efforts. Her eyelids would not flicker for minutes at a time. Often I fought off the temptation to shake her. At sixteen she had a style of her own: and knew what style was.

I never had an education myself. After second grade the school was closed down. Don't ask me why: in 1927 colored asked fewer questions than they do now. Sometimes Maggie reads to me. She stumbles along good-naturedly but can't see well. She knows she is not bright. Like good looks and money, quickness passed her by. She will marry John Thomas (who has mossy teeth in an earnest face) and then I'll be free to sit here and I guess just sing church songs to myself. Although I never was a good singer. Never could carry a tune. I was always better at a man's job. I used to love to milk till I was hoofed in the side in '49. Cows are soothing and slow and don't bother you, unless you try to milk them the wrong way.

I have deliberately turned my back on the house. It is three rooms, just like the one that burned, except the roof is tin; they don't make shingle roofs any more. There are no real windows, just some holes cut in the sides, like the portholes in a ship, but not round and not square, with rawhide holding the shutters up on the outside. This house is in a pasture, too, like the other one. No doubt when Dee sees it she will want to tear it down. She wrote me once that no matter where we "choose" to live, she will manage to come see us. But she will never bring her friends. Maggie and I thought about this and Maggie asked me, "Mama, when did Dee ever *have* any friends?"

She had a few. Furtive boys in pink shirts hanging about on washday after school. Nervous girls who never laughed. Impressed with her they worshiped the well-turned phrase, the cute shape, the scalding humor that erupted like bubbles in lye. She read to them.

When she was courting Jimmy T she didn't have much time to pay to us, but turned all her faultfinding power on him. He *flew* to marry a cheap gal from a family of ignorant flashy people. She hardly had time to recompose herself.

When she comes I will meet—but there they are!

Maggie attempts to make a dash for the house, in her shuffling way, but I stay her with my hand. "Come back here," I say. And she stops and tries to dig a well in the sand with her toe.

It is hard to see them clearly through the strong sun. But even the first glimpse of leg out of the car tells me it is Dee. Her feet were always neat-looking, as if God himself had shaped them with a certain style. From the other side of the car comes a short, stocky man. Hair is all over his head a foot long and hanging from his chin like a kinky mule tail. I hear Maggie suck in her breath. "Uhnnnh," is what it sounds like. Like when you see the wriggling end of a snake just in front of your foot on the road. "Uhnnnh."

Dee next. A dress down to the ground, in this hot weather. A dress so loud it hurts my eyes. There are yellows and oranges enough to throw back the light of the sun. I feel my whole face warming from the heat waves it throws out. Earrings, too, gold and hanging down to her shoulders. Bracelets dangling and making noises when she moves her arm up to shake the folds of the dress out of her armpits. The dress is loose and flows, and as she walks closer, I like it. I hear Maggie go "Uhnnnh" again. It is her sister's hair. It stands straight up like the wool on a sheep. It is black as night and around the edges are two long pigtails that rope about like small lizards disappearing behind her ears.

"Wa-su-zo-Tean-o!" she says, coming on in that gliding way the dress makes her move. The short stocky fellow with the hair to his navel is all grinning and he follow up with "Asalamalakim, my mother and sister!" He moves to hug Maggie but she falls back, right up against the back of my chair. I feel her trembling there and when I look up I see the perspiration falling off her chin.

"Don't get up," says Dee. Since I am stout it takes something of a push. You can see me trying to move a second or two before I make it. She turns, showing white heels through her sandals, and goes back to the car. Out she peeks next with a Polaroid. She stoops down quickly and lines up picture after picture of me sitting there in front of the house with Maggie cowering behind me. She never takes a shot without making sure the house is included. When a cow comes nibbling around the edge of the yard she snaps it and me and Maggie and the house. Then she puts the Polaroid in the back seat of the car, and comes up and kisses me on the forehead.

Meanwhile Asalamalakim is going through the motions with Maggie's hand. Maggie's hand is as limp as a fish, and probably as cold, despite the sweat, and she keeps trying to pull it back. It looks like Asalamalakim wants to shake hands but wants to do it fancy. Or maybe he don't know how people shake hands. Anyhow, he soon gives up on Maggie.

"Well," I say. "Dee."

"No, Mama," she says. "Not 'Dee,' Wangero Leewanika Kemanjo!"

"What happened to 'Dee'?" I wanted to know.

"She's dead," Wangero said. "I couldn't bear it any longer being named after the people who oppress me."

"You know as well as me you was named after your aunt Dicie," I said. Dicie is my sister. She named Dee. We called her "Big Dee" after Dee was born.

"But who was *she* named after?" asked Wangero.

"I guess after Grandma Dee," I said.

"And who was she named after?" asked Wangero.

"Her mother," I said, and saw Wangero was getting tired. "That's about as far back as I can trace it," I said. Though, in fact, I probably could have carried it back beyond the Civil War through the branches.

"Well," said Asalamalakim, "there you are."

"Uhnnnh," I heard Maggie say.

"There I was not," I said, "before 'Dicie' cropped up in our family, so why should I try to trace it that far back?"

He just stood there grinning, looking down on me like somebody inspecting a Model A car. Every once in a while he and Wangero sent eye signals over my head.

"How do you pronounce this name?" I asked.

"You don't have to call me by it if you don't want to," said Wangero.

"Why shouldn't I?" I asked. "If that's what you want us to call you, we'll call you."

"I know it might sound awkward at first," said Wangero.

"I'll get used to it," I said. "Ream it out again."

Well, soon we got the name out of the way. Asalamalakim had a name twice as long and three times as hard. After I tripped over it two or three times he told me to just call him Hakim-a-barber. I wanted to ask him was he a barber, but I didn't really think he was, so I didn't ask.

"You must belong to those beef-cattle peoples down the road," I said. They said "Asalamalakim" when they met you, too, but they didn't shake hands. Always too busy: feeding the cattle, fixing the fences, putting up salt-lick shelters, throwing down hay. When the white folks poisoned some of the herd the men stayed up all night with rifles in their hands. I walked a mile and a half just to see the sight.

Hakim-a-barber said, "I accept some of their doctrines, but farming and raising cattle is not my style." (They didn't tell me, and I didn't ask, whether Wangero (Dee) had really gone and married him.)

We sat down to eat and right away he said he didn't eat collards and pork was unclean. Wangero, though, went on through the chitlins and corn bread, the greens and everything else. She talked a blue streak over the sweet potatoes. Everything delighted her. Even the fact that we still used the benches her daddy made for the table when we couldn't afford to buy chairs.

"Oh, Mama!" she cried. Then turned to Hakim-a-barber. "I never knew how lovely these benches are. You can feel the rump prints," she said, running her hands underneath her and along the bench. Then she gave a sigh and her hand closed over Grandma Dee's butter dish. "That's it!" she said. "I knew there was something I wanted to ask you if I could have." She jumped up from the table and went over in the corner where the churn stood, the milk in it clabber by now. She looked at the churn and looked at it.

"This churn top is what I need," she said. "Didn't Uncle Buddy whittle it out of a tree you all used to have?"

"Yes," I said.

"Uh huh," she said happily. "And I want the dasher, too."

"Uncle Buddy whittle that, too?" asked the barber.

Dee (Wangero) looked up at me.

"Aunt Dee's first husband whittled the dash," said Maggie so low you almost couldn't hear her. "His name was Henry, but they called him Stash."

"Maggie's brain is like an elephant's," Wangero said, laughing. "I can use the churn top as a centerpiece for the alcove table," she said, sliding a plate over the churn, "and I'll think of something artistic to do with the dasher."

When she finished wrapping the dasher the handle stuck out. I took it for a moment in my hands. You didn't even have to look close to see where hands pushing the dasher up and down to make butter had left a kind of sink in the wood. In fact, there were a lot of small sinks; you could see where thumbs and fingers had sunk into the wood. It was beautiful light yellow wood, from a tree that grew in the yard where Big Dee and Stash had lived.

After dinner Dee (Wangero) went to the trunk at the foot of my bed and started rifling through it. Maggie hung back in the kitchen over the dishpan. Out came Wangero with two quilts. They had been pieced by Grandma Dee and then Big Dee and me had hung them on the quilt frames on the front porch and quilted them. One was in the Lone Star pattern. The other was Walk Around the Mountain. In both of them were scraps of dresses Grandma Dee had worn fifty and more years ago. Bits and pieces of Grandpa Jarrell's paisley shirts. And one teeny faded blue piece, about the piece of a penny matchbox, that was from Great Grandpa Ezra's uniform that he wore in the Civil War.

"Mama," Wangero said sweet as a bird. "Can I have these old quilts?"

I heard something fall in the kitchen, and a minute later the kitchen door slammed.

"Why don't you take one or two of the others?" I asked. "These old things was just done by me and Big Dee from some tops your grandma pieced before she died."

"No," said Wangero. "I don't want those. They are stitched around the borders by machine."

"That's make them last better," I said.

"That's not the point," said Wangero. "These are all pieces of dresses Grandma used to wear. She did all this stitching by hand. Imagine!" She held the quilts securely in her arms, stroking them.

"Some of the pieces, like those lavender ones, come from old clothes her mother handed down to her," I said, moving up to touch the quilts. Dee (Wangero) moved back just enough so that I couldn't reach the quilts. They already belonged to her.

"Imagine!" she breathed again, clutching them closely to her bosom.

"The truth is," I said, "I promised to give them quilts to Maggie, for when she marries John Thomas."

She gasped like a bee had stung her.

"Maggie can't appreciate these quilts!" she said. "She'd probably be backward enough to put them to everyday use."

"I reckon she would," I said. "God knows I been saving 'em for long enough with nobody using 'em. I hope she will!" I didn't want to bring up how I had offered Dee (Wangero) a quilt when she went away to college. Then she had told me they were old-fashioned, out of style.

"But they're *priceless*!" she was saying now, furiously; for she has a temper.

"Maggie would put them on the bed and in five years they'd be in rags. Less than that!"

"She can always make some more," I said. "Maggie knows how to quilt."

Dee (Wangero) looked at me with hatred. "You just will not understand. The point is these quilts, *these* quilts!"

"Well," I said, stumped. "What would *you* do with them?"

"Hang them," she said. As if that was the only thing you *could* do with quilts.

Maggie by now was standing in the door. I could almost hear the sound her feet made as they scraped over each other.

"She can have them, Mama," she said, like somebody used to never winning anything, or having anything reserved for her. "I can 'member Grandma Dee without the quilts."

I looked at her hard. She had filled her bottom lip with checkerberry snuff and it gave her face a kind of dopey, hangdog look. It was Grandma Dee and Big Dee who taught her how to quilt herself. She stood there with her scarred hands hidden in the folds of her skirt. She looked at her sister with something like fear but she wasn't mad at her. This was Maggie's portion. This was the way she knew God to work.

When I looked at her like that something hit me in the top of my head and ran down to the soles of my feet. Just like when I'm in church and the spirit of God touches me and I get happy and shout. I did something I never had done before: hugged Maggie to me, then dragged her on into the room, snatched the quilts out of Miss Wangero's hands and dumped them into Maggie's lap. Maggie just sat there on my bed with her mouth open.

"Take one or two of the others," I said to Dee.

But she turned without a word and went out to Hakim-a-barber.

"You just don't understand," she said, as Maggie and I came out to the car.

"What don't I understand?" I wanted to know.

"Your heritage," she said. And then she turned to Maggie, kissed her, and said, "You ought to try to make something of yourself, too, Maggie. It's really a new day for us. But from the way you and Mama still live you'd never know it."

She put on some sunglasses that hid everything above the tip of her nose and her chin.

Maggie smiled; maybe at the sunglasses. But a real smile, not scared. After we watched the car dust settle I asked Maggie to bring me a dip of snuff. And then the two of us sat there just enjoying, until it was time to go in the house and go to bed.

Contributors

ROBERT OLEN BUTLER (1945–)

A novelist and short story writer, Butler grew up in Granite City, Illinois, and was educated at Northwestern University. His novels include *The Alleys of Eden* (1981), *Sun Dogs* (1982), *Countrymen of Bones* (1983), *On Distant Ground* (1985), *Wabash* (1987), *The Deuce* (1989), and *They Whisper* (1994). His collection of short fiction, *A Good Scent from a Strange Mountain* (1992), earned the Pulitzer Prize. *Tabloid Dreams* (1996) is his most recent book of short stories.

RAYMOND CARVER (1938–1988)

The author of several collections of short stories and three collections of poems, Carver was born in Clatskanie, Oregon. He taught creative writing at several schools, including the University of California, Berkeley, the University of Iowa Writers' Workshop, the University of Texas at El Paso, and Syracuse University. Carver's short story collections include *Will You Please Be Quiet, Please?* (1976), *What We Talk About When We Talk About Love* (1981), *Cathedral* (1983), *The Stories of Raymond Carver* (1985), and *Where I'm Calling From*, which was completed just before his death.

SANDRA CISNEROS (1954–)

Born in Chicago, Cisneros's first book of poems, *Bad Boys*, appeared in 1980. Her novel *The House on Mango Street* (1983) won the American Book Award, and was followed by *The Rodrigo Poems* (1985) and *My Wicked, Wicked Ways* (1987). A short story collection, *Woman Hollering Creek and Other Stories*, appeared in 1991. Recent work includes *Loose Woman* (1994) and *El Arroyo de la Llorona* (1996). Cisneros is the recipient of NEA fellowships for poetry and fiction.

ANDRE DUBUS (1936–)

Author of the novel *The Lieutenant* (1967), several short story collections, and novellas, Dubus was born in 1936 in Lake Charles, Louisiana. He served as a captain in the Marine Corps before pursuing an M.F.A. in creative writing at the University of Iowa. In 1966 Dubus became a professor of creative writing and modern literature at Bradford College. His collections of short stories include *Adultery and Other Choices* (1977), *Finding a Girl in America* (1980), *Land Where My Fathers Died* (1984), *Dancing After Hours* (1996), and *Selected Stories* (1996).

LOUISE ERDRICH (1954–)

A poet, essayist, and novelist, Erdrich grew up in Wahpeton, North Dakota, and was educated at Dartmouth College and Johns Hopkins University. Her collections of poetry include *Jacklight* (1984) and *Baptism of Desire* (1989). Among her novels are *Love Medicine* (1984), *The Beet Queen* (1986), *Tracks (1988), The Bingo Palace* (1994), and *Tales of Burning Love* (1996). Erdrich is a member of the Turtle Mountain Band of Chippewa.

E. M. FORSTER (1879–1970)

A novelist, short story writer, librettist, historian, and essayist, Forster was born in London and educated at King's College, Cambridge. His books include *Where Angels Fear to Tread* (1905), *A Room with a View* (1908), *Howards End* (1910), *The Celestial Omnibus and Other Stories* (1911), *A Passage to India* (1924), *Aspects of the Novel* (1927), and *Maurice*, which was published posthumously in 1971.

MARTHA GIES (1944–)

Born in Salem, Oregon, Gies has published stories in a variety of literary magazines, including *Orion, American Writing, Northwest Magazine, Cream City Review, Other Voices, Left Bank*, and *ZYZZYVA*. Her work is also anthologized in *The World Begins Here: an Anthology of Oregon Short Stories* (1996). Gies teaches creative writing at Marylhurst College in Portland, Oregon.

ZORA NEALE HURSTON (1901?–1960)
Born in Eatonville, Florida, Hurston studied anthropology at Barnard College. After graduation, she continued her research into black folk traditions, writing *Mules and Men* (1935), stories about voodoo in the South, and *Tell My Horse* (1938), about the folkways of the West Indies and Haiti. Hurston wrote groundbreaking novels celebrating African-American oral traditions. These include *Jonah's Gourd Vine* (1934), *Their Eyes Were Watching God* (1937), and *Moses: Man of the Mountain* (1939).

STEPHEN KING (1947–)
Author of over twenty-five novels and numerous short stories, King was born in Portland, Maine, and was educated at the University of Maine at Orono. Many of his best-selling novels have been made into motion pictures. They include *Carrie* (1974), *The Shining* (1977), *Firestarter* (1980), *Christine* (1983), and *Misery* (1987). Recent work includes *Four Past Midnight* (1990) and *Nightmares and Dreamscapes* (1993).

MAXINE HONG KINGSTON (1940–)
Born in Stockton, California, Kingston attended the University of California, Berkeley. A novelist and short story writer, her first best-selling book, *The Woman Warrior: Memoirs of a Girlhood Among Ghosts* (1976), won the National Book Critics Circle Award. Her next book, *China Men* (1980), received a National Book Award. Kingston's other works include *Through the Black Curtain* (1987) and *Tripmaster Monkey: His Fake Book* (1989). She teaches English at the University of California, Berkeley.

JOY KOGAWA (1935–)
A poet and a novelist, Kogawa was born in Vancouver, British Columbia. She has authored four collections of poetry, *The Splintered Moth* (1968), *A Choice of Dreams* (1974), *Jericho Road* (1978), and *Woman in the Woods* (1995). Kogawa's novel *Obasan* (1981) won the *Books in Canada* First Novel Award and the Canadian Authors' Association 1982 Book of the Year Award. Recent fiction includes *Naomi's Road* (1988), a book for young adults.

JOHN L'HEUREUX (1934–)
Staff Editor and Contributing Editor to *The Atlantic*, L'Heureux was born in South Hadley, Massachusetts. He has published over a dozen books, including poetry, fiction, and a memoir. His novels include *The Clang Birds* (1972), *A Woman Run Mad* (1988), *An Honorable Profession* (1991), *The Shrine at*

Altamira (1992), and *The Handmaid of Desire* (1996). *Family Affairs* (1974), *Desires* (1981), and *Comedians* (1990) are his collections of short stories. L'Heureux is professor of English at Stanford University.

NAJIB MAHFUZ (1912–)

Born in Cairo, Egypt, Mahfuz was graduated from Cairo University. In 1938 he published *The Whisper of Madness*, his first collection of short stories. The publication of *Trilogy* (1956) brought Mahfuz critical acclaim throughout the Arab world and was awarded the State Prize for Literature in Egypt. He then wrote a succession of novels, short story collections, and plays, including *Children of Our Quarter* (1959), *The Thief and the Dogs* (1961), *Chatter on the Nile* (1966), *Mirrors* (1972), and *Love in the Rain* (1973). Mahfuz won the Nobel Prize for Literature in 1988.

BERNARD MALAMUD (1914–1986)

Born in Brooklyn, New York, Malamud taught writing at Oregon State University from 1949 until 1961, where he wrote three novels: *The Natural* (1952), *The Assistant* (1957), and *A New Life* (1961), as well as *The Magic Barrel* (1958), a collection of short stories. His later novels include the Pulitzer Prize–winning *The Fixer* (1966), *The Tenants* (1971), and *Dubin's Lives* (1979). Malamud also wrote many short stories that were collected in *Idiots First* (1963), *Pictures of Fidelman* (1969), and *Rembrandt's Hat* (1973).

VLADIMIR NABOKOV (1899–1977)

Born to an aristocratic family in St. Petersburg, Russia, after 1919 Nabokov lived in several countries, including England, Germany, the United States, and Switzerland. Author of numerous novels, short stories, poems, memoirs, and lectures on literature, he is perhaps best known for his satirical novels *Lolita* (Paris, 1955; U.S., 1958), *Pnin* (1957), and *Pale Fire* (1962); and for *Speak, Memory* (1966), autobiographical sketches of life in Czarist Russia.

FLANNERY O'CONNOR (1925–1964)

Born in Savannah, Georgia, O'Connor was educated at the Georgia State College for Women and later received an M.F.A. from the University of Iowa Writers' Workshop. Her two novels are *Wise Blood* (1952) and *The Violent Bear It Away* (1960). O'Connor's short stories are collected in *A Good Man Is Hard to Find* (1955), *Everything That Rises Must Converge* (1965), and *The Complete Stories* (1971), which won a posthumous National Book Award.

FRANK O'CONNOR (1903–1966)
Novelist, short story writer, poet, playwright, literary critic, and translator, O'Connor was born in Cork, Ireland. In 1931 he began to publish short fiction in books such as *Guests of the Nation*. Among his best-known collections of stories are *The Bones of Contention* (1936), *Crab Apple Jelly* (1944), *Traveller's Samples* (1951), and *Domestic Relations* (1957).

REYNOLDS PRICE (1933–)
Poet, playwright, novelist, and short story writer, Price was born in Macon, North Carolina. He was graduated from Duke University and won a Rhodes Scholarship to Oxford. Among his many novels are *A Long and Happy Life* (1962), *Kate Vaiden* (1986), and *Blue Calhoun* (1992). Price's *The Collected Stories* appeared in 1993 and was followed in 1994 by the memoir *A Whole New Life*. *Private Contentment*, a television play, was commissioned by *American Playhouse* and presented in its premier season.

PHILIP ROTH (1933–)
Born in Newark, New Jersey, Roth's first book of five short stories and a novella, *Goodbye, Columbus* (1959), won the National Book Award. The novels *Letting Go* (1962) and *When She Was Good* (1967) were followed by the best-seller *Portnoy's Complaint* (1969). Since then he has written many other novels, including *The Great American Novel* (1973), *The Anatomy Lesson* (1983), and *The Counterlife* (1986), winner of the American Book Award. *The Prague Orgy* (1996), *American Pastoral* (1997), and *My Life As a Man* (1997) are among his most recent works.

IRWIN SHAW (1913–1984)
A writer of plays, radio scripts, novels, and short stories, Shaw was born in Brooklyn, New York, and was graduated from Brooklyn College. His first play, *Bury the Dead* (1936), was followed by many others, including *The Gentle People* (1939) and *Sons and Soldiers* (1944). *Welcome to the City* (1942), *Act of Faith* (1946), *God Was Here But He Left Early* (1973), and *Five Decades* (1978) are some of his short story collections. Among his novels are *The Young Lions* (1948), *Voices of a Summer Day* (1965), and *Acceptable Losses* (1982).

LESLIE MARMON SILKO (1948–)
Born in Laguna, New Mexico, Silko grew up on the Laguna Pueblo Indian Reservation. After graduating from the University of New Mexico, she spent two years studying Eskimo-Aleut culture in Alaska, where she wrote *Cere-*

mony (1977), her first novel. Her second novel is *Almanac of the Dead* (1991). She also published *Laguna Woman: Poems* (1974) and a short story collection, *Storyteller* (1981). Recent work includes *Sacred Water* (1993) and *Yellow Woman and a Beauty of the Spirit: Essays on Native American Life Today* (1996).

ISAAC BASHEVIS SINGER (1904–1991)

Born in Poland and educated in a Warsaw Rabbinical seminary, Singer emigrated to the United States in 1935. In 1950, he published his first novel in America, *The Family Moskat*. His other novels include *The Magician of Lublin* (1960), *The Slave* (1962), *The Manor* (1967), *Enemies: A Love Story* (1972), and *Shosha* (1978). Among his collections of stories, *A Crown of Feathers* (1973) won the National Book Award, and his *Collected Stories* (1981) won the Pulitzer Prize. In 1978, Singer received the Nobel Prize for Literature.

JOHN UPDIKE (1932–)

Author of many novels, short stories, essays, and poems, Updike was born in Shillington, Pennsylvania. His highly successful second novel *Rabbit, Run* (1960) established his career as a novelist, and was followed by *Rabbit Redux* (1971) and *Rabbit is Rich* (1981), which won both the National Book Award and the Pulitzer Prize. Updike again received the Pulitzer Prize in 1991 for *Rabbit at Rest*. His collections of poetry include *Telephone Poles and Other Poems* (1963), and *Tossing and Turning* (1977). Recent books include *Collected Poems: 1953–1993* (1995) and *In the Beauty of the Lillies* (1996).

ALICE WALKER (1944–)

Winner of both the American Book Award and the Pulitzer Prize for her novel *The Color Purple* (1982), Walker was born in Eatonton, Georgia. A poet, essayist, and fiction writer, she worked as writer-in-residence at Wellesley College, the University of California, Berkeley, and Brandeis University. Walker's other earlier novels include *The Third Life of Grange Copeland* (1970) and *Meridian* (1976). Her stories were collected in *In Love and Trouble: Stories of Black Women* (1973) and *You Can't Keep a Good Woman Down* (1981). Her recent work includes *The Temple of My Familiar* (1990), *Possessing the Secret of Joy* (1992), and *The Same River Twice: Honoring the Difficult* (1996).

JOHN EDGAR WIDEMAN (1941–)

Winner of a MacArthur Fellowship and the John Dos Passos Prize for literature, Wideman was born in Washington, D.C. He was graduated from the University of Pennsylvania and won a Rhodes Scholarship to Oxford. His first novel, *A Glance Away* (1967), was followed by *Hurry Home* (1970), *The Lynchers* (1973), and *Damballah* (1981), a collection of short stories. Other story collections include *Fever* (1989) and *The Stories of John Edgar Wideman* (1992). *Philadelphia Fire* (1990), *Fatheralong* (1994), and *The Cattle Killing* (1996) are among his more recent works.

Credits

Grateful acknowledgment is made for permission to reprint work by the following writers:

Robert Olen Butler: "Mr. Green" from *A Good Scent from a Strange Mountain* by Robert Olen Butler. Copyright © 1992 by Robert Olen Butler. Reprinted by permission of Henry Holt & Co., Inc.

Raymond Carver: "Cathedral" from *Cathedral* by Raymond Carver. Copyright © 1983 by Raymond Carver. Reprinted by permission of Alfred A. Knopf, Inc.

Sandra Cisneros: "Little Miracles, Kept Promises" from *Woman Hollering Creek* by Sandra Cisneros. Copyright © 1991 by Sandra Cisneros. Published by Vintage Books, a division of Random House Inc., and originally in hardcover by Random House Inc. Reprinted by permission of Susan Bergholz Literary Services, New York.

Andre Dubus: "A Father's Story" from *The Times Are Never So Bad* by Andre Dubus. Copyright © 1983 by Andre Dubus. Reprinted by permission of David R. Godine, Publisher, Inc.

Louise Erdrich: "Love Medicine" from *Love Medicine* by Louise Erdrich. Copyright © 1984, 1993 by Louise Erdrich. Reprinted by permission of Henry Holt & Co., Inc.

Martha Gies: "Zoo Animal Keeper 1, REC-SVC-ZK," copyright © 1995 by Martha Gies, originally appeared in *Orion* (135 Main Street, Great Barrington, MA 01230). Reprinted by permission of *Orion* and Martha Gies.

Stephen King: "The Man in the Black Suit," copyright © 1994 by Stephen King. Reprinted by permission of the Darhansoff & Verrill Literary Agency. Grateful acknowledgment is made to *The New Yorker,* in which the story first appeared.

Maxine Hong Kingston: "On Mortality" from *China Men* by Maxine Hong Kingston. Copyright © 1980 by Maxine Hong Kingston. Reprinted by permission of Alfred A. Knopf, Inc.

Joy Kogawa: "Obasan" from *Obasan* by Joy Kogawa. Copyright © 1991 by Joy Kogawa. Reprinted by permission of Doubleday, a division of Bantam Doubleday Dell Publishing Group, Inc.

John L'Heureux: "The Expert on God" from *Family Affairs* by John L'Heureux. Copyright © 1994 by John L'Heureux. Reprinted by permission of Sterling Lord Literistic, Inc.

Najib Mahfuz: "God's World" from *God's World* by Najib Mahfuz. Reprinted by permission of the publisher, Bibliotheca Islamica, Box 14474, Minneapolis, MN 55414.

Bernard Malamud: "The Silver Crown" from *Rembrandt's Hat* by Bernard Malamud. Copyright © 1973 by Bernard Malamud. Reprinted by permission of Farrar, Straus & Giroux, Inc.

Vladimir Nabokov: "Christmas" from *The Stories of Vladimir Nabokov* by Vladimir Nabokov. Copyright © 1995 by Dmitri Nabokov. Reprinted by permission of Alfred A. Knopf, Inc.

Flannery O'Connor: "Good Country People" from *A Good Man Is Hard to Find and Other Stories.* Copyright © 1955 by Flannery O'Connor and renewed 1983 by Regina O'Connor. Reprinted by permission of Harcourt Brace & Company.

Frank O'Connor: "First Confession" from *Collected Stories* by Frank O'Connor. Copyright © 1951 by Frank O'Connor. Reprinted by permission of Alfred A. Knopf, Inc.

Reynolds Price: "Watching Her Die" from *The Collected Stories* by Reynolds Price. Copyright © 1993 by Reynolds Price. Reprinted by permission of Scribner, a division of Simon & Schuster.

Philip Roth: "The Conversion of the Jews" from *Goodbye, Columbus.* Copyright © 1959, renewed 1987 by Philip Roth. Reprinted by permission of Houghton Mifflin Co.

Irwin Shaw: "Act of Faith." Copyright © by Irwin Shaw. Reprinted by permission of the Estate of Irwin Shaw.

Leslie Marmon Silko: "The Man to Send Rain Clouds," copyright © by Leslie Marmon Silko. Reprinted by permission of The Wylie Agency, Inc.

Isaac Bashevis Singer: "Gimpel the Fool" by Isaac Bashevis Singer, translated by Saul Bellow, copyright © 1953 by *The Partisan Review,* renewed 1981 by Isaac Bashevis Singer, from *A Treasury of Yiddish Stories* by Irving Howe and Eliezer Greenberg. Reprinted by permission of Viking Penguin, a division of Penguin Books USA Inc.

John Updike: "Pigeon Feathers" from *Pigeon Feathers and Other Stories* by John Updike. Copyright © 1961 by John Updike. Reprinted by permission of Alfred A. Knopf, Inc. Originally appeared in *The New Yorker.*

Alice Walker: "Everyday Use" from *In Love & Trouble: Stories of Black Women* by Alice Walker. Copyright © 1973 by Alice Walker. Reprinted by permission of Harcourt Brace & Company.

Index of Contributors